Titles by

Robert Blake Whitehill

Cover designed by Carol Castelluccio at Studio042
Cover Photograph by Betty Fowler
Author Photograph by Michael C. Wootton

Cover art:
Copyright © Calaveras Media
Photography Copyright © Calaveras Media

Published by Telemachus Press, LLC
www.telemachuspress.com
and
Calaveras Media, LLC
www.Calaverasmedia.com

Visit the author website:
www.robertblakewhitehill.com

ISBN: 978-1-941536-48-3 (eBook)
ISBN: 978-1-941536-49-0 (Paperback)

Version 2014.08.21

For my new friend Bri, with
congratulations for winning the
WiLoveBooks giveaway for this volume.
I sincerely hope you enjoy your
read!

Tap Rack Bang

A Ben Blackshaw Novel

by

Robert Blake Whitehill

TELEMACHUS PRESS

PRAISE FOR TAP RACK BANG

Brimming with intrigue, mystery and the type of steady action that will keep any reader alert, TAP RACK BANG draws you in and holds you captive with every page.
Cyrus Webb, Host of Conversations LIVE, Editor in Chief, Conversations Magazine, www.conversationsmag.blogspot.com

Tap Rack Bang throws Whitehill's hero, Ben Blackshaw, headfirst into a terrifying new journey through one of the darkest secrets of our time—human trafficking. If you thought Blackshaw's previous adversaries were evil, just wait until you meet his newest nemesis. Whitehill weaves together intricate story lines that will leave you reeling—another brilliant Ben Blackshaw adventure that HatLine Productions can't wait to bring to the big screen!
Stephanie Bell, Producer, HatLine Productions,
www.hatlineproductions.com

Whitehill does it again with non-stop action, nail-biting suspense, nightmare-inducing villains, and high-caliber weapons. Ben Blackshaw is still in hiding when he stumbles into a human trafficking ring, which he addresses for his own reasons and with his own brand of justice. Blackshaw is the kind of hero who has morals, but is willing to do whatever it takes for those he cares about, and who earns the respect and trust of his friends. Unfortunately there is a high body count on this mission, and not all of the good guys make it though. A gripping read that I couldn't put down. The best Blackshaw book to date.
Brinda Glatczak, Editor in Chief, WiLove Books,
www.wilovebooks.blogspot.com

Robert Blake Whitehill writes about the Chesapeake Bay in the same style that Jimmy Buffet writes about the Caribbean. If his previous books were a thrill ride, Tap Rack Bang is the ultimate extreme roller coaster ride with several extreme stomach-dropping falls. The ending of his two previous books made the readers wonder "what is going to happen next?" This book will make you wonder "what just happened?"
Trey Shinault, Smith Island Crab Skiff Association

More complex, more disturbing than Deadrise and Nitro Express, Tap Rack Bang is a twisted but stirringly satisfying read.
Lowell Wilder

Incredible! Robert Blake Whitehill does it again! In his third Ben Blackshaw mystery series, Whitehill doesn't just tap you on the shoulder for attention, but from the very opening page, manages to rack you upon tenterhooks, to pull you into a web of intrigue as he bangs out another winning thriller! To me, Whitehill's writing style is like a Master's painting where brushstroke and color and texture are applied in just the right places to create a composition tantamount to … a poetic genius!
Really!!!!!!!!!!!!!!!!!!!!!!!!!!
Leslie Lakes

What can I say about Whitehill's latest novel, Tap Rack Bang???? Let's start with WOW, followed with AWESOME and finishing with BEST WORK TO DATE! This book shows how Whitehill has grown as a writer on so many different levels. First is his creation of a new litany of vermin (yes vermin, as in the lowest of the low) that will have you seething with a desire to see them all get their just rewards. Second you will find yourself cheering as each meets their demise, in sometimes surprising ways, even though the price will be high. A word of warning though. Do not plan on eating, drinking or being aware of the outside world once you start the final 80 pages or so. You will become totally immersed and completely helpless to put the book down until the final page. Speaking of which, the final half page will hit you square in the gut and leave you weak. This is a must-read and Whitehill's finest work yet.
Walter Whitehill, The Ice Man

Tap Rack Bang is a worthy successor to Deadrise and Nitro Express, and the action from all directions moves along quickly. As usual, the narrative is helped along by clever turns of phrase and an encyclopedic knowledge of ballistics, boating, and artillery. When the smoke finally clears, Ben may wish he hadn't followed the new thread—as it may have cost him that which he holds most dear.

Dave Pettit

Robert Blake Whitehill and Ben Blackshaw have done it again. Fans of the first two books will stay glued to the pages of Tap Rack Bang until the closing sentence. Whitehill not only continues the non-stop action and mayhem that our hero seems to attract like a magnet, but he takes us deeper into the quirky characters of Smith Island as he weaves a yarn that keeps us on the edges of our seats. For readers who enjoy a good story that combines fast-paced action and adventure with not a little bloodshed, humor and savvy political commentary, Tap Rack Bang will not disappoint!

David Wertheimer

The theme of Rack Tap Bang combines the disgusting enterprise of child abduction and snuff parties. And my favorite bad guy Chalk is at the center of it. (I love that name Chalk!) You will spend a weekend with it.

John Kopitz

Thank you, thank you, thank you. Tap Rack Bang: I loved it. Would have finished it in four hours, however, I went with my wife to drop our daughter off in Philly, and then went to dinner. Got to page three hundred twenty-nine in three hours. Loved the Havokker. It was another one-day read of an excellent book. Great writing.

John J. Francone

For my beloved son, Beau
Until the end of counting…

CONTENTS

Special Acknowledgments

I benefited from a great deal of crucial help in getting Tap Rack Bang ready for you, dear reader.

As ever, the accomplished poet, writer, editor, and coach, Cecily Sharp-Whitehill, a.k.a. Mom, was one of the earliest readers of the manuscript, and so it fell upon her shoulders to point out the more glaring deficiencies in the work. I hope I have addressed these, and then some. www.alliance4discovery.com

My patient and loving bride, Mary Whitehill, sat me down several times during her reading of the manuscript, politely mentioned the utter madness of a few things she discovered in the story, and set me straight that these ideas just would not do.

My son has no idea just how welcome his distractions are from the lonely press of writing. Thank you so very much, Beau, for remembering that I am locked away muttering to myself in the other room.

Matthew Bialer continues as a dear friend, bewitching poet, vivid painter, intrepid street photographer, as well as an insightful agent, and vociferous booster of all things Blackshaw. This series was begun, after all, at his insistence. www.greenburger.com

Karl Guthrie is also a great friend, as well as a consummate legal counsellor. His emails read like poetry, regardless of the nature of the news his communications might contain. It is such a great pleasure to discover folks who revel in English the way he does. www.theguthrielawfirm.com

Supervisory Special Agent Jonathan Zeitlin at the Federal Bureau of Investigation was very generous with his time providing me with insights into how the bureau handles investigations. That said, any errors where the FBI is concerned are mine alone. www.FBI.gov

Pete Lesher, Chief Curator at the Chesapeake Bay Maritime Museum provided fascinating information on fishing shanties, and fishing arks of the 19th and early 20th Centuries. These floating homes away from home helped waterman of a bygone age harvest the Chesapeake in pop-up shoreline camp communities that are forever lost to us now. www.cbmm.org

I must also thank George Moose, Rigger/Splicer at Fawcett Boating Supplies in Annapolis, Maryland for his insights into current materials used in marlinspike seamanship. www.fawcettboat.com

Suzanne Dorf Hall once again proved what a clear and sharp she has for proofreading! Thank you Suzanne!

My friends at Telemachus Press still meticulously build beautiful books for me. I am so grateful they also handle the distribution to fine booksellers everywhere, especially as new Blackshaw titles are slowly added to the list. www.telemachuspress.com

Shelton Interactive, with Rusty Shelton leading the charge, is simply the best public relations outfit to represent my work. Starting with the creation and upkeep of my snappy website, the team has managed to reach tremendously influential reviewers and bloggers, both amateur and professional alike. Dollars to doughnuts you know about Ben Blackshaw because of Shelton Interactive. Higher praise I cannot give, except to add a sincere thank you. www.sheltoninteractive.com

Adam Gubar continues to regale me over coffee and lunches with amazing facts from his private Ordnance Arcanum, and these ballistic titbits find their way into the manuscript currently under construction. I am grateful for his insights, suggestions, and enduring friendship.

My cousin, Walter Whitehill, has provided invaluable reflections on Blackshaw based on his own Special Forces service. I have never been to war, but Walt lets me know about the soldier's psyche both under fire, and on the home front. He is also the Robert W. Service of warrior poets, illuminating the crises and triumphs of going to battle and coming home again, which, because of his great sacrifices, and those of men and women like him, most of us will never personally have to suffer. Thank you cousin!

Betty Fowler is quite an amazing photographer. Her shot gracing the cover of Tap Rack Bang provided just the right claustrophobic creep-factor this story needed. You would not know it, but some of Betty's best work includes dazzling cloudscapes and seascapes around the Chesapeake Bay. www.flickr.com/photos/bfowlerfotos

I am ever grateful to Michael C. Wootton for my author shot, and so many other photographs for book covers, as well as images on the www.robertblakewhitehill.com website. I might never swap out those images no matter how decrepit I am fortunate enough to become. www.mcwphoto.com

Thank goodness Bryan Clardy is ever on the job over at Lightning Source where the print-on-demand paper books are created. His attention to detail always makes the Blackshaw canon look terrific from cover to cover and all the guts in between. www.lightningsource.com

Carol Castelluccio at Studio042 has maintained her very high standards with the cover design of Tap Rack Bang. I am always grateful that she is ready to capture not only the look, but also the feel of the latest Blackshaw mission in her work. www.studio042.com

Sam Codling at The Pie Store still bolsters the Whitehill table when life gets too crazy and entering our own kitchen feels overwhelming. We who are about to dine salute you, Sam! www.ThePieStoreNJ.com

It is once again my pleasure to report that the Montclair Ambulance Unit, to which the Tap Rack Bang characters Michael Craig and Vinny DeRosa belong in real life, continues to serve our community and other nearby townships in the crucial missions of emergency response and education. It is an honor to have served with you all. If you cannot work on an ambulance where you live, then please give all you can to ensure that the men and women of your Emergency Medical Service have all they need to take care of you and your neighbors. www.mvau.org

RBW
Independence Day 2014
Chestertown, Maryland

Tap Rack Bang

A Ben Blackshaw Novel

PART 1
MIDDLE PASSAGE

CHAPTER 1

THE SEARCHER FROZE in the darkness. A zephyr whispered through the pines all around him like a disembodied wraith; shadows and wan moonlight sifting through the lowering overcast made the trees appear to beckon. Chilled droplets ran down the back of his neck from the needles above, but he ignored them. He was one with the rain.

With discipline, with focus, he blocked the sound of water streaming nearby, but not before wondering what other noises the torrent might mask. His hunter's eye had filtered a movement that was no tree branch in the breeze. It might have been a squirrel, or raccoon, or a possum. It might have been his quarry. He waited, watching, and listening, but kept the LED flashlight that was strapped on his forehead switched off so he could be one with the night.

The woods were disturbed by another noise, an object whiffling through the air, followed by a light double-bounce of impacts with the ground to his left; maybe a pine cone falling from a branch. In the instant the searcher turned his head, training his rifle in the new direction along with his gaze, he got that dreaded, pit-of-the-gut sense he had been suckered.

Someone slammed low into his right side with a grunt, but he kept his feet and just staggered with a clunk of the grenades D-ringed to his H-gear straps. He pointed his rifle toward the new trouble, the real problem. He had already seen his prey in the light of day many times. This was not going to be a big deal, even if she were feisty. He was one with his target.

The hunter lowered his rifle, and was on the verge of cajoling his quarry into returning with him peacefully when he saw the pistol hovering in the darkness in front of him. He dropped a hand to the combat holster strapped below his right hip, and to his surprise, found it empty. He was looking at his own gun. He heard three rapid gunshots, saw their flashes, felt his entire chest punched with fire as the .45 caliber bullets destroyed him. He toppled, sliding limp down a steep hill slick with moist clay. Somewhere before he splashed into the stream at the bottom, he was one with the dead.

CHAPTER 2

BEN BLACKSHAW EXPECTED no company. As he rolled stiffly off the cot, his copy of Aldo Leopold's *A Sand County Almanac* dropped to the deck in a ruffle of dog-eared pages. Though it was still dark, like an automaton he stuffed his sock feet into the stiff, cold, unzipped paratrooper boots waiting on the chilly steel of the compartment's sole. He wished he had left the small foundry furnace on overnight. So much for the warmth of May. It seemed like April showers were still falling hard, in spite of the calendar. He could hear the dull hiss of the raindrops sheeting down on the deck overhead.

There was the thud again. It was not just a dream after all. The muzzy sensation of being awakened too early cleared, but the muffled gong still echoed from somewhere below him, likely near the No. 2 hold, well aft of the old Liberty Ship's bow.

Ben shrugged into his field jacket. As he carefully descended corroded ladders and stairways toward the hold, he knew the *American Mariner* could not have run aground. She had been intentionally scuttled on a shoal in the Chesapeake Bay during the Johnson Administration, and used for aerial gunnery practice by pilots out of Naval Air Station Patuxent River. The airdales of Pax River had quit strafing the hulk in the early 1970s. After serving all over the world, with a collection of registries from every branch of the United States Armed Forces, from training to tracking ballistic missile tests, this ship wasn't going anywhere tonight.

Ben's small flashlight was covered with a red lens to preserve his night vision, as well as to keep any stray beams from leaking through an inconvenient shell hole and alerting an observant boater to his presence. His heart beat faster as he maintained his slow stalk below. He wondered what the hell was smashing into his lonely lair in the middle of a watery nowhere. In the few months he had been hiding aboard the derelict ship, only once had a log floated into the hold through the twin waterline maws where decades of winter ice had partnered with brackish water and rust to gash in the hull clean through from starboard to larboard. That time, wave heights and tide had been perfect to roll the half-sunk tree trunk of several tons straight into the hold. It had been dangerous work extricating the log against wind and wave, where at any moment it might have rolled and crushed him against the serrated edge of the hull's wound, and sawn him in two. Leaving the flotsam bashing around the cavernous space was not an option. The booming impacts had been intolerable then, threatening his sanity like the roar of a perpetual storm.

Had Ben's own Inflatable Boat—Small broken loose from its hiding place behind a screen of wreckage in the hold? Not likely. As a former SEAL, Ben knew his business with lashings and mooring lines. He prayed that he was not hearing an inquisitive intruder's boat tied up and rhythmically tugging against its painter line, thumping hull to hull in the storm's rising waves. The rotten weather should have kept honest people on shore. Enemies wishing Ben harm had sprouted like toadstools since the previous fall, and like fungi, they would thrive on his carcass. Ben cursed quietly, wishing he had brought his Bersa Thunder 380 pistol below with him, but it was two in the morning, he was tired, and if he assessed himself honestly, of late he was getting careless.

Ben reached the bottom of a companionway stair that was missing its two lowest steps, and continued along the passage leading to the catwalk that ran all the way around the upper level of the hold. Knowing the rest of the way by feel from nights of patrolling the space, he turned the flashlight off. At times like this, a night vision monocular would have been handy. His friend Knocker Ellis Hogan, who lived on Smith Island on the eastern side of the Chesapeake, had promised to provide one for him. Ellis, at least thirty years Ben's senior, had nearly died of sepsis after being wounded during their last undertaking together, and was still making a slow recovery. Ben was not one to nag, nor would he insult Ellis by asking someone else who was more able-bodied to fill the order. Such was the life of a polite fugitive who depended on his friends for everything.

Ben moved forward with stealthy care. He had once heard that the visual neurology of a lifelong blind person was not utterly dead, but was in part commandeered to transmit a larger-than-usual share of auditory information instead, constructing a soundscape from nearby objects through which the blind could navigate. Ben believed it. First as a hunter on the marshes around Smith Island, then as a Navy SEAL, Ben had found he could listen his way through pitch darkness if he relaxed and allowed his ears to help him see by dint of a rude kind of echolocation. Instead of scrutinizing audible returns from the taps of a long white cane, he allowed the subtle alteration of the dynamics of breezes and footfalls reflected by his surroundings to help map the space immediately around him. Intriguing as this enhanced sense was in the abstract, tonight he was a civilian a long way from the peak of his training, and he did miss the promised night vision gear.

Shunting this regret aside, he let his ears and fingers go to work. He felt along the companionway wall, counting steps between bulkheads, until he reached his hand silently around the jam of the watertight doorway into the hold. He stopped. The hold's upper catwalk lay beyond the doorway, but Ben knew it let out a sepulchral, wrenching moan whenever the metal lattice took his full weight.

Ben listened. The cavernous boom of the striking object, whatever it was, sounded louder here, but now it melded with the rush of waves breaking athwartship through the double gashes in the hold's great space. Something was down there in the darkness. Ben needed to see it.

He crouched, and angled the flashlight down through the threshold of the doorway before turning it on for a one-second traverse of the space. He could not believe his eyes. It took all his will to rein in the compulsion to turn the light on again and stare at what lay below.

He thought it possible that shadows cast by the latticework of the metal catwalk played a trick on him, forcing his mind to incorrectly fill in the blanks of what lay beneath. Ben knew a boat when he saw it. It was definitely not his inflatable swirling loose in the flooded hold. It was an old white fiberglass dinghy with several inches of water in the bottom. Like the sodden tree trunk before, it must have been sluiced into the hold through the gaping wound in the ship's westerly, or port side. From Ben's quick glance in the feeble red flashlight beam, the boat appeared to be on the verge of washing through the jagged gap in the starboard, or east wall of the hold, and transiting out into the stormy Chesapeake once again. There, as the waves rose, it would likely swamp, and soon be gone.

Ordinarily this would not place Ben in the least moral dilemma. He had no need of the boat, so thoughts of salvaging it for his personal use did not enter into his mind. From recent hard-won experience, he knew that salvaging the boats of others brought far more trouble than they were worth. That said, he definitely did not want some searcher to case the *American Mariner* or its environs looking for the little tender.

The problem lay in the bottom of the boat, where Ben was sure he saw a small, darkly dressed human being, a castaway lying full length, head barely propped out of the water on one arm, and either unconscious or dead.

If Ben stayed where he was, it would be impossible to know whether the hapless intruder was alive, or past all hope. He risked flashing the red beam of light once more. The dinghy was now closer to the great starboard tear in the hold, even closer to sluicing away into the night forever.

Ben's instinct took command, winning out over every natural urge to lie low, do nothing, and let the problem float away. With the flashlight off, he pushed through the doorway and felt his way to the hold's starboard side, rationalizing that if a lost dinghy might arouse attention, a missing person would draw even more heat. Authorities around the Chesapeake would go on high alert if a corpse washed up. Ben would no longer be safe. No matter whether his morals were lofty or self-serving, he had to do something.

His left hand reached the second ladder on the wall of the hold. Defying the corroded rungs to part and fail under his weight, he lowered himself down the ladder as quickly as he dared. When his feet began to slip on the rungs' clinging tidal growth of algae, he used the flashlight for one instant more. To his horror, the dinghy had already washed halfway out of the hold. He kept the light on just long enough to sway out from the ladder and clutch the bow mooring line of the dinghy. From his lower position, he could not see over the gunwale to the figure lying there prone.

In the darkness, Ben strained against the wave action to pull the dinghy back inside the hold, and made the line fast to the ladder with an anchor hitch. By feel, he carefully stepped into the careening dinghy.

Ben lowered himself onto the narrow bow seat. He was about to turn on the flashlight one last time to help him look for a pulse point in the body lying just aft of his position. With no warning, he felt a blow, and saw bright starry flashes in his left eye as something cold and hard was jammed high into his cheek bone. He reckoned it was the frigid barrel of a pistol. This was confirmed when the snick of the hammer being cocked cut through the howl of wind and washing waves. Ben remained as still as the tossing dinghy allowed. A light hand fluttered along his shoulders and arms, and finally yanked the flashlight out of his grasp.

When the red light snapped on, Ben's good eye noted in the reflected, blood-palled loom that he was now the hostage of a child, a small girl of fourteen, if she were even that old. She shivered in the wind. What Ben had taken for dark, wet, clinging clothes was her black skin. The girl was utterly naked, and sheened with water shedding out of her hair. She stared at Ben, but the only thing he could see in her eyes, and in the fierce set of her jaw, was a pure and abject fury. *Aw hell no!* thought Ben. *Not like this—*

CHAPTER 3

THE RAGE-RACKED face of the girl, no, *woman*, struck Ben with a fresh fear he had never before experienced. Whatever had sent her into his world naked as the day she was born, yet so consumed with hate, he knew she was just one millimetric finger twitch from shellacking the bulkhead with his brains. It was all he could do to steady himself in the tossing dinghy, praying like hell she would not mistake any swaying fault in his balance as a hostile act, and end it.

He said, "I don't want any trouble."

When the pressure of the pistol barrel withdrew from his cheek, he thought for an instant she had pulled the trigger for his daring to speak. So, this was the nerveless nothing, the void, the quick dispatch to the unholy ground where all Ben's targets, the long dead, and the recently cooled, were waiting for him. She had killed him on principle. He was the handy target. He stood in for her true monster. Or perhaps she had read his guilty soul, and his bloody past, and rendered summary judgment that quickly? Now there was one less usurious coward of a man to infest her world. For surely only an evil man's anvil and hammer could have wrought her this way from the ore of a child's innocence.

An instant later, Ben realized he still breathed, could still hear the rushing swell of the Chesapeake's wash and flow into the No. 2 hold. He still felt the throb of pain below his eye where the woman had jammed the pistol barrel. Now came the jarring clack of his teeth as uppers and lowers met hard; not the castanet of fear, but from of a sharp blow under his chin. Ben rolled his head back too late, and in a daze spat blood from where he had bitten his tongue.

The ignominious fear of getting pistol-whipped in the dark by a child—no, a young *woman*—disappeared when she turned the red-lensed flashlight on again, and wordlessly pointed it at the ladder. The woman had retreated to the dinghy's stern, out of Ben's reach. Smart move. She pointed the pistol at his face, and flicked it upward to send the message home.

Ben slowly rose, and turned, drawing hand over hand on the mooring painter, pulling the boat back to the ladder. The moment he touched the lowest rung, the woman switched off the light again. Now Ben wondered if she were trying to keep him off balance, to keep from making use of the darkness for decisive action. Then it occurred to him that perhaps she was as worried as he about the light being picked up by someone abroad on the squall-dashed Chesapeake at night. Perhaps she too wanted asylum more than she desired blood.

There were still a hundred ways for this to go south, by intent or by accident. Ben climbed the ancient ladder slowly and stood on the catwalk, his hands held out from his sides. Another flick of the flashlight from below, and the beam swept, and held on the catwalk twenty feet from the head of the ladder. Ben walked to the place indicated. He glanced over his shoulder, and saw the pistol barrel hanging steady between his scapulae. His spine itched where the bullet would strike and shatter it. The woman turned off the light. Ben's soldier-mind said rush the ladder, kick her block off and let her drown in the water surging below. His survivor's mind, usually in perfect alignment with his inner warrior, held him in place for now, and very still.

After what seemed like mere seconds, the woman was up the ladder and standing on the catwalk shining the beam directly in his eyes again. She held the light and the gun toward him at arm's length to protect her modesty in shadows. She had untied the boat before ascending, and in the gloomy red, he saw its stern swirl out of the hold on a wave, and into the bay. Ben almost reached out as if he could stop the boat. It was gone now, to drift and be salvaged, or sink.

The woman twitched the gun with a quick twist that said *turn around and move*. Ben knew enough to add *slowly* to the message. The woman was better at this business than he expected. And all without a word from her.

Ben did as he was told, retracing his steps around the catwalk to the bulkhead door. The woman kept the light off most of the way as she followed. She moved without sound, without even a shivering intake of breath despite the chill, and never stumbling.

At the bulkhead door, Ben stopped. In a quick glimmer of red light, he saw the rusted metal stair ahead with the two lower treads missing. The woman behind him was naked, barefoot.

With his voice pitched just loud enough to be heard over the noise of the water in the hold, Ben said, "I live up there." He pointed up. Then he turned, slowly shucked off his coat, dropped it to the deck, stepped out of his still-unzipped boots, and climbed the stairs in his sock feet with that funny feeling of a gun's iron sights still hovering cold on his spine.

CHAPTER 4

QUICK AS SHE had been climbing the ladder in the hold, it was some while before the woman appeared at the door of Ben's bow compartment, which was formerly the *American Mariner's* sickbay. By then, he had a kettle of water, and a small pan filled with Dinty Moore beef stew warming on his small camp stove. A heavily shaded lantern threw deep shadows into the corners where the phantom bogeymen of Ben's nightly solitude seemed to have banished themselves for now.

The woman at the compartment door made quite a fashion picture. Ben almost smiled despite the danger of his predicament. She was little more than five feet tall. His field coat enfolded her in swagging drapes of heavy olive drab cotton, and hung down to the tops of the boots where he caught just a glimpse of her tapered, strong calves. With his artist's eye, he observed that, less one scowl of suspicion, her face would have been a perfect, lovely oval, in a hue of deep brown, with a wash of ochre. Her black hair was cropped short, curling tight to her head. Despite his peace offering of clothes and shoes, the young woman was still accessorizing with the pistol.

Ben said, "Plenty 'nough for two." He received no reply.

Behind the anger and fatigue, Ben noted an exotic look to the castaway's arresting brown eyes and strong cheekbones that seemed to explain why she had not spoken to him at all, let alone in English. He figured she was not from around here.

With her gun now leveled at Ben's head, the young woman took a single confident step into the compartment, but immediately froze when she noticed his Thunder 380 resting on the wooden crate he used for prepping more elaborate fare. She pointed at Ben's pistol with hers, and made it clear with a gesture that she wanted him to move away from his weapon. Girding himself for a bloody outcome if he guessed wrong, Ben shook his head. She gestured again, more emphatically. Ben looked her in the eye, and did not move.

The stew began to sizzle. The permanent below-decks draft wafted an enticing, rich aroma of heavy, warm, nourishing food through the compartment. Taking one of the greatest risks of his life, Ben scooped up a ladle full of stew, and dolloped it into a bowl on the crate next to his pistol. He ladled out more stew into a second bowl. He laid spoons on top of the paper towels that doubled for fine linen napkins. He wondered if she was going to take up the bowl, or his gun with her free hand. Or just shoot him and be done with it.

She drew closer. With the improved light, Ben noted the pistol was an M1911 Colt .45. It looked enormous in her small hand. Though it weighed three pounds, she ably repointed the big weapon as she shifted her gaze around the room looking for other occupants. Her eye always came back to Ben and his Bersa. This was not the first time Ben had been held at gunpoint in the old ship, and damn if it wasn't growing tiresome.

In a dash fit to rival a mongoose's strike, the young woman skipped up to the crate, snatched up Ben's smaller gun, and jammed her own big .45 in the field coat's cargo pocket. Then she whisked up the spoon and the bowl of stew, retreating to the bulkhead by the door. She squatted and began to eat, holding the spoon in the same hand she held the Bersa. To Ben, the gesture looked—practiced.

Interesting, he thought. She trusted his gun more than she was ready to rely on her own. Perhaps she had scavenged the Colt in a hurry, or emptied the magazine on her way out some dark door. Just as well. His Bersa didn't have any bullets either. Ben had unloaded it before he opened the can of stew. Standing down for the first time since the noise of the slamming dinghy woke him twenty minutes before, Ben picked up his own bowl and spoon somewhat confident, but not certain, he wouldn't be shot dead over breakfast. Just as well. He needed time to think.

CHAPTER 5

JOACHIM DEPRIEST HAD not seen natural daylight in three years, and for good reasons. The first reason was simple enough. He made his home below ground, and the room in which he spent all of his time had no windows. The lack of windows was not an issue for him. He saw all he wished of the outside world, and of the other chambers of his lair, through various satellite feeds and closed circuit camera networks displaying on numerous flat television screens paneling the walls from the floor to the ceiling.

Leaving this burrow might have been an option at one point, but from the very first time he descended into his home, he lost all interest in stirring forth into the world above ever again. Some who did not know him might speculate that he suffered from agoraphobia. If asked, DePriest would have smiled about his choice of accommodation, for in his mind, he did not suffer from anything at all. He regarded such petty diagnoses that ruled other, weaker men's lives as trifling, and meaningless to a personage of his greatness. His life down in the earth was a complete satisfaction to him. In a way, this was where he was born. Whatever he wanted from the world above could be purchased and delivered into his presence. Price was no object.

Voluntary choice had for a time been the only reason that kept DePriest from a life in light and air. Today there was another factor ensuring his sequestration from the rest of the world. Joachim DePriest was now too large to leave his chamber.

Always acutely sensitive to ridicule in regard to his girth, the only threshold he had crossed recently divided the overweight from the morbidly obese. DePriest was not merely large. He was a freakish human colossus, a tsunami of striated waves, folds, and creases that undulated as he laughed or raged.

He was not always this way. Joachim DePriest had long ago doffed a Bosnian name, Dragoslav Demirović. That moniker lay buried in Srebrenica, where he, and his father and two brothers had been shot down into a mass grave by the Serbian army under Ratko Mladić in 1995.

He should have died, but like the carbohydrate-gorged gladiators of old Rome, DePriest's fatty flesh, which was ample even when he was an adolescent, had borne the brunt of the slaughterers' attack. Though no vital organs had been touched, he had bled sufficiently from three bullet wounds to cause him to pass out for a time, persuading the killers on the pit's rim above that he was done, even though they certainly were not. The gasoline came next.

The executioners splashed gallon after gallon of fuel over the corpses before setting it alight. The infernal heat reached down to the dying young man through the tangle of bodies, instilling in him a primordial horror of burning alive. Then the roaring flames followed the sluicing courses of gas and found him. Some other victims who still had life in their veins began screaming, but they fell silent as more gunshots rang out. Dragoslav's face, head, and hair caught fire, but the weight of death on top of his limbs pre-vented betraying himself by thrashing. He struggled grimly to remain silent even while his ears, nose, and one eye were singed away. He inhaled smoky flames, scorching his vocal chords. Bodies burned, burst, and bled above him, and the running blood followed the fuel down and smothered the deeper fires; not before horrible disfigurement turned a young man into a hate-filled, otherworldly demon. Lying helpless beneath the corpses of his family incubated, and then spawned an unholy, grotesque, and vengeful soul.

As blood congealed around him in the pit, and the hot, suffocating stench of rot suffused and choked his lungs, he adopted a new name; one that rang of the Netherlands so he would never forget the United Nations Dutchbat peacekeepers who surrendered his family to their murderers. A bewildered, gentle eighteen-year-old Dragoslav had tumbled into the grave to be left for dead; but the new monster, DePriest, was exhumed and crawled out to despoil all he touched.

On the third day after the massacre, a young woman, who was digging at the scene of the carnage for her dead husband, instead found DePriest alive, and took him in to nurse his wounds. In repayment for her months of kindness, he brutally turned the grieving widow and her young daughter out into the street to whore for passing soldiers of any stripe. As DePriest and his family had been handed over to feral animals to be killed, so would he savagely exploit anyone he met, but for a *profit*. In this way he amassed a tainted fortune from human trafficking. But he also kept compulsively eating, packing on ever thicker layers of the fat that had saved him.

DePriest's voice, in contrast to his gargantuan size, remained a high wheezy whisper from the smoke and burn injuries, but because of his power, and whimsical, childlike delight in hurting others, even this soft tone struck fear into anyone who heard it. His two male servants, Armand and Wallace, were both attractive men in their late twenties, with delicate, feminine features they enhanced, at DePriest's insistence, with the judicious use of mascara, eyeliner, and blush. They snapped into action whenever DePriest's voice pitched up with anger into the shrill range of a boiling kettle's shriek.

The telephone began to tweet as Wallace and Armand were just finishing DePriest's morning ablutions. Ignoring the phone's fluting warble, the two men remained quietly grateful that the task of bathing DePriest no longer involved carting him to and from the spacious shower room. Even that restricted movement had become dangerous months before. DePriest had slipped and fallen on top of Armand in a calamity that came to be known as The Last Shower. It had taken an hour for Wallace, using the heavy-duty patient sling hoist (cleverly adapted from an auto assembly line robot used to move truck engines), to free the suffocating Armand and return the hyperventilating DePriest to his bed.

Today, as with every minute of every day since, DePriest reclined on a large custom-built chaise that allowed gentle, comfortable air circulation all around his body. He also slept in place, but sitting upright. His weight compressed his lungs too much when he lay down in any position. This chaise also permitted unhampered elimination and intimate hygiene without his ever taking a step. The boys, as DePriest called his servants, took care of it all. Wallace used a well-lubricated steel pizza spatula to gently lift DePriest's underfolds of flesh while Armand sluiced filth, sebum, and smegma away into the floor drain using a warm, gentle stream of water treated with antibiotics and moisturizing ointments that prevented infections, pressure sores, and unpleasant odors from developing between baths.

DePriest reached out with a massive hand, grabbed his bluetooth headset, and swung it over his domed hairless head. Touching a small switch on the wireless unit, he said simply, "Joachim." He pronounced it *YO-wukem*, gently harkening back to the name's Hebrew origin, meaning *raised by God.*

A voice on the line said, "Mr. DePriest?" The giant man did not correct his caller's more formal mode of address. DePriest affected a casual mien, but in his vanity, he enjoyed the strokes that came his way thanks to his wealth and menacing eccentricities.

"What is it, Maynard?" DePriest tried to inject a bored, bothered inflection into his piping breathy voice, but it was difficult. Conversations with Maynard Chalk always gave the afternoon a certain tingle. At the moment, Chalk was overseeing DePriest's most intriguing project to date.

Chalk was not happy about delivering his news. "Mr. D, we might have hit a little snagaroosky."

From the frown darkening DePriest's moonlike face, Wallace and Armand gauged that the domestic felicity of their evening was about to swan dive off a cliff.

DePriest said, "I don't have those *snaga'* things, whatever they are. I have *you.*"

"By the short-and-curlies, you most certainly do. It's about the herd. One of the prize head—always the maverick—ran off."

DePriest's extended pause was not for dramatic effect, but was a genuine result of his unhappiness. "I appreciate knowing every little detail of your day, Maynard. Truly I do. But this hardly seems worth mentioning, since I am sure you already have the stray back at the stockyard, safe and sound."

"I am a regular cow-poke, that is true, Mr. DePriest. But this time around, we might have to write down the loss. No way this little heifer survived jumping the fence."

"So you have a carcass. Freeze it until the event. Every little bit has value to the right person."

"Sorry again. Gone means *all* gone."

This surprised Joachim DePriest. "A runaway calf? You can't find her?" He chuckled and wheezed for a moment.

Chalk explained, "Not yet. Here's the thing. She went in the wrong direction. Likely got herself lost out in the dark. Trust me when I tell you, there's probably nothing left that you or anybody else will want to look at, let alone *process*."

Another pause from DePriest. This was no longer a matter for banter and laughs. "We picked our stock with great care, Maynard, and at great expense. *My* expense. It's so simple. You manage the yard. I bring the buyers. I rely on you. But now, I am embarrassed for you. I am wondering about your usefulness to my enterprise."

"We planned for attrition. We have reserves that'll likely do way better than this one, from beginning to end, so we shouldn't—"

"We have a runner," DePriest interrupted. "She is unaccounted for, with a head full of troubling thoughts. If this little one is alive, but outside your care, there could be loose talk. You see my position, I'm sure. Do you understand *your* position, Maynard?"

DePriest terminated the call without waiting for an answer. He took three breaths to calm himself, but he needed something else. Something *special*. He pouted, "Armand, I'm tense."

Wallace gave Armand a glance that said *better you than me*, and got busy. They were heterosexual despite the costumery DePriest made them wear; this gave them a mercenary view of all DePriest's requests. A job was a job, and theirs paid better than most.

Wallace lubricated the steel pizza spatula again, while Armand donned a latex glove on his right hand. Then, with Armand lifting DePriest's left thigh and ponderous belly rolls, Wallace gently began to work the spatula beneath the giant man, creating an adipose tunnel leading to the unseen objective. Armand had no consoling thought for himself except that the highly repetitive act he was about to perform would give his right triceps and forearm muscles tremendous definition. All in a day's work. He was a hired hand, after all.

CHAPTER 6

MAYNARD PILCHARD CHALK stared down in shock at the shattered remains of his cell phone. He had no recollection of throwing it against the cement wall of his office, but he was aware that he was too long a stranger to his antipsychotic prescriptions. That was the problem with psychosis: the disease lied to the patient that he was fine, and it often did so in the patient's own voice. Regardless, Chalk did not believe the meds helped him cope with the lethal encounters that were his stock in trade. In fact, he thought the crazy pills blunted his powers and slowed his reactions. Chalk sensed he was unique, and being uniquely crazy appealed to him, made him feel unpredictable. He wore chaos like a shield. *You can't kill a blur.* On the downside, noncompliance with the scrip did mean more messes for him to clean up when his temper flared. A high price, but a fair one, in his view.

Chalk understood the threat DePriest had made. He had no desire to dance with Armand and Wallace. Not this late in the game. Not this close to payday. DePriest's two boys might look dainty to some, but they were stone killers. They doubled as DePriest's personal protection detail along with God knows what else they did for that disgusting sperm whale behind closed doors.

As Chalk gathered himself, he felt the full weight of his new life as a fallen hero. He had saved Washington, D.C. from a terrorist's dirty bomb, or so the media had reported. When his boss, Senator Lily Morgan, (R) Wisconsin, scooped up the credit, and was appointed to the vacant post of

Secretary of Homeland Security (a post Chalk himself had helped make available to her with the unsuspected assassination of the previous Homeland Secretary by a subtle poison) she had forgotten all she owed him, and left him out in the cold. She simply quit taking his calls. When he persisted, she threatened to expose him to the world for what he really was: a brilliant black-ops strategist and tactician unburdened by morals, scruples, or the least respect for human life.

Chalk used to have money enough set aside in accounts all over the world for several lifetimes of abject dissipated luxury, but Lily had found it all, and frozen or taken it. Chalk told himself it was not about the money, that he was poorly suited for an existence outside of the trenches. Lily Morgan's projects had been a perfect fit for him, tinged as they were with her own brand of mental distemper. True, Chalk missed the action. He liked to keep his hands dirty, bloody, with the gouged flesh of his enemies crammed deep underneath his fingernails. So he had gathered up the few members of his black ops team who were still alive after the dirty bomb debacle. Operating under his shell corporation, called Right Way Moving & Storage, Chalk and his sadistic cadre had signed on for Joachim DePriest's fascinating venture. Action was good. The money helped.

Turning away from the wreckage of his phone, Chalk noticed he was not alone in the windowless office. *Surprise.* These psychotic blackouts did keep things interesting. He never knew where he was going to come to, or when, or with whom. Sebastian Kentish, a fit red-haired Brit in his thirties, and an MI7 wash-out, stood mouth agape and wide-eyed, his gun-hand poised to plunge underneath his open jacket toward his shoulder holster. Kentish had been brought in as a replacement from Chalk's Bangkok office, and despite hearing all the rumors, was still unused to his boss's erratic, eruptive behavior. That suited Chalk fine. He preferred his noobs and sea-soned hands alike to step gently around him with a Machiavellian mix of respect and fear governing their actions, especially when they were not un-der his direct orders.

Tahereh Heydar, another person Chalk did not expect to find present in the office, was a vicious Iranian woman of stunning beauty. She had once been the highest ranking female Jihadi in a stateside Al Qaeda cell. Chalk had intercepted her team on his most recent mission, and slowly but utterly destroyed it. Tahereh had become Chalk's lover, at first as a survival tactic, but later, she had come to admire his mad bravado. No threat, and no physical barrier stopped her from leaving his side now. Only her heart remained imprisoned. She stayed with Chalk out of a septic kind of love, the way a scab tried to stick to a gangrenous wound.

Tahereh was kneeling solicitously over the soon-to-be corpse of Matt Flynn, who was having some neck problems. Specifically, he was choking on his crushed trachea. *Whoops! Clean-up on aisle three*, thought Chalk. Must have been a juicy episode, for him to have spontaneously taken out one of his own. Such was the high cost of living on the rusty edge of madness.

Chalk quickly assessed Flynn's chances of survival and said to Kentish, "Ginger, get our boy here over to the cooler while he's fresh."

"Yes, sir," was the snappy reply.

Both Kentish and Tahereh knew better than to plead for a doctor for Flynn, even if they were so inclined. Only Tahereh knew that Chalk was not cheaping out on Flynn's medical care. During one of Chalk's more chatty, less violent psychotic breaks, which coincided with a blistering round of sex that would have been illegal in most states even without the presence of a baffled iguana, he had blabbed to her. It seemed that the physical examination every new hire received upon joining Right Way included full genomic and blood work-ups that were filed away to help with organ harvesting and sales on the black market. If the operative became a casualty, or as in Flynn's case, pretty close to it, Chalk reaped the death benefit. It sure saved a bundle for Right Way's pension portfolio. Even if an agent screwed the pooch on a mission, but was otherwise healthy, Chalk had been known to float the poor bastard's medical stats on several black market organ and tissue registries to see if there was a well-heeled recipient or two in dire need of spare parts. A bullet, and some handy work with a scalpel, effectively culled dead weight from the payroll, and turned Chalk a tidy profit. It also kept the current team roster motivated. Suspicions in the ranks would never be given voice. Rumors might endure forever unverified. No one had failed to notice a lack of Right Way retirees chewing the fat at the company Christmas party. Chalk thought of his quirky retirement protocol as the Crimson Parachute.

After Kentish hefted the still-struggling Flynn up on his shoulders in a fireman's carry and left the office for the short hike to the walk-in Arctipak freezer, Chalk's tone was abashed. "Pretty bad, I guess."

Tahereh could not help grinning. "You watch. Seb will come back in fresh pants."

Chalk valued Tahereh's good opinion. He was grateful she did not think less of him because of his lethal brand of psychotic whimsy. He told her, "DePriest says we have to round up that runner."

Tahereh sighed, and rolled her beguiling almond eyes. "So I gathered. I wish he'd let me put tracking chips in them when I wanted."

"Right? But I took his point. Anything we LoJack could get tracked by someone else. Plus, the cost would cut into the profit."

"More so than missing livestock?"

Chalk said, "You're pushing on an open door, honey. Saddle up a team. We'll ride the fence line, and see what's what. And no, we won't wait 'til sunup."

Tahereh shrugged. "It's a cowboy's life for me."

CHAPTER 7

BEN'S GUEST SNORED. It seemed unusual in so young a person. This was not some kittenish purr, either. The compartment resonated with the stertorous rhythms of her deep exhaustion. She had valiantly fought the onslaught of sleep, holding her gun on Ben steadily at first, then with the wavering droop of one wrist, which next she supported with her other hand. The heavy stew and warming cabin did just as Ben reckoned they would. Perhaps out of innocence, or trust, but more likely out of utter fatigue, she had not thought to bind or confine him so she could rest more safely.

Within a few minutes of the young woman's head lolling forward to stay, Ben placed her gently on his cot, and drew all his blankets over her. He had considered removing the salt-stiffened field jacket for her comfort, but as he carried her, the lapel fell back exposing the chilled Hershey's Kiss of a nipple. Suddenly, and certainly, Ben knew from the lightning thrum that coursed from his eyes to his loins, and then to his heart, that if she woke naked under his blankets, any trust he had cultivated since their meeting would rot straight away into hate. He remembered the rage inflaming her face below in the hold. He wanted no part of that again. So he left her in his coat. Neither did he take back his boots. In the one concession to his hands-off policy, he removed the .45 from the coat pocket for safekeeping.

Ben had a guest. He had a problem. He was supposed to be alone and inaccessible here on the hulk. Where in God's name had she come from?

Who would light out in a small boat onto the Chesapeake Bay in this chill wind, rain, and fog with no clothes, no oars, and just a gun? How come all this had seemed preferable to her instead of sheltering in place, wherever that place was?

He worked it over in his mind. If she slept in the nude voluntarily, it seemed strange that, even without a fresh change of duds close to hand, her clothing from the day before must have also lain out of reach. Perhaps she was caught in some compromising position. A jealous spouse came home too soon? Maybe. Had she been tossed out in the buff by an angry lover? That seemed cruel. It was possible, but Ben sensed it was unlikely. True, getting caught naked on the wrong side of a locked door happened more often than most folks realized, as the hallway surveillance videos of many hotels would attest. Those self-closing, self-locking doors did their mischief, even if all you were doing was innocently dropping a room service tray out where housekeeping could retrieve it. And that was nothing more serious than a matter of embarrassment on the guest's side, as well as a fair amount of mirth on the part of the clerk rousted out to bring up a spare key. Whether a hotel hallway, or even the front yard of a house, Ben figured a stranded naked person would stick close by the door they wanted to retreat behind. Unless the person feared what lay behind that locked door and wanted to get away, regardless of the cost in shame and dignity. He, or she as was the case tonight, would not hop into a boat in bad weather if help was at hand on shore. Unless perhaps she had started out aboard another boat. No, the hotel notion, and the idea of the woman as a guest somewhere, stayed with Ben.

He pulled on a pair of sneakers and a fleece jacket, and stole back down to the hold with his red-lensed flashlight. As he feared, the surging dinghy had washed away through the hold's leeward gash, and vanished into the Chesapeake night, and no trick of the currents and wind had brought it back.

As he ascended back to his compartment, Ben tried to remember details about the boat. Worn registration numbers were lawfully adhered or painted under the gunwale at the bow, but for the life of him, he could not remember what the numbers were other than they began with MD for Maryland. Something about having a gun barrel jammed in his face by a pissed-off naked woman addled his usually excellent recall. He would not be able to trace the number through a registry look-up.

Sifting through his fleeting recollections, Ben knew the boat had once been a thing of quality, but it was far from showroom fresh. His waterman's eye had instantly picked up that the fiberglass was crazed with cracks that had not seen fresh Gelcoat in at least a decade. There was still a powdery white smear of oxidation on the knuckles of his left hand. So it was a good boat some while back, but she had long ago been downgraded to rougher duty and indifferent maintenance. A yacht's tender? Perhaps at one point, but not today. Ben could not remember if there had been a load-bearing rectangle of marine plywood or mahogany mounted at the stern for seating an outboard motor, but that was standard on dinghies for the last fifty years and more.

He recalled no centerboard case, nor leeboards or their mounts, nor a step for a mast that would make it a sailing dinghy. If those elements were part of the boat, but he had missed them, it could be the woman had sailed the boat away, but rolled the mast out later in the weather. That was hard to do without swamping the little dinghy, and even if it had molded-in flotation cells, it would have been a job of work in the steep chop to bail the water down to the few inches he had noted sloshing in the bottom. Scratch the idea of a sailing rig.

As Ben reentered his compartment, he saw that the young woman had not budged an inch. And she still snored like a growling guard dog. Why had he not propped her on one side to quiet the noise? His wife had tipped him off his back often enough when they shared their bed. That would not work here. He dared not touch his guest while she slept. She would wake up all elbows, nails and teeth by the look of her. Ben figured he would pass on that fun. Let the poor woman snore.

Resigned to the noise, Ben sat down against the bulkhead and suddenly remembered the dinghy's oarlocks. That was something. There were two oarlocks, yes. Aluminum U shapes in the gunwales aft of the midships bench. Oxidized to the point of looking coarse and dull, but polished on the inside with the working forces of the oars. But there were no oars on the boat. Whoever owned the boat rowed it, did not look after the mooring line or the finish, but valued the oars enough to keep them somewhere other than with the boat. The missing oars were likely a replacement set, perhaps after the theft or loss of the originals, with their stinging cost a sharper recollection to the owner than the distant purchase of the boat itself. Ben knew from personal experience that not every decision a boater made was sensible. Neglecting the boat, but securing the shiny, expensive new oars would be deemed strange only by landlubbers.

With no oars aboard, the old dinghy was also safer from thieves. Likely the boat was already in the water when the young woman found it. This was no fancy boat-lift baby. She was not kept hauled out on davits, either. Those would have made the boat too slow to launch even for an experienced sailor, let alone a woman in a rush.

Based on the boat, the picture forming in Ben's mind was the woman making a hasty departure from somewhere she did not wish to be. Somewhere close to the shore.

Ben rose and crossed to the locker where he had stashed her .45. Assume the gun had come into her possession with the eight round magazine full. Assume, for good measure, there was also a bullet in the chamber when she was given the weapon, or when she took it. Upon inspection, Ben found one round in the chamber, and six rounds remaining in the magazine. The whole weapon smelled so strongly of cordite that neither the foul weather, nor the gun's immersion in the brackish water in the bottom of the dinghy could completely wash the scent away. So it was very recently fired. Had this slip of a gal pulled the trigger two, maybe three times tonight? Given the look on her face when they had met, and her ease in handling the pistol, he would not put it past her.

Gluing the few facts together with his experience and intuition, Ben felt this woman did not rack out naked of her own volition. Stripping away all clothing was a simple tactic to degrade and control another human being; a hostage. The recently fired pistol meant her departure from wherever she was detained came about with the help of deadly force. Her captor had been invested in keeping her in close, and was willing to break federal, state, and local laws, and abrogate every law of human decency to do it.

The noise of gunfire likely betrayed her escape. She had fled successfully to a point, but in the end, was too unfamiliar with her surroundings. She had run up against the shore, boxing herself in. She had stumbled into a pier of some kind, and found the boat. Such was her desperation, the boat's lack of seaworthiness in this sporty weather meant nothing to her. Tonight's stiff, variable breezes had done the work of the missing oars, pushing her from the pier and shore into a perilous unknown. Risking death from drowning or exposure was still an improvement over what she escaped. So she had likely come from the Chesapeake's western Maryland shoreline. How long had she fled naked in the rain and dark before her line of retreat was blocked at the water? How long had she drifted before washing into the wreck of the *American Mariner*? His rusting home, once asylum for his lonely sojourn, now reminded him of the prison hulks in Dickens' *Great Expectations*.

The woman might tell him more when she woke. She might not. Regardless, it was clear Ben did not have a guest. He was harboring a dangerous refugee.

She was also a loose end.

CHAPTER 8

DARKNESS AND RAIN cast a somber pall over Maynard Chalk's already miserable recollections of his last mission, which was a complete failure, save for his persisting heartbeat. Beyond that, his only consolation then and now was Tahereh's companionship. At least tonight she was not profusely bleeding from a cullet-slashed forearm, and fleeing with him from the imminent detonation of a dirty bomb, and all this on a crappy little boat threatening to capsize in the angry Chesapeake. It had been dark and raining hard then, as now. That fiasco had imploded just a few months before, and not that far from the woods where they were walking a search grid with the other two-man teams.

The melancholia from ruminating on the past, the losses, the shame, and his banishment from the privileged stratum of black-bag work with buckets of slush money to siphon off, had so far not devolved into another raging blackout tonight, but it was early. Like herpes, the worst psychotic episode was usually the first one, but it could flare just as brightly after an extended period of quiescence. Ever the statistical outlier, Chalk had proven that all his frequent crack-ups were violent enough to earn a super-max inmate in ADX Florence a life sentence locked up in isolation. He hoped Tahereh would see an eruption coming quickly enough to get the hell out of the way. With the nerve damage, her mangled arm was still all but useless to her, and Chalk would hate to dish her a setback. He was such a sap for this girl.

Chalk groused, "Did all our pickets check in?"

Tahereh stepped carefully through the pine woods, aiming her flashlight to either side of the grid line they were searching. "Still nothing from Sanders. He's now eight minutes overdue."

Chalk spoke into his encrypted radio. "Sanders! Where the hell are you?"

They heard nothing in reply but a gnat's buzz of electronic noise. Chalk pressed the transmit button again. "Sanders, I'm docking your pay if you don't hit me back right now, you lazy shit." Of course, garnishing an employee's wages was Chalk's euphemism for a severe beating and possible execution. Chalk was already totting up Sanders' black market value as an organ donor.

"He had sector Charlie, right?"

Tahereh answered with a distracted, "Yes."

"We should've got more dogs," vented Chalk. "Bloodhounds. Not those damn Rotties. I've seen gerbils with more spunk than our dogs. And why only two of them, anyway?"

Tahereh said, "Budget. Like tracking chips."

"Screw these grids. Grids are for punks. Let's head over to Charlie-Land and see what we can see."

Tahereh switched her radio to the search detail's common frequency to alert the other teams to their change of plan. They trudged through the misty woods for twenty minutes to the Charlie area where Sanders should have been patrolling. Two figures loomed out of the dark wet fog.

Chalk limbered his pistol and aimed it at the approaching shadows who doused two MagLite beams. Tahereh pinned them down with her own LED flashlight.

Chalk bellowed, "Wassail!"

"Drink ale!" came the countersign from one of the figures.

Chalk holstered his pistol. "Anything?"

A tall gunman, Felix Harrower, sporting two fragmentation grenades dangling from his H-gear, raised his hand in front of his eyes and squinted in Tahereh's beam. "No. No sign. He's just gone."

Harrower's buddy in the search, a shorter, wiry woman with a bedraggled brunette mullet jutting out from below her fatigue cap, came forward holding out a laminated terrain map. Earline Byrd swept her finger along a dark green section. "We've been all through here. Just about to work the ravine."

Chalk said, "We'll take over. You two boogie back and fill in for us in Echo." Chalk pointed at another area of the map. "We got as far as here, moving north."

Harrower asked, "Sanders? No word at all?"

Chalk barked, "Would I be standing here talking to you? Shove off. Double time!"

Harrower and Byrd snapped on their flashlights and hustled into the night accompanied by an unsoldierly clank of gear. Chalk wondered what strapped-on, ball-buster brain fart made them think grenades were really necessary on this detail, but he admitted he liked to march heavy himself at times. Better safe than sorry.

"Fucking amateurs," muttered Chalk. "Let's hit that ravine."

They ducked and wove through the stand of pine toward the west, with rain from the branches pattering off their jackets and down their necks. Chalk was infuriated. He did not care whether he found Sanders or the missing livestock first. There would be hell to pay tonight.

Ten minutes later, Chalk played his light over the steep edge of the ravine. The bottom was a rushing torrent choking and spreading from two feet to four feet wide as the snags and topography channeled the runoff. Chalk squatted and slid down the embankment, picking up more speed as pine needles topping the grass and clay greased his descent. Water broke high over his knees as he hit bottom. At first, Tahereh checked her descent better than Chalk had managed, but with one bum hand unable to help her clutch and balance, she still ended up sitting chest deep in the water.

She spat out a curse in Farsi. With Chalk's help, she got to her feet. She was soaked to the skin, chilled to the bone, with a fury burrowing deep into her soul, but she knew better than to gripe. "Upstream? Or down?"

Chalk mulled for a moment. The runoff was churning and turbid, offering no clues to which direction the maverick had fled. "Downstream, the current would help push her along wherever she was going. Are you thinking Sanders was in on this?"

Tahereh felt the rushing water excavating mud from beneath her boots. "She's been cut and stitched in the way of her people. What would she have to offer him?"

"Goddamn barbarians. But by my calculations, the funky body modifications leave her two holes, and two hands to the good."

"Your people are paid well enough," observed Tahereh. "Sanders wouldn't have to settle for damaged goods unless he was humoring her prior to killing her."

"He wouldn't dare sully the merchandise," seethed Chalk. "She was A-list stuff, especially with her mods. The pervs love that freaky junk. No way would he mess with her, if he planned to bring her in, that is."

"Then I believe she went upstream," said Tahereh. "She seemed like a clever one."

Chalk keyed the mic again. "Sanders, you godforsaken grunt! You keep your mutton-dagger out of my property, or I'll feed you your own goody bag! Sanders!" His warning earned only silence from the radio.

For the next fifteen minutes, they sloshed in the rain against the rushing current, playing their lights up and down the banks of the ravine. Chalk forged through the middle of the channel, while he helped Tahereh keep her feet along the shallow edges of the rain swollen ravine. The walls of the arroyo were often too steep for either of them to walk on the dry.

It was Tahereh's flashlight that first played over the obstruction lying up ahead. It seemed to be a deadfall tree that had tumbled down when the mass of mud beneath it calved from the bank into the flood. They slogged closer.

Chalk shouted "Sanders!"

The sentry's legs trailed loosely in the water, and already had snagged up a few small branches and a wad of leaves and pine needles. A half hour more, and he would have disappeared under the mass of detritus sluicing downstream.

"Please tell me he had a damn heart attack," yelled Chalk, as Tahereh clawed her way ahead to the fallen man along the right bank.

Tahereh reported over her shoulder to Chalk who lagged behind, "Three in the chest. His AK is here. I don't see his pistol. His knife's still here, too." Tahereh ignored the corpse's open, staring, rain-teared eyes. She always admired a sharp length of steel. She bent to recover Sander's coveted Gerber combat blade.

Chalk was still some distance downstream from Tahereh and the body when he shouted, "What about his poppers?"

Like an answer to his question, Chalk heard a tinny clank, a teaspoon dropped into the silverware drawer. Suddenly, Tahereh was jamming her hands blindly into the turbid water around the body, as if looking for a lost diamond earring. Her panicked shout came too late. "Grenade!"

The water next to Tahereh geysered into a gout of spray, accompanied by a low thump. Tahereh flew backwards up onto the bank and slid on her side in the mud back down to the water. Chalk felt something whirl past his head. Another thud. He turned to see what he assumed was Sanders's knife, which had hacked point-first several inches into a tree trunk a few feet behind his head. A boot-lace dangled from the hilt, with the wire loop of a grenade pin jiggling at the end. A simple booby trap.

Chalk chugged upstream to Tahereh and kneeled at her side. Both her arms were gone just below the elbows. Though badly pocked and slashed from her knees north, she had taken the brunt of the blast from her belly to her face. Her tattered, bloody fatigues were ripped away with her skin to expose shredded muscle fiber, and torn, perforated organs. Her thick mane of black hair lay scalped back from her face like a wig that had slipped askew in a wind. Tahereh's almond eyes were now little ramekins filled with raspberry preserves.

He tried to comfort her. "Honey, you sure stepped in it this time."

To Chalk's horror, a bubbling, wheezy whistle escaped the gash that had been Tahereh's mouth. Then came a barely discernible phrase, but with lips, teeth, and tongue battered to mush, he could not understand her. Wondering how the hell Tahereh could still be alive, he leaned in close to hear what she had to say for herself.

The stumps of her arms rose toward Chalk's face, clutched at his neck in a stiff, sticky embrace. In utter revulsion, he shoved the love of his life down into the mud with both hands. Tahereh did not move again. There was no sound but the rain, and the water flooding past in the ravine. Chalk figured he could ask Tahereh about her last words the next time they met up.

CHAPTER 9

BEN BLACKSHAW PACED the dark foredeck of his derelict home for about an hour, like a mad sea captain from a 19th Century yarn. The cold rain cleared his head. With the first subtle wash of dawn relieving the night's watch in the eastern sky, he went quietly below again. His guest still slept.

Blackshaw had to protect his solitude. He had to shield his presence on the ship from all but his few most trusted friends. He had to maintain the fiction of his death in a black-ops story where he would otherwise be the prey in a merciless hunt. In addition, there was his clandestine labor, transforming a cache of stolen gold bullion into works of art that could be slipped piece by piece into an elite market that cared nothing for his name, valuing instead the mysterious provenance of such rare work in such a precious medium.

Everyone on his home of Smith Island, less than three hundred souls, had a stake in his lonely efforts proceeding without interruption. There were tons of gold in this cache; so much work to do. He could not return home to a simpler life working the waters of the Chesapeake Bay, would not allow himself that peace, until every cursed ounce was rendered first into something beautiful, and then into cash.

He hefted the woman's .45 once again, considering his decision. There were already two bodies of unlucky operatives rotting to soup bones in the flooded bowels of the *American Mariner* from a violent wintertime incursion. Would one more make such a great difference? Then Blackshaw hesitated, recalling his vanquished targets' appalling tendency to return and offer him spectral company just as he was falling asleep. He knew this young woman would persist like a hypnagogic Fury long after her last breath.

"Ben?"

The voice recalled Blackshaw to his limbic self as he spun toward the sound, cocking the hammer behind the chambered round, and taking aim at the new intruder.

LuAnna, Blackshaw's beautiful wife, stood in the shadowed doorway to the compartment taking in the scene. He could not tell if the surprise on her face stemmed from seeing a girl snuggled deep into his cot, or from the unwavering gun barrel centered on her sternum.

She said, "Don't look at me like that."

"Like how?"

"Like I'm that annoying woman bringing over your favorite pair of titties for a playdate. Who's this piece of strange? 888 Outcall?" LuAnna sighed, teasing. "We're gonna have to take away your sat-phone again. Maybe for a week this time."

Ben said, "It's not what it looks like."

"Some might say it's too late for couple's counselling, but not me," said LuAnna with a chuckle in her voice.

Ben relaxed, flipped up the safety, and eased the hammer down. LuAnna stepped quietly into the compartment. "She don't snore like an old bear at all."

"Didn't cost me any sleep, neither," he likewise answered in the sideways syntax of Smith Island.

Blackshaw was glad LuAnna was here. After an unhappy stint keeping him company in his first lair in New York City, she had retreated to more familiar surroundings to live alone in their saltbox house on Smith Island. This morning, she had braved the expanse of the Chesapeake that lay between Smith and the *American Mariner* in an old crab skiff. The skiff drew so little water, some said it would float on dew. Its draft was definitely shallow enough to maneuver into the old Liberty Ship's waterline gash in all but the lowest tides.

Blackshaw said, "Sorry I wasn't there to help tie up."

"I managed all right for a girl." Like Blackshaw, LuAnna was born on Smith Island, and knew her way around any watercraft on the Chesapeake. Her career as a corporal in the Maryland Department of Natural Resources Police, with many long patrols under her belt, only added to her finesse on the water. The arrival of the gold bullion had brought with it her momentous decision to abandon law enforcement, and step into Smith Island's darker heritage of piracy with Blackshaw and many of their neighbors.

"This one got a name?" LuAnna teased.

"Reckon so. But she hasn't told me, nor said more than a mute's piece since she come calling."

"Bet she has her reasons."

Perhaps disturbed by the conversation, the guest stirred in her sleep. The blankets drifted to one side, revealing her strange pajamas. LuAnna's eyebrows twitched up in skeptical appraisal. Her tone was less lighthearted when she said, "Travels light, this one. Now's a good time to explain."

"Woke to a dinghy knocking around in the hold. She must've floated in at the hole, like that snag did before. Herself was laying in the bottom. I thought she was dead. She had a gun. Didn't catch me off guard none. Gave her some chow, and out she went."

At the mention of food, LuAnna shoved a wicker basket full of aromatic home cooked favorites into Blackshaw's arms. Then she knelt down next to the cot studying the young woman. "I don't like how you were looking at her, Ben."

"She earned a weather eye."

"There's a goose pie in the basket. And a cake."

"Chocolate? Seven layers?"

"Nine."

"Chocolate?"

"For the love of God, Ben, you sound like a child," chided LuAnna.

"Comforts are few here."

"Poor baby. You could always come home."

"Not yet a while. You know I can't. Still, it gets a little hairy out this way."

"Thought you'd spice it up deep-sixing this kid?"

"Crossed my mind. I'm not larking around on this boat. You know the stakes. You almost died for the gold, LuAnna. Rather not face that again."

LuAnna stiffened at the recollection of her near miss with the Reaper last Autumn. She rose to her feet, faced Blackshaw, and slipped the pistol out of his hand. "You saved my life. I thought it a most chivalrous thing. No one else would have done that for me." She kissed him softly.

"All in a day's work."

"You can't do this to her. The Ben I know couldn't do such a thing. Not for love or money."

"There's the work. It's not just for you and me."

"You mean the work you already left off once to go running around the world to help your old boss?" LuAnna was referring to Ben's recent hunting expedition for a rogue sniper at the behest of his former commanding officer.

"That was different. I was placed in a position. Low ground, and no damn cover. It was that, or lose everything we all worked for."

LuAnna removed the goose pie from the wicker basket, and set it on top of the electric furnace Blackshaw used to melt chunks of bullion to pour into his molds. She disappeared through the door. A few moments later, he heard the start-up coughs of a small, gasoline-powered movie set generator in the next compartment. True to its design, the jenny was inaudible after that. When LuAnna returned to the compartment, she switched the furnace on. It hummed with power. A new warmth rolled into the space enveloping everything. Soon, the goose pie began to steam.

LuAnna said, "Wait for it."

Soon, the pie's aromas wafted out to the corners of the compartment. The young woman stirred. She slowly opened her eyes, disoriented. Catching sight of Blackshaw and LuAnna watching her, she bolted off the cot, put her back to the far bulkhead, drew Blackshaw's Bersa from the coat pocket, and covered them.

LuAnna asked, "Is that your—?"

"Yep. Empty."

LuAnna ignored the terrified woman, and served up three plates of goose pie. The uninvited guest seemed to remember Blackshaw's earlier kindnesses. This time, she pocketed the gun while she ate.

Blackshaw watched with a small sadness as the young woman inhaled a second helping of his wife's ovencraft.

LuAnna said to their guest, "My name is LuAnna. I'm married to this knucklehead. He answers to Ben. What do they call you?"

The woman chewed, watched, and said nothing.

LuAnna asked Ben, "Not a word since she got here?"

"Suits me fine." This guest's anonymity had made hard decisions about her future less burdensome for Blackshaw's sprained conscience.

LuAnna persisted. "Look, Honey-Girl. You need to let us in on your big secret, or we can't help you. Honestly, you're putting us in a spot, showing up here. I can't vouch for your continued well-being if you don't uncork a little. You like that goose pie? I can teach you how to make it." To Blackshaw she said, "Maybe no English?"

"Crossed my mind. She wasn't out on a pleasure cruise. No idea how she got to wherever she was, that is, before she washed in here. That, plus the gun—"

"And a hasty job of dressing—"

"And that." Blackshaw hoped LuAnna would have let that go. "So, I think she's on the run."

"A fine pair you two make."

CHAPTER 10

JOACHIM DEPRIEST HOARFROSTED the room as he fixed Maynard Chalk with a disdainful one-eyed gaze. Chalk regarded the deformed colossus perched above him on the custom chaise and dais. He hated the monstrous figure at all times, but the spectacle of watching him eat was disgusting. The reflections of several news monitors across the globular abdomen gave DePriest the appearance of a multimedia asteroid.

DePriest swept a whole roasted chicken from the side table. In his great hand, the bird looked like a sickly sparrow. He sucked half the meat from the carcass at once. As DePriest chewed, his lipless mouth ejected large and small bones onto his belly. Grease slicked his mottled face to a sheen that reached his eyebrows.

Wallace, decked in a fetching vinyl French maid costume, cleared the bones away and tidied up with a linen napkin scented with rose water. Armand, sporting an androgynous scarlet latex catsuit, replenished the buffet, where five more pullets, a rack of lamb, a bushel of half-shelled oysters, and a washtub of mashed potatoes waited among other delicacies.

When the ravening anti-Buddha raged in his high-pitched voice, Chalk thought his ears might bleed. More partially masticated meat tumbled from the giant's glistening maw.

"The little one is gone!"

Chalk admitted, "Yes. For now."

DePriest shuddered with anger. "That was your *only job*, Maynard! The only thing you had to manage until tonight! And then for just a few more evenings after that, while the stock was processed, and during which your responsibilities were to be further reduced! Two of your team are actually dead?"

"Three. We anticipated attrition, Mr. DePriest, in the stock, and the personnel, too. This kind of operation—"

"Shut-up-shut-up-shut-up-SHUT-UP!" Waves rippled through the adipose rolls of DePriest's body as he screamed and flailed arms so large they might have been the hind legs off a blue ribbon state fair steer. "This event has been two years in the making! The word-of-mouth to qualified clients, surveys of precisely the right acts to conduct, the deposits I have collected, acquiring the facility, modifying it, stocking the yard, the servers, routers, and encryption; and the actors, all those fucking sociopathic actors we've had to vet—! You have no idea what it has taken to set everything in motion, to create it all, Maynard, to make everything ready. And now, with your simple lapse, we have a living, breathing, talking, heathen bitch roaming free out there looking for help, for the law, and for a reporter to hand over the story of a lifetime. Wisdom dictates we cancel. And all because of *you!*"

In his mind's eye, Chalk saw his profit share in the venture evaporate. Instead, the upfront costs of his security detail for the last six months loomed ruinously large.

"For Christ's sake, I never said I was Temple Grandin."

"You are Maynard Chalk! Your reputation and your resume made you the first and last person I approached to boss my hand-selected yard."

Chalk had enough. "Calm the fuck down, chubby." Armand and Wallace glanced at their boss for any sign that it was time to rein Chalk in as he brayed on, "We kick off in fourteen hours as planned. No deviation from the timetable. I'll find the runner. I swear I will. Meantime, nobody would ever believe her. She doesn't know enough to tell about any of it. Barely knows her own name. She has no friends here. We'll have our circus, and then by damn, I'll have my share."

DePriest's chest rose and fell as he tried to quell his fury. His eye glinted with cold light through a single porcine slit. Armand and Wallace stood like attack dogs, poised to tear Chalk in two at a word from their master. Like a volcano before the eruption, DePriest hissed, "I will make my final decision over breakfast. You have until then, Maynard. Make the most of it."

CHAPTER 11

BEN AND LUANNA speculated quietly while their guest ate the last bite of her third piece of Smith Island layer cake.

A soft, determined voice broke into their conversation. "L'Wana, Ben, thank you, but I must go now. Which way to my boat?"

The two Smith Islanders stared, surprised to hear their guest speak for the first time.

Ben said, "What's your name?"

The young woman grew impatient, even insistent, as she said, "Cheptalam. *Tally*. I need paddles. Do you have paddles, Ben?" Her words were clear, but heavily accented.

"Tally, your boat's gone," Ben told her. "Floated away. Sorry."

The woman's face fell when Blackshaw broke the news, but she certainly rallied. She drew Ben's Bersa, and aimed it at him. "Then I will need your ship. Please."

Blackshaw hated to share more bad news but there was no avoiding it. "Well, I'm not Captain Phillips. And that gun isn't loaded. I took out the bullets while you were napping. And if you look out any porthole, you'll see this ship is hard aground. Been on a shoal for longer than you've been alive. Maybe you missed the gash in the hold before."

Tally pointed the pistol at the bundle of blankets on the cot and pulled the trigger. The report in the confined metal compartment assaulted their ears. Blackshaw and LuAnna flinched, and stepped back as Tally trained the gun back toward them. Cordite melded in the air with the scent of goose pie.

"You said it was empty," complained LuAnna.

Tally was apologetic when she said, "I woke up and found the bullets while Ben was stomping around on the deck. This ship is really just a wreck?"

LuAnna said, "It's true. Can you put the gun down, please? Maybe we can help you." LuAnna had received an hour of hostage negotiation training in the Natural Resources Police. She had listened with half-hearted interest then, and was leaning heavily on empathy now.

Tally gestured toward Blackshaw. "This one wanted to kill me."

"And he might-could have, a hundred times," said LuAnna with a note of pride. "You're still alive because that's what he wants."

"You stuffed a gun in my face," reasoned Blackshaw. "Having you around seemed like a bad idea. Still does."

"Where will you go? The bay's right sporty," said LuAnna.

Blackshaw said, "So what? Let her go. I'll give her my RHIB. Your skiff could get traced once she ditches it, or swamps and drowns. Chesapeake's on our side, Hon."

LuAnna cast a disapproving look at her husband.

Tally said, "Please, there is something I *must* do. I must go back. There is no time."

LuAnna asked, "Back *where?* Honey, you've got the gun, so you can have a boat. Yay for you, and thanks for saying *please* and all, but even if you had the gawl-dang *Nimitz*, where the heck are you going?"

It was as if hearing the question for the second time allowed it to sink through Tally's emotional turbulence. She thought for a moment, recalling her hardships in getting to the *American Mariner*. She sat on the cot, deflated, as if exhausted anew.

LuAnna said, "Can you put the gun down, please?"

Tally pointed the gun at the blankets and pulled the trigger again. Blackshaw and LuAnna twitched as the hammer dropped on an empty chamber with a loud *snick*.

The young woman looked sheepish as she tossed the gun down, and said to Blackshaw, "You came back before I could load more bullets."

Blackshaw and LuAnna both released a deep breath of relief. Tally began to weep. She pushed at the tears with clenched fists. "My sister. I have to go back for her. I promised. She's waiting. They will kill her."

Tally's abject misery drew LuAnna into a desperate pity. "Who's going to kill her? Why? When?"

"Tonight," said Tally. "They are monsters. They are going to slaughter her like an animal, but what they will do to her before that—for hours and hours before that—Chamaiyo is twelve years old. Only *twelve*! We must kill them first, L'Wana. Ben, we must destroy them, every single one."

Heartrending as the story was, Blackshaw's mind was running down another dark byway. After she fired the last, the only round in his gun just now, the slide should have stayed back in the open position. Yet, after the shot, the slide had closed again, convincing Blackshaw and LuAnna there was at least one more round in the chamber. Yes, the same effect could come about if the magazine's follower were damaged, or if the magazine were cheaply made, but Blackshaw knew neither case to be true. The mag was new. He changed it out regularly.

In Blackshaw's view that left one other, more disturbing possibility. The intruder had depressed the slide release lever with her left thumb when she pulled the trigger, defeating the last-shot/hold-open function, completing the necessary deception. Tally was either very lucky, or her familiarity with guns lay well past pistol-whipping and squeezing a trigger. Blackshaw did not believe in luck. A gnawing sensation in his gut told him there was much more to Tally than she was letting on.

CHAPTER 12

THE *AMERICAN MARINER* was riddled from the Pax River gunnery practice. Looking back at her over the water and through the thickening fog, Blackshaw reveled with an artist's eye in the way the white hull paint ran to the corroded orange-brown of drying blood. The rude destruction of the old target ship that was begun with scuttling, and continued by bombs and bullets, was pushing ahead at a more natural pace by ensuing decades.

Blackshaw twisted the inflatable's outboard throttle all the way, and breathed deeply of the swift breeze and misting rain. There was no lack of air aboard the rotten wreck, if one did not mind it scented with fuel oil, rust, and voyages long since ended, their crews long since buried. For Blackshaw, there was something viscerally alive in the open Chesapeake winds that chilled his unshaven face, and watered his eyes.

LuAnna and Tally would be fine on the hulk, or that's what Blackshaw told himself. A quick glance from his wife before he left let him know without a word that she had her own suspicions about their guest. Unequivocal asylum was granted to Tally once she surrendered Blackshaw's Bersa. LuAnna kept both that pistol and the .45 in her custody. The former police officer also had a punchy little .25 Beretta Jetfire strapped to her ankle, but there was no need for Tally to know about that.

The inflatable was fast but brutal in the chop. Blackshaw would have liked to trim the boat with a second person sitting toward the bow, or at least amidships, to counter his own weight and that of the motor at the stern. He had positioned the portable gas tank as far forward as the rubber fuel line allowed. The tank was nearly full, and its weight and placement helped flatten the rise of the bow by a few degrees. Even so, Blackshaw was taking a sound beating. On the other side of the discomfort, he sensed the rough ride was shaking off a torpor that had slowly crept into his mind, muscle and bone over the last few weeks alone on the hulk. Rare visits from LuAnna bringing supplies helped somewhat to stave off madness from his isolation, but bay air and big water were the tonic for Blackshaw. He would not ease off the throttle until he got closer to where he was going.

He raced through the darker curtains of embedded squalls over places charted with names like Northwest Middle Grounds and The Old Hannibal. Here, around marks 72 and 70, a tide running in or out would push stripers, blues, and Spanish mackerel breaking toward the surface with gulls, white and wheeling overhead to show where to cast a line.

He pounded farther south cutting between Chumming and Mud Leads, which was known locally as Shell Hill. Still out of sight of shore, he passed the Martin National Wildlife Refuge which lay off Smith Island just north of the Big Thorofare, and across from the hamlet of Ewell. The refuge had been grazing and hunting grounds for Smith Islanders for hundreds of years until 1954 when Glenn Martin, the aviation pioneer, handed the first 2,659 acres of the parcel over to the U.S. Fish and Wildlife Service. Overnight, any Smith Island hunter who had been guiding, or gunning for his own family's table there, was branded a poacher.

He could not see his Smith Island house through the gray rain, but he felt the Siren pull of hearth and friends that set his heart keening in reply. One day he would step across his own threshold a free man, alive, and with his right name and no alias. But not today. Not this trip. For now, he was still listed as a dead man in all the databases that recorded such things, and in a shadowed oubliette of his soul he had to agree with the ruling. That would change. It must, or he would go insane with grief for his old life.

With the tide flooding, he ran between Cheeseman and Shanks Islands, which were now barely more than sandbars. Then he cut north up around South Point and Peachorchard Point. After another short run, he tacked northwest into the little gut where his friend Knocker Ellis Hogan lived.

Ellis's saltbox lay on higher ground that time, rising water, and a sinking marsh had cut off from the few hundred other fulltime souls on Smith who constituted all of civilization. Ellis could walk into Rhodes Point for necessaries across a long and complex series of footbridges and rough planked paths, but he preferred to take the deadrise named *Miss Dotsy*, which he was looking after for Ben until happier times. If passing within hailing distance of his own saltbox put Blackshaw into a remembering frame of mind, seeing *Miss Dotsy* riding high and pretty with bow, stern, and spring mooring lines perfectly set, cast his spirits into the mud. That boat belonged to his former self; really to a completely different man, from another bygone era.

In fact, several trying months and a hard winter had peeled off the calendar since he had walked on any part of the Smith Island archipelago. But nothing stayed the same forever, even there. On the marshy hummocks that Ellis called home, a few changes caught Blackshaw's eye right away. A large, old utility shed lay set back from the water about fifty feet. The shed sported fresh shingles. New glazing replaced the old shattered panes. Improvements were understandable since Ellis possessed fantastic wealth. The headscratcher was why Ellis's old push mower, rakes, shovels, his grass whip, and other implements stood leaning against the outside of the shed in the rain. Ellis was fastidious with his tools, even the prosaic and domestic ones.

The careless disposition of his friend's gear was not the only thing snagging Blackshaw's attention. A new lane had been cut out of the small lawn leading from the shed down to the water. The lane had been made passable in most seasons with a ton or two of crusher run gravel. At the water end of the lane, a four-inch-by-four-inch post of pressure-treated pine stood anchored in a footing of poured concrete. On top of the post sat a shiny new mailbox. Baffled, Blackshaw crossed the little patch of grass just reviving from a winter's brownment, and knocked on the water-side door of the saltbox.

Ellis opened the door so quickly it was obvious he had watched Ben's approach. Blackshaw noted how thin his friend had become fighting the sepsis he acquired from a late-treated gunshot wound to the thigh during their last sortie together. His black skin was drawn tight over the sinews of his throat.

Ellis spoke before Ben could greet his friend and break open the matter of Tally. He said, "Hey, Pilgrim," and snatched a Barbour Beaufort field jacket off a hook next to the door.

Ellis was in a rush as he donned it, explaining, "Got to get the mail. Then we can have coffee." The strange welcome earned Ellis a sharp glance, to which he responded, "Oh shut up. Aren't you already wet?"

Blackshaw's confusion was not cleared up at all as Ellis walked toward the renovated shed instead of toward the mailbox. Sensing consternation, Ellis called over his shoulder, "You'll see."

Ellis waited for Blackshaw at the front of the shed, and said, "Want you to eyeball something." He opened the garage doors, flipped on an overhead light, and watched Blackshaw's face closely.

"Lordy go to fire. Ellis, what *is* that?" Shoes, bikes, mopeds, and golf carts were the usual land transport on Smith. Blackshaw stooped to examine the sleek black sports car hunkered low in the shed's only bay.

"Bugatti Veyron. Fastest street-legal production car in the entire world. Not quite two million dollars. She tops out at two hundred sixty-seven miles per hour and change."

Blackshaw stared at his friend, "Once you hit two sixty-seven, I reckon *and change* is gilding the lily."

"And you'd know a thing or two about that, wouldn't you, Ben?" As Blackshaw's partner in salvaging the stolen gold from the bottom of the Chesapeake, Ellis gratefully accepted his full fifty percent share of the value of the artwork that Ben made from it. Blackshaw split his own half-share evenly among the rest of the Smith Island families, as well as with many men on Tangier Island to the south who had lent a hand in that bloody mission. This favorable arithmetic made Ellis the richest man on Smith, and for many miles around on the mainland.

"Swagger die, Ellis. What a thing." Then Blackshaw eyed the fifty feet of graveled lane leading from the shed to the mailbox at the water. There was no other road on this marshy patch of ground.

"Let's take her for a spin," suggested Ellis.

"Where are we going?"

"Done told you. To fetch the mail."

Blackshaw worked his way into the narrow space between the shed's wall and the car, noting the polished heat exchangers behind the cockpit. He was thinking of *Miss Dotsy's* serviceable Atomic Four engine when Ellis said, "A thousand plus horsepower."

"Plus?"

"And then some."

"Thank goodness for that. Isn't *Bugatti* owned by *Volkswagen* now?"

Ellis scowled. "I'm going to punch the shit out of you. Get in."

Blackshaw opened the car door, and squeezed into the snug tan leather racing seat on the passenger side. Taller and thinner, Ellis slid behind the wheel with practiced ease. He turned the key and waited as various lights came to life on the spare, curvilinear instrument panel. After a few beeps indicating all was in order, Ellis stabbed the Start button on the machined steel center console, and more lights blazed. The big engine behind them roared to life. The old shed shook with the power of it.

Ellis said, "Sixteen jugs. Four turbos."

Raising his voice over the engine, Blackshaw asked, "You don't pick up your mail at the Post Office in Ewell n'mare?"

"Of course I do," explained Ellis with great patience. "And then I put it in that new mailbox over there. Then I go in the house for a cup of coffee. I got a new espresso machine. Buckle up."

Despite the urgency of Blackshaw's visit, he did as Ellis instructed. Ellis made a few adjustments his friend could not see. Hearing a servo whine, Ben looked over his shoulder and saw the rear spoiler retracting into the body as the entire car seemed to squat even lower to the ground.

Ellis worked the finger paddles on the steering wheel, and the rumble of the engine changed notes. The beast moved forward slowly out of the shed. Blackshaw tensed for the moment his friend would surely floor the gas pedal, which would fill the shed with gravel and land them neck deep in the gut just ahead, or possibly in Brazil a little farther south. Yet Ellis did not accelerate past a cripple's limp.

Instead, Ellis made the most of the short lane, enjoying the view, glancing from time to time over at Blackshaw, moving the steering wheel with two fingers of his left hand. Within a few moments, they reached the end of the drive to nowhere, having barely dislodged a single stone along the way. With an easy application of the brakes, the starship-on-wheels stopped by the mailbox.

"She's got some kind of Hi-Fi stereo, but it's all about that engine sound for me," said Ellis. "Hang on." He climbed out of the car, retrieved a few junk mail circulars from the mailbox, and lowered its red metal flag. Regaining the cockpit, he craned his neck around, and backed the Veyron slowly up the lane to its place in the shed where he shut the beast down.

"Did you get Triple-A?" asked Ben. "You don't want to get stuck in a bad part of town in a whip like this."

"Run-flat tires," said Ellis, as if to an idiot.

"Should've known."

"Yes, you should have. And yes, I got Triple-A, too. I'm no fool."

"Belt-and-suspenders man."

"Yes indeed."

They sat in the car without saying anything for several minutes listening to the engine cool, watching the rain. With the strange outing done, Ellis seemed gloomy.

Blackshaw said, "What-say we try that espresso machine."

Ellis sat still for a few moments more before he nodded. Abandoning the mail there in the car along with several days' worth of previous pick-ups lying behind Blackshaw's seat, Ellis got out slowly.

Ben followed him to the saltbox. "You are very bored."

Ellis countered, "No, I'm old. But I am rich, and we are friends. You can borrow my car anytime."

CHAPTER 13

NO BARISTA WAS Ellis. Producing a few shots of coffee from the shiny tube-and-dome machine required the filling of reservoirs, some noisy grinding, the adjustments of hissing valves, and an acute risk of scalding. Soon there were two cracked mugs half-filled with an undeniably tasty brew. During the process, which seemed more complicated than a rocket launch, certainly more involved than starting the Veyron, Ben told Ellis what he could about Tally's strange and violent arrival at the old ship.

When Blackshaw paused, Ellis asked, "So she drops in out of nowhere buck-naked, whips up on you, and you give her food? You old softy."

"That was before I decided to put her lights out. And before LuAnna got there."

Ellis whistled low with mock surprise. "I remember a man not too long ago who wouldn't raise his hand in anger, lest it was overseas, and for our Uncle Sam, may he live forever."

"The stakes are too big now."

"It's not the stakes that changed."

Blackshaw rankled. "I remember your lecture on being true to myself, a self you thought I never met before. Be true to the song in my blood. And true to Smith Island's past, and future. Now, seems if I step left, you'd rather I danced to the right, Ellis. I'm telling you, this Tally is a mixed bag of tricks."

"'Song in your blood'? Now that's most poetical. You like the coffee?"

"Reckon it's hot enough."

Ellis started a chuckle, which grew into a hearty belly laugh. Blackshaw looked into his cup, and with a creeping disgust, recalled Ellis's penchant for finer things. "No! You did *not*! This isn't—"

Ellis was laughing so hard, tears ran down his cheeks. He was out of breath, could barely speak, but he tried. "Those beans came right out of a toddycat's ass, my man! Pip-pop-poop-pip! The look on your face—"

Ben had first heard of four hundred dollar-a-pound Kopi Luwak coffee when he was in Iraq. His longstanding private oath never to drink anything that had passed through the intestines of a civet, or any other creature, had fallen to Ellis's newfound delight in excess. Blackshaw tipped the rest of his mug out into the sink.

Ellis feigned heart failure, and whooped, "Oh my gawd! A fifty dollar shot, straight down the drain!"

After gargling and rinsing his mouth with tap water swigged from Ball jar glassware, Ben said, "You ain't right."

"Who is? You, for instance, are a reverse snob, all that wonderful gold notwithstanding. Now what are you going to do? Help that girl get her sister out of a jam? What's her name again?"

Ben rejoined Ellis at the kitchen table. "The missing little one? Chamaiyo. But I'm telling you, Ellis, big sister has serious skills."

Ellis sobered at the thought. "That does bother me. Where the hell did they come from?"

Ben said, "Africa. The accent sounds like she got her English out east, out Kenya way. I didn't ask. It was enough she stopped trying to kill us while she ate LuAnna's goose pie."

Ellis feigned disgust. "Kids today. That's just ungrateful."

"She can put it away. She's skinny. Looks like one of those marathon runners always winning in New York and Boston."

"Fair enough. If you're going to rescue this Chamaiyo, you need to know where Tally came from last night."

"I was racked out until she got to the boat. Wasn't watching the weather. Hard to reckon her drift. This morning, the wind had a little west in her, a little north in her. The tide was making. Toss in a squall or two overnight, and who knows?"

"And she was laying in the bottom of that boat asleep for the whole ride?"

"So she said. She talked about buildings and woods. Pines. Said she was running like hell to get away. Woods, dark, the pier, the boat and the Chesapeake. She's been traumatized some. Her recall isn't top notch."

Ellis pondered this for a moment. "And she didn't mention about the gun?"

"No more than to say she stole it from where she and her sister were held."

"Fishy. From *where*? Not from *who*? You said the gun had been fired."

"Swagger die, no doubt in my mind."

"And you asked her about that?"

"Denied shooting it. Never fired a gun in her whole life before that warning shot with my Bersa, which I think is a lie. We could ask her again, of course."

"*We*? As in you and I?"

"Yes, Ellis. Dubbin up your tackety boots. Weather's going to hell. Did I say something wrong?"

Ellis looked incredulous. "Ever notice how biding with you generally gets me hurt?"

"Nobody gets off the planet alive."

"I'd like some say in the matter of when I check out."

"Is *when* more important than *how*?"

"Big man, you can't separate the two. As to the way I die, I got no need for a blaze of glory. I got nothing to prove to anybody, least of all to myself, or to you."

"No argument there."

Ellis continued, "And I'm not convinced there's a big party waiting in the afterlife—"

"A barbecue, more like."

Ellis flipped up a middle finger. "—so I can wait to find out about all that. No rush."

"What's the worst that could happen?"

Ellis's laugh rang grim. "Famous last words. Right up there with, 'Watch this,' and, 'Hold my beer.'"

Ben said, "She's a kid. A young lady in distress, as LuAnna might put it. And a little princess held prisoner. Time's running out. It's got all the stuff we like."

Ellis slapped his hand down on the table. "That's it! You got it. The whole thing sounds like a fairy tale."

"I have a problem with folks who hurt kids."

"For the love of Christ, Ben, *everybody* does." Ellis sipped his coffee.

"It's the ones who like it that I mean to settle." Ben's jaw hurt. He found he was grinding his teeth. This was happening a lot lately.

Ellis suggested, "You should call up your buddy, and get better dope on the weather last night. I'll put a bag together. Maybe we go talk to this Tally girl."

Ben jibed, "Sure you're up to it?"

"I'm up to beating you down. Best remember that." Ellis rose and strode the few steps from the kitchen into his small parlor.

Ben followed, and found Ellis studying racks of exotic rifles on the wall. He asked his old friend, "That's twice you've threatened to do me mischief. Why so edgy?"

Ellis was so slow to answer that Ben thought he had not heard. Finally, Ellis replied, "Cabin fever. Same as you. We won't look any deeper than that for now. More coffee?"

CHAPTER 14

THIS WAS THE fourth, and most secluded, waterfront home Chalk and his team had checked out this morning. He was following a hunch. Ignoring the rundown ranch house, which lay set back from the shore under a copse of maples just leafing out, he surveyed the rickety old finger pier and the gray Chesapeake water before him. Twisted planks and canted pilings rucked the pier's deck into the contours of a nightmare roller coaster. Sunrise barely cast helpful light over the poorly maintained property, but Chalk could see there was no boat moored at the pier. Rope chafing marks on a piling said that had not always been the case.

Earline Byrd, Gläans Bellendre, and Felix Harrower stood behind Chalk at a respectful, even cautious ten feet. What with the runaway livestock, as well as the loss of Sanders, Flynn, and the revered Tahereh, they knew their boss was having an off day. Add rumors of the ass-chewing Chalk had taken from DePriest, and there was little doubt someone was going to get hurt. Someone was likely to die. Chalk might be his own worst enemy, but his flamboyant style of leadership did no favors for anyone serving under him either.

Jimmy Clyster approached from a small utility shed, one door of which was now split and hanging askew from a single rusty hinge. He was a stocky former Detroit cop who had been pensioned off the force after a few years on the bow-and-arrow squad. His undoing was a dicey shoot involving a minor. The DPD Professional Standards Unit never proved Clyster was shaking down the young drug mule, but for an officer who loved action, being Stellenbosched on administrative duty was worse than jail.

Clyster reported, "It was padlocked. Life jackets, a couple rods, some crab pots, and two oars."

Chalk grunted. He might have been on the point of offering more, but at that moment, an elderly man lurched out of the house. He wore yellowed pajamas and a ragged blue terry bathrobe loosely sashed over a belly which must have been many years and many beers in the making.

The man glanced back and forth between the strangers by the water, the shiny blacked-out Suburban parked in the driveway, and his violated outbuilding as he shouted, "Who the hell are you? My shed! Jesus!" It was hard for Chalk to understand the man. It seemed he had no upper teeth.

Chalk became stern and officious. "Homeland Security. You have a boat?"

The grizzled homeowner grew confused. "Yeah, right there—Hey! Where the hell is it? Godammit!"

Chalked kept his voice flat and professional. "When was the last time you saw it?"

The old man sputtered, "Yesterday. I was out on her myself yesterday!"

"You sure about that?"

"Of course I am, you idiot! Doc says I gotta exercise, and the boat's kinda like a rowing machine I figured." The mystified duffer was getting angry. Long-unresolved issues with authority were not helping him.

"Can you provide us with a description?"

"It's just a ten-foot dinghy. White. Fiberglass. It sure ain't new, but Jesus *dammit*!"

"You haven't reported this to your local police?"

"No! What the hell did you do to my shed?"

Chalk kept a straight face. "We think it was the thief."

"I think it was that asshole standing right there!" The old man pointed at Clyster. "Look at the door! I ain't deaf! I heard you! You're paying to fix that."

"Fair enough." Chalk drew his Glock G41 Gen4, and Byrd, Bellendre, and Harrower, who stood between their boss and the homeowner, nimbly sidestepped. Chalk fired once, hitting the old man in a thatch of gray belly hair. He folded to the ground, writhing and cursing from the pain. The light rain diluted the blood as it flowed into the nappy robe.

Chalk holstered the weapon under his jacket, then recalled something important. "Oh hell!" he blurted, and jogged over to the dying man whose eyes were losing focus. "Buddy. Hey pal, did you see anyone around here last night?"

In a moment that even an agitated Chalk could sense was surreal, the man actually whispered, "No!" before vomiting a pint of blood.

Impatient, Chalk asked, "Was that *No you don't want to die*, or *No you didn't see anybody*? Help me out here, compadre."

A shriek of terror from the back door of the rancher turned all eyes toward a girthy white-haired woman in a striped housedress flailing toward them across the grass.

The lady screamed, "Oh my God! Lester! Oh my *God*! What happened?"

Chalk drew his gun again, but waited until the woman was two yards out before he shot her in the face. She collapsed full length on the ground. Wisps of hair and gobbets of brain erupting from the back of her skull gunked Earline Byrd's slicker, neck, and face. The laconic operative did not flinch, or move a muscle to tidy up.

Chalk turned back to the man at his feet. "Lester? Hey, Lester! Still with me?" Chalk nudged Lester gently with the toe of his boot. The old man was done.

"Crap, crap, crap," said Chalk. He holstered his gun. "Any room in that shed?"

Harrower answered, "On it."

While his team stacked the bodies out of sight, and repositioned the broken door as best they could, Chalk stepped down to the water's edge. How he hated the Chesapeake Bay. The fishing, the crabbing, all those recreational delights masked a single grotesque truth. He had failed here once before. Failed mightily, and in a way that stripped him of his stature and status, his self-worth, and untold wealth, leaving him groveling for mercy in his humiliation.

Yes, he had been lionized immediately after the great act. Based on the lies he told, the media built him up to heroic status. He had saved Washington, D.C. from a terrorist's dirty bomb.

But the people closest to him remembered. It was not a clean win. The bomb had detonated harmlessly on a sand bar in the middle of the Chesapeake with no loss of human life; no casualties that the mucky-mucks knew about, anyway. Then someone started investigating what Chalk had known of the plot, and exactly when he had learned it. These questions begot more inquiries. Why had Chalk tried to take the terrorists down alone? Who exactly did he work for? Within one news cycle, the fetid odor of a career in black-bag operations began to pall around Chalk, and foul his limitless prospects. After a glorious life in the shadows, fame was his undoing.

His boss, Senator Lily Morgan, from the great state of Wisconsin, disowned him. While she was made Secretary of the Department of Homeland Security, Chalk had to crawl underground. He was told through intermediaries that he could avoid a Senate hearing only if he quickly disappeared.

For a time, he had naively believed he could transform his greatest blunder into his most dazzling success. In the end, no amount of spin, and Chalk had spent millions of dollars in bribes and on fruitless back-office PR campaigns, could change the fact that a dirty bomb detonating on American soil was so heinous it eclipsed the attacks of September 11, 2001. Someone had to pay. Chalk was no longer the man who had preserved the nation's capital. He had devolved into the goon who betrayed America.

Here he was again, on the shores of this giant cesspool, the Chesapeake Bay, chasing down a worthless little bitch just so he could hang on to a repugnant job as a death row jailer. His hands clenched involuntarily, squeezing imagined triggers, turning his enemies to ratatouille and splinters of bone.

"Gramma?" Chalk turned and saw a blonde girl, about five years old, and a boy who must have been her twin, standing by the back door of the house looking sleepy and bewildered. Clyster and Harrower were carrying the old woman's flaccid body toward the shed by wrists and ankles. Earline Byrd and Gläans Bellendre drew pistols.

For the love of Christ! Grandkids? I cannot catch a break, thought Chalk.

He threw a sharp look at Byrd and Bellendre, and said, "Do I have to do everything myself?"

The little girl started to cry as the two operatives stalked toward the house.

Chalk called after them, "Yo! On second thought, take them *alive!*"

Byrd and Bellendre holstered their guns and shifted into a trot.

CHAPTER 15

WHILE ELLIS LAID out his few sundries, some lethal, some not, Ben dialed a number on his encrypted satellite phone. He heard two measured buzzes; the call going out.

The tired voice of Michael Craig answered, "What."

The reclusive giant ran a discreet international consulting firm called Pemstar from an old hunting lodge in the wilds of northern Vermont. Weather analysis is a rough, impressionistic craft to most, but Craig's detailed models were rock solid in the most important way: persistence. His predictive assessments of wind, precipitation, temperature, dew point, humidity, and any kind of weather system, lasted not for hours, but for weeks. His accuracy and precision were godlike. From variable breezes to dust devils, from sun showers to hurricanes, generals and admirals the world over paid dearly for his work-ups when planning anything from small-team covert ops to full scale offensives. The more far-reaching the outlook they desired, the higher Craig's fee. Most of the Pemstar lodge, as well as a cavern in the hillside out back, were taken up with banks of servers running the most elaborate modeling software on the planet. Craig's proprietary software. It was all useless without the man himself making his final, uncanny review of the raw data he collected from sensors and satellites he hacked all over the world.

Ben had served with Craig in Iraq in Gulf War I. Craig's weird grasp of desert winds bearing the clotted plumes of black smoke from burning oil rigs had helped Ben exfiltrate like a phantom from a Fallujah shooting position infested by the enemy.

Ben said, "You know who this is?"

Craig's sigh carried all the way down the line. "We've talked about this, Your Royal Highness. I'm sure your daughter will make a wonderful bride someday, but as I mentioned this morning, I dislike bright sunlight, and there is just too much sand in your country. Sand, sand, sand. It gets everywhere. Your gracious thanks, your payment, the fine bonus, and an opportunity to serve you again in the future were, and will always be more than enough—"

"No," interrupted Ben. "But congratulations."

"Oh." Michael Craig paused, and regrouped. "I don't like talking with you. I talk to you, and things explode." Craig and *Pemstar* had played a crucial role on a delicate mission Ben had undertaken the previous fall.

"The sun's going to explode someday," reasoned Ben.

Craig griped, "Relativism is a rhetorical cheap shot, and you know it."

"Worth a try. You're turning down princesses now?"

"Would a *Wine of the Month Club* subscription be too much to ask? But no, when this guy is grateful, he's really, really grateful. You, on the other hand, are poor. Why am I talking to you?"

"Because I need your help. I need to hire you."

"The money you don't have is no good in my shop."

"And the money I *do* have?"

Craig considered what Ben said for a moment. "Also no good. What do you need? And the whole line's encrypted, so for God's sake, speak in plain English this time."

Ben could not overcome the need to obscure his meaning, just in case. "You know where I've been for the last few weeks?"

"Sure. You used that sat-phone, let's see—" Ben heard Craig working a keyboard. "At least once a week, to call certain people. By the way, how are the new mags for that Bersa working out?"

Ben was profoundly disturbed by Craig's intrusion upon his privacy. "I thought you were a weather guy."

Craig came close to giggling. "Sure. But whether your comms go out over copper, radio, or fiber optics, I know everything."

"Not possible. Even the NSA still has trouble word-sorting data packets over fiber optics."

"Those packets are nothing but light, Ben. Herds of photons. And every third photon on this planet works for me. Reports to *me*. They're like my tiny little dogs."

"You're creeping me out, Mike."

"Chill. I was at the Wiretapper's Ball last year—which I'm never going back to. I had spooks all over me dressed up like fresh-faced interns looking for a summer gig. *Kids*, Ben. They're still trying to figure out my VOIP intercept protocols because I can beat any anonymizer out there. See, I do more business than Silent Circle, Verint, Pen-Link and Narus combined. Sure, the NSA buys my stuff, even the Israelis, but I don't sell them my best. Never my *best* stuff."

"I have no idea what you said after *chill*."

Craig's voice got an edge. "What do you want, Ben? I have a life. I don't like you in it."

"Got a tough situation. I need a drift analysis for my sector for last night, from dusk 'til zero three-thirty. Twenty mile radius, maybe farther out."

"Okay. Starting with the whole Chesapeake, we're talking eight thousand one hundred fifty miles of shoreline, forty-four hundred square miles of water surface including eighteen trillion gallons of water, sixty-four thousand square miles of total watershed, as well as winds, currents, water and air temps, baro-shifts, thermoclines, tides, salinity, wave heights and frequency, tributary outflow volumes, factoring in Spring melt and precip' runoff volumes. I thought you said you had a real problem. For how big a thing?"

"Nine foot dinghy. Maybe ten feet. Fiberglass. Say, twenty inches of freeboard at the stern, and twenty-six inches at the bow. Flat bottom. Hard chine. Draws four inches, five at most. Think of a Crab Alley skiff, but smaller. No engine. No oars. No sail. Weight, about two hundred pounds. With a hundred pound load, inert, amidships."

"That narrows things down a little. Does this *load* have a name?" When Ben did not answer, Craig asked, "You want to know where this load, which is *inert*, ended up?"

Ben chafed as he said, "I already know that. It ended up on my damn stoop. What I need to know is where it started out."

"Backtracking. That's interesting."

"Come on, Mike. Life or death."

"Isn't it always?" Craig yawned. "What's the brisance of this particular gig?"

"I don't get you."

Craig sounded nervous. "You don't? Put it like this: based on what I give you, what's the likelihood you're going to start World War Three?"

"What's it to you?"

"Blowback. I don't need it."

"If everybody's reasonable, should be no problems."

"And when your natural charm tanks, and they don't play ball?"

"Small arms only."

Craig snorted in disbelief. Ben had an innate distaste for lingering on any kind of communication equipment. His impatience building, he asked, "Can you help?"

Mike did not answer. Ben pressed, "Can you do this for me?"

A few seconds later, Ben realized the line was dead.

CHAPTER 16

IT VEXED MAYNARD Chalk to drive so far south to the Calverton Marina in Solomons, Maryland, but that's where the best boat rental was. Not too close to the event site, yet not too far, and still open even in this miserable weather.

An inexpert field application of chloroform had kept the young twins floppy and quiet during the drive to drop them off at the venue with Byrd and Bellendre. Chalk kept Harrower and Clyster with him in the field. Harrower had a current boating safety course certification, which the rental joint would likely want, and Clyster could shoot straight as you please.

Pulling into the marina parking lot, Chalk saw Al, a skinny man in his forties, in a cheap rain slicker, oil-stained shorts, and worn boat shoes. His tan was so deep it had survived the winter. Al was waiting right where he said he would be, with the boat keys in his hand. His Silver Marine Piscator FRP 580 was plenty large at nineteen feet. He was happy to have a renter so early in the season, and his misgivings about letting the good ship *Thresher* go for a whole week was diminished with every hundred-dollar bill Chalk peeled off his roll of cash as an advance. Chalk even sprang for three fishing poles, lures, and a bucket of rancid bait to allay Al's unlikely suspicions.

Al did not need to know the generous rental fee was really a fire-sale purchase price. Chalk would never return the boat. Long before Al started looking for the *Thresher* to cruise homeward over the horizon, Chalk planned to vanish with his profits from the gig, and let the boat drift where it may. In the meantime, loathe the Chesapeake Bay as he did, Chalk felt that a rainy day on the water was preferable to even one nanosecond watching that giant cave maggot, DePriest, throw his considerable weight around over trifles.

The team cast off, and Harrower angled the *Thresher* down Mill Creek, out into more choppy water in the mouth of the Patuxent River, and north again around Drum Point into the bay itself. The waves were running several feet, with the hint of whitecaps frothing the crests. Harrower wanted to keep the speed down so they would not be beaten to death in the first ten minutes, but Chalk rammed the throttle forward with a look that said any reduction in RPMs was not welcome.

Stabbing his thumb at his phone, Clyster asked, "Any idea about the weather overnight? This app only works from now forward into the forecast."

"It was like this, only darker," quipped Harrower.

"He means for drift, you idiot," said Chalk. "Just keep north until we're off of Lester's place, and let's see what we see."

The men fell silent as spray flew over the leaping bow soaking them to the skin.

Abreast of *Dove* Point, Harrower suggested, "Should we put in to report?"

"Christ no. That's why we have phones and radios." Chalk found the cold water a bracing distraction from his other complaints. "And what would we say?"

Everyone aboard was wondering about the runner. From the stockyard to Lester's place on the water was a good five miles. That was a lot of ground for anybody to cover in great weather, equipped with the right gear, and with plenty of training. But lacking other solid clues, it appeared that heifer had knocked out the mileage, stolen the boat, and disappeared, and all of it barefoot, bare-assed, and without a friend in the world.

Chalk asked, "Where'd DePriest get that one?"

Clyster said, "The last jet from Africa, I think." He looked to Harrower for confirmation. "Wasn't that Kenya? Somalia?"

Harrower said, "Something like that. Part of a bigger group, but she came in with a kid. Her little sister, I think."

Clyster said, "A pretty hard case to ditch the little girl with us and split like that."

After a moment, Chalk said, "Unless she's coming back."

CHAPTER 17

JIMMY CLYSTER REVELED in the solitude the old wreck af-
forded him. When Chalk and Harrower had dropped him off from *Thresher*
onto the ship's rusting exterior passerelle stairway near the stern, he had
fully expected the old treads to fail under his weight combined with that of
all his gear. He was just happy to be away from Chalk's insane bluster.
Looking down, he could see the water through the holes that corrosion and
practice aerial gunnery had made. Clyster was not sure what Chalk expected
him to see now from this unusual observation post, what with the fog persisting far longer than anyone expected; the clag would eventually burn off.
The runner remained a problem.

Chalk, Harrower, and *Thresher* disappeared in the fog before Clyster
gained the relative safety of the main deck. There was no sentimental waiting around to be sure the passerelle held and he did not drop like a hanged
man through a gallows trap into the Chesapeake. Chalk had all the esprit de
corps of a wolverine.

Once on the deck, he scanned the ship fore and aft, and decided the
best view would come from the old wings of the bridge. He decided that
for his own safety, he would quickly reconnoiter the ship's interior before
heading up to his final position.

The fog made the ship utterly eerie. He could hear waves slapping the
outside of the hull, but the swish and swell also seemed to be coming from
inside, and from below. Now and then a rumble like distant thunder welled
out of a place he was unable to pinpoint. Perhaps Chalk's blather was not

such a bad thing. Clyster was not a superstitious man, but he disliked having his ability to see the horizon slashed by something so amorphous as this mist.

Stepping gently around the holes in the deck, he made his way toward the stern lying lost in the murk, and then entered the ship's interior. Moving forward, he carefully cleared one space at a time. He knew there was no one else here, but he had to be sure.

Stepping around collapsed overheads and dangling cables and pipes, Clyster penetrated deeper into the hull along rickety stairways missing treads until he found a vast space that had to be a hold. He was not surprised to find it flooded. He was surprised at how agitated the water's surface was. Then he saw waves pulsing into the hold from a companionway in the forward bulkhead. He was about to press on when he thought he heard a voice. A woman's voice with earnest tones. The watery sounds broke up the voice enough that for a few seconds he doubted his ears. This was likely some weird acoustic effect of the wind and water surging through corridors, shell and portholes, and innumerable jagged rusty fissures.

Clyster put his head through the hold's forward bulkhead just below the main deck level. Another hold. He was surprised by several things at once. The next hold had large gashes on either side which let the Chesapeake's waves roll through port to starboard without obstruction. Some of the wave energy radiated through the lower opening in the bulkhead he stood behind. That's what had roiled the surface of the last hold even though it was not directly open to the bay.

Except in this new hold there was an obstruction, of sorts. A boat. A white wooden boat, maybe fifteen feet long, with a small outboard motor on the back. Maybe it was the boat taken from the old man's dock. Whoever owned it must have brought it in through the port gash in the hold, and tied it up by that ladder on the port side, neat as a pin.

Then Clyster saw the women. Not just the one he had heard. She was a blonde, dressed in a dumpy, comfortable style of loose jeans and flannel with a coat. The clothes did not hide her sexy figure. He knew hers was the voice he had heard, because she was still talking. And she was talking to *the runner!*

Clyster ducked back out of sight. The women were on a catwalk at his level, and moving toward him. The blonde was making bullshit noise about helping, about getting the runner's sister back, and making everything okay. Clyster almost laughed at that. Remaining silent, his mind ranged afield into a fantasy about returning to base with that skinny bitch who had killed Sanders, killed Tahereh, and made them all look like chumps running around exposing themselves and the entire enterprise to stupid risks looking for her. Chalk would be profoundly indebted to Clyster for bringing a chance of revenge for all those insults within easy reach. And he might like the bonus piece of ass in the bargain.

Clyster steadied himself, slung his light machine gun around onto his back, and drew a TASER X2 from its holster. At this beautiful moment, he was completely vindicated that Chalk had taken his suggestion about picking up a few of these since their livestock on this gig was mostly doubled up two to a pen. This was the kind of nonlethal force the team needed, because it did not leave bruises. Used once, no troublemaker would want to feel it again. The best thing? The X2 allowed for a *second* pair of wired darts to be fired if the first pair did not do the trick on a single target. It was the only decent two-shot spazz-gun out there, and the beauty was, it could also work on two *separate* targets, like these uppity broads.

Half a moment before he thought he was going to have to take them both down on the catwalk, he heard their steps on the ladder descending to the boat. They were leaving this ship on that little skiff. Nope. Not on his watch.

He waited until he heard footfalls in the boat, then he struck. The hold reverberated the wave sounds so loudly that Clyster had dropped most of the way down the ladder before the women noticed him. Their eyes got really big, really fast. He activated the TASER's arc-warning function. Blue electricity crackled between two pins on the front of the bulky weapon. It sent the women scurrying to the front of the boat, but he noticed the blonde reaching for an ankle holster. The runner was pulling a pistol from her coat pocket.

Clyster pulled the TASER trigger once. The runner hit the deck jerking like an epileptic, screaming briefly until her head struck the gunwale and she went quiet. He shifted his aim slightly, and pulled the trigger again. The blonde went down shuddering with a low vibrato moan. It was that simple. It was beautiful. He was a hero.

He took a step toward the bow to inspect his prey, but his right leg buckled underneath him. Suddenly, blood was everywhere, and Clyster was falling out of the skiff into the deep black water of the hold.

CHAPTER 18

THE OPEN AIR of the Chesapeake seemed to do Ellis as much good as it had done Ben. They were mashing water in the inflatable back to the *American Mariner* mostly in silence as had long been their custom. Leaving *Miss Dotsy* at Ellis's place was difficult for Ben, who had a sentimental streak for the beautiful little deadrise, but her absence from Ellis's pier might excite gossip from watchful neighbors.

Ellis had his place at the inflatable's stern, managing the motor. Ben trimmed ship forward with his weight, sensing he could tolerate the exaggerated bounces in the bow far better than his ailing friend.

Knocker Ellis said, "You should have come home a long while ago. None of this would be a problem."

Though Ben saw Ellis's logic, he said, "You know I can't."

Snorting, Ellis fired back, "I know no such thing. Forget the business of your tortured soul. Look at it practical like. Gold's lost value since last fall. You could be sitting at home with your feet up waiting for the price to surge back into better territory."

"Pap did us no favors hauling that stuff to Smith," said Ben. "Brought plenty trouble with it. Friends died to keep that gold. You almost did, too. And LuAnna."

"Didn't we take care of business?" Ellis reminisced. "I never saw your neighbors so happy before a couple orders from you, and a few twelve gauge shells made them rich."

"The ones still breathing," said Ben ruefully.

"You dealt out some handsome death benefits, Mr. Moneybags. Whatever they thought of you before, and I admit it wasn't much, they like you fine now. They owe you."

"I filled a graveyard."

"With *volunteers*. You showed every last one of them how to put the metal to the meat, and they did just that, and proud."

Ben jolted along in the inflatable's bow for a few minutes. "Not something I like to dwell on."

"Everybody else does. You need to get home, Ben. Everybody on the council left a place for you. Head of the table."

Smith Island needed little in the way of elected leadership. A time-honored way of coexisting defused most problems between neighbors. The Smith Island Council, made up of mature, level-headed men and women, spent much of their time these days fending off property buy-out offers from the State of Maryland. Legislators in Annapolis fretted that climate volatility and Smith Island's slowly sinking substrate meant that the island's permanent residents could not wait to abandon their homes and move to the mainland, if only they could sell up at a decent price first. A collective, unanimous *hell no* from the Council quickly disabused the bureaucrats of that nonsense.

Ben scoffed. "Head of the table. Nice view, but it's just another way of skylining myself."

"You know how to keep your head down. And how about Poplar Island?"

The Smith Island Council was currently advocating that expensive dredging and spoil filling to reclaim the erosion of uninhabited Poplar Island back to its 1847 shoreline might better serve to build up Smith Island instead, where human voters actually lived.

Unbeknownst to the legislators, Smith Island now had a deep war chest for this campaign. Even if they could not divert dredging spoils from the Chesapeake shipping channel and Baltimore Harbor itself to Smith Island right away, the Poplar Island restoration was slated to finish in 2020. Someone in Annapolis would soon see the light. So what if it started with a glimmer of gold.

"You know me better, Ellis. I'm no part in a political machine—"

"—Said the former soldier. You were a cog in the works before. A tool for democracy, if you'll pardon the phrase."

"That was in another country, and besides, this wrench is dead. It's not like I can waltz into State Circle to whistle up barges full of spoil, and a few thousand yards of breakwaters, and hope nobody recognizes me."

When his father stole the gold from Maynard Chalk months before, it fell to Ben to secure and protect the bullion. Ben had done it, but at great cost. Now, he simply wanted the Smith Island families who followed the water to enjoy a financial backstop during the decades-long process of cleaning the Chesapeake Bay to a level where it could endure sustainable levels of pollution running into it, and a sustainable harvest coming out of it. The Chesapeake fisheries, including blue crab, oyster, clams, and rockfish were still wildly inconsistent from one year to the next. Restrictive harvest limits tossed many a waterman out of livelihoods that had sustained their families for generations. Ben had believed the Smith Islanders could work their hardest as ever they had, but with the gold as a hedge, they could rest confident that the brutally hard times were behind them. Still, to Ben it felt like his mission remained unfinished, and in that state, the task festered in his soldier's heart.

Ellis sat on his anger as best he could. "Just having you back would make a difference."

"Folks are fine without me."

"Beg to differ. I miss my friend. LuAnna, she misses her husband."

An adult great blue heron glided down close to the boat. This was unusual. These beautiful birds preferred quiet shallow shorelines, or pound nets, to make their living.

Ellis grinned. "And here's another one wishes you'd come to your senses."

"Lonesome George?" This particular bird had been encouraged over the years to visit Ben's *Miss Dotsy* for a daily oyster handout, freshly shucked. Sensing no food was forthcoming, the heron squawked, flapped, and peeled away into the mist.

"Reckon he's cadging from all the boats. Going to get himself in trouble, tame as he is. What have we done to him, Ellis?"

Ellis stared away into the middle distance, hard pressed to stop an eye roll as it began. "Oh my Lord! Is every little thing a sign of your Original Sin? Dry up, Killer!"

The old blood-and-white shroud of the *American Mariner*'s hull loomed in the distance.

Blackshaw closed the more esoteric topic with practicalities. "Would you kindly round under her bow and surf us into the big rip from port side? Seems to be my new front door."

CHAPTER 19

JOACHIM DEPRIEST RECEIVED news of the two young additions to his stock yard with mixed emotions. He was eating, and foremost, this visit from Earline Byrd and Gläans Bellendre was an interruption. The meal might have been called breakfast, or elevenses, mornos, or elva-kaffe, konkelstik, or brunch, or perhaps even an early lunch, but none of the names really mattered, because DePriest never really stopped feeding. Mouthfuls were verses in an epicurean lay without end. True, he tended to start the morning with sweeter foods, shifting to savories as the day wore on. Just before he began his apneic catnapping overnight, DePriest reverted to more sugary treats again.

Byrd and Bellendre stood front and center before the massive man surmounting the chaise's dais. There was some desultory shifting of weight between their feet. They were field operatives, and felt acutely uncomfortable underground in The Presence, as Maynard Chalk called it.

Despite the incursion of the underlings, Armand, decked in the costumery of a Louis XIV era lady-in-waiting, kept handing up Linzer tortes, which were DePriest's current obsession. They appeared no larger than ginger snaps in DePriest's hand. He devoured them just as quickly as if they really were wafers instead of a dessert that could cover a whole dinner plate before slicing into normal portions. Of course, slicing did not enter into the equation.

DePriest asked, "How old?"

As DePriest spoke, Wallace brushed crumbs of filigreed crust, dustings of powdered sugar, and globs of raspberry jam that spilled on his boss's hay mow of a belly. Wallace sported a surfer's Billabong Xero Furnace Wetsuit today. It had just the right amount of body-hugging kinky style, while protecting him from the offal emanating from either end of DePriest's alimentary canal.

Byrd, trying hard to forget the naked male genitalia buried directly in front of her beneath undulating waves of adipose tissue, answered. "When they came to, they said they're five, sir. They're cute. All blondy-blond. They cry a lot, but they're kinda cute."

DePriest condescended to smile at Byrd's assessment of the children. "And they are twins?"

"Like two peas in a pod, but one's a boy, yes sir."

DePriest marveled that his handpicked yard contained no twins before now, especially children. An oversight on his part. His mind reeled at the possibilities for one of the opening night acts. Then his brow furrowed deep enough to stash several rolls of quarters in the folds. "Rookard will like that. So will our subscribers. But they are local?"

Gläans Bellendre sensed the thin ice cracking beneath them, and said, "Yes, but nobody's looking for them. Chalk saw to that."

DePriest was no longer comforted by the thought of Maynard Chalk seeing to anything important. The enormous man had taken great care to procure his subjects from distant countries. It was traditional of him to do so, in one sense. The United States was a nation of immigrants. He felt that carrying on with this historic schema in his work was his genius. These days the United States Government maintained black sites well offshore where the all-holy U.S. Constitution held little sway to protect covertly renditioned combatants and foreign operatives.

Working his plan in the opposite direction of travel, DePriest hearkened back to the time of slavery in American history. He felt there was nothing to be lost by having his coyotes bring the talent onto the shores of the Republic from parts foreign, where oceans, vague diplomatic treaties, and pewling international legal remedies reduced a lone immigrant to abandoned status even if he had the most powerful interested parties working form him back in his home country.

In the final analysis, Chalk's international connections had helped with the acquisition phase, but perhaps he was getting too old, and was in over his head serving both as warden and defender of the venue.

DePriest asked, "So, the two little white Yankee born-and-raised tow-heads are held where, exactly?"

Bellendre was ready for this. "In isolation. They don't know a stupid thing."

Byrd gave a small cough. DePriest shifted his eyes to bore in on her. She said, "They did see what happened to their grandparents. Pretty clearly."

"Which is why they're in isolation," added Bellendre. "Can't bother up the rest of the stock."

DePriest was still a few steps behind his minions. "You said, *grandparents?*"

Byrd swallowed hard before she said, "Yes, sir. It's what the kids said."

DePriest went on, "And you're going to tell me the children were with their grandparents because the parents both died tragically in a car accident?"

"The 'rents went on a trip to the Grand Canyon," said Byrd. "Not coming back for a few days. Just the two of them. A getaway kind of thing."

"How many days?" DePriest's voice was rising.

Byrd wanted to cover her ears. Bellendre took a half-step back. He was tracking his boss's line of thought now, and the mood in the room was growing bleaker by the second.

Bellendre confessed, "Two, or three days. I don't know. The kids said they were checking off days on a calendar on the fridge. I did not confirm this. My apologizings."

"A *calendar*," sneered DePriest. "We are in possession of domestic stock with parents who will shortly be wondering why the grandparents aren't picking up the phone when they check in to say good-night prayers with their wee ones. *This* is why we choose orphans, or *make* orphans, to work with. *Because no one will come looking for them!*"

"We could disappear them now," offered the helpful Earline Byrd.

DePriest weighed the more cautious choice of taking the twins out of play now against the profit of leaving them in isolation for a few more hours until the games began.

After a pause, during which he mashed another Linzer torte down his gullet, DePriest said. "The curtain goes up tonight. We'll stay the course. Keep the new ones in strict isolation. How is Maynard doing finding the runner?"

Wallace nipped up close to crumb the great belly.

Gläans Bellendre brightened. "These snot-fuck kids came from a place on the water. On the Chesapeake. A boat was tooken from that place overnight. It's our goodest clue. Could be the runner is a swimmer is a drowner."

"Are you certain she is dead and drifting on the bottom of the bay?"

"Not certain. No," said Bellendre. "But the odds—"

DePriest rose raging halfway to his feet. Shuddering curtains of striated abdominal flesh swagged around his knees like human bunting, and dark malodorous matter flowed down his legs onto the chaise from the canyon of his colossal rump.

"Find her!" he screamed. "Now go!"

CHAPTER 20

SENIOR RESIDENT AGENT Pershing Lowry was about to step out of the barber chair, when Kyle, the elderly haircutter, held up a large teardrop mirror to help his customer inspect the total picture, front and rear.

Lowry's expression did not change as he said, "I bring you less and less work every time, but the price just keeps going up. It's robbery." The narrow ribbon of black fringe that horseshoed around Lowry's gleaming dark brown pate was hardly worth the weekly stop, but Kyle fussed and fretted over the tight curls as if they made an unruly snarl many years from its last encounter with scissors, blade, and comb.

Kyle suggested, "You could get away with coming in every *other* week, sir. I'm starting to see grey. There's an effective camo that could blend it in naturally. It lasts for weeks, especially if you use a shampoo for color-treated hair. I do have some of that."

Agent Lowry, who was four years at the FBI's Maryland Metropolitan Office at Calverton, was keenly sensitive to the fine line between grooming and labor-intensive cosmetic artifice. In his fifteen years with the bureau, his presentation was viewed by other agents as conservative even by the standards of a government culture proud of its monastic code of business dress. A fully shaved head might be the next, albeit radical step, but definitely not a dye job. He would never live that down.

Lowry simply said, "I think not."

Kyle did not press the point as he moved over to the old mechanical cash register and waited for Lowry to settle into his suit coat.

Lowry held still for a moment, then another moment, looking at the old, chipped rocket ship chair where Kyle took care of children's hair. Then he studied the small gumball machine in the corner, with its glass globe decorated like a comet with corroded chrome. Perhaps the chair and the gumball machine had been purchased as a set sometime in the 1930s during the heyday of Buck Rogers. After removing a twenty dollar bill from his wallet, and a ten, Lowry said, "Business picked up lately?"

Kyle turned toward the rocket ship and said, "Yes, we recently had a banner day, but I can't figure how you'd know that."

"We have your place staked out during business hours, Kyle."

The look of concern on Kyle's face was priceless. "You don't say!"

Lowery cracked the slightest smile, and said, "No. I was trying to be funny. But your bubble gum machine is full. It's been *nearly* full for four years, which is obviously fine with you."

Kyle hastened to explain, "Gumballs never go bad, but—"

"It's true," affirmed Lowry. "They don't. No expiration. So, you must have sold a lot of them lately to drop the level enough to make you want to top the machine off. A *whole* lot of them."

Kyle smiled with admiration. "And for this, the big bucks are yours. You're right on, sir. Lester Thompson brought his grandkids in on Tuesday. Sweetest little twins. Now, you know Lester wouldn't let me touch a hair on his own head, more's the pity, but we got the babies shaped up meet and proper."

Senior Resident Agent Lowry said, "The twins must like gumballs a great deal."

"Yes, they each had one. But it was those kids on the field trip just before the twins who really cleaned me out."

Lowry held onto the bills he had just taken from his wallet. Though Kyle was working alone today, no one was waiting for a trim right now. "Really? Haircuts on a field trip?"

"They were headed down to St. Mary's City to see the historic waterfront. Walk around on the *Dove*, the old three-master there. The kids were underprivileged, as we used to say, though I'm sure it's put differently now. *Urban*, more like. And the lady said they were going to have their picture taken. So they stopped in here to spruce up first."

"Really? How many kids? How old?" Agent Lowry was relying on a deadpan expression practiced over years to keep his questions in the harmless realm of friendly banter.

"Nine children. Five boys and four girls. Age five, up to about twelve. One other girl was in her mid-teens, I guess, but she didn't get a style. Lovely children. Thank goodness both my freelance cutters were in that day. Those little ones gave us a very busy hour and more. And yes, they depleted my stock of gumballs."

"One lady chaperone? Besides the teenage girl?"

"Yes. And the young fellow with a crew cut who didn't say much. The lady bought the gum, paid for the haircuts, and tipped, too. But she had what they call a mullet that I could have fixed up very nicely. Thin, straight, brown hair, longer in the back. A little layering would have given it more body, and loft, more than her little puff-ball up front. You must think me terribly indiscreet discussing folks who come in here this way."

"On the contrary, I'm always glad when a friend has an upswing in business. I suppose they were traveling on a school bus."

"It was one of those short busses they used to keep for the, you know, the *ree-rees*, the Special Education kind. But I guess now every town, every nursing home uses them for senior access, for day trips to the shopping center. How it passed inspection I'll never know, smoky as it was. Seemed it was from up north a ways. Montgomery County?"

"It said that on the side of the bus?"

"I couldn't be sure. But it was blue, with white trim, not yellow and black. Is everything all right, sir?" This was the longest that Lowry had ever lingered to chat.

Perhaps Agent Lowry's own sensitivities were making more of the story than was warranted. But this shop was well away from anything a GPS or a map would suggest as the best route of travel from north of Washington, D.C. south to St. Mary's City. The driver needed local knowledge to find the place. Kyle's shop had no website, though it might have been listed on a chamber of commerce internet roster of businesses. Lowry tried to be reassuring, but with his habitual monotone, even *Merry Christmas* came out like a death notification.

"I'm sure everything's fine. Did all those kids behave themselves, at least?"

Kyle was always careful to gauge when a customer was a shut-in, or otherwise lonely and happy to talk, and who was distracted by cares into companionable silence that needed respecting. There was still no one waiting for a trim, so he ventured into the next natural stanza of conversation with Lowry.

"I saw them come in, and I admit I was worried at first. Back in the day, most of our customers were adults of course, with parents and grandparents who brought in a child or two, which was usually manageable. Though that's no guarantee with kids today, I don't have to tell you. But since that specialty kid's stylist opened at the mall, with those princess thrones and jet airplanes, and dragons and what-not for chairs, and DVD players, and X-Box and TV screens at every station, we see almost no children here. So, like I said, I was worried with this bigger group, but, Agent Lowry, they were perfect. Not a peep out of them. No horsing around. No cutting up. Waited like sleepy darlings, before, during, and after their haircuts, and never squirmed. Moved not a muscle. I couldn't have asked for better behavior from my own children when they were little ones."

Agent Lowry handed over the twenty-dollar bill along with the ten, and glanced at his tidy horseshoe of hair again in the mirror. "You had quite a Tuesday, indeed," he said. "Thank you, Kyle. Keep the change."

With any luck, Agent Lowry looked like a normal man at the end of a pleasant storefront grooming ritual repeated thousands of times every day in small-town America. That is what he sincerely hoped.

The old barber depressed a key on the register, and its drawer sprang open with a chime from another age. As he placed the bills in their proper slots, he said, "Thank you, sir. See you next Thursday."

Agent Lowry did not hear Kyle. He was already standing on the sidewalk imagining, as he often did, what his sister's son would look like today. His nephew, Nathan, a clever, charming boy of seven, had been abducted from a church sleepover in Malvern, Pennsylvania. A few minutes, and an unescorted potty break was all the kidnapper needed. All leads had been exhausted. The child was never seen again. No ransom was demanded. No word came. No remains were ever recovered. A terrible void of pain still existed all the way through his family, like an old bomb crater in a cherished garden that nothing could refill; not denial, nor confusion, not time, not tears, not even the heartbreak of a generation. That case had been cold for fifteen years.

Slowly emerging from his dark reverie, Agent Lowry remained still for a moment more. He was trying to recall exactly where he had parked his car.

CHAPTER 21

BEN BLACKSHAW AND Knocker Ellis Hogan realized they had shared a simple unspoken expectation upon arrival at the *American Mariner*, but they understood it only when this expectation was flatly and perhaps fatally dashed.

As Ben had asked, Ellis waited until a larger wave rolled toward the long gash in the ship's hull. When Ellis gunned the small engine, the inflatable surged forward just in front of the wave's crest. The RHIB's bow broke out of the drizzle and into the darker shadow of the great hold's interior; he nimbly idled the engine and raised the still-spinning prop out of the water. With the snaggled lower fangs of the hull's maw safely cleared, Ellis dropped the prop back into the water, and threw the engine into reverse to arrest the inflatable's forward motion.

With lower RPMs, Ellis deftly guided the RHIB behind the handcrafted screen made from the hold's detritus to hide the boat from any casual trespasser. Ben quickly tied off the painter to the ladder opposite where he had moored Tally's dinghy earlier that morning.

With the engine shut down, Ellis said, "What the hell?"

"I don't like it," replied Ben.

LuAnna's crab skiff should have been moored in there still. It was gone.

CHAPTER 22

WHEN ELLIS CAUGHT up to Ben in the *American Mariner*'s converted sick bay, he was winded. Ladders and stairs did not figure much in his life during winter on Smith Island. That fact, plus his recent spate of ill-health was making this a difficult junket for him already. Perhaps Ben had asked too much of his friend inviting him out to play.

Neither LuAnna nor Tally was there. Dirty dishes from the meal LuAnna had brought still lay on the crates. A fussticular house-proud woman, in Ben's view, LuAnna would never have left a mess like this unless something important had taken her attention. Perhaps Tally's very presence was enough to do that. Ben hoped that was the case.

At the moment Ellis puffed into the compartment, Ben was checking through his belongings. Two boxes of ammunition for the Bersa and a spare magazine were laid out. Ben had already flipped back the tarpaulin covering the gold bullion to take stock. Ellis knew this was not a crass prioritization of worldly goods on Ben's part. That stack of gold bricks was motivation enough for an intruder's mayhem, and despite their best efforts at silence, word might have gotten around. Smith Island was a small community, and gossip traded like cash. A tourist might have heard something, and come calling.

"Gold's all here. Still, she left in a hurry." Ben corrected himself. "*They* did. Nothing seems to be missing."

"Damn. Why wouldn't she sit tight?"

Ben said, "Tell me if she left of her own accord, and maybe I could answer that."

He pulled his sat-phone out of his jacket, and hit a two-digit speed dial. Ellis caught his breath while the call to LuAnna went out. Ben gave it a full minute's ringing, then disrupted the call without getting an answer. He grabbed his spotting scope and headed for the door.

Ellis warned, "For God's sake, don't skyline yourself topside."

"Right now, elevation's all I've got to work with on this wreck, and I mean to use it." With that, he was gone.

Moving like an old man, Ellis found Ben just outside the bridge on the starboard wing slowly scanning the Chesapeake Bay through the rainy murk. He paused to wipe the monocular lenses clear of water with his shirt, but it was damp, too, and the result was a pair of smears. He continued the scan anyway.

Ellis could not help but ask, "Anything?"

Ben did not answer.

"Do you think she took Tally back to your place on Smith?"

Ben was agitated. "Why? I know she felt sorry for the girl, but she sure didn't trust her all the way either. We both figured containment here was the best thing, at least until we brought you along."

"I'm flattered, but this isn't good."

Ben crossed to the port bridge wing, and repeated his scan westward as thoroughly as he could. The monocular offered a large field of view, but in the featureless waters of the bay, it was hard to maintain any kind of orderly grid for his search. A trained sniper, he relied on minute, regulated changes in his arm position to describe anything like an organized pattern, but he knew that in his worried state he was making a poor job of it.

Finally, he lowered the scope.

Ellis said, "She'll call."

"Sure she will. If she's able."

"Come in out of the weather, Ben. Let's think. What if they're still aboard?"

"Then LuAnna would have shown herself. She knows we were coming."

Ellis said, "We could still look around."

Together, they descended back to the sick bay. They both gave the space a more careful study.

Three minutes later, Ben picked it up. "The picnic basket. LuAnna brought the pie and cake in the picnic basket, and it's not here now."

The relief was evident in Ellis's voice. "There you go. Tally told her something helpful, or she got some kind of brainstorm, and they took off to check something out. And we should, too. I hate it here. Can't blame LuAnna if it this wreck had no appeal without you."

With the extra magazines and ammunition in Ben's coat pockets, they returned to the catwalk in the No. 2 Hold. Ben helped Ellis descend the stairway past the two missing treads, and wondered again if rousting his friend out had been such a good idea.

To Ben, the strangest thing about the interior of the *American Mariner* was how all the bullet and bomb holes allowed even the most diffuse daylight to illuminate the ship's interior. He halted on the catwalk as a thinning in the cloud cover unleashed rays of light down through the water in the hold. A moment later, Ellis saw it, too.

They both stopped walking and held still, each fighting a desperate, quiet war of denial about the truth that gently surged a few feet down below the surface. From this vantage, it was so clear. It was the outline of LuAnna's crab skiff, sunk. They had missed it before when they came in. Seeing no skiff moored in the hold had meant it was simply, inexplicably gone, not swamped. They never would have seen it now if the little boat hadn't come to rest on a snarl of collapsed ship's wreckage that littered the flooded space. Otherwise, the skiff might have dropped all the way to the bottom of the hold to be lost in the depths of the brackish ink.

Ben gripped the catwalk rail with both hands to steady himself. Fear choked his voice to a whisper. "She best not be down there."

Ellis wanted to assure Ben that LuAnna was safe, but his mouth refused to form a single comforting lie.

CHAPTER 23

SENIOR RESIDENT AGENT Pershing Lowry returned to the
FBI's Maryland Metropolitan Office at Calverton. Now he scanned the
morning emails, while sipping a mug of black coffee. His office door was
closed. He worked his computer's wireless mouse mechanically. The emails
gliding past his eyes received no real attention. For distraction from his own
oppressive thoughts, he brought his mug to the break room for a refill, took
a moment to start a fresh pot brewing, and was retracing his steps; he
changed course, knocking at the open door of Special Agent Molly Wilde.

Wilde, who was in her second week of trying to quit smoking, smiled
briefly at Lowry to let him know he was welcome, then returned to dis-
guising a fevered effort to shell a square of Nicorette gum out of its foil-
and-plastic bubble.

Lowry sat in the small bent wire chair and courteously sipped coffee,
pretending the view out the window was intriguing until Wilde got the gum
softened up, parked, and working to quell her nicotine craving.

Wilde confided, "I feel like a damn cow. This stop-and-start chewing."

Agent Lowry thought Wilde was anything but bovine. She was lean,
lovely, with large brown eyes and thick brown hair snatched back into a
simple barretted ponytail. She was several years Lowry's junior, and he was
almost certain she was single. She was dressed in one of her tailored suits,
by St. John, or Donna Karan, or Armani. He could never tell which unless
he got a glimpse of a label when she threw her jacket over the back of her
chair. Her clothes were an important investment from her personal budget,

but she never strayed beyond plain dark colors and discreetly patterned weaves.

Wilde was the first woman who made Lowry unhappy to recall all the bureau policies and common wisdom that made even broaching the matter of his admiration cause for actionable scandal.

He had quit smoking many years before, and asked with unfeigned sympathy, "How is it going?"

Wilde gave a low throaty growl before she said, "Peachy. I feel health and well-being running through my system like a jolt of electricity."

And with that, she had done it again; made Lowry smile in a way that exposed more of his gleaming teeth than had seen daylight in a long while, absent a toothbrush in his hand. Special Agent Molly Wilde noticed his smile, and enjoyed it until she sensed she was staring at her boss, and with a silly expression on her face.

Lowry asked, "Is vaping not an option?"

"E-cigarettes? God no. Way too close to the real thing." She squinted her eyes and said, "I'd feel—trendy."

"Heaven forbid."

As best Lowry could recall, Wilde had never seemed to suffer from the few cigarettes she indulged in each day. She was always fit, never lagging in the field. Along with nicotine, the cigarettes had offered her a few minutes of respite in which she could let her mind roam freely around cases that the bureau would prefer her to doggedly attack straight on. But during a recent physical, Wilde's blood pressure was found to be elevated above normal. That was all it took. Her romance with tobacco ended abruptly, but not without irksome pangs of regret.

Lowry asked, "How goes CETF this week?"

The FBI had merged newer cybercrimes analysis methods with traditional investigative techniques. Now there was a Child Exploitation Task Force in every bureau office coordinating efforts with local, state, and other federal agencies. Child pornography sites based in China were going dark. Wanted fugitives tracked overseas were being extradited with increasing success. But this difficult, discouraging job was never-ending, and Agent Wilde missed real cigarettes.

The question made her demeanor shift to business so abruptly that Lowry winced. Special Agent Wilde was again sitting before him reporting to her superior. Molly had disappeared. "The New York office is getting traction in the courts in an interesting way. When the pimps buy condoms made out-out-state, it's an interstate transaction at its most basic level, and for sex trafficking, given that they buy in bulk, so it's a foot in the door. The task force attorneys are moving slowly with it, but like in New York, there are no condom manufacturers in Maryland, so it might be a good angle for us here."

Lowry mused, "The kinder, gentler pimp makes his girls use condoms."

"They have recruitment and retention issues, same as us, I suppose."

"Molly, you have your ear to the ground," said Lowry, "and you're hep to the cyber side of things, too, of course. Is anything happening locally right now? Any sporting events, or conventions, say in St. Mary's, that would draw traffickers? North to south? The pimps move like circuses these days, following the crowds."

Agent Wilde said, "St. Mary's is never going to be Bangkok, or even The Block in Baltimore, which was quite a scene there for a while, but we do have activity."

"Are minors involved?" Once again, Lowry was deadpanning, but Wilde was too long in the game to disregard even the most general inquiry from her boss. And his questions were getting fairly specific.

As ever, Wilde's answer was thorough, but she got to the point. "We're passing our active leads directly to the St. Mary's County Sheriff's Vice/Narcotics gang, giving them the busts, and getting some decent interagency cooperation in return when they get a line on any through-trafficking toward D.C. out of the south. Some of the 'tutes are underage, yes. We're still trying to reduce sentencing trends in the courts so the girls, especially younger ones, will cooperate more freely. That's helping. But by minors, I take it you mean—"

"Yes, children. Kids. Including males."

"What's on your mind, Pershing?" Only when Wilde said it did Agent Lowry come close to liking his first name.

"I got a haircut this morning," explained Lowry. "My barber said he had a bunch of kids through his shop a couple days back. Tuesday morning. Nine or so younger children, some black, but I'm not sure at this point if all of them were. They were docile. Kyle said they were well-mannered, but I hear that, and I think *afraid*. Two adult chaperones, one male, and one female, with an adolescent female in the mix somehow. They were tired, he said, though it was morning, supposedly on a field trip to see the *Dove* in St. Mary's, traveling out of someplace to the north. And it didn't feel right."

Agent Wilde's antennae were out and waving. "Okay. Can I ask around on this?"

Agent Lowry was disappointed that Wilde was not brushing off his concern as trivial. He would prefer if he were making too much out of nothing. Perhaps Wilde would take any question he raised seriously. He was her boss after all. He said, "As I have it from Kyle, they were traveling in a short bus, blue and white, likely an older model. It's the whole north-to-south aspect that makes me feel like I'm bothering you with something unnecessarily."

Wilde thought for a moment before she spoke. "I agree, on this coast, the trafficking flow often follows the illegal guns and dope, from south toward the mid-Atlantic cities and the northeast."

Agent Lowry smiled apologetically, and was about to get to his feet when Agent Wilde continued, "But as you know, a pornography site can be located anywhere. It doesn't depend on actual foot traffic for revenue. *Visits* are cyber. And so are payments. Customers can be anywhere in the world, in two places at once, really. On the site, and at their home or their office or wherever."

"How do you read this?"

"Without some basic follow-up, we won't know for sure."

Agent Wilde had said we won't know. Lowry appreciated how she was taking ownership of his concern. A strong tactic to build rapport with him.

She went on, "There is one thing that worries me. The kids might have been drugged, not tired. Or they might really have been tired from being on the road. How *long* on the road then becomes the question. Yes, the north-south flow is atypical for trafficking to cities we usually think of, and to the truck stops and sports arenas in between them, but I'm afraid that leaves at least seven other possibilities."

"I'm not sure what you're thinking."

Wilde explained, "Assume the chaperone let slip the actual direction of travel to your barber. And he says the kids were knackered, for now let's say to an unspecified degree. The seven possibilities we have to include are the international airports."

Agent Lowry reflected on Wilde's suggestion. He felt less silly bringing the whole matter up, but his relief was quickly replaced by worry. As he rose to his feet, he said, "Whatever else you're working on, would you please take some time right now, and do your thing, just so we can be sure? We might need to data-mine a lot of airport surveillance footage."

"Of course." A moment later, Agent Wilde's voice stopped him at her office door. "Pershing?"

"Yes?" Lowry turned back to her. Was Pershing such a terrible name?

Wilde was giving him a taste of his own professional deadpan. "Your barber. He does nice work."

Lowry left immediately, without another word, unsure whether Wilde was mocking his paltry fringe, or flirting. Whatever his uncertainty, the fire of his blush radiated an unfamiliar hope as he went back to his office. It felt good, enlivening, the sunburn after the first day of a tropical vacation.

Within seconds of sitting down at his desk, his phone chirped. He was getting a call from Agent Wilde's extension.

Perhaps she was going to apologize for the personal remark about his grooming. After all, if he had misjudged and made a similar comment to her, the harassment claims could have cost him precious time fielding inquiries from HR, if not lost him his job altogether.

He answered with care, his tone betraying no interest, as if this were their first conversation today. "Yes?"

Wilde was also businesslike, very direct. "I made a call. The *Dove* replica in St. Mary's is out of the water for maintenance. They hauled her last fall, Pershing. They found rot. Lots of it. The economy and donor fatigue made fundraising soft, delayed the repairs. She doesn't go back in the water for three more weeks."

CHAPTER 24

BEN AND ELLIS had boarded the inflatable, but the engine was quiet, the painter was still lashed to the ladder in Hold No. 2, and Ben was rummaging through the big bag. He hated pulling his old wetsuit up from the depths of the duffle. He unrolled it to find his face mask and snorkel tucked inside one shoulder.

"Thanks for bringing all this," Blackshaw said.

Ellis knew his friend was anything but grateful in the usual way. This gear could only help with answers, and if things went very badly, with closure. Ellis checked the dive light, and pulled out Ben's old pair of ducted Seavenger Rocket diving fins.

The wetsuit was worn out, with many fraying tears repaired with a strange mix of gums and glues. It had been Blackshaw's outer membrane in earlier times, and struggling back into it felt like a fight against evolution, against progress in his life. Even pit vipers do not put on old skins.

Ellis asked, "You okay to do this?"

"I couldn't ask you to."

"And I wasn't volunteering, believe me. But you have a history of turning up folks you know under water, and I think there's an old enemy still down there in at the bottom of this hold."

"Another word for a history is *practice*." Blackshaw spat in the mask and smeared the lenses to prevent fogging.

Yet, Knocker Ellis had a point. There had been a fair amount of killing aboard this very ship a couple months before, and Ben had notched up his share. The most easily accessible remains from the melee had been recovered and carted away, but two of his enemies still lay aboard, deep and out of the way, and he had not been able to muster whatever it took to risk his life again to see they received the least honors. Perhaps their spectral appearance late at night when he was alone would finally cease once he took care of that grisly job, but for now, they were scum, they had tried to kill him, and they could rot a little longer.

Ben hooked the fins' straps over his heels, secured the mask on his face, and with the dive light in hand, rolled over the side of the RHIB into the flooded hold. With every twist and kick, cold water ran into the wet suit at cuffs, along the poorly sealed zipper, and through new holes still wanting repair.

Lacking any appreciable body fat, Blackshaw had no need of a weight belt, even near the surface. The closed neoprene foam cells of the wetsuit held him almost at neutral buoyancy. Gentle sweeps of his hands and easy flicks of his fins were all he needed to keep him from sinking onto the swamped skiff. He scanned LuAnna's boat with quick passes of the dive light. At the stern, he found it. A bullet lodged in the transom.

At the surface, Ben exhaled, and said, "Knife."

Ellis handed the unsheathed dive knife to Ben, who grabbed it and ducked back down to the transom of the skiff. He made an ugly job of it, but finally a large caliber rebated boat-tail spitzer bullet tumbled free of the wood into his hand.

Tucking the round into a thigh patch-pocket of his wetsuit, Blackshaw dived deeper. The No. 2 Hold was a jumble, with open spaces leading into snags and traps of old structural members and machinery. There was no sign of LuAnna.

Using the wreckage as handholds he drew himself further down toward the aft bulkhead of the hold, below the catwalk that encircled the space just under the upper deck. A few passes of the light, and he found what he expected. A skeleton decked in rotting tactical gear lay ensnared in a morass of old hoist cables. The bones looked like their owner had been drowned in the tentacles of a sea monster conceived by Jules Verne. Blackshaw knew the truth.

A single flick of his fins sent him gliding close enough to see the five inch steel dart Ben himself had fired from a Russian SPP-1 Underwater Pistol. He could still see most of the projectile jutting forward from the fourth cervical vertebra, a forty-penny nail in a cut-rate crucifixion.

Blackshaw angled the light toward the bottom again. There, he noticed a more recent addition to the macabre cast. A man, looking fresh as his dying day, lay there supine, pinned by the weight of arms and supplies strapped to his H-gear. He seemed completely uninjured until Ben passed the dive light over the corpse's right thigh. The femur was shattered by a large entry wound. Turning the body, he saw the meat of the thigh had been ripped away posterior to the long bone. The exit wound was more like a full avulsion of the flesh. The leg twisted loosely in the eddy of Ben's manipulations, dangling, barely attached to the distal end of the femur by lax quadriceps. This guy had bled out in a few desperate minutes.

Ben cherry-picked a few items from the dead man's kit, wallet included, and with his lungs burning for air, he carefully eased his way through the wreckage back to the surface.

Ellis's eyes widened when Ben grabbed the sponson and rolled two round fragmentation grenades into the RHIB, along with a Glock 21, three spare magazines, a long pair of Secuvox binoculars, and finally, an HK MG4 Light Machine Gun trailing three feet of ammunition belt. Then he pulled himself aboard. Next, Ben took the bullet out of his thigh pocket and passed it to Ellis. "In the skiff's transom."

Ellis hefted it, turned it over in his hand, and said, "Copper-nickel alloy. .408. Over four hundred grain, by my guess. CheyTac?"

"Might-could be. There was a fresh-looking fellow with his leg blown half off down there. Some of CheyTac's systems could surely do that. A .408 is anti-materiel."

"This dude down there. Was he anyone we know, Ben? Sorry, but I have to ask. You understand."

"Stranger. Who rolls out on U.S. soil carrying a belt-fed machine gun and grenades?"

Ellis reminded Ben, "You and yours have stepped out with quite the arsenal, from way back, even before we came into money. I swear, by the size of those old fowling pieces in the museum, y'all went after duck and goose like they were the Kaiser himself."

Ben sorted through the wallet for the driver's license. "Who's James Clyster when he's at home?"

Ellis said, "Don't know the name. Question is, why'd Mister Clyster come here, and how. And where's LuAnna and that girl?"

"These are big," Ben said, examining the binoculars. "With one hell of a zoom. Like he was here to watch, as much as kill."

Ellis poked at all the materiel on the deck. "No comms?"

"Not that I saw before I come nigh on drowning to scavenge up all this tasty gear."

Ellis pursed his lips, and slightly raised his eyebrows. Ben knew what that meant. He spat in his mask once more, fitted it over the scowl on his face, snatched up the dive light, and once again rolled over the side into the dark and cold.

Two minutes and eighteen seconds later, by Ellis's watch, Ben surfaced, and tossed a milspec satellite phone into the inflatable, and pulled himself back aboard. Ellis picked up the phone. "Wasted enough time down there."

Ben said, "It wasn't on him. That should be good in water down to thirty meters."

"How deep did you find it?"

"About twenty-five feet, give or take."

Knocker Ellis said, "And it's turned off."

"You turn it on, and it could get triangulated," said Ben. "And the Clyster Blister might not have wanted that."

"Set check-in times with the home office?" asked Ellis.

"Reckon. I guess now he's going to be off schedule for, say—forever."

"But if we fired it up, we could check the call history." Ellis put his thumb on the power button.

Ben warned, "Not here. Not now. Don't want to tip our hand just yet. We have a fair notion Clyster is mobbed up with a tough crowd. We need to think first. Might have nothing to do with LuAnna and that Tally, or why they're not here."

Ellis looked discouraged. "You thinking it's old business that's back on somebody's agenda?"

"We've had our troubles. Like as not we've made some loose ends around here. Foolish to think we wouldn't be called to account one day."

After their decision to keep the dead man's comm powered down, both men were startled to hear a faint sat-phone's warble. In a moment of confusion, Ellis said of the unit in his hand, "This one's still off. And I never turned mine on."

In a rush of hope, Ben dug his own phone from where it was stowed in his coat's pocket. He checked the screen. Not LuAnna.

CHAPTER 25

JOHN TURNER FROST could not keep himself from stealing away from his meeting to look at the on-line brochure yet again. His chemical company, FerdeLance Industries, was firming up an extension of a contract for its defoliant CoproLite; the stuff was growing in popularity with what he suspected was an Al Qaeda faction in Southern Sudan.

Of course, an herbicide was of little use in that part of the world, but CoproLite's poorly hidden off-label property of killing livestock and gravely sickening adolescents and children was making it the hot new arrow in the *au currant* Jihadi's quiver. Anybody with a crop duster and a drum of CoproLite could scorch the earth of an unsympathetic village with a single low pass, devastating a potential enemy while ensuring the cooperation of the neighboring hamlets for all time. Even though it was concentrated and highly toxic, it was selling by the ton overseas.

Frost was the founder, and served as the CEO of FerdeLance, so he felt obliged to put his grey head in at the meeting, shake some murderers' blood-soaked hands, and be on his way after a few good-natured laughs. Subordinates took care of completing the new contract's details.

During a measured stroll back to his opulent corner office, Frost's heart rate surged with excitement. Perched on the edge of his plush office chair, he typed in a web address he knew by heart. Then he tapped out the interminable passwords, nine in all, six of which were issued by the site itself in a file that self-deleted within ten minutes of delivery, and which could not be replaced without a payment of two hundred thousand dollars.

His fingers trembled so much he muffed the last password on the first try. Failing a third time would block him from viewing the site ever again, without hope of a refund or other recourse. Frost thought the ground rules were intense, even by defense industry standards, but with all the hugger-mugger access protocols and exorbitant fees, he also felt a young adventurer's thrill. He was like a spy, which was true from one point of view. He would soon be peeking through a cyber-keyhole at love, lust, and death.

Finally, he typed the last careful keystroke of the last twenty-five character password, and the encrypted brochure came up on the screen in all its unspeakable glory. Frost was transfixed, utterly beside himself.

He had struggled to route the site's five million dollar subscription without his wife's knowledge; no easy feat. His bride of so many decades was Department of Homeland Security Secretary Lily Morgan. Granted, she was always able to shunt federally funded projects to FerdeLance and its subsidiaries, but outside of business, they now led separate lives.

Ever the modern girl, Lily had not even taken his last name when they married. After their engagement, she had babbled something about her affection for her father that nothing short of a Freudian intervention would ever completely explain. And now, she was simply growing too erratic to spend any time with at all. Early on, Frost had assumed her personality deficits were caused by her rise through local politics to the Senate, and then to her current exalted post, but these days she was weird beyond all understanding. He wondered when her superiors would encourage her to resign to *spend more time with family*. Her underlings did not seem to notice the hallucinations. So be it. If Lily Morgan could still funnel greenbacks his way, John Turner Frost had been taught not to care about everything else that was wanting in the marriage; he took this lesson to heart. Sexual forays outside the Frost-Morgan bedchamber were now commonplace, but the events tonight were going to be something else again.

As the week of despoiling drew closer to its start, the teaser images on the site's screen became more graphic. There was more blood. The talent portrayed was younger and younger. The unspeakable acts to be found on the menu were bizarre, offensive to Natural Law, and just so darn *creative*. Frost had to admit, the marketing had been excruciatingly seductive, mercilessly tantalizing. The guarantee was that everything he would behold would be absolutely real. This was no ordinary gore site. No fake blood made of Karo Syrup and red food dye. No Hollywood special effects of any kind. The physical damage, the cries of the participants would be genuine. So would their long, drawn-out deaths. God, what fun!

It all began when a whispered word from a stranger over the stall partition in the Senate lavatory had dug its fetid hole into his mind. Usually a phlegmatic soul, Frost had barely been able to rush back to his office computer without arousing suspicion. That is where he first learned about *L'Abattoir*, as if calling a slaughterhouse by its French name would make the goings-on there classy, sophisticated. Over the course of a few weeks, the increasingly horrific images had drawn him further down the rabbit hole, from one level of commitment to the next, until the big money pitch had been made. Frost must have been screened and qualified for an approach by virtue of his age, his vast holdings, and more than a few indiscrete web searches he was wrong to believe were totally cloaked. Perhaps the fee was really a blackmail payment. Frost smiled at the thought. After all, it was only extortion if you weren't enjoying yourself.

Frost had taken great care and never mentioned his growing enthusiasm for the week of *L'Abattoir* to anyone, though a partner to share in what was to come might have heightened the astounding level of anticipation even more. Earlier that morning, a good friend of his, another captain of industry, had cancelled their usual weekly dinner tonight, and that sent Frost into a paroxysm of speculation that his pal was going to be riveted to the same site online as he, instead of quaffing martinis and wolfing filet mignon as was their habit. It was possible. There were those college adventures in Singapore they had vowed never to speak of again. How many white men today could say they had actually owned a slave, if only on a school holiday abroad? What larks! Fifty years later, Frost wondered if a leopard could really change his spots. Regardless, Frost remained determined not to broach the matter with his friend.

Frost might have joined the North American Man/Boy Love Association, or The Glockenspiel Society, that preeminent BD/SM community, long ago, but they proved so tame, and frankly, so stridently vocal and self-righteous that he could not bring himself to sign on. He did not need their validation nor, God forbid, did he wish to have his name floating around on some bleating perverted advocacy group's membership list. He regarded his predilections with a connoisseur's individual snobbery. Frost was not a joiner.

Like an item for sale on a television shopping network, *L'Abattoir*'s site boasted a number reporting that there were already more than one hundred subscribers, each blissfully anonymous to all the others; the number was climbing every day. Perhaps that figure, whether it was accurate or just fraudulently totted-up window dressing, would provide enough of a sense of community to keep Frost content until the fun began. *Enough to know he was not alone. There were many others like him in L'Abattoir.*

He was mousing slowly through the dark site's splash pages, trying to decide; he could view the events broadcast live, and in the order prescribed by the host to bring off the most powerful impact, or he could schedule a mix of live and delayed happenings on a program of horrors custom-tailored to his own peculiar tastes. This reminded him of picking out his dinner selections from menu during breakfast aboard a luxury cruise, only much more exciting. Whichever way he chose, and he still had to submit his requests for each of the seven nights, he would miss nothing. He would get his money's worth.

Suddenly, an instant message window opened on the lower right-hand side of his computer screen.

HOST: Hello Jack ;-).

Frost froze. They knew who he was! No one who respected or feared him used his old nickname. He had fired valued employees and abandoned the most exotic lovers for this sort of insult. He moused the cursor into the empty field below the disturbing salutation, typed, and clicked ENTER. He was deeply annoyed to see that his side of the communication was also la-beled JACK. The impertinence!

JACK: What do you want!

HOST: Are you excited about tonight?

JACK: I don't like this. It was supposed to be anonymous. I want my money back.

After hitting ENTER, Frost sensed how ridiculous his umbrage must have appeared to his mysterious correspondent. But it was true. He was furious! Yes, he was as excited as hell, but he was now personally in touch with someone who was party to all the sick, awful, disgusting, wonderful things that were going to take place on his screen this evening. Frost felt dirty, betrayed, and out in the open. Yes, he was elated the circus was in town, but by damn, he did not want to shake the ringmaster's hand.

HOST: I have something special for you.

Frost did not know which way to turn, but his hand, driven by a sense of danger, was slowly reaching for the mouse to close the screen.

HOST: Please don't do that. You'll want to hear about this.

Horrified, Frost realized that HOST was watching him through his computer's web camera. That was quite a hack, given FerdeLance's hardened double firewall. He snatched the spherical camera off its perch on the top of his large flat-screen monitor and fast-balled it across the room trailing wires. It smashed into a beautiful solid gold, life-size sculpture of an adult Canada goose. At 24 Karat, the soft metal neck of the goose dented and twisted with the impact.

A passing accountant who had heard the clatter knocked urgently on Frost's office door, and trying the knob, found it locked. He attempted to peak around the half-closed vertical blinds of the small interior window. Frost waved the meddler off with savage gestures. Now the good Samaritan would be trembling with terror, waiting for his pink slip. Fortunately, Frost had no idea who the man was.

HOST: Relax Jack. That goose really was something beautiful. I suppose now it will be a memento of this wonderful week we are about to share.

HOST had somehow seen the camera, the *unplugged* camera, strike the sculpture! Frost suddenly felt hemmed-in. That *person* was still watching him through at least one other camera planted in his office that Frost had not known about. What else might this voyeur have seen? *Plenty* thought the old man, as he recalled his office antics, particularly after the priapic quickening his libido had received since he had subscribed to *L'Abattoir*. Oh, they had screened him well.

JACK: This is an outrage!

HOST: Agreed. Anything less would be worthless to a man of your tastes. Care to hear my offer?

Frost typed nothing, but braced himself for the blackmailer's sting. What he got instead surprised him.

HOST: You are invited to watch *in person*. I mean live. Every night. From beginning to end. We will provide the limousine, and luxury accommodations, and gourmet foods the likes of which you have never before enjoyed. Interested?

Frost was dizzy with the prospect. How often had he wondered what it would be like to watch a death row inmate's execution? God how he envied those lucky witnesses who retained their innocence while watching a legal murder. They got to see it! Frost had never been to war. Death held a dilettante's fascination for him. He had witnessed such proceedings once before, on a very special night overseas. But this would bring it home! Make it viscerally real. Did he dare?

JACK: How much?

HOST: Triple again.

JACK: Done.

HOST: Congratulations! Watch this space, as they say. Wiring instructions will follow. And pack a rain poncho, or two. I guarantee it will get very, very messy.

The small direct message box disappeared from his monitor. Frost leaned back in his chair. He had some work to do. Slushing fifteen million additional dollars in one day toward this wonderful possibility was going to be very tricky, but he could do it. Setting the financial concern aside in a sudden flight of fancy, he wondered if he should wear an outlandish mask to this strange fete, as he had once seen in an otherwise lethally dull Stanley Kubrick movie. Oh dear, he was becoming a complete idiot, but by God, he did not care in the least. He felt so alive!

CHAPTER 26

SENIOR RESIDENT AGENT Pershing Lowry was driving his bureau Impala back to Kyle's barber shop to learn more about the visit from the kids on the field trip when Special Agent Wilde, riding shotgun, got a call on her cell phone. By the sound of Wilde's end of the brief conversation, it was the office. Wilde jotted down a phone number in a small notebook, ended that call, and dialed.

As she waited for the call to go through, she said to Lowry, "County. One second." Then someone picked up the line, and she spoke louder into the phone. "Sheriff Williams, this is Special Agent Molly Wilde returning your call to my Calverton office. If you don't mind, I am going to put you on speaker so Senior Resident Agent Pershing Lowry can hear you. That okay?"

Wilde got the right answer, pressed a button on her phone's screen, and said, "Go ahead, sheriff."

Williams had a smoker's rasping voice. Add to that, he sounded tired, discouraged, or just world-weary. "Can you hear me?"

Lowry nodded once, and Wilde said, "Just fine, sheriff. What's up?"

"We got a call from a local couple vacationing out west. Their kids are staying with their grandparents near here during the trip. The parents check in with the kids every morning. This morning, nobody answered. That was around eight, local. They tried every so often after that, and nothing. Parents swear the old folks weren't going anyplace because they're hardcore homebodies. Both retired. So that was four persons old enough to answer the phone out there who aren't doing that. We've checked area Emergency Departments, and doc-in-a-box clinics. Nothing."

Lowry said, "Sheriff, excuse me, this is Lowry. How old are the kids?"

"Five. Both of them. Twins." said Williams.

Lowry knew that these days, with the success of *in vitro* fertilization, twins were much less an exotic rarity than in times past, but he wondered what the odds were that this was the second pair of five year olds he had heard about today.

Sheriff Williams was still talking. "Anyway, we sent a car around to do a well-being check. I'm on my way there now myself, but my deputy says the owner's car is there, and the place is empty."

Lowry said, "Only one car registered to the address? The parents didn't leave a vehicle there, to save parking fees at the airport?"

"Affirmative on the first. Les Thompson has one car. And negative on the second. The parents drove to the airport in their own car. I wouldn't have bothered you, but Deputy Mangione said the place feels wrong, and she didn't want to go any further with this until there were more eyes-on. I trust her instinct. That's why we're talking."

Lowry immediately remembered that Thompson was the name of the man who brought in the twins to Kyle's barber shop.

Agent Wilde was saying, "Would you like to check back with us once you've had a look around? You can use this number."

Lowry shook his head and mouthed *mute* while pointing at the phone.

Wilde said, "Stand-by one, sheriff."

With the mute function activated she looked at Lowry. He said, "Get the address, please. Kyle can wait."

Wilde almost asked why, but sat on it. Instead, she brought the sheriff back into the call and got the address, which she wrote down into her notebook under the phone number. She also noted the date and time.

Lowry said, "We appreciate your call, Sheriff Williams. We're heading over there right now, so if like you said, you want to hold off on the walk-through until we get there—"

"Appreciate the assist," answered Williams.

Wilde ended the call politely.

Lowry said, "Usually they call us long after the wheels have flown off the investigation. I wanted to encourage their reaching out."

"Okay," said Wilde, but in a drawn out way that meant she was not one hundred percent clear on the decision.

Lowry filled her in. "A Lester Thompson brought his twins in to Kyle's on Tuesday just before that bunch of kids. If anybody tells me coincidence, I say bull."

Wilde was speechless. She passed Lowry the notebook. He slowed down just enough so that entering the address in his personal GPS was not completely suicidal. After what seemed an eternity, the GPS calculated the route to the Thompson residence.

Lowry hit the gas hard. The Crown Vic's modified engine, transmission, and suspension launched the vehicle forward like a carrier catapult. Wilde flipped on the strobe light package concealed in the grille and rear lens assemblies.

"Thanks," was all Lowry said as he sped up.

CHAPTER 27

BEN BLACKSHAW AND Knocker Ellis Hogan were already several miles west of the *American Mariner* when Ben's personal sat-phone sounded. He checked the screen, then opened the line. Ellis throttled back so Ben could hear.

It was Michael Craig, the weather man, sounding tired as ever. "You're in some trouble."

"More than usual?"

"I told you, it's not all about forecasts for kiddies' birthday parties over here. You picked up some comm gear almost an hour ago. It's shut down now, I can see, but it still has a hailing chip on a side-frequency that's pinging a position every two minutes. *Your* position. Your own sat-phone is powered up, and the two signals are on top of each other ... in case you were wondering how I did that."

Once again, Ben was disturbed that Craig might know so much about his movements. With no one to blame but himself, he said, "I should throw it over the side."

"No," said Craig. "I'm familiar with that gear. The new unit just pinged. Switch it on. We have two minutes. Let me walk you through the shut-down sequence on the hailing chip. Then at least Off will really be *off.*"

A few moments later, Craig confirmed that the dead man's sat-phone was no longer betraying their whereabouts. Then he said, "I checked the last three calls on that phone. One went out, and two came in, and in that order. The same contact number all three times—"

Blackshaw's patience was wearing thin. "—That's great, Mike, but I need to focus on the drift trace we talked about. Got anything for me?"

Craig's annoyance bounced down hard from the satellite. "No. Listen to me, Ben. The gear you grabbed, and its friends-and-family contact unit, they both come from a tenth generation block that fell off a truck, but the routing went close to Langley before the trail cooled."

"Langley? That's some crap news. How many sat-phones went wide?"

"Total? Two dozen," said Craig. "That's two-four."

This was not what Ben needed to hear. "Maybe the bogies like to have spares."

"Sure. Or maybe one unit goes to every four-man team. Suck on *that* math."

Ben asked, "Is LuAnna's sat-phone powered up? I assume you got her dialed in."

There was a brief silence. Mike Craig came back, "Negative. Off. No activity at all since a few days ago, and that was a call to your unit, as always."

"Keep that number flagged close for now."

Craig said, "I always do. You two spatting?"

"I wish," said Ben. "This bogey gear. Where is the unit that it called up last? I mean right now?"

Craig answered after a moment. "It's on, and its hailer chip says it's actually on the water out there with you. Yes, about three klicks northwest of your position. Moving north at, looks like fifteen knots." Craig rattled off the longitude and latitude, which Ben relayed to Ellis, who went to work pinpointing the coordinates on a laminated chart of the Chesapeake.

"Okay," said Ben. "What about that drift trace?"

"Not going as fast as I'd like," reported Craig. "Your rain is skewing some of my data. It's really strange. Working on it."

"Work faster," said Ben.

CHAPTER 28

MAYNARD CHALK FUMED, in spite of the wet, cold ride on
Thresher. An observation post out on the water had seemed like a great idea,
the spooky old wreck was just the place, and Clyster seemed like the right
man for the job. Except that Clyster's check-in was overdue. The hailer
chip had completely quit for an hour, then had come back up for thirty
minutes, but moving west from the old ship, like Clyster had gotten on the
water again. Chalk knew Clyster had no boat. And now the hailer chip was
down again. Missing team members was becoming a theme in the last
twelve hours, and its lack of variation was pissing Chalk off. Maybe the
units were defective.

Felix Harrower turned from a small GPS accessory that tracked all
their security comms and said, "Still nothing on the screen. Maybe he's below decks out of the rain, and the signal's blocked. Want to circle back?"

"No. And that doesn't account for the time the unit was away from
the old ship's position. Keep going. I want to see the water from where that
old fart's boat was taken."

Harrower could not help saying, "We were just there a couple hours
back."

Chalk's hands flexed. He took several deep breaths. "I would like to
feel where she might have gone from that place, you shit-piston!"

Harrower went on, "Getting pretty foggy for that. Anyway, what if she
cut that boat loose just to mess with you, and then stayed on shore?"

Now *that* had not occurred to Chalk. He felt sure that the runner's first order of business was to shake pursuit at any cost. Would she risk staying local? She knew about the dogs in the security detail, had certainly heard them bark now and then. Only water could break the airborne plume of skin cells, the rafts, with their unique hormones, sweat and fungi that flaked off from a human in an expanding cone by the tens of thousands every minute. For the second time Chalk wished he had a real bloodhound on the damn payroll, instead of just barkers, growlers, and biters. If the runaway's scent had definitively terminated on the old man's pier, he could be sure Harrower was wrong. But Chalk's instincts told him the bitch had put to sea. She was out here, and that pig man wanted ocular proof that she did not pose a threat, dead or alive.

Chalk punched two buttons on the sat-phone to reach out for Clyster and waited. The fog rolling in around him was nothing compared to his internal confusion.

Harrower said, "Viz is getting pretty low. Maybe I should take the speed down a notch." He reached for the throttle.

Holding the sat-phone to his ear with one hand, Chalk rested the other hand on his pistol. "Steady as she goes, laddybuck. Steady as she goes."

CHAPTER 29

THE GPS ANNOUNCED that Lowry was on short final to the Thompson place. He dropped down below Mach speed to turn into the drive. Agent Wilde flexed the cramp out of her hand from holding on too tightly to the arm rest. Lowry pulled in on the grass near two clean late model Chargers; the County Sheriff's cruisers idled with their light bars fully ablaze.

It was tight lips and brief, firm handshakes all around. Greetings were terse but not rude. No one jockeyed for turf. There would be time enough for that later. Right now, children were missing.

Agents Lowery and Wilde followed Sheriff Williams and Deputy Sheriff Mangione into the house. On the way, Lowery passed his hand over the hood of Thompson's venerable Coupe de Ville out of habit. It was cold. Of course it was cold. It had not been driven for many hours. The dry patch of ground underneath made it likely it had not moved since the rains began the day before.

Sheriff Williams was gray-haired, fit, barrel-chested, with the carriage of a man who could knock out a few one-arm pushups, but he had the mien of one who would never do such a thing for an audience. None of that fit with Williams's smoky rasp, but his job came with long stretches of administrative boredom punctuated by calamitous pressures. Lowry amended his impression right away. Williams was confident, but not arrogant. The power of his command came from his competence and bearing, not the insignias of his rank. Okay. Lowry could work with a guy like that.

Deputy Sheriff Mangione was tall, dark-haired, with a neat, no-fuss hairstyle, and sharp movements in her eyes and in her step, like a much younger person eager to show something to interested strangers, but not sure how to begin. The place was stressing her. Lowry understood. She was right. It felt all wrong.

The house had all the hallmarks of a neat housekeeper's work undone by an invasion of two active children. There were toys strewn around the living room, and in a spare guest room with twin beds. Some of the toys in the bedroom bin were clearly meant for kids younger than five, likely purchased by the grandmother as welcoming bait for their first few visits.

They stepped carefully around oversized plastic baseball bats, golf clubs, and balls like they were holy relics not to be profaned or disturbed. A worn plush rabbit on one bed had likely been brought from home, likely by the girl. The other bed had a robot soldier abandoned in it, with a laser rifle aimed toward the ceiling from beneath the pillow. Lowry marveled at the way young kids could imbue anything with a guardian's life force that offered comfort, allowing sleep to descend even in less familiar surroundings of their grandparents' house. He gently pushed away the inevitable thoughts of Nathan, his missing nephew, and refocused. These beds were unmade. The woman of the house might have helped the children tidy up before starting the day. This basic habit was likely an important teaching for her to impart. That is how Lowry's grandmother had taught him.

The king size bed in the master bedroom was made up. A full set of uppers still floated in a glass beside a bookmarked thriller on the nightstand. Mr. Thompson's nightstand. The reading material on other side of the bed ran to bodice-rippers and *People* Magazine.

The four investigators gathered again in the kitchen and looked it over carefully. The important toys lay next to two of the four place settings; electronic gaming consoles. Their switches were positioned to On, but the units had long since powered themselves down automatically to save the batteries after too much idle time. Brightly colored rings of cereal dissolved in two bowls of milk turning grayish pink.

Lowry studied the stove, the sink, and the toaster, which had four slices of toast still sitting in it. He confirmed the setting was for very light, soft, toast that could take a spread of butter without falling apart, but still be an easy chew. One stove burner was still alight, but with a flame so low, it was almost invisible. In the sink lay a frying pan with a full recipe of soft scrambled eggs floating in water.

Lowry said, "There was a woman here. In her late forties. Not Mrs. Thompson. I mean another one. Mrs. Thompson was drawn away from cooking eggs for the grandkids, or for herself and her husband. She expected to be back very shortly, and left that burner on. She did not come back. If she knew she were leaving in a hurry for an extended period, she would have turned off the burner and dumped the eggs in the trash."

Sheriff Williams said, "Someone else came in here later, but not too much later, saw or smelled the eggs going on the stove, and tossed them in the sink. But that person couldn't know Mr. Thompson's likes his scrambled eggs soft because of his bad teeth. They'd have noticed if the burner was turned up higher. How do you figure a woman?"

Agent Wilde agreed. "A man tosses pans in the sink."

Deputy Sheriff Mangione said, "That's right. But only a woman in a hurry, who knows she's not coming back, and who doesn't care about the housekeeping, puts the pan in the sink runs the water to stop the cooking right away. To prevent a fire that would attract attention. And that's a very different agenda from a woman who stepped away, but expected to come back quickly and dish up. Mrs. Thompson had already hit the toaster before she left because those mushy eggs were very close to being done just how they liked them."

Williams asked the first jurisdictional question. "Who's going to get prints off that burner knob and the frying pan handle?"

Agent Lowry said, "If it comes to that, we could do it. Would you have any objections, sheriff?"

"I have a very bad feeling that if there is a case, it's going to be your case," said Williams. "It would shorten the chain of custody on the prints, and anything else, if we started with your techs, and your lab, from the jump. Why did you say the unknown woman was in her late forties?"

"A hunch," Lowry answered. "She did the thing with the water in the frying pan as Deputy Mangione said. It's almost a reflex. Saw my mother do it enough times. But this unknown woman is out of touch, because she does not have contact with younger children of her own, or with young nieces and nephews. She did a fast sweep before she left, but didn't know to take the video games with the kids, or how the games would've kept the children calm for an extended period. What I'm seeing here is a very sudden thing, at a crucial moment in Mrs. Thompson's breakfast preparation. It feels unplanned. Opportunistic. The kids would have taken those consoles along if they had time, and if they had any say."

Deputy Mangione answered a call on her cell phone, listened for a moment, and said, "Let's keep eyes-on until further notice," and hung up. Then she said, "Still nothing from the hospital emergency departments, or the quack shacks."

Agent Lowry said, "Let's take a look around outside."

•

CHAPTER 30

CHALK'S STOMACH CHURNED. Here he was in a fog bank close to shore, but there were red, blue and white strobes making a blinding psychedelic carnival out of his destination. Cops. The water vapor hanging in the air refracted the strobe light everywhere, surrounding him, bathing him in the harsh brightness of petty authority. It stabbed his eyes, giving him a smashing headache. It felt as though the light was flickering from inside his skull.

On the one hand it did not matter so much, because he had no intention of setting foot on dry land. But the light reminded Chalk he could not bull his way through an encounter with the fuzz because these days he had zero reach-back support. He had none of the identification cards that used to strike terror in the hearts of the local po-po. If he were detained, there would be no liberating phone calls from government gods who loved him. His only recourse under questioning would be a stony silence. That would cost him time he did not have. If he read DePriest correctly, it would also cost him his share.

Without an order, Harrower had throttled down to idle, thrown the engine in neutral, and was now setting up two fishing rods, and inserting them in the angled chrome tubular holders at the stern.

"Nice touch," Chalk said. "Cut the engine. Let's give a listen."

CHAPTER 31

SPECIAL AGENT WILDE stood at the foot of the old pier. The engines of the two County Chargers idled far enough away so as to be unobtrusive. There was a boat on the water somewhere close. She heard the motor at low RPMs. The source of the sound was hard to pinpoint out in the fog.

Lowry, nearer to the Thompson house, called, "Molly?"

She held up her hand to indicate she had heard him, but that she would not respond at the moment. Lowry watched her. Soon, Sheriff Williams and Deputy Sheriff Mangione were also paying attention.

The motor sounds from the water stopped. Wilde thought she saw the shadow of a boat with a forward cabin, two men, and an outboard on the stern. She called to the fog, "Hey, how they biting?"

There was a pause of a few moments before an older man answered her. "Not so great with all the yelling."

Something in the man's gravelly voice made Wilde's flesh crawl. She ignored the veiled complaint and called back, "What you fishing for?"

The same man replied, "A little peace and quiet, and maybe a bass."

Wilde picked her way toward the end of the pier over loose and missing planks. "Sorry. Just curious. What kind of bait?"

"Now, that would be telling," came the answer.

Agent Wilde said, "Okay. Have a nice day."

There was another moment of quiet, then the man's voice sifted through the fog again. "Is there trouble over there?"

Wilde shot back, "That'd be telling."

She heard eerie chuckling on the water, along with the whine and buzz of a fishing reel unspooling fast. Something flew out of the fog and dropped into the water ten feet from where she stood on the pier. A fishing lure. The man had intentionally cast in her direction.

The sound of the reel ratcheting in reached Wilde, and little *Vees* etched the surface like waterbugs; the line hopping and settling over and over as it was wound in. At the same time, the boat's engine started, and was shifted into gear at low RPM. Nobody had three hands for those tasks. Definitely two men aboard.

Wilde turned to find Lowry at her side. She said, "They aren't fishing. That guy said *bass*, not stripers, not rockfish, like a local would say. And stripers are close to spawning. They're in the rivers now, or at the mouths of creeks. No river here, and no creek. And the lure he cast at me was light colored. In the rain, you go Henry Ford."

"Any color lure you want, as long as it's black," said Lowry, impressing Wilde. "But maybe the lights attracted them, and they were curious."

"Even if you're right, it doesn't make *them* right. They aren't fishing. Not for fish, anyway."

CHAPTER 32

HARROWER EASED *THRESHER* away from the shoreline deeper into the Chesapeake fog. He was navigating blind, but for the GPS. Chalk was reflective. He had enjoyed twitting the cop; he had no doubt that, with the whole skull-blasting strobe light show silhouetting her, that's what she was.

But why the hell was she there? What tipped her to the kerfuffle that was barely hours old? Dead oldsters often rot for weeks without anyone checking up on them. Chalk relied all his life on American indifference to previous generations. It's what made new wars possible, and the endless profits that came with them.

Must have been the two kids they lifted that prompted the sudden interest. White kids. Yankees lose their ever-loving minds when a white kid gets a splinter. A child of color has to hit the Emergency Department twenty times for stitches and splints before a social worker looks in to entomb the tot beneath a welter of forgotten case files. And Chalk had disappeared *two* white kids. Twins, no less, for the love of a merciless God! If Chalk's security detail was not careful, his tweaked-out moment of inspiration might lead to years of regret.

Maybe that woman was not a cop. He could not remember catching a cop hat or a cop belt in her misty outline. In fact, from what little he could see, she looked well-tailored, not boxed-out, like a veteran doughnut-muncher in a ballistic vest. It hit Chalk all of a sudden. *Dammit!* That bitch was a *Fed!*

CHAPTER 33

MIKE CRAIG BUZZED Ben's sat-phone with an update. "Still tracking that third party phone. Your target boat stopped just offshore. It's weird."

Ben had to agree that was unusual. This was the kind of weather you mashed through to tie up in a safe harbor, or at least to a protected anchorage where you could drop the hook and ride it out. This mess was not something you lingered in, unless it was important. He said, "*A little off shore* could mean the boat's at the end of a pier."

Craig answered, "Negative. I checked a recent satellite photo-mosaic of that exact position. There's an old pier, but it terminates thirty feet from where the target is. And the visibility between your position and the target is down to about that, thirty feet. You're in fog."

Ellis had already slowed the inflatable boat down to a walk for that reason.

Ben scanned the gray murk and replied, "Thank you for sharing."

"Look sharp, Blackshaw. I'm saying you and the target aren't that far apart, and you might not spot it until you're on top of it. But that's not the weird part."

"I'm listening."

"You better be. My drift analysis finally hawked up a data-loogie. I triple-checked it for precision and accuracy. All good. Using last night's weather, and all the other factors I told you before, the drift solution narrows my circle of confusion down to a diameter of fifty yards. The weirdness is this, the circle is centered right over that pier. That's where a dinghy like the one you described, with an inert load, would have started out. And inside that circle is where your target boat was just stopped."

Ben asked, "*Was* stopped?"

"It's moving now. South. Fifteen knots again. Crazy fast in that fog, unless your ass is on fire."

Ben jotted down the target boat's last position and course as Mike Craig fed him the numbers. He passed the info to Ellis, who doped out an intercept solution on the chart, plotting that into his handheld GPS.

"What's around there?" asked Ben. "What would set some girl running scared as hell in an open boat in dogmeat weather around there?"

"Right now, I got bupkus. But I'll take a look."

"I appreciate this, Mike."

"Wine of the Month, Blackshaw. Remember that. No honeys."

Ben ended the call, and filled Knocker Ellis in.

"So, LuAnna's skiff is swamped with a nice big bullet in it," said Ellis. "And there's this deader packing heavy lying underneath the skiff, with a radio that leads back to the same place that girl Tally's cruise disembarked from."

Ben pressed his lips together hard, then asked, "Reckon them's coincidence?"

"Hell yes, Ben. Happens every day."

CHAPTER 34

SENIOR RESIDENT AGENT Lowry and Special Agent Wilde were walking away from the water, back toward the Thompson rancher. They were not speaking about the disembodied voice on the boat; the encounter clawed too deeply into their psyches. Neither of them could discern whether their gut reactions were enhanced by their errand, the eeriness of empty property, and the fog, or if the chat had simply been strange unto itself.

Lowry noticed Wilde halt abruptly midstride. An instant later she said, "Stop." and pointed at the ground five feet to their left.

Then Lowry perceived it, too. He called, "Sheriff! If you please."

The sheriff and his deputy approached as Wilde made an inventory of what she observed in the grass, "Blood spatter. White hair. Gray matter. Bone fragments."

Sheriff Williams said, "A head shot. Somebody wasn't barking possum."

"Depressed grass," observed Deputy Mangione. "Rain beats grass down, but this bigger patch looks like a heavy weight, like a body."

Wilde turned around slowly in place twice before she pointed at another area lying ten feet away, back toward the water. "Is that pinky-brown stained grass over there?"

Mangione said, "A-firm that."

Lowry squatted down at the first spot of gore, and studied the surrounding grass. He said, "It's hard to be sure, but I make two parallel press-down tracks about eight feet apart. Occasional drag and pressure signs between. For rest intervals?"

Wilde said, "Same from the staining over here. Far enough apart to be two adults carrying another adult by the ankles and wrists. Grabbing your own hands around the front of the body would offer more leverage and control in the carry—"

"—but you'd get lots of blood on you," finished Sheriff Williams. "From a head wound at least."

Still squatting, Lowry said, "I can't see from here. Molly, please point where your set of tracks leads."

She complied, and Lowry indicated the line of his faint trail. The grass was not so much pressed down as slightly bent at different angles from the surrounding blades.

Wilde said, "I'm pointing at that shed."

"That makes two of us," confirmed Lowry. "Shall we?"

The four of them took paths toward the shed that kept them wide of the tracks in the grass.

As they approached the shed, Deputy Mangione said, "The door hinges."

Lowry said, "I see what you mean. Let's be careful here, friends. The overhang of the roof might've kept the rain off, and saved some prints. See there? The door's ajar. Sheriff Williams, you have a good flashlight. Would you mind?"

The sheriff drew a black metal Krypton MagLite from his duty belt, and switched it on. It was the big model that used four D-cell batteries, and was also known in law enforcement as the Junkie-Be-Good light for the way its weight, when judiciously applied, could quell trouble during a lively arrest. He took off his hat, and passed it to Deputy Mangione. He stepped up to the door, shined the beam into the six-inch gap, and peered inside. Sheriff Williams' shoulders stiffened. Then he squatted, and lowered the angle of the beam.

Williams uttered a quiet, "*Shit.* Definitely two adults. One male. One female. Elderly. A bath robe over pajamas, and a house dress, respectively. Stacked up one on top of the other. I see drying blood. And lividity on both. The male is supine. Single GSW. A gut-shot. Female also supine. She got the head-shot." He sounded disgusted when he said, "They shot her in the *face*."

Barely restraining his impatience, Lowry asked, "And the children?"

"I can't see any children, but I can't see behind this other door either."

"Please go ahead and open the damaged door enough so you can," Lowry said evenly.

The sheriff used the MagLite to push the door open one foot. He was careful to stop before it jutted out from beneath the protective eaves of the roof. Redirecting the light, he looked behind the door and exhaled. "No kids. Plenty of room for them, but they aren't here."

Lowry said, "That's it. I don't care if they skip out of the woods in the next ten seconds, we're done looking for them by ourselves. Agent Wilde, put out a SAME. Charlie Alpha Echo."

Wilde was already dialing her mobile phone. Within two minutes, a Specific Area Message Encoding protocol would flash a Child Abduction Emergency to local, state, and national authorities. This would also activate the AMBER Alert so TV and radio broadcasters to spread the word; it would also post crucial details on digital highway signs. AMBER was a backronym, for America's Missing: Broadcast Emergency Response, originally named for Amber Hagerman who had been abducted from Arlington, Texas and murdered in 1996. Pershing Lowry had activated this system himself only once before. Like that small pale flame on the kitchen stove, he held out hope this time it would turn out differently.

Despite their many collected years of experience, everyone suddenly jumped at the unmistakable sound of distant gunshots from offshore, then crouched low by reflex. One—two—three individual reports, followed by a brief pause, then two quick bursts of automatic fire.

Deputy Mangione summed up everyone's thoughts. "What the *fuck*!"

CHAPTER 35

THE LITTLE FISHING boat had materialized fast out of the fog. Ellis had swung the outboard's tiller hard over just in time. Whoever was at the helm of the other boat had cranked the wheel in the other direction and cussed a blue streak. With a combined closing speed of thirty knots, the two vessels had swept past within two feet of each other.

Ben recognized Maynard Chalk sitting in the boat's stern right away. They had a history. It was not good. The way Chalk's eyebrows relevéd into his receding hairline, it was plain Chalk had an idea who Ben was, too. Chalk's limbering his pistol and shooting at Ben three times confirmed it. The flashes spitting from the barrel refracted in the fog over the inflatable's stern.

Ben's response was rash, irrevocable, and unforgiving. As the inflatable bounced over the fishing boat's wake, he snatched up the eighteen pounds of Clyster's HK MG4, jerking the barrel over the transom. He racked it, and without a glance at the selector switch, he squeezed the trigger, letting two bursts fly at—nothing. The fishing boat had vanished in the fog, much as Ben hoped the inflatable had evaporated from Chalk's view.

With a slashing motion across his own throat, Ben told Ellis to cut the outboard. In the immediate quiet, they heard the fishing boat's motor recede, then circle back.

Ben and Ellis lay low in the inflatable, trading fast glances to see if the other man were hit.

Ellis, in a voice that might have carried farther than he meant, asked, "You good?"

"Reckon. You?"

"So far, okay," bellowed Ellis, "But given you're around, my odds for seeing sunset are dropping fast."

After making doubly sure he and Ellis had all the holes they woke up with and no more, Ben said, "Toss me the patch kit." There was one casualty after all. Ben had both his hands clapped over through-and-through bullet holes in the inflatable's right sponson.

Ellis handed Ben the kit, and the tossed forward a small manual air-pump from its stow under the back bench. To make a quick seal, Ben threw his wetsuited legs over the holes while he broke out two patches glopped with an adhesive that would rival a sticky mousetrap.

As he worked, Ben said, "That was him."

"Him who?" said Ellis in his overly loud voice.

"Chalk. The guy who hit Smith Island last fall."

"The way you were shooting, I figured it wasn't a long lost buddy. You said he was dead."

"Don't yell. I said I *hoped* he was. I said it was *likely* he was. But then he was in the news, wasn't he."

Patches in place, Ben got to work with the air pump, and topped off the damaged sponson as best he could. He could still hear the fishing boat's engine.

Ben barked, "He's coming back. You hear that?"

Ellis groused, "You shot off a machine gun next to my squash. I can't hear shit." He tried to shake the ringing out of his ears. "I can barely hear you, not that I want to."

Ben trained the machine gun out into the fog toward the sound of the other boat engine. Now the thrum seemed to be receding again. "Sorry. It happened fast."

Ellis said, "You must be pretty sure LuAnna wasn't on that boat."

Ben's heart sank as he realized how foolish he had been to fire.

CHAPTER 36

MAYNARD CHALK RAGED inside. A blizzard of emotions and sensations whited-out his already challenged thought processes, with a paralyzing hate drifting uppermost. It was all he could do to train his pistol over the boat's wake in case the fiend in that inflatable circled around to kill him. Then he managed to notice his own boat's wake was still carving tight to starboard from Harrower's evasive jink of the wheel.

Chalk hated inflatable boats. They always brought trouble in the form of tactical skirmishes that augered ill for him. And he hated the man he recognized aboard that particular boat. Ben Blackshaw couldn't really be alive! That bastard, not to mention his conniving klepto father, had cost Chalk nearly a hundred million dollars in gold bullion not too long ago. That is why Chalk had fired. He could not help himself. He was ever the *imp* in impulse.

These Blackshaw men had authored the first chapter in his fall from grace as a public servant. There would be a reckoning. It could not be now. Why in God's name was Harrower turning back?

He pivoted toward the helm to find Harrower clutching his left shoulder, his face twisted into a rictus of agony. Assessing the misfortunes of others only in so far as they hindered fulfillment of his own ends, Chalk groused, "Well, fuck my life!"

Chalk staggered forward against the hard banked turning forces. Before the boat could broach, he backed the throttle down to a canter, and rolled the helm out on a southerly heading. Bullet holes spiderwebbed the forward and port windscreens of the boat's cabin.

He mercilessly pulled Harrower's injured arm out of his slicker, ripped open the sleeve, and inspected the injury.

Harrower flinched. "Damn! Easy there, pops!"

A groove less than a half inch deep, but two inches long oozed blood at the shoulder, but there was no arterial spurting. Still, a venous wound like that could suck air into Harrower's bloodstream and finish him.

Chalk pulled his pistol, cocked it, pointed it at Harrower's head and shouted, "Are you going to live, or die?"

Harrower responded well to Chalk's method of triage. Cowering away from the gun barrel, he yelled, "Live!"

"Then stop whining, you big sissy!" Chalk holstered his gun, pulled out his personal IFAK, opened an H bandage, and lashed a hemostatic dressing in place. He felt it was overkill, but he had nothing smaller in the Individual First Aid Kit to work with. "I got plugged like this one time, and not a peep out of me, compadre, so sack up."

Reaching back into the kit, Chalk pulled out a single use morphine auto-injector, and stabbed Harrower in the arm above the wound.

"Ow!" yelled Harrower.

"Felix is your first name? That means *pussy*, right? Listen up. I was saving that dose of poppy for a quiet Saturday night, so you say thank you and pipe the hell down before I change my mind and suck it right out of your arm again, because I *will* do that. Mor*phine* equals more *fun*!"

Chalk grabbed up the sat-phone in his bloodstained hand and barked, "For the love of almighty Satan!" He held the phone up in front of the crazed windscreen, and could see daylight through a bullet hole in the unit's electronic vitals. He tried to power it up and got a few sparks and some static for the effort. The main comm to his base was dead.

He squinted at Harrower and hissed, "I needed this phone one ass-load more than I need you. Do not disappoint me, boyo."

CHAPTER 37

BEN BLACKSHAW HAD held a northerly course in the RHIB by virtue of Ellis's handheld GPS, but maintained a sedate pace. The fog kept visibility down to a short distance. He cut the engine every few minutes to let his ears assess the soundscape around the boat. Every noise, even the waves, seemed muffled as if his head were stuffed in a bag of damp cotton wool. Ellis was examining Clyster's weapons. The HK machine gun was obviously still functional after marinating in the brackish Chesapeake water of the *American Mariner*'s hold, but since there were only three rounds left on the belt after the encounter with Maynard Chalk, it would not be the go-to iron in another hostile meeting.

During one of the pauses with the outboard shut down, Ben said, "If LuAnna was aboard Chalk's boat, she was below decks, and I was pointing higher than that. I didn't see her. I didn't see Tally."

Ellis said nothing. Ben needed to believe he had not just accidentally shot up his wife, and there was no way to know the right of it from here. Ben's impetus to leave the service had come from the mistaken belief that his last shot in Gulf War I had clipped his target, an Iraqi general, but had also passed on to kill the target's wife and unborn child. Though Ben found out later that the death of the wife and child were brought about by Sadam Hussein's minions to make a minor military public relations win into a fiasco for the United States, Ellis knew the event, false as it was, had bitten deep into Ben's soul. Even learning the truth of the circumstances surrounding the mission and its outcome did not spare Ben endured a guilt-suffused hangover persisting to this day. The former SEAL still believed that in following his orders, he had precipitated the death of two innocents.

"You don't want to swing around and make sure? Cap that bastard in the bargain?" asked Ellis.

"Nope. For now, I'm operating on the idea LuAnna is alive, where-abouts unknown. It's LuAnna we're talking about. She's a survivor."

"Oft times, she survives because of you. Most times, she survives *for* you. It's a crazy kind of love you got with her."

Ben did his best to ignore Ellis's unabashed sentimentality, and said, "We need to see that pier Chalk was clocking. He's in this business with Tally up to his neck."

"Seems low-stakes for him."

"That it does, but we don't know the whole story." Ben started the engine, put it in gear, and continued north.

As he drew closer to the circle of confusion Mike Craig had defined with the results of his drift analysis, the fog began to flash, flicker, and wink. It was like watching a distant artillery battle through a grey dust storm, but there was no mistaking the bright spasmodic palette of emergency, caution, and danger.

"Damn," said Ellis. "I'm breaking out in handcuffs already."

"You're innocent. You have nothing to hide."

Ellis glanced down at the RHIB's sole. It was strewn with arms no civilian could legally own; not just Clyster's gear, but also the items Ellis had brought from his home.

Ben was adamant. "We need to see what's happening there right now."

With a sad anger on his face, Ellis lowered the machine gun over the side first. Clyster's grenades and pistol followed. Then Ellis's duffle with his own gear sank in their wake. Ben changed out of his wetsuit into his clothes and foul weather gear. Then he dropped his Bersa over the side.

Ellis observed, "Like a burial at sea. Next time, I'm not even bringing a pocket knife."

"And the fuel," reminded Ben. "And the GPS. And the damn phones."

CHAPTER 38

THE FBI TECHNICIANS had started with the doors of the shed, and were now finished working in the Thompson's kitchen. They had fingerprinted the remains of Lester and his wife on site to speed their elimination from the scene. With the help of the quick, the dead were now bumping across the lawn in body bags on gurneys toward the Medical Examiner's meat wagon.

For a moment, Agent Lowry considered how, in his line of work, bodies were immediately cadavers until the state took full charge of their examination and disposal and made them victims. Lawyers would one day make them into decedents or victims once again. Long before that, funeral directors would dress them, casket them, and cosset them with wax and cosmetics, and for a day or two, they would become the dearly departed. Lowry concluded that in renaming death, we somehow bent it to our many disparate purposes, but its finality could not be altered.

Agent Wilde approached him from the party of technicians recovering evidence from the grass where the Thompsons had been murdered.

She said, "Is it just me?"

Lowry was about to ask what she meant, but then he heard it, too. Another boat on the water. This sound was from a smaller engine than the earlier fishing boat carried, but its noise was not moving up or down the shore. It seemed to be heading straight in to the Thompson's waterfront.

A small inflatable boat bearing two men, cruised in past the length of the pier, and nudged up to the bulkhead at the shoreline. The white man,

who sat forward, dropped a loop of painter line around one of the creoso-
ted, verdigris-capped pilings that buttressed the bulkhead's heavy lateral
timbers. The black man cut the engine, and began detaching hose fittings
and mounting fasteners from the small portable fuel tank.

"Morning, friends. My name's Ben, and that's Ellis. We saw your
lights, and figured it was our lucky day."

Agent Lowry produced his flip wallet and identification. Wilde was
doing the same. Lowry said, "I'm Senior Resident Agent Lowry. Federal
Bureau of Investigation. This is Special Agent Wilde, and this is not your
lucky day. This is a federal crime scene. Please cast off and leave the
premises."

Ellis said, "We'd be happy to oblige, but this here fuel tank is nigh
empty. We got all disorientated in the fog, and we burned up way more
than we thought trying to get straight."

Ben chimed in, "Truth is, I thought *he* topped her off. He thought *I*
filled her up, and it's my boat, and I didn't eyeball it this morning like I
should've, so shame on me."

"Is there a gas station close?" Ellis held up the disconnected tank. "We
could stay out of your way walking to it, unless somebody could give us a
ride."

Wilde asked, "Where did you come from?"

"Tangier Island," said Ben. "Somebody get hurt?"

Ben and Ellis had climbed out of the boat, and were standing deferen-
tially on the bulkhead's cap rail. Lowry noticed Wilde studying Ben's rain-
coat.

She said, "We heard some shooting out on the water about a half hour
ago, maybe forty minutes back."

Ellis gave a shrug. "Hard to hear much over the motor."

"Is that what brought y'all here?" asked Ben. "You got an ambulance.
County mounties. Federals. Reckon that's one heck of a show of force
'cause of somebody letting fly on the water."

Wilde ambled closer to the men and cast a glance down at the inflatable. "What brought you out on a morning like this?"

"We got a tip from a friend about an old decoy. Captain Curtis Johns?
Karen Ray II?" Ben asked as if they really should have heard of this guy and

his boat. "No? He runs a deadrise out of Crisfield. The best fishing trips. Said he saw one washed up over to the refuge."

Lowry asked, "An old decoy?"

Ellis smiled. "Not old, so much as *antique*. The Ward brothers carved decoys in Crisfield for gunning long before they started doing them for decoration and art shows. Find an antique one, and there's collector folk who'll pay thousands for it even if the paint's marred, or long gone. Tens of thousands, even." Ellis gave a quick finger twirl by his ear.

Wilde understood him. Ellis thought these collectors were crazy, but if he got lucky and found something they wanted, he would take their money quickly enough.

"Which refuge?" asked Wilde.

"Martin, north of Smith Island," said Ben.

Lowry frowned. "You're a long way from there."

"Fog is fog," said Ellis, as if that explained everything.

Wilde said to Ben, "And you could sure use the money. Your coat has a few holes in it. Excuse me."

Wilde pulled Ben's coat away from his side. There was a bullet hole in the right front of the coat, and another in the back, with two more on the outer flank. "Those are pretty fresh, but you weren't in that coat when it got hit, or you'd be bleeding, maybe dead. Were you wearing that wetsuit down in the boat at the time, with your coat rolled up and stowed? Are you also a long distance swimmer or something?"

"Oh my blessing," said Ben in genuine consternation. "Wow. This is my lucky day after all."

Wilde continued, "And your boat's trailing a slick, like a lot of your gas went over the side very recently, and got drawn along in your wake."

"A two-stroke takes an oil-and-gas mix. Some oil's going right through without burning, I guess. I'll have it checked out. Hate to pollute the Chesapeake," said Ben.

Wilde said, "Oh, but you got a four-stroke there. No mix, just straight gas. You're lying to me, Ben. Or you think I'm stupid. Which is it?"

Lowry said, "Could be both. Gentlemen, I believe we need to have a conversation."

CHAPTER 39

BEN WAS SATISFIED. Ellis was less sanguine about the start of the interview with Lowry and Wilde. Catching the watermen in obvious lies meant the agents felt they had an advantage. It remained to be seen if this false sense of superiority would lead the feds to reveal more about what was going here on than they intended, or just waste precious time. It was going to be tricky from here on out.

Wilde had asked Ben and Ellis politely to turn out their pockets, and then patted them down anyway. The watermen had not kicked up a fuss. Cooperation might earn them more intel.

Agent Lowry asked, "Why are you here?"

"I think we explained that," said Ben.

"No, you trumped up some crap about decoys and running out of gas," came Wilde's rejoinder, "but you're both here at the scene of a double homicide, without identification. You have recent bullet holes in your coat. I can grab a sample and check you both for GSR."

Ellis said, "Gunshot residue? Without due process, and no probable cause?"

"Find a waterman without GSR head to toe. That'd be a neat trick," said Ben.

"And that'd be when your two new friends, who come to you hat in hand, down on their luck, and lost in a fog would likely lawyer-up," said Ellis. "Seems like we're the ones who caught the odd stray bullet. We didn't shoot it. What would we shoot it *with*?"

Lowry said, "I'm not sure you're friends of mine."

"No, not friends," agreed Wilde. "You're persons of interest at the very least."

"Just to be clear, we're not under arrest," said Ben. "Not suspects in your double homicide."

Lowry considered this for a moment. "I can live with that for now."

Agent Wilde, who was clearly bad-copping today, took a few more moments before she begrudgingly muttered to Lowry, "If you say so."

Ben went on, "Okay. All that being said, a double homicide is a terrible thing, but it's not FBI turf."

Wilde bridled. "That's none of your concern."

Ellis shook his head in frustration. "Suit yourself. How about that ride to the gas station? Just drop us, and we can walk back. Sorry for the imposition and whatnot."

Lowry called, "Sheriff Williams!"

An older man in a crisp county uniform abandoned a conversation with a female deputy, and made his way over to the four-way confab by the water.

Lowry said, "These gentlemen are in a tight spot. They saw all the lights and commotion and came here looking for help. I realize you're not Triple-A, sir. And I wouldn't ask you to assist with a courtesy transport in the middle of what's going on here. Is it possible you have a can of fuel in your cruiser? If so, you can count on being reimbursed for it in full by the bureau. I wouldn't ask if it weren't important."

The downcast sheriff studied Ben and Ellis, weighed them, and found them wanting. The burden of reams of additional paperwork for the reimbursement gave his face a further discouraged air. "Five gallons do you?"

Agent Lowry raised an inquiring eyebrow at the watermen. Ellis said, "Very neighborly."

Lowry broke a small smile of approval toward the sheriff, who walked back to the trunk of one of the cruisers. He opened it, hauled out a first responder's medical kit, and with that out of the way, removed a red metal jerry can. He hoisted it out one-handed, but it hung solidly through its transit to the ground as if it were full.

Ben noticed the sheriff was in no rush to bring the can over. Instead, he seemed to wait by the cruiser for a signal from Lowry. This is already a tight-knit crew, thought Ben. Something bigger than murder was on their minds.

"Now then," said Lowry. "We have your fuel. No need to hitch a ride in the front of a cruiser to get it."

Wilde added, "Let's make sure you don't need a ride in the back. What do you know?"

Ben said, "Convenient as a waterfront place might be for it, I'm going to bet these killings weren't a drug sale, or some dope-runners' falling out. Not to bring the two of you here at this stage of things."

"Granted," said Lowry.

"A missing person," said Ellis.

Lowry reluctantly conceded, "Two for two."

"The murder victims were collateral to someone going missing." suggested Ben.

Wilde was impressed, but that only made her more suspicious. "I'll ask you again. What do you know?"

Ben cast his eye around the property. A few toys lay in the yard, but not enough to make this place a child's home. He noticed the children's wooden swing set near a stand of trees. It sported a yellow fabric canopy over an elevated platform that was reached by a ladder, and evacuated by a sliding board. This was a typical grandparent's expenditure to make the place appealing for visits by cherished children. He nodded toward the apparatus. "A kid?"

Wilde looked out at the foggy bay to hide her growing uncertainty about the line this conversation was taking.

Lowry took a breath, and let it out slowly. "To save time, I will go out on a limb here with you, Ben. Two five-year-old children, a boy and a girl, are missing."

"No ransom?" asked Ben.

"There has been no contact from the person or persons who did this," said Wilde.

Ben caught sight of the black shadow of fingerprint powder on the doors of the shed. The ruts in the wet yard leading from there to the ambulance were plain. He asked, "What about that shed?"

Wilde said, "The vics were dumped there."

"That leaves two options," said Ben. "Serial killer, or trafficking. Serial killers might work in pairs, which the body dump suggests, but they don't often team up. Managing two kids alone is hard, too. Unless the one who did this is known to the kids."

Ellis asked, "Anything else?"

"Isn't that enough?" asked Wilde.

"It's plenty," said Ben. "But I think Ellis is asking if the bodies were all that was in there."

Wilde did not refer to her pad when she recited, "Lawn care items. A push mower. Two-cycle engine, and a two gallon can with a gas-oil mix." Her eyes glared at Ben with a glint of triumph on that point. "A weed whacker, also two-cycle. Weed killer. Garden tools. An open bag of fertilizer. Two oars, and four life jackets. Two adult and two children's."

Ben turned and studied the twisted pier. Wilde followed his eye-line. After a moment she said, "Where's the boat? Ben? Who was in that boat? Do you know?"

Ben ignored the questions, and said, "Could you ask the sheriff for our fuel please?"

Wilde said, "We should hold these guys."

Lowry said, "We can't hold them for noticing things we failed to see." He signaled to the sheriff, who hoisted the jerry can one-handed, and trudged it over.

Ellis lowered himself into the inflatable, reattached and mounted the tank, and made a clean steady pour of fuel from the can to the tank despite the waves lapping at the bulkhead. The fuel tank was smaller than the jerry can, but Ellis did not pass the unused fuel back to the sheriff.

Lowry patted the air at the first sign of the sheriff's agitation. "Full reimbursement, sheriff. For the can, too."

Wilde said, "Their boat's not even registered."

Lowry said, "We won't assume the Coast Guard's job today, Agent Wilde, but I take your point. Ben, you've given us very little here."

Ben answered, "I know it seems like that, Agent Lowry, but there's no grapevine among us watermen. No rumors to speak of, nor gossip, at least not such that a Smith Islander nor Tangierman might mention out of school. But still, a person might hear things."

"I understand. One hears things on the breeze."

"Like a name," said Ben. "A name like Maynard Chalk."

Wilde had her notepad and pen out. "How do you spell that?"

"It's like *Satan*. There's only one way."

Ellis started the motor. Ben climbed from the bulkhead into the inflatable and cast off. The boat eased away from the bulkhead.

Ben said, "Again, a serial killer, or human trafficking?"

Agent Lowry was getting frustrated. "We agreed on that. With no answer, the question adds nothing new."

The fog enveloped the shoreline. The strobes made shadows of the receding agents.

As they disappeared from view, Ben called out, "What about *both*?"

CHAPTER 40

JOACHIM DEPRIEST GAZED down at the man standing before him. Sam Rookard seemed so ordinary. In his late forties, with thinning blond hair, he did not even have a calendar boy's physique. His appearance was positively average, forgettable, even banal. But there was something feral in his eyes that DePriest found captivating.

Retaining Rookard's services had been simple enough. An internet registry of sexual offenders, complete with links to mugshots and court documents, made DePriest certain this man was the perfect choice to work directly with the talent. His crimes were not so egregious that he had been locked away forever. He was escalating, true to his ilk, in the deviant nature of his moral turpitude, but he still retained a certain *je ne sais quoi*; perhaps it was the element of creativity that his training as a physician's assistant lent to his body of work.

Rookard hated the registration requirements that made him a pariah to every neighbor wherever he went, simply for being himself. He wanted a second chance, but not at redemption. DePriest could offer him that special preferment, and so much more. Rookard wanted desperately to evolve from the petty world of animal torture, subway rush-hour frottage, and peeping through windows at children, to more hands-on opportunities. In this secluded facility, there would be no risk of being caught. His contract with DePriest included a new identity and the documents to back it up, in addition to a sum of money that would keep him comfortable for the rest of his life no matter where he decided to put down his gnarled roots.

Though a bit late in the game for DePriest's temperament, Rookard was still developing the finishing touches on the Opening Ceremony of *L'Abattoir*, which were thematically based on torture techniques employed by those madcap brothers of the Spanish Inquisition. Special archaic equipment had been built to Rookard's order, with many modern touches. There would be interrogations. The talent would of course have no idea what answers might possibly save their lives. DePriest believed that their confusion and hope, as they were dehumanized by suffering, would be a wonderful counterfoil for the audience who would know the situation to be absolutely hopeless.

"You still want the Audience Choice segment, right?" Rookard sounded hopeful. This had been his most important concept. A portfolio of photographs of the talent would be available to the subscribers with opportunities to vote upon who was to be interviewed first, what they were to suffer during the conversation, and how they would be finished.

"Yes, of course," said DePriest. "But with a twist."

Rookard's face looked as though he had swallowed a live insect. Creative freedom had been so important, but DePriest was the boss. Afraid of what nonsense he'd hear, Rookard asked, "What do you have in mind?"

"When you learn the talent order that the subscribers have voted for, don't display it. Massage the list a bit," said DePriest, grinning like a gargoyle. "Divide it in three equal sections from top to bottom. Start the night with something from the high middle-tier talent group. Fill in after that with talent from the bottom-tier. Then finish the Opening Ceremonies with a top vote-getter."

"I get it. You want to hold back the best for last. To hold their eyeballs on the whole night."

"Exactly," said DePriest, his tone unctuous, and self-satisfied.

Rookard said, "You're not going for ratings, are you? And you already have their money."

"What's your point, Rookard?"

"I'm saying that regardless of whoever goes out the gate first, and whoever goes last, I will hold the subscribers' attention every minute. You don't have to worry about that."

"You misunderstand me. We have to look at the bigger picture. We must put on a great event lasting seven wonderful nights. We need to use the voting results in the most creative way possible, to keep the subscribers' anticipation keen."

"And we will! I've pulled a team of helpers together that you'll have to hold back with cattle prods. They're animals. Monsters. Single-digit IQs. They're excited to do this. They'd do it for free. Seriously, every thought they have is a war crime. And with my work in between, your subscribers will pee on the floor rather than leave their screens for a single hot second."

"That's why we've formatted for the mobile applications, for devices large and small," explained DePriest.

"Jesus Christ, what if someone watches on a Smartphone in public, or on a tablet?"

"The encryption makes the streams untraceable. And what casual observer would believe it's all real? Regardless, I sincerely believe the subscribers will want to drink in all your work in a very private setting. And, please do not take the Lord's name in vain again, or it will be the last thing you do."

Rookard checked DePriest's stern face closely for the joke. No, the big man was not kidding.

DePriest went on, "My point, Mr. Rookard, is that if we are successful, there will be an opportunity to do this sort of thing again in a year, perhaps two. Think of that. Would I be able to drag you out of retirement to help with *L'Abattoir Redux?*"

In spite of a desire to appear calm and businesslike in Joachim DePriest's presence, an unpardonable quiver racked Rookard from his scrotum to his chest. He took a moment to collect himself before he asked, "What will you call the *third* version?"

DePriest's smile split his broad, scarred face; a fissure in a meringue. "Let's put on a good show, and we can discuss it."

CHAPTER 41

HOMELAND SECURITY SECRETARY Lily Morgan was having a bad day without quite knowing why. Variant Creutzfeldt–Jakob disease, first acquired from the mad-cow-infected bone meal with which she fertilized her beloved prize-winning roses, continued to kill nerves and bore holes in her frontal lobes. Usually an efficient killer, vCJD seemed to be taking its sweet time bringing Lily down. Like unbridled power, the nasty, invasive prions were making her quite insane in the meantime.

Lily's office had been mercifully quiet this morning, and unburdened by many of the usual hallucinations that troubled her, but by no means was it completely mirage-free. Matters deteriorated when she heard the deafening squawk of a large chicken. She looked up from her computer game of solitaire, a game in which the face cards sometimes lectured her about the vital importance of toenail hygiene, to see an enormous wingless bird resembling New Zealand's extinct moa, with a vivid spray of tail feathers composed of red flares and dazzling blue and yellow fireworks of an oddly smokeless, and inextinguishable nature. Lily relaxed when she realized she could understand that the squawking, burning moa was only trying to tell her to answer a phone. At that point, the giant bird faded away.

Piecing the information together carefully, she looked at her hand, saw a noisy cellular phone clutched in it, fathomed what it was, soon divined it was her own, and reasoned that yes, she should see who was calling. She did not recognize the incoming number.

After opening the line and giving what she thought was an appropriate greeting, Morgan heard, "Lily, dear? Is that you? You sound like a pardoned Thanksgiving turkey."

The Secretary of Homeland Security wisely reverted from bird-speak to English. "Who is this?"

"It's John, dear."

"I'm speaking with farm equipment."

"No, Lily. It's your husband, John."

"Oh." *Husband* rang a distant bell, but she was having trouble putting a face to the voice. "It's been a while."

"Since breakfast? Yes, a few hours, I suppose. I wanted to talk with you about an idea."

"I'm very busy." This was not exactly true, but Lily Morgan did not know it. Lily's post running the third largest cabinet office in the nation was maintained on life-support by a cadre of expert advisors and assistants who were fervently interested in keeping their jobs in spite of toiling for a boss who was abjectly bonkers. Secretary Morgan's tenure was only a few months old, after all. No one felt it prudent to abandon ship quite yet, though lots had been drawn among the top staffers to decide who might resign first, second, and so on. The exit strategy among her juniors was more solidly laid out than Morgan's own work agenda for her first year in office.

"Of course you're busy, Lily. But I was thinking about a getaway."

By this point in the chat, Lily was as close to alert and oriented to time and place as she was ever going to be, given her neurological disease process. "What did you have in mind?"

The man claiming to be her spouse asked, "Do you remember our trip to Romania back in '83, and all the fact-finding fun we had there together?"

Lily smiled at the first crystalline recollection in the dialogue. "Do I *ever!* Who knew orphanages could be so damn exciting? The little ankle-biters never knew what hit 'em, and if they did, the squealing really gave me a tingle. Yes, good times, Bill."

"It's *John.*" The man on the phone sounded exasperated. His voice took on a more endearing, affectionate note when he said, "I felt very close to you on that vacation. It was like a second honeymoon."

Secretary Lily became practical. "We were younger then, and Nicolae and Elena were fantastic hosts. They fought all the way to the firing squad, the madcap scamps. It's a nice idea, Tom, but how can we break away now?"

After a pause, the gentleman caller said, "It's only for a week. And it will be even more fun because we don't have to leave the country. The place I have in mind, it's just a couple of hours from here. You can keep tabs on things at the office. Stay in touch. Call in sick, sweetheart, and let's do this. Together."

"It sounds very romantic. When were you thinking?"

"Tonight."

"That soon." Lily Morgan consulted the rubber plant next to her chair. "The schedule looks pretty light. Let me move a few things around. Okay. This will be fun."

CHAPTER 42

ELLIS WAS ANGRY. "That was a nice lateral pass."

In the bow of the inflatable, Ben had poked a finger through the bullet hole in the front of his coat. "Reinforcements are a good thing."

"You have no control over if or when they'll ever show up," observed Ellis.

"They have resources we don't."

"They're hamstrung by laws."

Ben laughed. "You believe that."

"I'd like to believe it, but point taken. Where to now?"

By Ellis's best guess, the inflatable was still traveling roughly east, perpendicular to the shoreline they had just left behind.

Ben said, "Hang a forty-five right. This fog has to burn off soon."

Using the boat's wake as a reference, Ellis pushed the motor's throttle arm to port, timing his turn by habit, until he judged the disturbed water trailing off the stern was disappearing to the northwest.

"What's down thisaway?" Ellis asked, a genuine satisfaction lifting his mood.

"Home."

PART II
SKIPPING THE GALLIVANT

CHAPTER 43

WADE JOYCE LAID aside the end of the new three quarter inch spring line he was whipping with Consolidated Thread Mills #3 Waxed Marine Polyester. So far, this was the sole extravagance of a Smith Island waterman who had come into considerable money; fresh dock lines for his big deadrise, *Varina Davis*.

The knocking at the door had been polite enough the first go-round. A tall man with a girth that nearly matched his height, Wade gathered annoyance rather than speed when the second round of banging came quicker and louder. His petite wife Mary strode to meet him at the door as he opened it.

Wade beamed when he saw who was darkening his stoop. "Get in here Ben! Mary's already got the pot on, and none of that cat piss brew we hear Ellis's ladling out." As an afterthought he added, "You can come in, too, Ellis."

Ellis looked hurt as he said, "Technically, it's cat *shit*."

Unable to help himself, Ben gave a proprietary glance around the Joyce home for a sign that money had changed his friend. Seeing no new furnishings, no flat-screens, and no trinkets, he picked up the new line Wade was working on and had to admire the tight whipping. A master marlinspike seaman, Wade would never let the *Varina Davis* leave port with lines finished out by melting, or God forbid, with just a lubber's knot.

Mary brought mugs of coffee from the kitchen, and said, "The others should be along any minute. Make yourself at home."

Ben was puzzled. "The others?"

Wade said, "Kimba Mosby called Mary ten minutes back. Said she saw you and Ellis tolling in. Reckon there's nigh on five coffee pots abrewing around Ewell right now, since nobody knew for sure where you'd tie up."

Ben said, "We might need *Varina Davis*. I didn't mean to stir up a fuss."

"Good luck with that," said Mary. "Where's LuAnna?"

Ben said nothing.

Ellis looked grave. "There's a situation."

Mary caught Ellis's tone, and recalled an incident in the island's recent history in which things had gone very hard on LuAnna.

There was another knock at the door. Wade brought Art Bailey and Orville Hurley back to the parlor. These two men were also loyal veterans of the recent fracas that had netted the gold bullion for the islanders. There were handshakes and greetings between the blooded campaigners, but a quiet descended as soon as it was understood that the arrival of Ben and Ellis was no social call. Not wishing to make Ben chew his cabbage twice, they sipped coffee and waited until the full Council of Smith Island had assembled.

While Mary Joyce was caught up in finding extra mugs and brewing another pot of coffee, Wade shuttled his massive form several more times between the parlor and the door. Soon, the present company also included the Reverend and Kimba Mosby, Julie Nuttle, and Sonny Wright, all part of the informal island leadership, as well as irregular soldiers primed for clandestine work after hours.

Wade Joyce seemed content with the headcount, so Ben asked, "You expecting Ephraim?"

Ephraim Teach, who, true to Smith Island's early pirate heritage, believed he was descended from Blackbeard himself, was a particular friend Ben had hoped to call on for help today. He had been an ardent soldier in the fight to keep the gold bullion they had salvaged the previous fall.

Wade looked suitably downcast when he said, "Ephraim's got the pip, and sends you his regards. A real bad cough. He said he'll be keeping to his bed today."

Ben digested the disappointing news. Then he carefully related to the present company the strange encounter with Tally early that morning on the *American Mariner*, and of her little sister's captivity and death sentence. No one said a word as he described returning to Smith Island to meet up with Ellis to work through what to do next. Word of LuAnna and Tally's strange disappearance from the old Liberty Ship, followed by the discovery of the swamped skiff in the vessel's hold, and the armed dead man lying below it, evoked confused, angry murmurs. Eyebrows rose when he told of their being directed by Michael Craig's drift analysis to the waterfront property where Tally had stolen her lifeboat, and his signal triangulations that put their old enemy, Maynard Chalk, close by there as well.

A few voiced angry epithets, moderated no doubt by the presence of Reverend Mosby, when Ben described the close call and exchange of gunfire on the water with Chalk. Silence fell again, perhaps with inward doubts of Ben's judgment, when he told of his brief parlay with Agents Lowry and Wilde of the FBI.

Julie Nuttle, who took a practical view of Ben's story, said, "I feel for the girls, I do. But the only thing that's bothered me in all this is, where's LuAnna?"

Sonny Wright said, "Hold on here. Forgive me Reverend. Likewise you, Ben. We let Maynard Chalk get away once already. I followed the why of it back when we done it, but LuAnna's troubles today can't be nothing but part and parcel of that fonny boy still drawing breath."

A rumble of assent moved through the group.

Orville Hurley boiled it down. "Asides fetching LuAnna home, who you coulda seen to proper yourself, Ben, if you was living where you live, instead of skippin' the gallivant to parts foreign, or hunkering like a hare in places peculiar, I don't see a nickel in this business."

Reverend Mosby cut in, "Orville, we all know why Ben sojourns away, and we all have benefited powerfully from his sacrifice. Holding himself apart from *his* rightful place among us was not his choice, but it was the *only* choice."

A strange, soft chorus of *Amen* overtook the assembled company. Even Reverend Mosby seemed surprised to have struck a Sunday-go-to-meeting chord.

Art Bailey slurped his coffee loudly, and said. "Question is, can we afford trouble just now?"

Ellis corrected, "What *can't* we afford, thanks to Ben?"

"Orville's got the right of it," said Art. "It goes double for you, Ben. There's many on Smith, and Tangier too, with a jumbo stake in your health. I mean orphans. The sick and infirmed who can't work. Widows whose men followed you to the fight and bled out in sand and water. We can't take a gold brick to Walmart for sundries and expect them to make a hunnerd thousand in change. People would talk."

Kimba Mosby, the reverend's wife, nodded agreement. She studied Ben, and said, "There's such a high-humming market for your golden widgeons and ducks and geese. We are so lucky to see these creatures alive every day, but some folk won't ever give them a second glance lest they get their hands on your beautiful work, Ben."

"For top dollar," said Ben with an edge of disgust in his voice. "So, now I'm Jacky-Jim Audubon for those with a spare million or three."

Ellis's impatience surged. "Is there anybody else you wish might've bided here for longer, but who went on to do the difficult thing? The *right* thing?"

"Meaning Ben's pappy?" asked Julie. "I was so fond of that man when we were kids. But there was no stopping Dick Blackshaw if a whim took him and shook him." She smiled in sensual reminiscence. "To the rascal go the spoils. But now we got ours, and now hanging onto it is the smart play."

Reverend Mosby *ahemed* and said, "I think friend Ellis refers to the path of our Lord and Savior. It was hard for him. His sacrifice was utter and entire. We were all rewarded by it in the end."

"Hold up!" barked Ben. "I am *nobody's* savior. I value my hide the same as any sane man. What little good I ever mean to do is strictly while I'm up and around right here. The Here*after* is none of my concern. No offense, rev'."

"Aye," said Art Bailey. "Plenty good works to do here and now. Ben's a bona fide *artiste*, his wonders to perform. I can't drink n'mare, so changing water to wine don't help me none, but turning gold to cash is something else again, swagger die."

"Chalk is unfinished business," declared Sonny. "You think he clocked you, Ben? You think he's still runnin' hot and means you mischief?"

Without thinking, Ben's finger found the bullet hole in the front of his jacket.

Sonny noticed the gesture, understood what he saw, and said, "Lordy go to fire, that's good enough for me."

"You're bored, Sonny," said Julie. "You got a mean temper, and an itch to blast something or somebody, never mind. You need a hobby in the worst way 'til goose season comes 'round again."

Sonny snorted a short laugh. "It's always goose season where I'm at. Sonny rhymes with *money*, doncha-know."

Wade Joyce's telephone tweeted. There was a moment of quiet among the assemblage while Mary hunted up the cordless handset. It was not lying in its cradle on the end table by Wade's easy chair. The house was small. Mary soon returned from the kitchen holding the receiver to her breast. A mystery clouded her brow.

"It's for you, Ben." Mary handed him the phone.

He put it to his ear. "Who is this?"

"Don't you know?" asked Michael Craig.

"How'd you—"

"All your comms went down. Even the sat-phone on that target boat. I got worried. Ninety minutes later, your hometown lines blow up with chatter about the return of the *prodigal son*. Sometimes two and two really are four."

"Ellis and I had a little trouble on the water."

"You're talking, so it wasn't all that bad. Ben, the Feebs down in southern Maryland are rattling on about your old friend Maynard Chalk. Did you dime him?"

"We might've had something to do with that." Ben rose and stepped into the Joyces' kitchen. A sepulchral quiet in the parlor meant everyone was not only listening, but could likely hear his side of the conversation. To make matters worse, Mary bustled in with a few empty coffee mugs, busied herself at the pot with refills. She took her time getting the creams and sugars and cheese just right.

"Depending on how you and yours plan to handle matters," Craig was saying, "you might find yourself tripping over G-Men."

"Too late for that. But it was a risk I was willing to take, especially since folks closer to home are a mite balky on mustering out." Ben was okay with Mary Joyce hearing that as she returned to the parlor with the coffee.

"Did the drift analysis help?" asked Craig.

Ben looked out the window over the sink. The fog was still there. The rain was light, but steady. "It got me shot at, and interviewed by some Feds. Is that what you mean by help?"

Craig chuckled. "Sounds productive. There's something else. I don't know if it relates."

"If you're onto it, Mike, I'd give a listen," said Ben.

"There's some weird shit going down."

"Lord, I'd never call you to bore you with the day-to-day."

"I'm actually not joking. I've hacked some of the EPA water monitoring stations, including the Maryland and Virginia Departments of Natural Resources, plus a few more non-profit water quality testing sites that sample and transmit data remotely. There's an intense bloom in fecal coliforms hitting the Chesapeake."

"So you discovered there're more than three hundred million chickens farmed on the Eastern Shore," explained Ben.

"Yes, and I've accounted for their one-and-a-half *billion* pounds of guano. That's one hell of a phosphorous problem, but what I'm talking about is localized at the western edge of the bay, near the start of that drift analysis point. A few miles to the south."

Ben said, "It's been raining for a while. Some town sewers overflow and bypass the treatment, putting the stuff into the bay raw. Might be a small chicken farm, or dairy, or an over-fertilized field."

Michael sounded worried. "But it's not. There's no town near the bloom's effluent. No sewer or treatment outlets. No factory farms. No farms at all. What got me was that the goop is made up of ten to fifteen percent fiber, which is a lot, and the insoluble amino acids, the ash, is coming in at one-point-two, which is the high end. It's definitely human. What's odd is, like a farm, the diet is just one food. Like oatmeal."

Now Ben was interested. "A cheap way to feed a large bunch of folks. Where is this?"

"Dove Point. I know you've seen the piers. It's not too far from the Calvert Cliffs nuclear plant."

"The LNG transfer facility. It's defunct."

Craig corrected Ben. "We're fracking so much domestically, developers are looking at it hard again, this time for *exporting* natural gas from Dove Point, not importing like it used to. But yeah, at the moment, nothing's going on there. For sure nothing that would put that much human scat in the water. It's mothballed. With offices, big underground engineering spaces—"

"Who puts a liquid natural gas terminal so close to a nuke plant?"

"It was zoned an Energy Corridor. Taken through eminent domain. The federal NIMBYs didn't want it any closer to D.C." Michael Craig paused for a moment. "Dammit, Ben. You're keeping to your whole *small arms* promise, I assume"

Ben ignored the remark. "You're sure about all this."

"That was rhetorical, right?"

"Wine-of-the-Month?" Ben glanced into the parlor. He did not like the expressions he saw fouling the faces of his friends.

"Affirmative," said Craig.

Ben ended the call and returned to the parlor. "Sorry about that. So who's in?"

Wade Joyce looked uneasy when he answered. "Ben, we all follow the water as hard and close as ever we did, but your pappy and you brang us peace of mind, which we never had before. Faith is fine, but maybe you could say it got us a sturdy bank statement, and that is surely something fresh, begging the reverend's pardon."

Julie Nuttle simpered, nodded in complacent, complicit agreement.

Ben was taken aback, but he still had to ask, "If you aren't in, then could you lend me *Varina Davis*?"

"That's asking a lot, Ben." Wade looked abashed. "I make my living off her. *Miss Dotsy* pretty much always did for you before."

"There is a kid in trouble," Ben reiterated. "I have intel saying it's likely more than one kid."

Orville Hurley shook his head. "I, for one, never met this Tally girl. Who knows what's true and what's not?"

Ellis sucked a tooth loudly and with disdain. "Seriously? *Peace of mind.* You won't lend a man your boat if he asks, though he's the very man who got you your stuff and things. We got no *picaroons* in here? None at all?"

Ellis had invoked the ancient Smith Island slang for a pirate. The first settlers on the archipelago hundreds of years ago had hearkened back to their old, opportunistic ways on the coast of Cornwall for their living, where sometimes a fat harvest came sailing by on top of the water, not schooling below. Devout Methodism was now the order of the day on Smith and Tangier, but sometimes a nefarious past and the God-fearing present put the islanders at loggerheads.

With a darting glower, Julie cast deep shade in Wade Joyce's direction.

Wade buckled down, and dutifully said, "Art's right. So is Orville. Ben, there's no percentage in this business. I'm sorry about LuAnna, but she does get herself into tangles, and well you know it. And before that, she was Natural Resources Police. Ain't a man in here she hasn't busted at least once, and most of us plenty more. Undersized oysters. Oversized catches. Them fines hit hard, at a time and in a way we won't soon forget. Sorry, but she's your woman."

Ben filled with fast anger. "She's from *here*. She damn near died to help you get your *sturdy money*. And she resigned off the NRP first thing, and threw right in with us, so there's no disloyalty. At least not from *her*."

That made Orville Hurley and Art Bailey squirm.

Ben barreled on. "Put it to a vote. Right now. All those in favor of sitting tight, and leaving LuAnna and me hung out to dry, put your hand up where I can know every one of you plain."

All hands but Ellis's rose slowly. Then Ben noticed that Sonny Wright's palms were both resting flat on his knees.

Ben eyed the others, his face blank in disbelief.

CHAPTER 44

BLACKSHAW HELMED THE inflatable, which he and Knocker Ellis Hogan had chosen again over *Miss Dotsy* for speed. Ben had asked Sonny Wright to stay behind on Smith Island to keep watch over the Council members in case their passive stance burgeoned to the point of interference in his doings. Ben's untimely death, after all, would also kill the local exchange rate.

Then they had stopped by Ellis's home to re-kit. Ben was still not ready to cross the threshold of his own saltbox, especially with LuAnna away.

The weather in the middle of the Chesapeake was clear for a few miles, but mist and fog still surrounded them on all sides. The breeze had freshened. Ben wondered how this fog could hold together in it. The gray seemed to have a substance more dense than mere vapor.

Ellis broke a silence of more than half an hour. "I'm sorry about them, Ben."

"Oh, that didn't surprised me, or shouldn't have. It does read like a fairy tale. Whuppity Stoorie, or Rumpelstiltskin. Those people have a big stake in keeping me out of trouble and spinning cash. What'd happen if I spoke to other folks? What'd they say?"

"We're short on time for going door-to-door. At least Sonny feels you."

"There was a time he wanted me dead."

"That time is clearly past. He wants a piece of Maynard Chalk."

Ben said, "He's looking out for his interests."

"And he likes a skirmish, too," said Ellis. "You bring those on something fierce, even if there's no money in it."

"All part of my charm."

They porpoised across the bay at an unhealthy clip, slowing only when the fog closed in again to cut visibility.

At the *American Mariner*, they took a calculated risk that the weather was not going to deteriorate further. Using a crude block and tackle rigged in the hold, they hoisted the bow of LuAnna's crab skiff out of the water. A few more pulls using their combined weight, and the boat hung in the space like a side of beef. With no time to dry out the guts of its outboard motor, they removed it. Shy of the motor's weight, it was easier to lower the boat back to the water's surface with little bailing left to dry her. Then they transferred the more powerful motor and fuel tank from Ben's inflatable to the crab skiff.

Ellis said, "You know I don't shy from work, but *Miss Dotsy* was ready to go."

"We've got to fit in," said Ben, "but we've got to be right quick. Neither *Miss Dotsy*, nor that RHIB give us both. And if LuAnna spies out her own boat somehow, she'll know we're in the neighborhood."

With the inflatable moored once again in the hold behind its purpose-built screen of detritus, they set out again.

Within an hour, the piers supporting the big heavy transfer piping for the *Dove* Point natural gas terminal appeared like a black lattice work in the gloom ahead. A two-story structure on the main pier housed pump and valve controls, and empty offices where cargo had once been registered. Even a few orange Survival Systems International lifeboat capsules still hung from their single cables in case fire or some other disaster cut pier workers off from the safety of land. The rest of the structure disappeared in the foggy distance toward shore.

Ben slowed the skiff down to a walk. Ellis made sure dirty tarps covered their gear in a slovenly manner. He draped the painter line over the bow so it danced in the water like a living thing. It took some careful negotiation of the waves to keep the bay from rolling over the skiff's low freeboard.

Ben rounded up to the north for a slow pass fifty yards from the end of the piers. The kept their body English to a slouch. Ellis put his feet up on the opposite gunwale, crossed his ankles, and though he faced the shore, and slightly aft, he let his head loll with the swells like a man dozing. They made an unseamanly, yet nonthreatening presentation to anyone who might be watching; just two men on the water moving slowly past, prompting no one to wonder where from, or where to.

The vast array of pilings supporting the complex's enormous plumbing system seemed to take forever to file by. Great ships used to tie up here to off-load over a hundred thousand cubic meters of natural gas that had been compressed into less bulky fluid at minus two hundred twenty degrees Fahrenheit. The facility appeared deserted as advertised, with gulls crying and flapping, challenging one another for space though there was plenty to go around; the herons rested like sentries.

Ben muttered just above the engine's noise, "You see that?"

A thick-bodied, box-chested Rottweiler with a security harness and looped leather hand grip had bounded onto the end of the pier, and was matching the crab skiff's ambling pace along the T end. The gulls and all but the most distant herons took flight at its menacing approach.

"I'd rather meet *you* in a dark ally," said Ellis.

They heard a man shout, "Brutus! Sitz!" The dog sat immediately.

"That critter speaks German," observed Ben.

The Rottweiler's handler appeared out of the foggy distance and growled, "So ist brav, Brutus."

The crab skiff was leaving man and dog in its wake, but not before Ellis said, "Brotherman's packing an MP5."

"And those aren't crabapples on his chest," said Ben. "He's tricked out like that fonny boy floating in the hold."

"So much for *Observe and Report*. That's no rent-a-cop." Ellis's hand slowly snaked low under the tarp toward a long, narrow hump in the fabric. "I could drop him in the water. We could fish him out and have us chat before we throw him back all catch-and-release style."

"Crossed my mind, but we need more soft intel before we raise the roof." Ben kept the skiff pointed north.

Ellis pulled his hand from beneath the tarp. For now, it held only a sandwich. By the time the skiff was abreast of the white tower of the Dove Point Lighthouse, the snack was half-eaten.

CHAPTER 45

JOHN TURNER FROST was thrilled. His conversation with his bride had made him happier than he had been in a long while. By tonight, he and Lily Morgan would be watching their first evening of entertainments that promised to outdo the festivities in Romania so many years ago.

He drew the blinds to his office, and turned on his computer. It took him all of five minutes to leverage and wire into a numbered holding account the twenty million dollars for Lily's subscription. Then he carefully logged onto *L'Abattoir*'s site. This time he did not miss a single keystroke of the many passwords.

Frost discovered that in addition to his selection of activities and proclivities, he had further votes to cast about his preferred order in which the candidates would be handled each evening. There were men, women, and children of all descriptions to be considered; even a lovely set of twins, and a pregnant lady, too. He paused for a moment before making a selection until he realized Lily's taste and his own jibed perfectly. She would be delighted with any order for which he voted.

Where before he had been taken aback, he was actually relieved when *L'Abattoir*'s instant message window opened on his screen.

HOST: Hello Jack ;-).

Frost was more polite this time around.

JACK: Good morning.

HOST: I have your wiring instructions for your additional, up-close-and-personal fee.

JACK: Very good. There has been a development. I am happy to inform you that my bride will be joining me for the full week.

There was a pause that made Turner fear the connection had failed.

HOST: She was not invited. This is highly irregular.

Frost was prepared for resistance. It was understandable that *L'Abattoir*'s security measures might be tight for attendees who had not been vetted in advance.

JACK: What in God's name is regular about any of this? Lily will be my guest. I assure you we both swing that way. I'll have you know we were hosted by none other than the Ceausescus once for similar revels. Yes, the Ceausescus. A terribly misunderstood couple, but they were fun-loving, just like Lily and me. There won't be any problem unless the diversions disappoint.

There was another long pause.

HOST: There is no two-for-one special offered. Absolutely no discounts. You do understand the fee is now double?

JACK: I would expect nothing else.

HOST: In that case, we are honored to welcome your wife to attend.

JACK: I have a special request. A simple one.

HOST: I hope we can oblige.

JACK: Lily and I would enjoy ourselves even more if you would be so kind as to place a bed for our use close to the staging area. Very close.

HOST: Interesting.

JACK: With rubber linens.

HOST: You realize you might be in full view of other subscribers of our small in-person audience as they move about freely to achieve the best viewing angles.

JACK: Like we give a tinker's damn.

CHAPTER 46

SAM ROOKARD INSPECTED the stock. While DePriest was tabulating the subscribers' voting results for the talent, there were the aptly named last-looks to undertake to be sure the talent was appropriately clean and spruced.

The underground cells had been hosed out but still reeked of piss, shit, and fear. Extra rations of gruel were ordered for the day. The pinched look of hunger would not suit the performances. A strenuous HAZMAT-level decontamination shower was also in store to remove filth and give the talent that fresh-faced glow.

Rookard lingered at the cells of the children. They were his very special charges. His twisted fondness did not extend to compassion or mercy, of course. It only meant that he gave his intended treatment of them extra consideration. He was keenly aware that kiddies were particularly susceptible to the phenomenon of compensated shock, which made them appear to be quite lively right up to the point they quickly deteriorated into an unrecoverable state and died. Rookard had extra monitoring equipment in place to make sure a child's performance did not end prematurely. Touches like this made him the perfect man to oversee this event. He complacently reflected that DePriest had chosen well in him.

These lovely, adorable twins presented him with a problem. There was no time to get additional monitoring gear for their simultaneous performances. He had planned to fugue the action back and forth between them until the final coups. He would simply have to use his well-honed instincts which had ably served him in the past. With that thought, he returned to his makeshift shop to his whet his blades with extra sharp edges.

CHAPTER 47

EARLINE BYRD AND Gläans Bellendre were as unsure how to find the runaway as Maynard Chalk had been. Since their boss was not on scene to direct their efforts personally, they weighed the risks of calling him for orders versus operating independently according to their own ideas. Integral to that decision was an ongoing assessment of who they feared more, DePriest, or Chalk.

"The big man said to find her," said Byrd.

"They both said that, for fucking's sake," snorted Bellendre.

"You cuss like a moron, Gläans."

"I learn from the best, monkey-*beyotch*. I'd like to tap that young black girl myself. You saw her rack? Sweet little bubbies. Then after, *bang!*" Gläans pretended to kill his victim, mimed a pistol with his fingers.

"That's not what *tap-rack-bang* means."

"I made joke."

"You're an idiot. Please shut up and dial."

They were puffing cigarettes outside the facility's main entry. The smoke helped scour away the combined odors of DePriest's body and mass human captivity in spite of the operatives already having liberally dabbed Vicks mentholatum ointment under their noses.

Vast spherical tanks loomed around them in the murk like three new planets about to smash into Earth. In better weather, at least one of the tanks always seemed to eclipse the facility with unending shadow, depending on the sun's position in the sky.

Gläans pulled out the sat-phone, and speed-dialed Chalk. After ten rings with no answer, the he broke off the call.

"Now what?" asked Gläans.

The absence of Chalk, Clyster, and Harrower brevetted Byrd to the unenviable, unwanted rank of commanding officer of the security detail.

She tried to see the top of the nearest tank. She traced the helical staircase that wound around the exterior of the great sphere to its north pole. Halfway to the top, the frail-looking stairs disappeared in the chilly haze.

She tried using her field glasses, and asked, "Is Firesbaugh still posted up there?"

"I suppose so."

"I can't see him. He probably can't see a damn thing either. High ground won't do us any good."

"But the girl ran. She would be super crazy-brain to come back."

Byrd made a decision. They could blunder around in the crap weather and further deplete the security staff covering the facility, or sit tight until Chalk returned.

"Fuck DePriest. If you think Chalk's pissed off now, he'll go apeshit if we lose any more stock. Let's head back down and keep track of the ones we've still got."

They refreshed their Vicks nosegays, pulled the heavy door open, took a deep breath, and descended.

CHAPTER 48

BEN AND ELLIS tied up the crab skiff north of the Dove Point Light Station. The restored light was still in active service, and had been since 1828. They would infiltrate Dove Point for reconnaissance of the gas terminal from there.

First they made their way south again on foot, stopping short of the white tower. Summer hours that opened the historic landmark to the public had not yet commenced. That did not mean the keeper's cottage would be free of bed and breakfast visitors. The light itself was managed remotely from Baltimore. Ben was glad the blatting old horn and the later electric diaphone fog signal were no longer in use. A few minutes' quiet observation of the place let them know they had the property to themselves.

Ellis was about to swaddle the tower door's lock in Ben's coat to damp the sound of their break-in when he saw the lock was already parted from the splintered door frame. Vandals taking advantage of a deserted property, most likely. Ellis picketed a position just inside the door.

Ben started climbing slowly, keeping his steps on the triangular treads inside the tower as soft as possible. He had the feeling of ascending around the helix staircase toward the inmost parts of a tall chambered nautilus. For a few moments his entire world consisted of the gently tapering white masonry walls, and the delicately fanning stairs above and below bolted on ornate iron supports that were fixed into the central column. John Donahoo's design remained a marvel of beauty to Ben almost two hundred years on, but the fifty foot climb was winding him more than he would care to admit.

With his head even with the top of the helix stair, Ben instinctively halted his ascent, but was not certain why. The fifth order Fresnel lens was clean, as were the cupola's windows. The light was operating, in all likelihood out to its nominal twelve mile range.

All at once, two things struck him as wrong. The half-door from inside the cupola to the circular outside walkway around it was ajar. And through that door he could hear nothing. Second, there was a raw funk of guano in the high space, but where were the shrieks of the gulls themselves? He finally heard something, but it was no bird.

The sound was a human exhalation. The wafting sour musk scent of a cigar that soon followed let him know a smoker was taking his ease in the fresh air outside the cupola. Ben was aware he had no business in that lighthouse. Like as not, his unknown companion was also out of place. Drawing his borrowed knife, Ben continued his ascent in absolute silence, and with extreme prejudice.

Taking a full circle's scan, he saw no one standing above the masonry half-wall that supported the cupola's glass housing. Whoever was up there must be seated below the sill toward the south, diametrically opposite of Ben's approach to the tower with Ellis, which explained why they had not noticed the stranger before.

Ben slowly stood just until he could look over the sill. And there he was. Ben saw the top of a man's head; his shoulders were clothed in the same color uniform of the guard a mile south on the terminal pier. The muzzle of an automatic weapon lay propped on the other side of a thick window mullion. From the muzzle brake's slanted opening and black phosphate finish, Ben figured it was a sweet TAPCO number likely retrofitted to an AK-47. The sentry took another drag, and exhaled a contented stream of smoke.

From his slightly higher vantage, Ben made another scan to be sure this man was alone. Check. There was no one else on that deck.

The half-door giving access onto the deck faced east, almost ninety degrees counterclockwise from the sentry's position. For Ben to duck low and scramble onto the deck ready for business would take time; the sentry could finish his cigar, charge the rifle, check his Facebook page, and line up his shot long before Ben could hope to subdue him.

The sentry's cigar's ember was burning down to a stump. Ben was left one option. He slowly took off his coat and wrapped his left arm in it, hoping for the best. In one fluid movement, he stood and smashed out the window directly over the stranger's head. The shards of glass were still falling as Ben reached down and forward and wrapped his right arm tight around the startled man's neck. Reflexes took over his opponent's body. The cigar fell away as he grabbed Ben's arm with both hands. Ben let the sentry get his feet underneath him, let him struggle to a crouch. Ben eased the pressure a little more, and the man stood a little higher. Then Ben quickly released the sentry's neck, and with his left hand, he pushed hard. The man flailed, but the low railing caught him just right. He tumbled overboard with a long scream that ended in a crunch fifty feet below.

Ben carefully unwrapped the coat from his arm, letting the embedded shards of glass drop away on the stairs. A few slivers had made their way through the cloth and cut him, but none too deeply.

He heard Ellis's voice from below. "I do declare. It's raining men."

CHAPTER 49

"HALLELUJAH," MUTTERED CHARLIE Firesbaugh. He was on top of his small world. The north pole of the enormous natural gas sphere where he kept watch was chilly in the fog that shifted now and then to a drizzling rain, but this was far better than duty down in the stifling, fetid holding areas underground.

The mist lay so dense around him that he could see almost nothing. It was as if he floated in a cloud. The exterior stairway helixed down off the platform which also supported the tank's internal pump column. Sounds from below were muffled up here, like standing watch in a ship's crow's nest, but without the lulling sway of waves. He meditated on the distant lighthouse flashes a mile away, one every ten seconds. The beam was a peaceful, metronomic measure of his tour.

Then it happened. Firesbaugh thought he heard a scream. It was faint. An instant later, he realized that just before the scream, the light station's flash that he had been waiting for had not radiated forth in the murk according to its schedule, which had been unaltered over the last several hours. He wondered if he had blinked because of the scream and missed the distant flash. No, the flash usually endured longer than the human eye's reflex. Perhaps a thick waft of clag had overwhelmed the light for a moment. No again. The light was made to penetrate exactly this kind of dirty weather.

Firesbaugh knew that Earline Byrd had detailed Arnie Campobasso to keep an eye on things from the tower earlier that morning. Campobasso could handle himself. He had bragged that he was trained well by the Deltas, but who the hell knew what a man would do if he were in a real jam? Blocking the light might draw attention in weather like this. Campobasso knew better than to do that. And there had been a ball-shriveling finality to the scream.

No, Firesbaugh's gut said something was wrong at the light station a mile north. He took out his sat-phone, and dialed Byrd's number.

CHAPTER 50

ELLIS HAD DISARMED and dragged the sentry inside the door to the lighthouse by the time Ben descended the stair from the cupola. The man's legs were re-articulated at odd angles, as if he had extra joints. Several compound fractures in his lower extremities bled into his pants where jagged bone jutted through skin. His eyes were open, but unfocused.

Ellis said, "He came down like a cat. Landed on his feet." Ellis slapped the sentry in the face twice.

Ben said, "If one whack on his squash put him out, how do you reckon another smack'll wake him up?"

"I've always questioned the logic myself," said Ellis, "but it felt so right."

"Really?" Ben struck the sentry, whose head whipped through a short arc. "How about that. I do feel better."

The sentry groaned. Ben and Ellis looked at each other and smiled.

"Go figure," said Ben.

The sentry lifted his head and mumbled, "Medic—"

"Medic's incoming, soldier," said Ben. "What's your outfit?"

"Can't feel my legs."

Ellis said, "A good thing, too. They're FUBARed something awful."

The sentry focused drunkenly on his legs first, then on Ben, then on Ellis. Then he chuckled gently. "I get it."

"I don't think you do," said Ben. "You work for Maynard Chalk?"

"Fuck off."

"I'll take that as a yes."

"I got rights," groused the fallen operator.

"That's cool, except we're not cops," said Ellis, "meaning you got every right to die."

The sentry's face fell for a moment, then hardened to a defiant resolve.

Ben asked, "How many in your unit?"

"Way more than two, John Boy."

Ellis struck the sentry again. "This goes one of two ways. We converse. We get along. We leave an anonymous tip that somebody needs an ambulance here. And then there's the other way."

Another mordent laugh from the sentry. "I signed on with Chalk—he took an ICE number."

Ben said, "Seriously? You get in trouble, and Chalk calls a relative for you?"

"Didn't think about it at the time, but no," muttered the sentry. "Way it works, I give *him* trouble, he *visits* my relatives."

"I heard of some stupid deals—" said Ellis.

"Doesn't have to play out that way," said Ben. "Did you see a honey-blonde woman, thirties, traveling with a young black woman, late of Africa?"

"We've got all that, and lot's more like it for the big show," said the sentry. "Something for everybody. The ones you're talking about, you can't afford them now."

CHAPTER 51

MAYNARD CHALK STARED at the small screen of the unit that displayed the position of each of his security team's satellite phones. Though his own phone had been destroyed in the recent exchange with that Blackshaw bastard, the separate command/control module still worked fine. Harrower was landing *Thresher* at the floating pier next to the much larger T pier at the LNG terminal.

"Virgin of Guadalupe! What the hell is going on!" barked Chalk.

He watched agog as all the sat-phone icons exploded from the central access door of DePriest's dungeon facility, radiating out from it like an incendiary star shell. In less than a minute, two icons stopped moving and took up what he assumed were defensive positions at the perimeter. All the other icons were leaving the terminal compound altogether and heading north. Expanding the command/control module's map, he saw the pip representing the sentry at the lighthouse was out of position. That must be where the trouble lay. But who was looking after the goods?

Chalk ordered, "Hold on, laddybuck. Head out again. Go back north."

Harrower hesitated. He had fantasized about receiving actual medical care for the gunshot wound in his shoulder, rather than going into the field again with nothing more than Chalk's slap-dash swipe at first aid. The morphine was already wearing off. His whole arm was catching fire. The expression on Chalk's face, and his twitchy, angular body English clearly told Harrower that this was not the moment to cadge for another hit of poppy. He veered *Thresher* away from the floating dock, pressed the throttle forward, and got on course bearing down on the flash of the Dove Point Light Station.

CHAPTER 52

ELLIS RETURNED AFTER emptying his canteen, and siphoning it full again with gasoline from the crab skiff's fuel tank. Blackshaw was puffing on a cigar liberated from the sentry's pocket. It had been crushed out of shape a bit from the fifty foot drop, but it still drew nicely.

The sentry was bound now, his wrists secured with the AK-47's sling around the tower stair's central column. His head still lolled and bobbed. From a history of difficult interrogations, Ben could tell the injured man was sandbagging, much closer to compos mentis than he was letting on.

"Any luck?" asked Ellis.

"No." Ben took the cigar out of his mouth, and jammed it between the lips of his captive.

Then Ellis opened the canteen, and dumped its reeking, chilly contents on the floor all around the sentry, saving the last of the gasoline for his uniform. This made the man stir and wake. His grenades clacked on his chest as he struggled. He took in his situation in short order.

Speaking around the cigar, the man said, "You can't do this!"

When Ben and Ellis were standing near the tower door by the sentry's gear, and beyond the wet patch of fuel on the floor. Ben said, "You sure could try to spit that cigar clear of the gas. You might make it, but in your condition, you might not. So how 'bout it? How many operatives, and did you see the women I described?"

"Think I'd waste a Montecristo?"

Ellis said, "It'll be your last. Talk to us a little, and you could always get more."

The sentry sneered, "I like this one fine."

Blackshaw shrugged, collected the AK-47, the sentry's sat-phone, and left the tower with Knocker Ellis.

CHAPTER 53

HARROWER NOSED *THRESHER* up to the beach south of the light station's rocky rip-rap. Unable to contain himself, Chalk imprudently leapt ashore off the bow with no cover. Harrower followed more slowly, burdened by his injury, his gear, and the little day hook which he jammed into a gap in the rocks, tugging hard on it once to check its placement.

Chalk trotted across the beach to the grass. The command/control module displayed the light station sentry's sat-phone about eighty yards ahead in the woods backing the property. Was the guy out of position taking a leak? Chalk was going to give his overpaid operative holy hell.

Or he would have, if the situation had not blown up in his face. To his right, the *whump* of an open-air ignition blasted forth from the door at the base of the lighthouse tower. Then came the screams of agony. Then from the woods, a burst of automatic gunfire erupted. Bullets tossed dirt divots high out of the grass. His man had lost his mind!

Chalk recognized the rhythmic mechanical clang of the gun's action cycling in amongst the reports. Years of experience told him it was the sound of Campobasso's favorite ax, an AK-47. So who was screaming in the lighthouse? These thoughts raced through Chalk's addled mind as he threw himself full length onto the grass, pulling his pistol as he fell. He loosed a barrage of suppressing fire at the woods. Oily black smoke began to pour out of the lighthouse's cupola. When would the screaming stop! Chalk simply could not work under these conditions.

To Chalk's left, more gunfire erupted. More divots danced out of the earth around him. Now his own security detail from the LNG terminal was throwing down on him.

"You goddamn idiots!" Chalk yelled. "It's me! Hit the woods! The fucking *woods*!"

The shooting from the south continued, but was now redirected at the trees. Chalk turned as Harrower finally opened fire at the woods as well, but his shots went wide because he kept glancing at the smoking lighthouse tower. The screams from that sector were hitting a miserable high pitch; a thoroughbred race horse keening in its death throes after foundering in the home stretch.

Chalk yelled at Harrower, "Get to the top of that tower! Shoot down into the woods from there!"

Harrower balked. "It's on fire!"

Chalk changed his pistol's magazine and aimed at Harrower. "I couldn't hear you over all the noise! You really want me to nut you? Sure, I could do that from here."

Harrower wised-up and ran for the tower door. He halted at the threshold for a moment. The screaming faded to nothing. The smoke from whatever was burning in there was now sucked up the tower as if it were a chimney. He stepped inside.

Two quick explosions blew Harrower back out the tower door an instant later; the burning Campobasso's grenades cooking off in the flames. A collection of human limbs flew past Harrower and landed smoking in the yard. Some were the Campobasso's. Some were Harrower's own. His dismembered torso convulsed. He coughed up a bright gout of blood onto spring-green grass and went still.

"Damn wussie pissant!" bellowed Chalk. He stood up, oblivious to the bullets zipping past him, and marched toward the woods firing as he went. When his pistol was empty, he dropped it, swung his MP5 from his back to his front, and loosed a magazine-voiding barrage at the trees. When the MP5 magazine was spent, he tossed that weapon aside, drew his knife and ran screaming toward the woods like the madman he was.

By the time Chalk was a full twenty feet into the woods, he came to his senses out of his Berserker's fury to realize no one was firing at him anymore. His comrades to the south had respectfully ceased their fusillade as well for fear of hitting him. Chalk looked around, and caught sight of the ejected brass his attacker had left on the ground. Two magazine's worth, he figured. "Sloppy rubes," was all he said.

Chalk examined the command/control module, and found the satphone chip he had been tracking was gone from the screen. Perhaps an unlucky shot had damaged his man's unit as Blackshaw's shooting had ruined Chalk's out on the water. He emerged from the copse of trees to find his team mustering on the grassy yard. Without a word, everyone converged on the smoking tower to make sense of the carnage there.

Gläans Bellendre gamely put his head in at the door, and quickly pulled it back. "One of ours. Jesus hell-shit! Can't be sure looking at it. Smell's making me hungry. Byrd put Campobasso here."

This got Chalk moving. He poked around the mess on the ground outside the tower, bent over a severed limb for a moment, and stood again, strapping on a gore encrusted watch.

He grumbled, "Patek Philippe, for Chrissakes. Glamor-pants nimrod had no business with a fine timepiece like this in the field." To his assembled group he went on, "Am I paying you all too much? You all losing your ever-loving edge? And if you're all here, who, in the name of Garryowen's bristling tallywhacker is watching my store?"

CHAPTER 54

MARYLAND'S METROPOLITAN OFFICE of the FBI at Calverton was abuzz. Sheriff Williams was checking in by phone with Lowry and Wilde every thirty minutes to confirm the children had not yet been found, and that no ransom demand had been made.

Three partial sets of latent prints from the Thompson crime scene had already been run through the bureau's IAFIS, or Integrated Automated Fingerprint Identification System. Despite receiving more than sixty million ten-print sets per year, it could return a hit in no more than twenty-seven minutes. The NGI, or Next Generation Identification system was slowly phasing-out the IAFIS. Unfortunately, neither database produced a hit from the Thompson scene.

Lowry conferred with Wilde in her office about the disappointing result.

"It seems incredible," mused Lowry, who could not help but appreciate that Agent Wilde's cheeks were rosy, and her eyes were fetchingly agleam after their time at the chilly shore.

"I agree. Nearly everything about the scene was so—organized. Except for that burner on the stove. They can't be noobs and virgins to this kind of work."

"What about that name our mysterious friend Ben dropped?"

"Maynard Chalk." Wilde referred to printed reports and newspaper articles. "He was credited with keeping the dirty bomb out of D.C. until an investigative journalist started asking how he came to be so close to it, and what agency he was working for at the time. The thing is, despite the hero-ics, nobody claimed him. Maybe because the bomb still went off?"

Lowry said, "Maybe. Success has many fathers. Failure is always an or-phan. But it seems odd. Nobody disses a bomb squad tech if a controlled, or in this case, isolated, detonation is the safest method of disposal. There has to be something more."

"Chalk had a company called Right Way Moving and Storage. The journalist already proved it was a shell."

"Who sussed that out?" asked Lowry.

"Colleen Tsu. I love her."

"At the Washington Post?"

"One and the same," confirmed Wilde.

"We should speak with her," said Lowry. "My bet is Chalk was left out in the cold because he was up to his armpits in other business that might blow up much closer to D.C., and which some agency could not credibly deny. Christ, I hope he wasn't on the bureau's payroll."

Wilde was working her computer keyboard. Her face took on a look of grave concern. "That's not good. How did I not hear about this?"

"What've you found?"

"Colleen Tsu's WaPo obituary."

"Oh dear."

Wilde angled her screen toward her boss. "There."

Lowry leaned close, taking in the scent of Wilde's hair, and read. "Car accident. Single fatality. Patch of ice. This past Christmas Day?"

Wilde pointed. "See here? They're actually referring to it as suspicious, like it was a hit and run by another vehicle."

"Where has Chalk been since the bomb?"

Wilde was annoyed. "I've come up with zip since Tsu first published that all might not be kosher with him. That was 29 November last year."

"He dropped off the face of the earth. Molly, what do we know about his affiliations before that?"

"Just the usual work history. Then I checked with State. He traveled to some hot areas in the world. Mozambique. Falklands. He was Army way back in Bible times. In Vietnam."

Lowry took a breath. "Molly, I'm authorizing you to run those prints from the Thompson scene through MiSLED. My order to that effect will be noted in this case file." He jotted briefly on a notepad and showed it to Wilde. "My password."

The Military Security Law Enforcement Database was an international archive of all public and private sector personnel who carried firearms. Right after it was first created, access to MiSLED was granted only to those who obtained written consent from the highest levels of federal and state governments in order to prevent frivolous lawsuits and the exposure of undercover operations in progress at home and abroad. Four times a year, the MiSLED database was *congruenced*, in the tortured parlance of bureaucracy, with the IAFIS and NGI records to weed out criminals who were also trusted, armed public servants. There were enough hits on those occasions that access had gradually flowed from loftier strata down to men and women with Pershing Lowry's mid-level security clearance.

Wilde opened MiSLED with the password, and pushed the notepad back to Lowry, who put the entire pad in his pocket for shredding later. Then she cross-fed the three incomplete sets of fingerprints from the Thompson scene into the system.

After a few moments, Wilde's eyes widened. "Hat trick!"

"We got Chalk?" Lowry leaned close to Wilde's screen again. Her hair. That scent—

"Not exactly," said Wilde. "But we do have, Earline Byrd, U.S. Army, lieutenant. Gläans Bellendre, from the DCRI. That's France's Central Directorate of Interior Intelligence. Last but not least, James Clyster, late of the Detroit PD. And they all left their positions under some pretty dark clouds."

"How did that motley crew hook up at the Thompson place?"

"Now they're all listed as employees of Right Way Moving and Storage." Wilde said what they both were thinking. "I put my money on Chalk."

CHAPTER 55

BLACKSHAW INFILTRATED SOUTH toward the LNG terminal as soon Ellis started rolling out the flanking fire from the cover of the woods by the light station. He was forced to speed up his stalk, but he did so with care in case the larger detail that would soon be moving in behind him from the lighthouse had left a soldierly rearguard.

Something was rushing in quick gray dashes through the small, bright green leaves and tendrils of the underbrush. The squirrels were on the hump, looking for mates. A pair sprinted and stopped, scooted and stopped again around the trunk of a maple tree. Ben saw the operative seated at the base of the trunk only when the man craned his head back to glance at the ritual love chase above him. Then he returned his attention to the gunfire at the light station.

Ben slowly backtracked to a shallow depression which led to a muddy stream bed swollen with rain and fallen leaves latticed with winter decay. He eased into the chilly water, just a few inches deep, and kept his head low as he crawled. From time to time, when new growth on the streambed's bank allowed him cover, he looked over the edge to check his position relative to that of the sentry. The freshet was taking him gently toward the LNG facility and its enormous spherical storage tanks, but the stalk line was so indirect it was going to eat up time Ben did not have.

He considered passing the sentry without engaging him, but that would leave an enemy immediately on his six for trouble later on. After another few yards, Ben pulled a Beretta that had come from Knocker Ellis's handy saltbox armory, and threaded a noise suppressor from the KEH Skunkworks to the barrel. It would keep the racket down for several shots before the steel wool guts started burning out of it. After that, the gun's report would get progressively louder.

Again, Ben peered over the edge of the stream bank. He could see the top of the sentry's head over an intervening fallen log, but at thirty feet, even with the suppressor balanced on his forearm, he deemed it too small a target.

The gunfire at the light station kept the sentry focused northward. Blackshaw's chance to thin the ranks came with two explosive cracks, the not unexpected detonation of the cigar lover's grenades. The sentry in front of Ben stood as if curiosity was about to send him running toward the fight. Ben squeezed the trigger, but he had rushed the shot. The innocuous pop of the gun was quickly followed by a spray of bark and splinters from the tree trunk in front of the sentry's face. He reeled backward clutching at his eyes, staggering like a drunk as he tried to clear them.

Not sure if the homemade suppressor would still perform as quietly as Ben needed, he drew his knife and dashed in on the blinded man, bowling him over onto his back. Two slashes of the blade and a deep jab into the jugular notch took the sentry off the board, but Ben's front was now wet with copious jets of arterial blood.

He continued south toward the terminal.

Within ten minutes, and still surrounded by trees, he took cover behind a garage, which, by some planner's gaff must have been built all the way out to the facility's north property line. An old ten foot chain link fence with a frisee of shiny new razor wire on top butted the east and west ends of the garage, but did not pass behind or over the structure. That left a single unbarred window in the garage wall open to any enterprising intruder.

Ben wedged his knife under the window's sill, and tilted it open. He crawled inside. Light from his entry point and from the row of windows at the front of the garage revealed large-property commercial mowing equipment at least fifteen years out of date, an old blue bus with white trim, and a much newer black Suburban.

Then he saw it. The dim light exposed someone sleeping in the back, easterly corner of the musty space.

He crept closer, and realized he had been horribly wrong in his first impression. The truth was worse. There was no sleeper. It was a heap of discarded clothing.

Ben approached the pile and kneeled beside it. Dresses. Small pairs of jeans. Tiny shoes. Little sneakers, and flip-flops. Sweaters with rockets, and train and duck motifs. There were other clothes for adults. Brassieres. A woman's camelhair coat. A black pair of high heels. Blouses and shirts. Tradesman's workboots. A barn coat. Panties. A thong. Jeans and slacks. There was even a single small glittering cardstock disk with a tassel. It was backed with an adhesive that was still tacky to the touch. An exotic dancer's pasty.

These were the barriers that good folks chose to cover themselves, to attract or repel, to protect themselves in so many ways, from weather, from ridicule, to hide their scars, their indulgences, and deficits. These chosen articles were the public and private statements of modesty and pride, symbols of station, of employment, of wealth and want, of style and strata. And here they all lay, stripped off, heaped and strewn in an old garage reeking of earthen mildew and thickened motor oil; their naked owners were never meant to return and claim them.

With fear gnawing at his gut, Blackshaw sorted gently through the intimate remnants of so many lives for anything his wife had worn that morning.

CHAPTER 56

KYLE WAS SURPRISED to see Agent Lowry enter his barbershop again so soon, and accompanied by a woman. With concern evident in his voice, and an eye on his work from that morning, he asked, "Agent Lowry, did you find something amiss?"

Lowry said, "What? No, my haircut's fine. This is Special Agent Molly Wilde."

"Charmed," said the chivalrous Kyle, bowing slightly over her hand. "How may I be of service?"

Wilde said, "Agent Lowry told me about a group of children who came in here a few days ago."

"Tuesday. Yes," said Kyle. "It was unusual, but a welcome spate in this difficult economy. Has there been a complaint about our work?"

"None whatsoever," said Agent Lowry.

Wilde removed a photograph from her jacket and held it up where Kyle could see it. Kyle took the photograph and stepped toward the shop's front window for better light.

After a moment, Kyle said, "The woman with that troubling mullet. You'll remember, Agent Lowry, I told you we did not style her hair. Just the children's. Is everything all right?"

"Wish I could say yes," answered Wilde.

"If this woman should return, with other children, for instance," warned Lowry, "I want you to play it cool, leave the shop immediately, and call us as soon as you are safe."

"Oh my. Who is she?"

"We consider her extremely dangerous. It's likely she's armed," Wilde said, taking the picture back.

Lowry said, "The same goes if you see the bus. The blue and white one you described. Call us, alright?"

"Of course I will. This woman is actually taking care of children?"

"She is," said Wilde, "but not in a nice way."

Lowry's cellular phone sounded. The ringtone was a faithful digital rendition of an old Bell landline unit that at one time had been hardwired to the wall of every home and office in America. He answered and listened for a few moments before ending the call and replacing the phone in his jacket pocket.

Lowry said, "Thank you again, Kyle. Remember, look sharp."

Kyle nodded as he removed a folded straight razor from a beaker of blue Barbicide. He whipped drops of fluid off the instrument, and tucked it into the pocket of his white tunic.

Outside the shop, Lowry said, "That was Sheriff Williams. Something's happened at the Dove Point Lighthouse."

CHAPTER 57

BLACKSHAW EXFILTRATED FROM the garage's rear window, dropping to the ground outside in such an inelegant heap that he was glad Ellis was wrangling the crab skiff by now, and not watching him. The shooting at the Dove Point Light Station had stopped. Chalk's operatives would be coming back to the LNG terminal shortly. Leaving the rear-guard's corpse in plain sight was a tactical choice. Investigating the body would hold them up for a time. The one saving grace of the last few minutes was not discovering a single stitch belonging to LuAnna.

This did not quell the dread Ben felt for the owners of the clothing he had found; touching their things had brought these missing victims close in a way that deeply disturbed him, and disarmed his powers to concentrate. Who would gather humans to kill them? There was an efficiency about all this that reminded Ben of grotesque precedents in history. Nazi Germany, and the Holocaust. The Khmer Rouge, and the Killing Fields. Still, it felt completely beyond his ken, like the ocean once appeared to be in the eyes of early seafarers. *Here There Be Monsters.*

CHAPTER 58

GLÄANS BELLENDRE OVERSAW the loading of
Harrower's and Campobasso's remains onto *Thresher*. The distasteful chore
required several trips from the light tower to the beach. Now he was taking
the boat south, solo, while Chalk and the balance of the team patrolled
through the woods back to the LNG terminal hunting more signs of their
attackers.

Chalk, and operatives Luther Flegg, Martin Jasper, Wendy Peltier,
Twei Yoo, and Rolly Mulgrew moved carefully among the trees.

Chalk said, "Didn't anyone see *anybody?*"

Jasper said, "Sounded like one guy."

"But which guy?" asked Chalk. "It wasn't cops. Cops like to negotiate
'til you give up from fucking boredom."

"Then they beat the heck out of you," chimed Rolly Mulgrew.

"And if they do shoot," said Yoo, "they don't take your own weapons
to do it."

"And no booby traps. Somebody's got a major side of beef with us,"
said Chalk. "I was sure Blackshaw was dead 'til today. We traded shots out
there on the bay less than two hours ago. He's got every reason to fear me.
But we're nowhere near his turf."

One of Chalk's operatives might have asked who this Blackshaw was,
but the whoop, bark, and wail of distant sirens called through the trees. The
cadre picked up the pace. An automated fire alarm must have notified a
local ladder company that their landmark lighthouse was heating up.

Mulgrew said, "Maybe it's the runaway."

Chalk laughed. "She's a thousand miles from here." Then he remembered how she had rigged Sanders's grenade, which had killed Tahereh. She was a devious little bint, that's for certain, but all her mayhem was directed on her trip outbound, away from the terminal.

They were spread out with five yards between them, but when Jasper uttered a clear, succinct, "Aw crap!" they gathered on his position at the west end of the line abreast. He was looking down at a body. It was one of their own.

Luther Flegg was disgusted. "It's Meeker."

"His head's damn near cut off!" Mulgrew admired a thorough job of work no matter who paid the price.

"Don't you touch him!" ordered Chalk. "In fact, I want all you clowns to put your grenades in Jasper's ruck, nice and easy. I don't know whose idea it was carry those things."

No one mentioned that the frenzied order to do so had come from Chalk himself while in a Vietnam-themed schizoidal blackout.

"Jasper, we're going to step away for a moment while you give our buddy here a good once-over for booby traps," said Chalk. "They seem to be going around. When you give the all clear, you and Rolly will hump his body back to base and get him on ice. For a proper funeral, I mean. With a little duct tape and a turtleneck, it can still be open casket."

Chalk heard Wendy Peltier emit a sniffle. He suspected she had been sweet on Meeker. His death likely put a cramp in her plans to hook up.

"Peltier, you buck up right now or I'll bite off your nose and play your skull like an ocarina," Chalk snarled.

Flegg gamely asked, "An ocarina?"

"A fat clay flute with holes, idiot!"

"But wouldn't the brain get in the way of the sound?" Flegg's ignorance was tireless.

"For Wendy? Not so much," said Chalk with resignation.

He and the rest of the team kept the line moving, more alert than before. After a few yards, he mumbled, "Yoo, you said something about guns and cops."

"They don't shoot you with your own gun. Not usually."

Chalk marched on. Blackshaw had thrown down on him with a machine gun. Every weapon had its own song, and despite his surprise at seeing Blackshaw among the living, Chalk recognized the tune of the gun going off in his face over the transom. That was Clyster's HK MG4. Had to be. Blackshaw having the same weapon as one of Chalk's own misfits was possible, but damn remote. And Clyster's sat-phone was definitely off-line, with no side band tracking signal. Just like Campobasso's unit: gone. If Blackshaw got hold of Clyster's gun somehow, it must have happened out at that wrecked ship. That rust bucket would bear a closer look in the very near future.

They arrived within sight of the north fence line, and Chalk called another halt.

"Somebody's been sleeping in my bed—" he whispered, pointing to the rear of the garage. Under the one window in the wall was a rufous smear of mud and blood. A few quick hand signals, and his operatives were taking up positions surrounding the garage.

"Gotcha, you fucker!" growled Chalk.

CHAPTER 59

SENIOR RESIDENT AGENT Pershing Lowry strode quickly toward the firefighters deploying hose from their truck for the smoking lighthouse. Sheriff Williams intercepted and fell in beside him and Agent Molly Wilde.

"Gunfire," said Williams. "At least one and maybe two explosions. The guy who called it in was a veteran. Said it sounded like Khe Sanh."

"Have they hit that tower with water yet?" asked Lowry.

"Not yet."

Wilde said, "Can they hold off until we see it? I mean, it's not still burning, right?"

Sheriff Williams's expression was pinched. "It's a landmark. We can't let it—"

"It's brick," said Wilde. "Just for a second."

The captain of the firefighters gave a shout of complaint as Lowry and Wilde stepped into the smoky ground floor area of the light tower.

Lowry bent his knees and leaned his face as close to the floor as he could. "Gasoline?"

Wilde swiped a finger through the edge of a patch of tarry substance coating the floor. "Cooked blood."

Lowry nodded. "See the walls? The damage to the stair treads? Shrapnel."

Sheriff Williams, who watched from the doorway said, "Explosives. Your turf again?"

Agent Wilde was looking up the helical stairway when she said, "Now that's interesting."

Agent Lowry and Sheriff Williams followed her gaze. A disarticulated hand stood upright on its trauma-tattered wrist, leaning against the masonry wall on a tread about eight feet above the floor. Most of the blast-torn fingers seemed amputated or curled by tendons that shrank in the fire. The middle digit was extended in a final message of protest.

CHAPTER 60

THE TWINS WERE terrified. They sat close to each other in a dim cement room with a barred metal doorway. Barry remembered being bundled into a big truck, and then the lady with the gun who had acted nice held a smelly rag over his face. He and Nicole had awakened in this cold little room, and their clothes were gone. The lady was gone, too. This was not right, not having clothes and being here together. He didn't even take baths with his sister anymore. He was glad Nicole was there anyways.

A soldier, not the lady, had pushed two bowls of oatmeal into the room through a slot by the floor. Barry had shouted that they needed spoons, but nobody came back for a long while. Then someone rolled two little bottles of water in through the slot. They sat scooping the oatmeal with their fingers, shivering, pressing back to back with their legs tucked up for warmth.

Nicole said, "We're in big trouble."

"I didn't do anything." Barry got in trouble a lot, and was angry that he hadn't broken any rules, and was still getting punished.

"Mom-Mom and Pop-Pop got hurt." Nicole could remember that.

"The soldiers hurt them." Barry was worried. Mom-Mom and Pop-Pop were boring, but very nice. Everybody seemed to be in trouble. The soldiers had different rules, really hard rules, and even Mom-Mom and Pop-Pop had broken them. Barry could not figure out the new rules.

"Mommy and daddy are going to pick us up." Nicole was more grown-up than Barry. With Mom-Mom and Pop-Pop hurt, she knew their mother and father were the next friendly faces they could think to look for.

Somebody was always looking for them, making sure they were safe, and not cutting up, or running too far away.

Barry said, "They're on a trip."

"Three Xs left on the calendar. They come back in three days." Nicole did not want to wait three days in a place like this.

"How will they find us?" Barry had asked a good question.

"I don't know. But they will."

That is when Barry noticed a rude man staring right at them through the barred metal door. The man did not say anything. He was staring at them, and he was smiling.

In all of Barry's short life, never had a grown-up's smile made him feel like crying.

CHAPTER 61

CHALK WAS BAFFLED. He had taken care to position his operatives in front of the garage, and in the rear as well, with weapons charged, fingers on triggers. On Chalk's signal, Rolly Mulgrew had ventured close to the front door of the garage and pressed the button on the big junction box. With the loud electrical snap of a high-amp relay closing, the door had rumbled and jerked upwards slowly, revealing the tires, then the bumpers and bodies of the Suburban and the old bus.

In dashed the operatives, training their guns left and right, collapsing their sectors. Within moments, the chorus of *Clear!* was sung by everyone inside. The garage was empty of intruders. The heap of clothing concealed no one. No one cowered inside or beneath the vehicles.

Then Chalk noticed the back of the old bus. In the thick soot and dirt near the exhaust pipe, someone had left him a handwritten message. It said. R.I.P. MAYNARD followed by a six digit date. Today's date.

CHAPTER 62

BLACKSHAW RENDEVOUED WITH Ellis and the crab skiff where the north property line of the LNG terminal met the Chesapeake shore. The big T pier was a half mile to the south, and nearly out of sight around a narrow spit of land covered with trees leaning toward their deaths as soil washed from under their roots year by year.

Ellis beheld the monster who stepped aboard the skiff. "You should see yourself."

Ben was caked in mud from his skull drag through the streambed. His chest and face were also coated in drying blood.

"You should see the other guy," said Ben. "Mike Craig was right. This is the place. There's a garage with a pile of clothes in it. Little kid's shoes—" For a moment, he couldn't say anything more. His hands shook. He clasped them behind his back as if he were stretching his shoulders, but Ellis was not fooled.

Ellis advocated for the Devil. "That's not much to go on."

"Tally was buck naked when she washed into the ship. You know as well as I do that's a dominance tactic, to break the will of a prisoner. Judging by the outfits in the pile, we're looking at a total of maybe twenty individual hostages. At least half of them kids."

Ellis hated to ask. "Did you see anything of LuAnna's?"

"No, but come to think of it, that's exactly what Chalk's crew did to *her* last fall, plus a beat-down. Stripped her, I mean."

"How many jailers?"

"Close on one-to-one. Tally reckoned ten from what-all she could hear, but we have to figure more."

"We thinned 'em by three at least. Any reason I shouldn't be heading north right now?"

"It's as good a direction as any for aught we can do," said Ben. "Enemy's bunkered in, like as not below ground, and with superior forces, and there's a score of prisoners just sitting there to sponge up the crossfire."

Ellis had his eyes out over the bow and said, "You're not going to believe this."

The visibility in the oppressive fog had lifted out to half a mile. Ben looked where Ellis indicated. In the distance, with gunwale barely cresting the whitecaps, he saw the same make of boat that Maynard Chalk had been using earlier that morning, with one man at the helm.

Ben said immediately, "Let him pass—"

Ellis frowned. "And opportunity knocking twice like this?"

"I was going to say let him pass, then we'll round in behind him. With any luck, he can share some thoughts with us."

CHAPTER 63

SPECIAL AGENT WILDE hated helicopter rides. Of course she had done her research, and read all the statistics, including the fact that the *Jesus nut* attaching the main rotor to the rest of the aircraft was in fact a highly reliable, oft-inspected fitting with a history of remarkably few failures despite millions of hours in the air. This did not help allay her terror. She was flying over the Chesapeake, which was masked by a layer of fog. She knew the cold water was roiling down there somewhere below the clag. She also knew the Eurocopter in which she flew was equipped with skids, not floats. If the Tangier Island Airport was socked in below instrument mini-mums, her pilot, McCourt, would simply turn back without landing and recross the bay to the Meers Creek Airfield. She shelled a second square of Nicorette to bolster the work of the first piece she chewed with little calm-ing effect.

To distract her mind from a cold watery death, she focused on Senior Resident Agent Pershing Lowry. Her breathing deepened, and a heat flooded her body from her toes to her throat. He could make trouble for her if he wanted. She sensed his attraction to her. Without doubt, it was flattering. The real problem was that she reciprocated in full. Lowry was handsome and smart, completely honest, and unflappable in a way she could not help but admire. He was so utterly humorless that his stunted attempts at levity were somehow endearing. She liked his baldness. It was a virile look, but Wilde wished he would commit to a full shave down to the wood, and do away with the carefully tended fringe which she felt made him appear older.

Yet there was no hope for them as a couple. Her career came first. She had already discarded well-heeled men who spoke too quickly and enthusiastically about marriage and family and her future as a stay-at-home mother. She wanted more. She needed a man who understood her deep attachment to the bureau without wanting her to completely shift gears and sacrifice it. She and Lowry had no argument on that point. She sensed he respected her intellect, her work ethic, and that meant everything, regardless of his physical appreciation of her. But any dalliance with her direct report would be actionable grounds for termination for them both. She would not wish that on him. She preferred to think he would not place her in the same position by making advances she would not, could not accept.

A short spate of sickening turbulence wrenched her thoughts back to the case and her reason for risking her life in this eggbeater. Wilde was gratified that Lowry had come to share her sense that the mysterious Ben who had cadged fuel from them at the Thompson murder/abduction scene was worth a second look as a person of interest. But they had no last name for this Ben. There was no one on the Right Way Moving & Storage roster, past or present, with the first name of Ben, or Benjamin.

Tangier Island was the only lead they had on him. A check of the online White Pages listed no one named Ben on Tangier. That did not preclude his living off the grid with no phone or with an unlisted number, but a search of Tangier's tax records likewise showed no one named Ben.

It was possible that Ben was an alias, and stating Tangier as his home was a lie. The only verifiable fact was the name of Maynard Chalk. Ben's tip had come up all cherries, connecting prints from the Thompson scene to Chalk's corporate front. Perhaps Ben had lied with the best of them about needing gas, about hunting the old, that is, *antique* decoys, by staying close to the truth. With a population of seven hundred, smaller than many high school graduating classes, someone on Tangier Island had to know Ben by description if not by name. Before taking off, she had located a Tangier Island elder who was willing to speak with her.

McCourt found the visibility he needed at the Tangier Island airstrip. Offering thanks to God for a safe landing, and ducking low beneath the still-churning main rotor, Wilde sprinted through the gale toward the field attendant's shack.

Inside, she was met by the woman who had monitored the airport's Unicom frequency, and also by an older fellow, small and wiry. His crow's feet gave his eyes a jovial cast, but as Wilde held his gaze, she saw a keen intelligence assessing her.

Wilde flipped her badge out, and introduced herself. Then she asked, "Are you Mr. Robert Crockett?"

"In the flesh. Ye come a long ways in that whirligig to say hello. Least I can do is let ye call me Bob like nigh ever-body else. And this here's Agatha Elburn. Miss Agatha looks after the field. Mows the grass, and hollers over the wireless to the flyboys about the wind'n weather."

"Ms. Elburn. Bob, thank you for meeting on such short notice. Would you call me Molly?" She tucked the badge wallet into her jacket.

Crockett grinned. "Reckon I'd settle for that."

"I wouldn't have come so far if it weren't important. The fact is, the bureau needs some help."

After a self-effacing chuckle, Crockett said, "I'll help ye if I can. What-all's the particulars."

"As of this morning, we're investigating a double homicide in Calvert County, and an abduction of two children. Five-year-old twins."

"Lordy go to fire. Ain't that something nasty."

"It's terrible," agreed Wilde in all sincerity. "It may sound strange to you, but we got some very helpful advice on where to focus our investigation from a neighbor of yours. A man named Ben."

Bob Crockett furrowed his brow, and exchanged a puzzled glance with Agatha Elburn. He asked, "What last name?"

"Well, Bob, he didn't say. The crime scene is on the opposite shore of the bay near Dove Point. This gentleman pulled into the bulkhead out of the fog, said he and his friend needed fuel, and while we were chatting about why the bureau was there, he gave us a name."

Agatha poured two cups of coffee that smelled burned and yet somehow delicious after such a long morning.

Bob asked, "What was the name he mentioned?"

"Maynard Chalk," said Wilde. She watched Crockett closely for a reaction. If the name rang a bell, the old man masked all but the most general signs of recognition well.

"This Chalk fellow. He was in the news, warn't he?"

"There was the dirty bomb. Chalk was credited with saving Washington, D.C."

Crockett became wry. "That's it. Thought the name was familiar."

Agatha set out a jar of non-dairy cream powder, plastic spoons, and a bowl of sugar. Then she gathered up her purse, excused herself, and left the hut.

After she was gone, Crockett asked, "Now, who's the friend this Ben fellow had along with him?"

"Our chat was so brief, and so unusual," explained Molly, "I admit we didn't make proper introductions. I think Ben said he was called Ellis. I can tell you that his friend was an older black man. Do you know Ben? He's about six foot four or five. Looked very strong. Brown hair that was not very neat. A week's growth of beard, too. Blue eyes. Handsome enough. He carried himself like he'd been in the military. Bob, we could really use a few more pointers from him on this case."

Crockett asked, "Ye reckon he done the deeds?"

"He knows more than most about what's going on, and that's something we don't fully understand. The person he mentioned, Chalk, is a known associate of three individuals whose fingerprints we found at the crime scene. We think those three people are involved. That was an enormous help. It's why I wish I could speak with Ben again."

"I hate to break it to you, but I don't know anybody name of Ben on Tangier." Crockett seemed genuinely sorry, but the glint in his eye betrayed a crafty understanding.

A pretty girl about six years old, with black hair, fair skin, and dark eyes that sparkled like Crockett's, banged in through the door of the hut. She dashed into Crockett's open arms and said, "I saw the helicopter, Pop-Pop!" From the safety of her grandfather's arms she looked shyly at Agent Wilde, and said, "Did *you* fly it here?"

"Oh, not a chance, sweetheart," said Wilde with a note of gratitude in her voice. "There's a nice pilot who flies it for me. My name's Molly. What's your name?"

"Avery, ma'am. You staying to supper?"

"I wish I could, Avery, but I have to leave before the weather gets any worse. Bob, you're absolutely sure nobody named Ben lives around here?"

If it were possible, Avery's eyes brightened even more as she said, "Ben Blackshaw?"

"Who is Ben Blackshaw?" Molly felt like a hunter closing in on prey.

Crockett barked at Avery, "Ye run along, child. Molly and I are having us a chat on grown-up matter. Now git, afore I make ye cut a switch to suit your wicked ways."

Avery laughed at Crockett and his threat, but after kissing him on the cheek, she obeyed, banging out through the hut's door as fast as she had come tossing a *nice-to-meet-you-ma'am* over her shoulder.

A thick silence hung between Agent Wilde and Crockett. She said, "One of the missing children is a girl about your granddaughter's age. Are you telling me Avery knows Ben Blackshaw, and you don't?"

Crockett was not rattled in the least. "Ye asked me about a body named Ben from Tangier. Tweren't any lie there's nobody of that name from here."

"Okay. Fair enough. Where is Ben *Blackshaw* from?"

"Best I recall, he's from up around Smith Island, or maybe over to Crisfield or Deal."

Wilde pressed. "Do you know how I could get in touch with him?"

Crockett's expression grew rueful. "That's the real shame of it, Miss Molly. Ye'd want the holy power of the Lord to talk to that one now, 'cause I heard Ben Blackshaw's done drowned sob-wet and gone to his reward. Like as not, whoever ye talked to was yarnin', and warn't at all name of Ben, nevermind."

Wilde let that sink in. "Okay, what about the black man with him?"

Crockett grinned. "Swagger die, Miss Molly. Daresay I don't know any man half right in the head, neither black, white, nor pink, nor blue who'd pass the time of day with a dead man, let alone go for a boat ride with one, doncha know."

CHAPTER 64

GLÄANS BELLENDRE FINALLY eased back on *Thresher's* throttle. Without Maynard Chalk aboard bossing irrational speeds through the foggy weather and brick-wall chop, the going was much easier. He would have preferred to tip the burned, blasted remains of Felix Harrower and Arnie Campobasso over the transom, but Chalk wanted every part iced down in DePriest's walk-in freezer.

Gläans kept his eyes trained keenly forward, as much to avoid fouling his prop on early crab pot sets and trot lines as to spare himself looking directly at the carnage gunking up the cockpit behind him. Even though the weather was far from perfect, for a few peaceful minutes, he was a pleasure boater enjoying the Chesapeake Bay, and not the ghoulish captain of a charnel scow bringing out the dead.

When he felt the hand grab his shoulder, he was certain the dismembered deceased had risen to accost him. He turned, astonished to see the fist of a living man jabbing for his chin. The impact fired off meteors and comets in his brain, and his legs came unstrung beneath him. He did not so much fall, as the boat rose up around him.

Gläans had no idea how much time had passed when he woke to a sharp stinging slap electrifying the whole left side of his head. He sat with his legs pointed aft, bound at the ankles. His wrists were bound together behind him.

As *Thresher* rose up the face of one wave, he could see two skiffs surfing down the leeward slope of the wave just behind. The little wooden boats were in tow, secured to *Thresher's* own stern cleats. His face shuddered beneath another wallop. Gläans moaned and tried hard to focus his eyes. The two skiffs realigned into just one as his double vision cleared.

A black man holding Gläans' shoulder said, "See? Works every time." Clenched in the man's other hand was a disarticulated forearm, either Felix's or Arnie's, he could not be sure. Apparently this was the blunt instrument with which he was beaten.

A second man, white, stared down at Gläans with an unholy fury, and growled, "How many are you?"

Gläans was still stunned from the wicked jab and macabre clubbing, and could not make sense of the question. He managed a, "Fucking-shit-fucker!" which sounded confused even to his addled brain.

The black man hoisted Gläans up and draped his head over the transom. The prop was churning. Suddenly his head was underwater, and he was drowning. When he was sure he could not hold his breath any longer, he was lifted, drenched, out of the water only to inhale lungsful of oily engine exhaust. Gläans felt as though he vomited everything he had eaten for the last several weeks.

The white man said, "Ease up, Ellis. How many operatives are you working with?"

Despite the admonition from his partner, the black man cocked the bloody forearm for an obliterating blow.

Gläans' head was already splitting. He got the picture. No money was worth this kind of punishment. Clearly these men were not American law enforcement, and were in no way bound to kiss his ass during questioning. He coughed and said, "Twenty. A couple more?"

"How many hostages?"

"About the same. I don't know. I'm outside on watch but for sleeps and eatings, not down at the jail, thank shitting God. The stinkings—"

"When's the killing time?" asked the white man.

"Tonight," admitted Gläans, as the man called Ellis reared back the arm for a strike.

The black man relaxed.

The white man said, "There're children. How many children?"

"They cry and cry and cry," whined the afflicted Gläans. "So many."

"All down below ground?"

Gläans nodded, a mistake which stirred up a maelstrom of pain in his head and neck. His world began to spin. The exhaust and waves were going to make him vomit again. Between reflexive precursor gags, he said, "Guards outside and inside."

The black man dragged Gläans back into the cockpit and let him fall onto the corpses.

The white man said, "I think we got the smart of it."

The black man raised his hand. The heavy forearm came down hard, with its projecting radius and ulna cracking into Gläans' temple. There was another flaring starburst in his skull. After that, darkness.

CHAPTER 65

IN HIS OFFICE, Agent Lowry received a file from his lab containing one good fingerprint from the disarticulated hand Wilde had discovered at the Dove Point Light Station. With his expectations low, he repeated what the lab had already done, introducing the prints into the IAFIS and NGI fingerprint databases. Like the lab, he got no hits.

Then he used his password to open MiSLED, checking the prints against the military, security, and law enforcement database, and was immediately introduced to Campobasso, Arnoldo J., who once worked for the Servizio per le Informazioni e la Sicurezza Militare, or SISMI, Italy's intelligence agency. Lowry was only half-surprised to learn that, since SISMI's reorganization in 2007, and Campobasso's forced ouster, the operative had been in the employ of Right Way Moving & Storage.

Lowry picked up his desk phone, and he listened as the call he placed was routed via satellite through the radio of Agent Wilde's helicopter and into her David Clark headset. He could not help but smile when he heard her voice.

He asked, "Any luck?"

"This thing hasn't crashed yet." He could tell she was profoundly uncomfortable, but was putting a brave in-charge tone in her voice. The gallows humor only added to her appeal.

She said, "There is a Ben, last name Blackshaw, but he's from Smith Island or some other place nearby, not Tangier. And he's dead."

"Since this morning?"

"Since last fall."

Lowry said, "Damn. Okay. The blown up hand from the light station got a hit. Former Italian secret service. And before you ask, the answer is yes, he was working for Right Way."

Wilde said, "That's two scenes within ten miles on the same morning leading to the same company. Does Right Way have an address?"

"Annapolis. Levy just called in from there. The place is cleaned out. Neighbors said nobody but a pissed-off leasing agent has been there in three months. There's a BOLO for Chalk. I was putting together a sketch on Ben and another sketch of his friend. The parents of the twins are meeting me here in two hours. Will you be back for that?"

Wilde hesitated, "You know how I enjoy meeting traumatized parents when I've got nothing useful to offer them—"

"It's your intuition in an interview I would appreciate. Your empathy is not in question. In fact, I think it would help."

"If it's an order, Pershing," said Wilde, "I'll change course."

"Where are you going?" Lowry realized that he was leaning on Wilde. His mind raced, assessing whether his request was professionally based, or instead lay in his deeply personal pleasure in having her close by.

"McCourt says there's a helipad on Smith Island for medical emergencies, and it's okay for weather right now. I thought I'd pay my respects."

Lowry said, "Understood. No, it's not an order. Carry on. Oh, and Molly, about this dead man's hand—"

"Yes?"

"Arnoldo J. Campobasso. The bigger question about that guy is, where do you think the rest of him might be?"

Wilde signed off the call with assurances she would give that some thought, and provided she survived the day's flying, they could discuss it further in person. Then, with just a few more minutes before landing on Smith Island, she fired up her tablet, somehow got out to the Internet through the Eurocopter's satellite uplink without jeopardizing the pilot's ability to navigate, and typed *Benjamin Blackshaw* into her browser.

She read his obituary in the *Somerset County Times* closely. Blackshaw had died with his bride on their honeymoon cruise of the bay in a December storm. That was tragic, and weird. She wondered why anyone would cruise the Chesapeake in such chilly weather. He had served in the Navy as a SEAL with distinction. Highly decorated, he had received an honorable discharge later in the proceedings of the first Gulf War.

She was about to use her FBI access to look more closely at his military record, when she realized there was a tab on the browser page for Images. The Eurocopter's skids touched down as she swiped the tab. In the first row of pictures was the man she spoken with this morning, holding a bronze sculpture of some kind of duck, and a blue ribbon. The caption said the photograph was taken at a waterfowl festival in Ocean City, Maryland several years before. The artist, Ben Blackshaw, was from Smith Island.

She dropped the tablet into her briefcase, closed the flap, threw the strap over her shoulder and climbed out of the helicopter. There had been no time for her to call ahead to arrange an interview with anyone, but now it appeared there was no need. A very large man stepped out of his golf cart that was parked a healthy distance from the cracked cement helipad, and gave Wilde a wave. She headed over to him with her bureau identification open and held up in plain sight.

She shouted over the helicopter's din. "I'm Special Agent Molly Wilde with the Federal Bureau of Investigation."

She was angry, certain that Bob Crockett had stonewalled her on Tangier. She did not care if she sounded more businesslike than usual now.

"Wade Joyce," the big man replied. "Let's get out of this weather." He gestured toward the passenger side of the golf cart, and Wilde took a seat there.

Wade wedged his bulk behind the wheel. The golf cart groaned under his weight, which elevated Wilde's seat several inches. As soon as they had rolled a few listing yards out of the worst of the rotor wash, Wade said, "This's sporty weather for flying."

"Mr. Joyce, you've likely already heard I was just on Tangier Island making inquiries."

"That so? What about?"

This guy was playing it very cool. Wilde could not believe that no one on Tangier had alerted friends on Smith Island about her meeting with Crockett. She proceeded with every intention of appearing to take this man at face value. "I'm working on a double homicide case that also involves the abduction of five-year-old twins. A man named Ben volunteered some information to the bureau that has direct bearing on the case. I need to speak with him again."

"That sounds awful. But, Ben who? How can I help out?" Wade stopped the cart in front of a small grocery store. He went on, "There's coffee here that won't kill you. And I reckon the griddle's hot by now if you want some eggs or a burger."

"I'm not hungry. What I need to know is where I can find Ben Blackshaw."

"Oh. Ben *Blackshaw*. In that case, sit tight."

Wade stepped on the accelerator, made several sharp turns that threatened to pitch Wilde into him, or out of the golf cart entirely. She relaxed her grip on the cart's front roof support once they got onto a longer straight stretch of narrow paved road.

"Blackshaw is here?" Wilde asked.

"Oh, he used to follow the water, like his pappy," explained the big man. "He was a soldier before that, also like his pap. He's here full time these days."

The cart passed a wood frame Methodist church, and Wade Joyce braked to a stop in front of a burial ground. Without further comment, the goliath nimbly dismounted and walked down a crushed oyster shell path toward the back of the cemetery. He halted next to a family plot fenced in low with cast iron balustrades.

Wilde followed him, noting that nearly all the graves had flowers, American flags, tidy borders, or other tokens of recent and loving attention.

Wade Joyce's hands were folded in front of him in a prayerful manner fitting the place. Wilde followed his downcast view to a headstone. The stone marked the final resting place of Benjamin Fallon Blackshaw and his wife, LuAnna Bryce Blackshaw. Their death dates were the same day the previous December.

Wilde summoned her patience and asked, "Mr. Joyce, the remains of Ben Blackshaw are in this grave?"

"And his poor LuAnna. Both cremated of course."

"Cremated. Of course."

"Water does terrible things to a body," averred Wade.

"The man I spoke with earlier today was in excellent health. He matches a photograph captioned with his name on the Internet." Wilde could not wait to hear what the big fellow would tell her next.

"There's family resemblances on Smith that run to cousins, even second cousins. Like mirrors some of them. Spittin' images. But why somebody'd claim to be somebody else beats me. And clean on the other side of the bay, too."

"Somebody who looks like Ben Blackshaw—exactly like the artist-waterman-soldier I just saw on at least one picture on the Internet, stopped by and told me his name was Ben, said he was from Tangier—"

"See now, Agent Wilde, there's proof positive he was a liar who couldn't keep his facts straight, or he would've said he was from Smith Island, doncha know."

"Take me to his house."

This surprised Wade Joyce. "Pardon?"

"Show me where Ben Blackshaw, deceased, and his wife LuAnna, deceased, used to live until last December."

Wade slowly let out a breath, turned, and walked back to the cart. Wilde followed and took her place in the passenger seat again.

They drove along narrow cart paths for five minutes before Wade Joyce applied the brakes in front of a ramshackle saltbox. The windows were open, and sheer curtains billowed out as if the place were straight out of a Walker Evans dustbowl photograph.

Wilde said, "You leave the windows open in this weather?"

"I guess a neighbor might've aired the place out for springtime," suggested the big man. "Out of respect and remembrance."

"I'd like to go inside."

"You likely need a warrant or some such."

"Are you kidding me? The man's dead."

"Well, don't dead folks have rights, too? For aught I know, the place is in probate."

Wilde withdrew the tablet from her briefcase. She spent three minutes accessing a few relevant databases, casting a glance now and then at the house number and the street sign at the intersection a few doors to her left. Then she looked several doors to her right.

Then she turned to her companion. "Mr. Joyce, for the last ten minutes, you have been serving up bullshit by the shovelful. Tax records show this is not Ben Blackshaw's house, and never was. And I highly doubt whoever's name is on that headstone, that Ben Blackshaw or his wife are interred there. I want to thank you for your time. I can make my way on foot from here. Before I do, I want you and your buddy Bob Crockett to think about something called hindering a federal investigation. There's serious prison time for that, and I can make sure you serve it in a supermax. You might come through okay, big as you are, but as old as Crockett is, he might not see daylight again unless he's very, very good at sucking cock. And gosh, I sure hope he doesn't suffer from hemorrhoids, because they're not likely to get any better in jail, if you take my meaning."

Wade Joyce was stricken aback. Agent Wilde marched off down the narrow road to her right. After a few moments, she heard the golf cart sputter to life and accelerate. Wade slowed down beside her. She kept moving.

"Miss Molly—"

"It's Special Agent Wilde, and I'm done with you."

"Ma'am, we got off on the wrong foot. It could be I got turned around with the address—"

Wilde failed to contain her anger. "It could be you've got some racket going that means more to you than the truth, more than helping me locate two missing children, and that pisses me off."

She stopped in front of another saltbox. This home had a well-tended yard, and an array of unusual found-object animal sculptures installed there. Though the sculptures' components were just welded junk from cars and other mechanisms she could not identify, there was an obvious grace in the pieces that vividly captured the movement of wild creatures.

Wilde said, "*This* is Ben Blackshaw's house. Maryland property taxes already paid in full. For *this* year. By a dead man."

Wade Joyce's entire demeanor had changed, darkening with hostility. "Ma'am, you best remember where you are."

"And you best remember who you're talking to." With the hairs on the nape of her neck springing up, alert to danger, Agent Wilde took five steps back from him, drew her Glock and aimed it at his belt buckle. "Get out of that fucking cart."

"What?" The giant was truly stunned now.

"I'm commandeering it," said Wilde. "Are you stupid *and* deaf? Get out! Now!"

Wade Joyce dismounted. Following a jerk of Wilde's head, he stepped well away from the cart, and even raised his hands to shoulder level unbidden. Agent Wilde got behind the wheel and drove back toward the helipad. Without the big man's weight, the cart was much faster than on the trip to the burial ground.

Wilde did not holster her weapon until McCourt had their bird in the air. She could tell he wanted to ask what had happened, but he prudently kept his eyes on the business of flying.

She took time to quiet her breathing, and used her thumbnail to pry loose two pieces of Nicorette gum; they seemed to do absolutely nothing for her nerves which hummed like piano wire.

This entire trip had raised many more questions than it had answered. Trying hard to put her last two encounters behind her, she returned to Pershing Lowry's question about the dead man at the light station. Where indeed was the rest of Campobasso, Arnoldo J.? More importantly, who killed him? Why? Was he blown up to silence him? Was he dead because he got in someone's way?

Something had prompted their only source, Ben Blackshaw, to come forward with the name Maynard Chalk. Something about this case had made Blackshaw break cover, a cover that many people had a significant stake in maintaining, on Smith Island at least, and perhaps on Tangier Island as well. It was the cover of a grave. An empty grave.

As she often did, Wilde let her mind wander beyond the facts of the case. She mused that in Ben Blackshaw's strange way, he had enlisted the help of the FBI, perhaps as a good citizen, or maybe as a direct stakeholder in the outcome of the case. She wondered if he were invested in the Thompson murder. Perhaps his interest lay in the abduction of the children. But he had learned of the murder and the abduction from his conversation at the Thompson scene with her and Lowry. That meant he came forward to parley with authorities before he had any details of the abduction. He must have floated in out of the fog on some other pressing matter which was tied to their case. It all rolled back to Maynard Chalk, and Right Way Moving & Storage. Damned if she could figure out what could possibly be bigger than abduction and murder.

CHAPTER 66

THE CRAB SKIFF bashed white spume off the waves as it coursed over their crests. More often, Knocker Ellis nimbly navigated through the rolling mounds of water like a snowboarder carving among moguls on a slope. He wove a course toward the *American Mariner*. Blackshaw wanted to case the ship again, given the real possibility he had missed a lead on where LuAnna and Tally might be. He studied the bullet he had cut from the skiff's transom. Despite the heavier weapons they were discovering on the operatives they met, none were packing a CheyTac .408.

Ben could only conclude that Clyster had not been killed by one of his own. Nor had the FBI randomly put Clyster down and taken LuAnna and Tally. In the past, the bureau had been embroiled in a few drawn-out headline-grabbing cases with well dug-in megalomaniacs and their sheeple, but despite fatalities on all sides in those tragedies, its agents did not abandon bodies strewn about the countryside. If she were with the feds, LuAnna would have found a way to reach him by now.

The Natural Resources Police did not field such high-powered arms. Who would put a bullet into an operative's leg rather than making a clean CBM, or center body mass, shot? Granted, even a flesh wound from such a big gun qualified as major trauma, but anybody who picked up a sophisticated weapon system like that, with its price tag north of ten thousand dollars, would likely know to make a CBM shot.

He reflected on his own final mission in Iraq, when he was convinced that a fragment of his bullet had flown through an interior doorway and killed the pregnant wife of his target. He had been showing off for his spotter, snipping the seated target's brainstem just below the basal skull through a window from three hundred yards out. Had Ben taken a less risky CBM shot, any through-flight of bullet fragments could have lodged in the heavy wooden back of the target's chair.

It occurred to Ben that LuAnna and Tally might have been in the skiff when Clyster boarded it and likely attacked them. Someone had laid down the ideal shot to disable Clyster, and also terminate the bullet in the wood of the skiff's transom. Strike Clyster higher, and the through-flight of such a big chunk of metal clanging all around the hold might have hurt LuAnna and Tally. Ben had to wonder who would take such care with a shot. Who would want Clyster dead, but also want LuAnna and Tally alive? Only an extremely dangerous person could tolerate living witnesses to a murder. Otherwise, Ben would have found his wife's body on the bottom of the hold right next to Clyster's.

The buzz of Ben's newly-issued phone interrupted his musings. He grabbed it out of his coat pocket and opened the line.

Sonny Wright's voice was almost lost in the noise of the outboard engine and rush of water beneath the skiff.

Ben clapped a hand over his other ear and shouted, "Sonny! Say again!"

"I said you need to step on back here right quick! We got us a development!"

Ben rang off and passed the word to Ellis, who looked apprehensive as he swung the motor's throttle arm to starboard, and dead-reckoned a line for Smith Island.

CHAPTER 67

AFTER A MISERABLE half-hour aloft, Agent Wilde noticed the fog below was thinning in a few places. She had the vantage of a bird's eye view yoked to a personal curse, her obsessive need never to waste any resource, especially one as costly as helicopter flying time, loathe it though she did.

She felt drawn to the water even though descending would slash the helicopter's margin of safety, which she cherished right now. She pushed the foam head of her microphone stalk close to her lips and asked McCourt, "What's the bearing to the Thompson scene?"

McCourt, a full-time FBI employee, had gotten a complete briefing on the case so far. He consulted a chart, and made a chopping motion toward the northwest. "Eight miles." He held up the chart, and indicated a place. "And we're here," he said.

Wilde took this in. "Okay. I got a feeling. Take us down to that clear area of the fog."

McCourt answered by the book. "We're on an instrument flight plan back to Meers Creek."

Wilde said, "Not anymore, friend. Refile it, or deviate, or whatever you need to do, but start your descent toward the visible water now, please."

Whether it was her obvious agitation when she returned to the helicopter at Smith Island, weapon drawn, or his usual spirit of cooperation, McCourt spoke a few words over the radio, disconnected the autopilot, and gently lowered the collective.

Then he asked, "Looking for anything in particular?"

"Anything at all. I'm just sick of looking at clouds."

A few minutes later, the pilot said, "One thousand feet."

Wilde immediately said, "Make if five-zero-zero."

She heard McCourt say, "Wish I'd brought a fishing rod," as he lowered the collective once again.

The water's whitecapped turmoil came into focus below. Turbulence buffeted the helicopter. Agent Wilde clutched her briefcase to her lap to keep it from levitating into the cyclic or the instrument panel. She could do nothing about the upheavals threatening her stomach.

The helicopter descended into a clear area of the fog over one mile in diameter. It was like flying down into a gray volcanic bowl. Wilde marveled for a moment at the way the walls of the bowl seemed well-defined, almost solid, the way a hurricane's eye appeared in a satellite image on the Weather Channel.

Then she turned her attention back to the water. She saw waves, and nothing else. It was a small, empty ocean within the fog boundary. She made the pilot fly its circumference twice. Twice she saw their helicopter's shadow cast onto the fog bank's wall by the wan sun above.

The pilot asked, "Okay. I got nothing. We good here?"

Agent Wilde nodded. McCourt brought in power, eased the cyclic forward, and gently lifted the collective. He banked the helicopter left so that it initiated a climb inside the clearing, putting Wilde on the low side of the turn. The water filled her window.

Then something caught her eye and held it as the helicopter flew on, forcing her to crane her neck around to her left, until she was looking out the back seat window.

She yelled, "Did you see that boat?"

"Where?"

"Turn around! Turn back! It came out of the fog, and turned back into it." Agent Wilde glanced at the compass. "If north is noon, it came out around six o'clock, and disappeared around seven o'clock. A tight turn. Evasive. It was fast."

The pilot banked the helicopter harder, and Wilde was terrified as her face and the pit of her stomach were first to feel the loading G forces.

The pilot confirmed, "It headed into the fog south southeast? We can call that in, but why?"

Wilde said, "There were people lying down in the cockpit. I think there was blood."

"A big fish, maybe? Rockfish can get pretty—"

"They weren't fucking *fish*!" snapped Wilde. "There! There it is again! It's back. It came back!"

"I got it. It's still turning. Jesus!" The pilot noted the GPS coordinates of their current position.

"There it goes!" said Wilde. "Like it's circling part way in this clear area, but mostly in the fog, like an autopilot. Did you see the people in the cockpit?"

McCourt was pale when he said, "Those aren't people. Those are bodies."

CHAPTER 68

SONNY WRIGHT'S CRAB shanty, which he used for sloughing soft-shells in their season, lay behind his home on a navigable gut reached through Tangier Sound. Wright's place lay well away from the three hamlets on Smith Island. With no gossips to witness and announce the approach, there was no reception committee other than Wright himself when Blackshaw and Knocker Ellis tied the skiff up at the finger pier by the shanty.

Wright's movements were tight, jerky with stress, but he refused to say anything until he hustled his visitors toward his house. Ben noticed Wade Joyce's golf cart parked in the yard. Once inside, Wright made no customary offer of coffee though Ben and Ellis were clearly thrashed from their time on rough water. He just paced, beginning and restarting his news several times before Ellis broke in.

"Take a breath, Sonny. Sit down. What's going on?"

Sonny did not sit, but he blurted, "The FBI was here. A woman agent choppered right down onto our pad like an avenging angel. She went to Tangier first, and talked to Bob Crockett, and then she come here, and talked to Wade."

Ellis asked, "What'd she want?"

"If it's that Agent Wilde, I told her I was from Tangier this morning," said Ben. "Didn't think she'd hop on it so fast. What happened?"

"Crockett put her off right enough," said Sonny, "but she got a line on your last name. Avery spilled them beans all over creation. She don't know nothing from nothing, simple little thing."

"I used to like that child," said Ben.

"So, next thing, the lady puts down right on our pad, and Wade is nice enough." Sonny was getting more wound up as he unraveled the story. "He shows her where you're buried, but she Googled you, saw your face, and ain't buying neither thing Wade's selling. He shows her where you live, at Tyler's old place, but she Googles some more, finds your real saltbox, and gets all uppity that Wade's yarnin'. The he gets *his* hackles up, 'cause he don't like being called a liar especially 'cause he *is* one, and she pulled a gun on him, took his cart straight on back to her chopper, and you know Wade don't like walking nevermind. He picks up his cart at the pad, and comes right over here to complain, knowing I threw in with you."

Ben asked, "Where's Wade now?"

"I'm gettin' to that. Wade's mad as hell you even talked to the FBI. Starts going on about how you're a loose end, and I need to call you up so he can talk some sense into you."

"Sonny, where is Wade?" asked Ellis.

"I tried to put him in mind of all you done for us, and how we should be pulling together to get through the business to find LuAnna, maybe help that negro child. You ain't found her yet, have you, Ben?"

"No," admitted Ben, watching Sonny's agitation grow.

"That's what I told Wade. Then he starts in about how we don't need you running around making up to the feds. Then I get the picture, 'cause don't he start saying we got enough in the bank for now, and can't we fig-ure out how to sell gold on our own without you helping like you do. Said he plain didn't trust you to keep your mouth shut n'mare."

"Sonny, are you okay?" Ben did not like where this was going.

The old waterman's speech sounded pressured, too quick, even for him. His mouth was barely keeping up with what appeared to be a trauma-tized mind. "Then I saw it. Wade had his old Smith & Wesson in his belt under his shirt. He was all het-up, talking about how he didn't like you, and we didn't need you. Nothing I said would change his mind, try as I might. Anybody could see that. I'm sorry, Ben, but for five seconds, I told him I agreed with him. Told him I was putting on some coffee so's we could lay a plan to fix you."

Ellis said slowly, but firmly, "What'd you do, Sonny?"

Sonny did not speak. He stood rooted there in his parlor for a moment. Then he stepped over to a closet, and pulled the door open. Wade Joyce lay on his back with a ragged shotgun wound where his heart had once beat. His eyes were half open, as if he were waking from a dream.

CHAPTER 69

AGENT WILDE'S HELICOPTER did not have sufficient fuel remaining to hold on station until the Natural Resources Police patrol boat arrived. Instead, McCourt soon set the bird down back at their destination, the Meers Creek Airfield. Wilde hoped the coordinates they had provided the NRP would hold until they got a solid radar return on the gyrating vessel and could intercept it.

She climbed out of the helicopter, but held onto it until her feet got the message that this was in fact solid ground, and she could let go to walk on her own. It had been one hell of a ride for the reluctant flyer. Before she could get her land legs back, her investigator's eye was involuntarily drawn to a flaw in the paint of the chopper's left rear door. She leaned in for a closer look and stopped breathing.

Collecting herself, Wilde put her head back in the cockpit and told McCourt, "You're going to want to take a look at this. I don't think it's going to buff out."

The pilot was running a thumbnail down the Eurocopter's shutdown checklist. He asked, "What do you mean?"

"This bullet hole. Was it there before? I don't think it was there before."

McCourt just stared at Wilde. She turned and walked as steadily as she could toward her car.

CHAPTER 70

WHILE ELLIS HELPED Wright tidy up after Wade Joyce's untimely death, Ben's sat-phone buzzed.

Ben answered. A voice on the line asked, "You know who this is?"

"I've been trying to leave you be, Mike."

Michael Craig's voice was uncharacteristically rushed. "Did you case that LNG terminal?"

"We might've looked in."

"What about that light house near there? There's been some crazy chatter on the official freq's."

"We might've looked in there first."

Craig said, "The ATF got a call. Something went boom, didn't it. Were there explosives?"

"*We* didn't bring 'em. We're still looking for LuAnna."

Ellis and Sonny were grappling Wade Joyce's bulk into a loose cocoon made from a plastic drop cloth retrieved from the half-painted parlor.

Suddenly, Ben was party to their curses at the same time as Michael Craig was swearing over the phone. "Dammit Ben! I told you this was going to get out of hand! For you! For me! I don't need this kind of exposure."

Ben soothed, "You super-encrypt everything."

"I thought I did," complained Craig. "Then I got a load of the people you're messing with. Do you know what the hell is happening at the terminal?"

Ellis attempted to roll Wade's body into the drop cloth, but at the same time, Sonny was trying to pull the cloth around the big cadaver. In the confusion of efforts, the body gave a mournful belch, tipped off its precarious balance on its side, and flopped onto Sonny, pinning his legs, and soaking him in a cataract of blood.

"Get this bastard off me!" shouted Sonny.

"He's coming back for you!" teased Ellis.

Ben tried to ignore the macabre wrestling match, and said to Michael Craig, "Best we can figure, there's about a one-to-one guard-to-hostage count, about twenty on each side. I'm all for buying in bulk, but what I don't get is why kidnap so many? It's hard to manage that big a bunch. You picking up anything about ransom?"

"Remember I told you, the photons and I have a thing."

"You got to get out more, Mike. Too late to marry the princess?"

Craig managed to sound indignant. "If you must know, I'm in love already. Her name's Nicole, and when *you're* not harshing my mellow, I've never been happier in my entire life."

An exuberant Michael Craig was about as boisterous as Eeyore locating his tail, but Ben let it go. "Congratulations. The photon thing?"

"Right," said Craig. "There are black holes in cyberspace, same as in outer space. Imagine empty servers, and even fat-pipes where nothing appears to be going on, like worm-holes. Black pipes. But Instead of *light* getting sucked in, it's *money*."

"For ransom?"

"No! That's just it." said Craig. "I've been watching the area in question, in Southern Maryland around that terminal, and I'm seeing evidence there's huge cyber capacity that's been constructed there, but it's doing absolutely nothing."

"Is the NSA involved?"

Craig laughed. "Are you kidding me? Those poor bastards max out their storage capacity with data-mining before their latest, greatest servers even come on line. They burn petaflops of space, and it's still not enough. Put it like this, the NSA is the only thing keeping the guys building super-computers in business, but even so, for them it's a perpetual game of catch-up."

Sonny got one leg free, and pushed Wade Joyce's body off his other leg—rolling the big dead man onto Ellis's arm. Ellis wrenched his neck aside as the body's chest wound tipped toward his face.

"Somebody's overbuilt the neighborhood," said Ben, "and that's got you worried?"

"Very," Craig shot back. "The server capacity sits there all quiet, but I backtracked, like the drift analysis. Starting a few months ago, every few days, a chunk of big money blows through. The increments are always the same, five million bucks. You don't need that kind of capacity to move money. You could do it off a smart phone. But today, a few tranches came in at fifteen million bucks, and then another one for twenty million. These are weird, round numbers, right?"

"If you say so."

"The increasing amounts feel like something is building up. It's like a growing calderas dome, but financial pressure is pushing it up. But this money, it blows past that LNG terminal. It doesn't stick around long. Whoosh! In and out. It stops there long enough for somebody to decrypt and peak at it. Like opening an envelope and checking on a payment. So far, I can't figure out where these tranches come from, or where they go, but I'm telling you, it's millions already, and growing. Except for this basic data I deciphered so far, nearly the whole route is encrypted. But the encryption key isn't an elliptic curve-discrete logarithm thingy like usual for most businesses and credit cards. This is literally twisted. Maybe like a Möbius strip, with a single—or it could even be a triple-twist. I've never seen anything like it. Somebody does not want these transactions discovered."

Ben summed, "So, something's for sale, but the only things there are the hostages."

"Not exactly. I looked into the redevelopment of the LNG terminal for gas exporting. At first I thought all the mystery money was for that deal. Get this: turns out that Tank One was never purged and recharged with carbon dioxide. It's still full of natural gas."

This puzzled Ben. "That sounds right sporty, Mike. The terminal's been closed a while."

"I went deeper on that. See, fracking caught on so hot and fast that that imported tankful never got sold domestically. A crooked exec' saw the writing on the wall, decided to keep it, paid some engineers to turn a blind eye so he could turn the load around, and put it right back on the first export ship out when the joint gets going again. And he would have made a nifty profit. He's in jail now, but the gas is evidence, and they've got no place in an evidence compound for it. So they left it right there in Tank 1, closest to the main building. At least that's what the internal memos say."

"But you're sure there's no ransom demand for any of the hostages," confirmed Ben.

"No," said Michael Craig. "Just money in and out. Maybe a sale, but not of a *thing*. It feels like an *experience*. A ball game. A concert. Tickets for an experience of some kind. With scalping, as the event gets close. Ben, I don't think the hostages are ever meant to go home."

"You might have the smart of it, given what I saw. Just wondering, Mike, how big is Tank One?"

"Not sure on that yet, but the whole facility is rated at fifteen BCF. That's fifteen billion cubic feet. Ben, why do you want to know that?" Craig paused, then shouted, "Ben! No! I told you, there's a fucking nuke plant just up the road!"

"Sorry Mike. Gotta go." Ben ended the call and put the phone down to help his friends.

Wade Joyce was already giftwrapped, a human sausage encased in clear plastic, bowsing line, and duct tape; but Ellis and Sonny were covered in blood. They both stood still, out of breath, and eyeing Ben malevolently.

"A little soda water'll get that right out," said Ben.

CHAPTER 71

THE PIER'S END was an island in the fog. Maynard Chalk and his team had found no one in the LNG terminal's garage; Chalk felt a powerful need to step away for a breather. His operatives were now mounting the day's second search of the property, but with orders to limit the sweep to a one hundred yard perimeter around the main building.

He had been wrong to set a picket so far to the north at the light station. Campobasso had been completely useless there in this weather, and had effectively become separated, vulnerable, and a liability. This weird mist was like something off a Scottish loch, and damn if there weren't beasties lurking in it. Chalk prided himself on being the biggest fiend of them all, but that, he realized did not make him the only one. He was on the pier to meet Bellendre and the *Thresher*, and make sure Harrower and Campobasso were properly bagged, tagged, and dragged to cold storage.

Chalk hated running a defensive game. He was in his element when he was on the attack, hitting his targets with a flurry of punches that seemed random, but that were calculated with precision by a subconscious steeped in forty years of wetwork. This idea of protecting a single position was anathema to him. Nothing, no one, and no place should ever loom so important strategically that he should have to sit on his hands and get his ass mauled for a paycheck. He was used to big jobs. International gigs. Wholesale slaughter of worthy opponents. This was so local. So puny. So *retail*.

The fog was putting him off. A Chesapeake Bay fog had killed a whole planeload of his reinforcements one night. He felt blinded, cursed. This scud was alive.

He remembered a short story he had read back in the '50s, in a rag called *Astounding Science Fiction*, when he was very young. It was called *Marshmallow World*. The hero of the story is this man of incredible strength. The strongest man alive. He can burst ball bearings between his thumb and forefinger. He's like a god. But then a world leader starts to worry that this strong man could take him down without a whole lot of trouble. So the boss lures this amazing human being to an island in the middle of a marshmallow sea, and maroons him there in the one place his strength could do him no good. He can't swim, or walk away. The poor bastard can't push against the soft, yielding marshmallow cloud, because it got him no equal and opposite reaction. He was trapped. A mighty phenomenon in human form denied to the world because of fear and jealousy. Chalk could relate. That was how Chalk saw himself; a threat to the highest offices in the land, pinned to a single spot on the map, and surrounded by this amorphous mist that he could swear hated him more than his own mother, and that was saying something.

Chalk heard the guttural growl before the dark low shape lunged at him out of the thick haze.

A voice hailed Chalk from beyond the gray void. "Halt! Fuss, Brutus! Hier! Sitz!" The invisible operative's peremptory zeal together with his German accent made Chalk freeze like a Stalag escapee caught in a spotlight. The dog eyed Chalk's crotch like dinner before trotting back to his handler's side.

Helmut Wagner lowered his MP5 as he stepped into view. "Mr. Chalk. I'm sorry. It's dangerous to be out here."

"Thanks for the concern, asshole. Any sign of Bellendre?"

"Not yet. The fog has been in and out. One minute, I can see a boat two, three hundred yards away. The next minute, I can't see my hand in front of my face. All morning it is this way."

"Hold on. What boat? A black inflatable?"

"No, sir. A small, white boat." Helmut Wagner went on. "Crazy to be out in a little boat in this kind of weather. You see the waves? Waves and fog do not so much like each other. Waves mean wind, and wind blows fog away. Not *this* wind. Not this fog. It stays and stays in the wind."

"Buddy, you sound like a bad vampire movie. Who was in the boat?"

"Two men. This was long ago. If they are not on shore now, they are dead in so small a boat, or they are lost, and that's the same. As for Bellendre? Ich drücke meine Daumen." Wagner pressed his thumbs together, the Teutonic equivalent of crossing his fingers, despite his grim assessment of the weather.

Chalk waited half an hour more for Bellendre to bring *Thresher* into the LNG pier as ordered, but the operator did not show. He was overdue. Chalk left Wagner at his post, and trudged back toward shore to report to DePriest.

CHAPTER 72

SPECIAL AGENT WILDE almost made it to her office. Five minutes was all she had wanted. Five minutes to pull it together, gnaw on a piece of Nicorette until it screamed, or she did, and then she would meet Abigail and Mark Thompson, the parents of the missing children. At least Mark, who had lost his father and mother as well as his kids, would likely manifest a more masculine kind of stone-faced shock about his folks. He would be comforting his wife, putting up a front for her, the pillar of strength in this crisis. That is how it played out on the one other kidnapping case she had worked years before. Abigail would be the basket case.

Senior Resident Agent Pershing Lowry intercepted Wilde before she could close her door. Groaning inside, she smiled, let him in, and they sat. He stayed quiet, keenly aware that the flights and the interviews had been challenging for her, not to mention the treat of discovering the small fishing boat with the bodies.

Wilde said, "Heard about the bullet hole in the helo'?"

Lowry raised his eyebrows, which constituted utter shock in the muted palette of his facial expressions. "Are you hurt?"

"No, but I'm fucking offended. I get the runaround all day, then somebody takes a shot at us just to let us know where we stand."

"A rifle?"

"No, a slug from a shotgun. A *pumpkin ball* is what they call it locally. McCourt preflighted before we left Meers Creek, and Tangier, and again before we left Smith. It happened after we lifted off Smith."

Lowry said, "That was a love tap, Molly. The way those people can shoot, if they were serious, you and McCourt would've been swimming. Until they fished you out, of course. And then—well, they don't kill you. They *keep* you."

Molly was exasperated. "One minute we're being steered, the next minute, we're getting herded. We had linkage between the kidnapping scene and the light house before I even left. The whole thing took years off my life. It was a waste of time, wasn't it."

"That's not true. You got the last name Blackshaw. I grant you, he looks like a bigger can of worms at this point—"

"He's the one who really pisses me off, Pershing. He drops his hint about Chalk and disappears, but he muddies every scene."

"You like him for the light station?"

"*We* didn't blow it up!" Wilde fumbled the Nicorette capsule. It sprang off her fingertips and landed in Lowry's lap. He handed it back to her.

"Molly, he wasn't armed. Neither was his friend."

"Somehow, I don't think that's an issue for him," she said. "We should have busted him."

"It's the guy who chatted with you out of the fog I'd like to speak with. The one who cast that line toward you."

"Like a *fisher of men*. That guy still makes my skin crawl." Molly suppressed a shiver. Then she sat up straight. "You think that was Chalk!"

"The one I'd really like to bust. We need to talk about the boat," said Lowry. "That was an important find."

"Please, I need to know this was worth it."

"The boat was rented locally by three guys this morning. We're running pictures of Chalk down to the owner now. The remains belonged to Campobasso, and one other man. We haven't got prints off that one yet. Then there's the third party."

"Anybody we know?"

"He's not talking," said Lowry.

"It's hard when you're dead." Wilde finally got a thumbnail into the Nicorette capsule, levered out the gum and popped it into her mouth.

"Agreed, yes. But this one's alive."

Molly smiled for the first time in hours. "No! How?"

"You're not going to like it."

Her smile faded. "Tell me."

"He was trussed up like a turkey. He's severely traumatized, and that boat was pounding around in circles in very rough seas for a while before the NRP intercepted it. So, he's a mess. The water cops said he babbled about a ghost attacking him out of the fog. They said he sounds French, which fits Chalk's international recruitment profile. He's sedated now."

"Who tied him up?" demanded Wilde.

Lowry said nothing at first. "The NRP noted that the knots on this man's ligatures were straight out of a marlinspike seamanship manual, implying maritime experience. No granny knots. A former Navy SEAL might fit. Or a waterman. Maybe both."

Agent Wilde muttered, "Blackshaw."

"I'm sure I don't know," said Lowry after a moment. "The Dungeons and Dragons squad is dusting the boat now. When Frenchy comes to, we'll definitely show him a photo of Blackshaw." Lowry stood to leave. "When you're ready, we should speak with the Thompsons. Conference Room Two."

CHAPTER 73

JOACHIM DEPRIEST GORGED on goose sausages from a serving platter that Armand held up for his boss. From time to time, Armand jinked the platter to one side or the other to avoid having his fingers skewered by DePriest's fork, which was the size of outdoor barbecue equipment, and very sharp. Chalk watched the man eat, and worked hard to choke back the urge to vomit. He noticed that Armand's make-up seemed to have been hastily applied. DePriest was running roughshod over everyone without budging an inch.

DePriest sucked another sausage lewdly before drawing it into his maw and smacking his tattered lips. Chalk wondered if he even chewed those things.

"Where do we stand, Maynard?"

"As to what, exactly, big chief?"

DePriest ignored the casual mode of address, destroyed another sausage, and said, "I'm thinking about personnel right now."

"Oh that. Tahereh, Sanders, Flynn, and Meeker are in the fridge. Harrower and Campobasso are definitely dead, but their remains are missing with Bellendre on the boat. Clyster is also missing at this time. The runner hasn't been seen since last night, but we're up a sweet pair of twinsies, which should be great for the show."

DePriest rolled the food around inside his mouth thoughtfully. "Maynard, am I counting aright? Since yesterday, or this morning actually, you have lost *eight* members of your security detail?"

"Two are MIA, so make that six confirmed, yeah," begrudged Chalk. "But we have more than enough crew to get us through tonight and the rest of the week."

"You don't feel we're being persecuted? Or perhaps your squaddies are utterly incompetent, profoundly unlucky, and otherwise unfit to save themselves, let alone protect my interests. What is going on?"

Chalk struck his most collegial tone, though he wanted to pull his Glock and empty its magazine into the massive walrus dressing him down. "Point taken, Your Bigness. So, I want a look at the talent list, as well as the guests who will be coming here, and the other subscribers. I need to see if you didn't rustle some stock that's special to somebody else. Catch my drift?"

"Out of the question!" DePriest's greasy jowls shook with umbrage, and partially masticated goose bits flew from his mouth onto the floor at Chalk's feet. Armand strategically positioned the sausage platter between himself and his boss, but food struck him in the face anyway. At least Chalk's question about DePriest's chewing was answered.

"All due respect," said Chalk, "it's very much *in* the fucking question. There should be no reason under the sun for anybody to pay this op' one iota of attention, but as you pointed out, a totally underground, completely encrypted cyber venture has brought me one hell of a lot of personal inconvenience. So I need to see what's attracting it. It's not the view down here, and it's sure not your winning personality, or your good looks, or your tranny fucktard goony-girls. There has to be something else. I want the lists. Now."

Chalk was prepared for a full-on ear-splitting tirade. Armand was certainly braced for it. DePriest huffed and puffed for a full minute before he said, "The only thing above-ground on this event is your team." Then he added, "So be it. Wallace will see to the lists. But Maynard, if you fail me, I will see to it that Armand and Wallace deal with you personally, with no interference from me. I think they'd like that. I think I would, too."

Chalk turned to leave, took three steps, then stopped. Squarely facing DePriest again, he said, "I've noticed you like to make threats every time you and I have a chat."

DePriest ruminated on a piece of sausage. "I can't help myself. You seem to need motivation."

Chalk smiled indulgently. "That might work for some, but threats aren't my style where you're concerned. You've figured that out, right?"

"You baffle me, Maynard."

"That so?" Chalk walked for the door again. "Bet your ass I'll be there when the penny drops."

CHAPTER 74

ABIGAIL AND MARK Thompson were shattered. Agent Wilde felt awful for them. Their vacation had ended abruptly that morning with the worst possible news. Mark's parents were dead. The couple's children had vanished. Despite pen register watches on every possible number associated with the entire Thompson family, no ransom call whatsoever had come in. All pertinent email addresses were also under surveillance. Nothing had come in through those channels, either.

The Thompsons looked gutted, haunted. Their reddened eyes and bloated faces revealed they had both done a lot of crying on the bureau jet that had returned them to Maryland. That was understandable. Nothing of the life they had left behind for their trip to the Grand Canyon remained except an inner void larger than the canyon itself. Senior Resident Agent Lowry knew that nothing would fill it but the safe return of the children.

Lowry said, "There was a degree of professionalism at the scene—"

"Scene. The *scene*—?" bridled Abigail Thompson. "That's my father-in-law's *home*! Mark and I got married there!"

"I meant no disrespect," said Lowry. "But there is an opportunistic aspect to the children's abduction."

"What are you saying?" pressed Abigail. "Somebody meant to kill Les and Linda, and just took our kids?"

Wilde said, "We believe there was a conversation between whoever did this, and either your mother-in-law, or your father-in-law, but it became a confrontation, and from there, it escalated further."

Agent Wilde passed Mark the second box of Kleenexes. Wilde had misjudged. He was the inconsolable one. For the moment, Abigail's spirit was stiffened by a fury that Wilde admired. Abigail's answers to questions were crisp and precise. Her own questions in return seethed. She wanted a piece of whoever had done this. That would sustain her, if only for this early, crucial stage of the investigation. She would buckle soon enough.

Mark's voice cracked as he said, "Dad isn't exactly a people person."

Lowry noted Mark's use of the present tense. The situation had not sunk in yet. "I know you've been asked this several times already, but can you think of anyone who bore either of your parents ill-will. Anything at all. Did he have any business dealings with anyone? Any partners?"

Mark shook his head. "Retired. Lusby."

Abigail filled in the blanks for her distraught husband. "He was running the Lusby Township Department of Public Works when he retired. There was a guy who lost a quarter acre of his place to eminent domain, for a catch basin Les helped build so half the neighborhood wouldn't flood every time it rained. One lousy quarter acre! Out of five acres total. And he got *paid* for it! The guy got a lawyer, and named Lester in the suit against the town. It didn't go anywhere. It was years ago. What the fuck has this got to do with finding our babies?"

"We're trying to eliminate possibilities here," said Wilde. "Did Lester ever mention anyone trespassing? Did anyone ask if they could use his pier, even casually?"

Abigail eyed Lowry, and settled her red-rimmed glare on Wilde. "You think somebody was running dope through his place? And he was in on that? He had an old dock, not an airstrip in a jungle. For God's sake, check his bank accounts! They were living month-to-month on his pension and Social Security! They put every damn penny of their savings into buying a place on the water. *That* was their dream. Ending up shot in a fucking shed was not part of the big plan, lady."

"It's distinctly possible your children were taken because they witnessed those crimes," explained Lowry.

"Oh Christ," whispered Mark, grabbing another Kleenex and blotting his eyes and nose.

"You're not following," said Wilde. "Your children were not found at the scene. Do you understand me? They were not in that shed. They are very possibly alive somewhere."

Lowry and Wilde let the atmosphere in the conference room decompress for a few moments. They both understood that silence in an interview made a powerful demand to be filled. Often, the result was useful information no one might have thought of. Privately, Lowry felt the technique was a bit too Zen-voodoo, but Wilde believed in it.

"How early do you think this happened?" asked Abigail.

"There's evidence that Mrs. Thompson was in the middle of preparing breakfast," said Lowry.

Mark looked sharply at his wife. Abigail said, "Barry will go barefoot all day, and Les and Linda would let him. But Nicole, she likes shoes. She got a bad cut once on a piece of glass. Her flip-flops are her favorites. Puts them on first thing in the morning, and takes them off for bed, but she'd wear them to bed too, if we let her. Did you find her flip-flops at the house?"

Wilde cast a puzzled look at Lowry, who said, "I'm not sure. Why are you asking about them?"

Abigail's eyes grew wide with stunned disbelief. "Because Nicole's got guts. Because she's fearless, and if you take your eyes off her for two seconds, she's gone. She's five, but she's little. They both are. Her feet haven't grown very much since she was three. Oh my God! She gave us heart attacks running away to look at things. Bugs. Salamanders. Exploring."

"Mrs. Thompson? Abigail?" Wilde was thinking this was it. The woman was finally and completely cracking up. *Salamanders?*

Mark seemed to stir out of his stupor. "The chip?"

Abigail said, "We put a chip in her flip-flop. What was it? A Kindertrek. The device thing is at home." She half-rose from her chair. "We have to get it."

"Honey, the battery," said Mark Thompson. "It's been two years."

Looking hopeful, Lowry asked, "Mrs. Thompson, what's the range on the chip?"

"Two miles," said Abigail. "It's not much, but I don't care. If she was wearing those flip-flops, and there's any juice in that battery, it puts me two miles closer to my babies. Right now, I'll take that."

"And I assure you," said Lowry, "so will we."

CHAPTER 75

SAM ROOKARD DESCENDED to the holding pens. He wanted, felt compelled to inspect the stock again. Meditating on his living charges always inspired new and interesting ways to transition them to their finish. Of course, nothing in his plans involved the talent going unconsciousness for very long, if ever. He knew the subscribers wanted to see reactions to pain, to witness the terror, to see hope blossom in the talent with Rookard's carefully crafted lies, and his false promises of rescue and freedom; and then the onlookers would thrill to watch that hope die again when Rookard himself, or the monsters he had recruited, resumed their ghoulish work. This was going to be Rookard's finest hour. This would be the realization of an art form he alone would perfect. The week of *L'Abattoir* would never be forgotten.

Rookard took the next stairway down, but halted a moment to listen. Someone was running toward him in the corridor below, but the lights there were off. He could hear the footfalls, the heavy boots, the jangling clank of gear. It was one of Maynard Chalk's men double-timing closer.

Luther Flegg flew out of the darkness, hit the bottom stair running, and almost bowled the spindly Rookard over with his momentum. A zing of adrenalin raced through Rookard's body, converting instantly to umbrage. He shouted, "Idiot! Watch where you're going!"

Flegg did not apologize. He blurted, "She's out!"

"Who's out?" asked Rookard as he disentangled his limbs from Flegg's.

"The little black girl!" Flegg was pale. He tried to stand, but again sat hard on the stair.

"Which one?" Rookard noticed his hands were wet, greasy.

"Don't know her name. The sister took off this morning," said Flegg.

Rookard looked at his hands, at his shirt. "Jesus! You're bleeding all over me!" He pushed Flegg away. "Give me your keys."

Flegg patted his belt where his key loop was usually belayed, and finding nothing, he desperately frisked himself. "She threw up in her stall. Laying there in the mess. I went in, and—" He pulled his hand away from his side. No keys. More blood. A lot more.

Rookard was a wilting physical coward at heart, but with a blade in his hand, and a sense of his victims' powerlessness before him, he became a demon. "Give me your knife." He would teach that skinny bitch a thing or two.

Flegg reached for his sheath. There was nothing in it. His head lolled to one side, and he passed out.

Rookard felt for Flegg's carotid pulse. It was still. He looked down the stair into the dark corridor and shuddered. He stood, and dashed two steps back in the direction from which he had come. In a moment of clarity, he stopped, returned to Flegg, took his pistol and his machine gun, and resumed his pell-mell climb toward the light.

CHAPTER 76

THE LISTS FASCINATED Chalk. He was studying Wallace's printout in his little basement office in the LNG terminal. The livestock represented a hand-picked collection from the abject fringes of world-wide humanity. The local talent was culled from hookers, odd-jobbers, strippers, and others who *never would be missed*, in keeping with Ko-Ko's compilation of the condemned in Gilbert and Sullivan's *Mikado*. Even if their absences were noted by a fellow skell, the authorities would not exactly hop to it to locate them as they would if the President's brat had been nabbed. Choosing from this outcast stratum bought time for the venture to proceed to its unnatural conclusion. Plenty of time. Woe betide the friendless and the lonely if DePriest's creeps came knocking.

Some of the exotic and imported meats didn't even have last names, other than those in their forged documents, and then only if they were brought into the country through traditional ports of entry, where Customs and Border Protection were on the lookout for freeloaders who thought that access to the thirty-seventh ranked healthcare system in the world was worth the trouble. Others, Shanghaied in locked shipping containers or other unsavory modes of transportation, were only noted on the list with Xs for their names, then gender, race, and approximate age. The document read like a slaver's bill of lading from by-gone days; days that did not seem all that *gone by* when he thought about it.

And yet, Chalk found the list bereft of an essential facet; it did not tell the full story. He had done many a walk-through of the pens as part of his quality assurance protocols. All the meat was simply beautiful. Bright, lively, and well-marbled. Male or female, there was something captivating about each of DePriest's subjects. It was for the diabolical destruction of this beauty that the subscribers were paying so much. Chalk knew what they didn't. Even if they lined up all the pageant princesses on the planet and slaughtered them each and every one, DePriest's subscribers would feel no better about the ugliness inside themselves. There was no exchange of virtue on the other side of these sacrifices. No quality of grace would be conferred on the subscribers, and certainly no salvation. Their black hearts would not rise a little closer to being God's anointed for having chainsawed a little of the intervening competition out of the way. No, instead they'd be dropping fast in the ranks toward hell. Chalk looked forward to their company—and his share of their thirty pieces of silver.

Chalk knew Rookard was having a field day making up stage names for all the meat as part of his dumber-than-porn scenarios and pantomimes that he believed would help each evening's narrative hang together. For the subscribers' sakes, Chalk hoped there was a Fast Forward function to help them breeze through Rookard's dreck to the juicy parts. Rookard had all the innovative showmanship of a brain-damaged Sunday School teacher.

Only the runner stood out in Chalk's scrutiny, and only because she had in fact bolted and successfully disappeared. That escape was her only distinguishing trait. The fact that she had abandoned her poor little sister to shift for herself, suffer, and die horribly was merely one more aspect that made the runner otherwise quite ordinary. Screw all the cat posters on social media; Thomas Hobbes got it right in *Leviathan*. The way humanity truly lived it, existence was indeed solitary, poor, nasty, brutish and short. End of story. His dear departed Tahereh had reminded him of that once before. Chalk took comfort in the predictable nature of people. He kept his expectations managed down to a minimal *quid pro quo* with his fellow man.

Chalk spent more time with the subscriber list. The clients, after all, were the financial engine of all human trafficking, whether they were duping a Filipina nurse into a life of underpaid, punishing hardship sluicing bedpans in the States, or pimping one's ten year old daughter to the man in the next village to cure him of AIDS, the multibillion dollar trade in suffering began with a man seeing something helpless with a pulse that he lusted after, and reaching into his pocket for the scratch to obtain it. Sometimes it only took pennies, or a few dollars, to get it. On rare occasions, the freight ran to millions for a turn, like on this venture he was working with DePriest. Some called it exploitation. Chalk knew it was actually a brutal trade in rape and murder, or slower, grinding servitude to the death, and the wheels started turning any time folks snapped up what the pimps and bawds had on sale. And they called it a *free* market economy. Like hell. One thing was certain to Chalk; humans were the original renewable resource.

Chalk was impressed by this subscriber list. He recognized the names of oligarchs from around the world. DePriest was incredibly well-connected. There were quite a few men on the roster who were publicly known as philanthropists. Seeing those names made Chalk smile. So many of them had founded environmental causes, railing and spending against the volatile climate. You'd stand a better chance with them if you were a low-land gorilla, or an apex predator getting reintroduced to an ecosystem that humans had overrun. But if you were a human little girl or boy in their clutches, you were fucked and far from home. There were even doctors listed who ran big hospital systems, or who financed research to cure ravaging diseases; one might assume they had pronounced the Hippocratic Oath at some point in their rotten, stinking lives, the pledge to do no harm. The hypocrite's oath, more like.

Of course, Chalk recognized many other names of well-heeled reprobates, the arms dealers, the environmental poisoners, the big-money grifters scamming the populace with their pork-barrel lobbies, and stacking the highest courts in the land to be sure their interests would never be hindered by anything like jurisprudence. Chalk was pleased to note there was even one subscriber from the ranks of the U.S. Supreme Court.

And given a few other names, the venture capital financiers, apparently there were many ways to hedge one's funds. Offshore accounts were merely foreign mattresses in which to stash money, compared to what these boys could do legally right here at home. Wall Street was merely a gang of cock-wagging pantywaist stooges in service of the real international power structure. It seemed every category of scum and do-gooder was represented on this list. Chalk began to see enriching possibilities for blackmail after the curtain came down on *L'Abattoir*'s stage.

In the much shorter group of in-person attendees, Chalk's eye came to a sudden and full stop on one particular cockroach. John Turner Frost. He had an unnamed plus-one on the guest list. Chalk's heart beat faster. Frost ran FerdeLance, a chemical wildcatter's outfit that would have made Upton Sinclair scream diatribes; *The Jungle* would look like a kiddie's picture book of nursery rhymes in comparison to a single paragraph on FerdeLance. What excited Chalk was knowing Frost was also Department of Homeland Security Secretary Lily Morgan's better half. Was she the plus-one? Chalk almost said a prayer that she would be darkening *L'Abattoir*'s door.

Lily Morgan, Chalk's former boss, had severed their lucrative partnership, destroyed his career, and abandoned him to rot in the pillory of public opinion. He could not avenge himself on Morgan in the circles she usually traveled. But here, in this secluded lair, which was designed and equipped for large scale torture and murder, anything was possible. What would the other subscribers think if Chalk tossed Lily up on the stage, and cut Rookard loose on her? That would blow their fucking minds! At the moment, there was no celebrity component to the meat scheduled for butchering. Chalk's brain fizzed at the prospect of Lily Morgan getting her due in such a debauched and public way.

Chalk felt his grip on reality swirl down the drain of his paranoia. Of course she was coming to *L'Abattoir*! Doubtless she was responsible for his encounter with Ben Blackshaw earlier that morning. She used the line of Blackshaw against him, like spies and *agent provocateurs* detailed to thwart his every effort to find a little happiness in this sordid life. The walls bloomed with eyeballs watching him, as if he could see every subscriber peering at him closely, judging his achievements, his failings, assessing the quality of his death. Lily Morgan's lavender peepers studied him most closely of all the orbs, and they twinkled with a sick delight.

With no idea how much time had passed, Chalk was roused from his fevered visions by the pitter-pat of panicked feet approaching down his quiet corridor. Were the footsteps real, or auditory hallucinations? He could not be sure. Dwelling on Lily, he realized, was a trigger for a psychotic mini-episode. At least there were no bodies lying at his feet, neither expendable friends, nor hated foes. He was not sure why the hell he was holding his sat-phone in his hand. A second later, Chalk was surprised to see Rookard himself skid to a stop in front of the office door which, based on proven principals of good leadership, Chalk always left open. Rookard was upset. He was drenched in a Jackson Pollock of fresh blood.

"Maynard, we have a containment issue."

CHAPTER 77

CHAMAIYO WAS TERRIFIED. She hated the dark, and she missed her big sister Tally very much. But being afraid did not mean she was weak, or stupid. She had forced herself to throw up, and then to lie down quietly next to the mess. The guard had come right in the minute he saw her unconscious in her pen. She had gambled he would not call for help first. She had won that bet. She was not the least surprised when, instead of trying to help her immediately, he first tried to touch her. That was his second mistake. A few seconds later, she had his knife and keys, and he was very badly hurt. She covered her retreat from the pen by turning off the big light switch a few feet down the hall. That had sent the guard sprinting and squealing toward the illuminated stairway at the corridor's end. He did not want to be alone with her in the dark anymore. That was his only good decision in the previous minute.

Not for the first time, Chamaiyo knew it was lucky she was small. Even when the lights came back on, and they would very soon she knew, she could tuck and fold herself into impossible spaces to wait out the search. They would never find her. Even if she had to hold still as a stone for hours and hours at a time, she could do it. She was Kalenjin. She was raised by her family, by her people, and by her culture to endure great pain without a flinch, without a whimper. She would run, she would suffer, she would kill, and she would welcome any of that hardship rather than sit quietly in her cell waiting to be used like a ceremonial cow.

CHAPTER 78

LILY MORGAN LEFT her office early. She was getting excited about the special week-long getaway her husband had in store. She was touched he had invited her to go with him. Her surveillance on him made it clear that he was a whore-hound who strayed once, sometimes twice a month. At least he was discreet. Not every call girl would submit to his proclivities for any amount of money he offered. And when Lily wanted a bit of extra attention from John, she simply made his flavor du jour disappear forever. By the time he recruited someone fresh and willing, Lily was tired of his doddering and moping around the townhouse, and once again, if only for a time, it would be all right if he sought his pleasures with a tramp on the side.

She opened her closet door. She needed a selection of dresses for the cocktail hour before each evening's entertainment began. Lily was unfazed when a dragon scaled with playing cards poked its head out from between her black Armani, and the deep blue Halston Heritage number she was eyeing. Her Variant Creutzfeldt–Jakob disease played hell with her ever weakening ability to discern what was real, and what were images bubbling up from the Swiss cheese of her brain. Her hallucinations sometimes ran to mythic creatures, but this one took the cake.

She was surprised when the dragon spoke. "You forgot about me."

Lily's answer was quick and sure. "I've never seen you before."

"But you have." Smoke curled out of the dragon's nostrils. "And I really thought we were friends. But when things got a little tough, you betrayed me. Is that any way to treat a compadre?"

"You must have me confused with someone else. Are you absolutely sure you've got the right closet?"

"What do you think this is, fucking Narnia?" The dragon's eyes blazed red, and every scale on the beast's head became a joker card.

"Go away! Shoo! What do you want from me?" Lily Morgan found herself trembling in this strange presence.

"I want to sit down with you and talk about old times." Flame licked out around the dragon's tongue.

The beast's massive head thrust closer to Lily, and she could smell the acrid stench of her hair smoldering. "We don't have old times. We don't have any times to talk about."

"We could have run the world!" growled the creature. "We had everything we needed, the power over life and death, the money, the abject terror of the masses. You were a woman of ideas. And you gave it all up for what? For the next shit-stained rung on a career ladder, that's what. You traded in partnership with a god for a new desk!" The dragon groaned, pained with the insult.

Lily was defiant. "I do okay, buster. The view's pretty good from that desk. And if you're such a holy bigshot, why don't you go and do all that world domination stuff on your own?"

The dragon's head lunged at her, smoke from its snout and the rasping denticled tongue curling around her terrified face. "We need our humans, Lily. Without you clay-footed dipshits, we gods are just notions. You make us real. I'll come see you again. We'll sit down and drink a nice steaming cup of blood—"

"Lily?"

Lily Morgan turned from the dragon to see her husband standing in the bedroom doorway. She was not certain he was actually there, so she hedged and said, "Hello, John."

He said, "With whom are you speaking, dear?" He had that familiar, mistrustful look in his eye, so she knew he was real.

"This dragon, of course." She turned back to the closet, but the beast was gone.

John seemed sad, but he was looking at her hand. She dropped her gaze, and discovered she was gripping her mobile phone. Examining the log, she noted that a call lasting several minutes had ended only seconds ago. She did not recognize the incoming number.

CHAPTER 79

SONNY WRIGHT HATED the idea of remaining behind on Smith Island yet again. Ben and Ellis were barely able to persuade him to hold the fort. Without condoning Sonny's killing of Wade Joyce, they made it plain staying put was a crucial rearguard action. Joyce's death was not the first Smith Island loss in service of preserving the gold and its exchange into cash. Even Reverend Mosby had once lifted a bloody hand against a neighbor who had murderous, selfish designs against Ben and the treasure. That righteous example did not settle Sonny in the least. He was not so much in fear for his eternal soul as he was worried about lingering among suspicious friends when Wade Joyce was declared missing.

Together, the three men drove the body in the golf cart to a secluded point of marshland, and with three shovels going hard for an hour, they interred the big man there in the reedy waste. Sonny said he was up to the task of ditching the cart far from any home or hamlet among the cattails, but everyone knew all these efforts were temporary measures. Someone would be answering for this crime one day soon. Until then, ever the man of action, Sonny wanted to get back on the water and into the real fight beside Ben and Ellis.

A glance at the deteriorating weather confirmed that the time for open inflatables and low crab skiffs was past. The work that Ben had in mind would require all the freeboard and capacity of his beloved *Miss Dotsy* deadrise.

With Sonny receding into the mist enveloping Ellis's pier, Ben was tortured by the mystery of LuAnna's disappearance. The presence of Chalk and his ilk infesting the bay, regardless of his link to Tally and her tale, was deeply troubling. If Chalk had LuAnna, and if she were somehow part of the show Tally described, her prospects were dim. Why would Chalk stay quiet, and not try to bargain with Ben for LuAnna's return? Perhaps because Chalk had tried it once before, and the gambit had utterly failed. LuAnna had survived. Chalk's force had been slaughtered nearly to a man, and he had lost significant property and prestige for his trouble. Ben did not negotiate. But this mission was different.

Ben asked Ellis, "Say it's fifty-fifty hostages to operators at that terminal, what would you do?"

Ellis said, "What is your ideal outcome? You want Chalk dead at most any price."

"Not at any price. Not if we lose LuAnna."

"LuAnna's missing. You don't know anything about where she is. What if she and Tally are blowing up your credit card shopping in D.C.? Her problems might be completely separate from Chalk and his crew, and might-could have zero connection to Tally and her sister's troubles. It's like Schrödinger's cat. Cat ain't dead for sure 'til you give a look inside the box."

"You want to operate that way," asked Ben.

"That's up to you, buddy. I'm single."

"That's cold," said Ben.

"Oh, I get it," said Ellis. "You want the fairy tale ending. All bad guys dead. All hostages freed without a hurting hair on their heads. Plus, of course you and I come out just fine. LuAnna's home making coffee and whatnot. You know that's not happening."

Ben said ruefully. "Don't forget the part about all that going down with just the two of us on the case. I admit there's been some mission creep since I rolled out this morning."

Ellis said, "Don't I know! And here I took you on a drive in my nice car, hosted you the extra special coffee, and this is the thanks I get."

Ben eased the tiller back and forward again to meet each wave at the healthier angle. The breeze was blowing against the tide, slowing the first waves, allowing following waves to catch up and merge with the slower ones. Rogues were building steeper.

"You haven't asked where we're going," observed Ben.

Ellis came close to a guffaw. "Turn to port. Turn to starboard. We're headed for trouble any which-way with you at the helm."

Ben bore north, and soon the hummocks and hillocks of a low island began to show over the waves. Ellis fell silent. He knew the place. The waves of the bay settled in the lee of the marshes surrounding the island. Ben guided *Miss Dotsy* into a series of streams that narrowed to barely navigable guts.

When *Miss Dotsy*'s wheel started churning up too much mud in the final constricting waterway, Ellis cut the engine. They had avoided the island's ancient stone landing. It was too exposed to the open bay and the casual or prying eye. Ben slipped over the bow with the painter line in hand and started towing the deadrise deeper into the reeds.

Ellis finally said, "You look like something out of *The African Queen.*"

"Bogart, or Hepburn?"

"In that wetsuit? More like the leeches."

Eroding and subsiding into the Chesapeake Bay like so many other nearby features, MacCatheter Island was more bog than dry ground, except for several acres deep in the interior. Higher elevations there drained better, and gave more solid footing. Closer to shore, the best access to their goal was through the series of streams and guts that had been planked below the water's surface by poachers to allow rapid, untraceable escape should the Natural Resources Police launch a raid to spoil the fun. Ben Blackshaw knew the way.

"You remember what I said about a good death?" asked Ellis as he slogged the gut in his rubber boots.

"And you say *I'm* being a drip."

"I want to amend my earlier remarks with a preference for expiring in one, and no more than two, pieces."

"Duly noted."

Ellis went on. "I mention it because this particular island isn't good for making my fond little hope come true."

Nevus MacCatheter, the island's former owner and namesake, had made his mark in the late 19th Century buying up the leftover or obsolete munitions and ordnance from various wars and skirmishes around the world, including many in which the United States had fought and prevailed. He would sell his discounted goods to less developed nations, or belligerent, cash-heavy warlords of every stripe, with an arms dealer's studied disregard for their politics.

With his business based in Washington, D.C., a prescient nervousness among town fathers about storing things that go boom within the city limits forced MacCatheter to find new space for his expanding inventory. A hunting trip on the Chesapeake led to his discovery of the island, its purchase, and the start of its most unusual and volatile chapter in history.

With the island's deed of sale signed, the higher ground was immediately riven with reinforced bunkers and tunnels for securing the touchy wares. MacCatheter, who was either fearless or a fool, even built a small castle in the Moorish style for his wife, Nelly, to serve as his family's summer home, and as a lodge for the fowling season.

MacCatheter also stocked the island with a herd of deer for his hunting pleasure and that of his friends and clients. The island was not large. Game could often be baited and taken from any of the castle's verandas. The gentle deer had prospered to such an extent that when their natural diet of plants was quickly consumed, they began devouring Nelly's prized garden. This enraged her to near apoplexy. The resulting argument sent her husband forth in a spiteful fury of his own that evening, rifle in hand, pockets stuffed to overflowing with cartridges, to dispatch the troublesome pests wholesale. He would show her. And he did.

After a certain hour of the evening, the war monger's pleasure in single malt scotch made any but the closest deer safe from his wavering aim. That did not stop MacCatheter, who fancied himself a marksman sober or squiffed, from potting at the skittish creatures; they simply gamboled away from his fusillade into impossible distances downrange. Undaunted, MacCatheter kept shooting.

An account of the tragic evening was pieced together from the disjointed mutterings of Nelly MacCatheter before she succumbed to her injuries. Based on what she told her rescuers, it is supposed that a stray bullet from her husband's gun found its way into a bunker storing heavy Howitzer shells. The bunker's iron door was unfortunately left ajar by a negligent employee.

When the unlucky round struck its explosive big brother, the chain re-action of detonations throughout the warren of bunkers leveled everything on the island more than four feet high, whether natural or manmade. The castle was razed to the brick. Nelly was discovered dying in the fallen boughs of an oak tree on the opposite side of the island. Nothing was ever seen of Nevus MacCatheter again.

The dead and injured were taken away from the cursed place. An as-sumption was made that all MacCatheter's goods had gone up at once, a safe wager given that the holocaust was observed from as far away as Baltimore harbor. Down through the decades, no one wanted to test that theory by poking around the island for saleable scrap or souvenirs. Rumors that the ghosts of a mad Scotsman and his harpy bride troubled the place also kept the feebleminded well clear.

Blackshaw pressed on toward the interior of the island. Ellis began to notice the overgrown craters where bunkers had erupted a century before. He had observed the like on a pilgrimage through the Ardennes of Belgium, France, and Luxembourg, but with more trees, and fewer cattails.

"Ellis, you worry too much."

"We're wasting time. I know you and your scavenging ways. There's nothing here. Unless you're going to hurl that old arch at somebody." Architectural fragments of the castle dotted the marsh.

"That's not exactly true," confided Ben. "I progged around the place some when I was a kid. There's a couple-two-three bunkers that didn't go off like Fourth of July. We're up against the worst kind of folks, Ellis, and plenty of them. Don't fail me now."

Ellis was quiet for a moment beneath the weight of Ben's veiled insult. Then he said, "What the hell am I doing here? I have money. I've got peo-ple for this."

"No one we could trust."

"You're overreaching, friend. Let's just look for LuAnna. Let that Tally girl work out her own salvation."

"With Chalk around, I'm telling you, Schrödinger's cat or not, there's no way the two aren't bound up somehow."

"A score isn't settled if you die, too."

"There's some honor in it."

"I've lived forty years under a cloud," said Knocker Ellis. "Shame is my old friend. You get used to it."

"There." Ben pointed to a mound of earth entangled beneath thick briars. He levered the rusted leaf spring of a destroyed munitions cart out of the ground. Ellis found a length of old pipe. Together, they smashed the briars back several yards, until a low iron door came into sight.

They knelt and dug soil, moss, and grapevine away from the door. It hung askew in its frame, likely because of the primordial blast that had driven humanity from the place. Ben worked his fingers around the edge and pulled hard. The door lurched with a groan that might have come from the earth itself or the soul of either man.

"Gimme room," ordered Ellis.

Ben rearranged his footing so Ellis could get a solid purchase on the door beside him.

"On three," said Ben.

On the count, the men pulled. The door howled open a few inches. They counted and yanked again, and again, to a chorus of metallic squawks and squeals made weird by the acoustics of the bunker's interior. Finally, the door was open wide enough to allow a wash of light to bathe the maw. They peered inside.

"Oh my blessing," whispered Ben.

After a long silent moment, Ellis said, "Orpheus, you *got* to leave that bitch down there."

CHAPTER 80

LUANNA CAME TO from a twitching stupor to see Tally cowering on the far side of a small wood-paneled galley space; the refugee was trying to get as far away from a large Doberman Pinscher as she possibly could, even though the dog was fast asleep. Tally would have climbed out through the genteelly curtained port above her head if she had the presence of mind to figure out how to open it.

Every muscle of LuAnna's body felt sore, as though she had run a marathon. At least the rocking sensation was not an artifact of her addled nervous system, which had taken the full brunt of a military-grade TASER calibrated for a big man in thick, heavy gear. She gradually recalled boarding her skiff with Tally inside the hold of the *American Mariner*. Then the man had shimmied down the ladder, and tased Tally before any weapon could be drawn in self-defense. He had quickly done the same to LuAnna, whose body and brain had exploded in a welter of brutal spasmodic pain and bright light from overstimulated optic nerves. Likely she had imagined the man falling overboard in a limbic bid for fulfillment of her wish for rescue. The rest of the images she retained were an impressionist's blur that refused to hang together in any kind of sensible order.

A quick scan of the galley told LuAnna she knew this particular boat well. The two-burner gas stove, which was bringing a galvanized coffee pot to boil, was warming what little space was not occupied by two human beings and the dog. As her mind cleared, she recognized the animal; Gertie, the big bitch, dozed, dreamt of love, and occasionally farted into her jumbo heat diaper on the cabin sole at their feet. The atmosphere was close.

They were aboard her Uncle Conrad's *Winnie Estelle*, a sixty-four foot Chesapeake Bay oyster buyboat, her keel laid in Crisfield in 1920. This boat, and vessels like her had plied the bay serving as the Mack trucks of their day during the first half of the Twentieth Century, before the great estuary was girdled by bridges; they hauled melons and corn in the warmer seasons when their holds and decks were not heaped with oysters. In fall and winter, watermen in skipjacks and deadrises would sell their oyster catches to buyboat captains out in the Chesapeake far from home. The crews of smaller, slower boats could stay out dredging and tonging bivalves for a full week, spared the expenses of time and fuel to return home at the end of every day. It was the buyboat operators who would put into port to sell the harvest.

The galley door opened briefly, bringing a welcome change of air with the woman who entered. To Ben's wife, the stranger appeared to have some Asian ancestry to compliment certain other qualities that LuAnna found oddly familiar, but could not quite place. The newcomer tossed half a can of coffee into the pot, and left it on the stove to boil.

The woman said, "Conrad's watching the radar. It's getting interesting out there."

LuAnna said, "You're *her*. Annie Vo. Ben's sister."

"Guilty. Half-sister, but who's counting."

Dick Blackshaw, Ben's father, had enjoyed a liaison with a local woman during his tours in Vietnam. Only much later in life had Annie Vo found her father, and they had struck up a strange partnership as fellow mercenaries in the years since.

LuAnna asked, "You still having nightmares?"

Annie Vo's face darkened. "Every once in a while. I see Ben's been talking out of school."

LuAnna smiled at Annie Vo and said, "He said you're married to a very nice girl."

Annie Vo relaxed her martial mien for a moment. "Janie. She's the best. She's going to have a baby in a couple months."

LuAnna beamed. "Really? I'm going to be an aunt?"

"Wow, you jump right in, don't you. Sure. Aunt LuAnna. Sounds okay." Annie Vo scrutinized her half-sister-in-law, and seemed to approve.

"How do you know Uncle Conrad?" LuAnna asked.

"Pap knows him, of course. He gave me a lift," said Annie Vo, who was now scrutinizing Tally.

The girl also seemed to measure up well, now that she was drowning in a warm change of Annie Vo's clothes with cuffs rolled to fit. She still wore Ben's field jacket on top of everything. There was something of the distressed waif about Tally in the oversized rig, and it appealed to Annie Vo, and made her wish to help.

Tally said, "You took that shot back at the ship?"

Annie Vo smiled with unalloyed pride. "You're not complaining, I hope."

"If you had missed—"

Annie Vo sounded deflated when she said, "I didn't. And you're welcome." She poured three mugs of coffee.

LuAnna asked, "You always hang around on my uncle's buyboat?"

Annie Vo explained, "I have some unfinished business with brother Ben. It's all about the DNA at this point." The lovely mercenary had recently quit working for Homeland Security Secretary Lily Morgan's black bag Meme Displacement Unit as a hired assassin. But there had been a serious falling out between Annie Vo and her handler. She meant to settle things permanently with Lily Morgan, and wanted Ben to help out. She asked, "Is Ben sleeping okay? No visions? No horrors or hallucinations?"

"All the time," said LuAnna. "The wars, they never end, do they? So, that's how you came by the old ship. Looking for Ben."

Blackshaw had left the *American Mariner* to bring Ellis up to speed on Tally, her escape, and the pressure to save her younger sister, Chamaiyo.

Absent Ben, time had weighed heavily on LuAnna's hands, and with the coming daylight, Tally expressed the hope that if they got back on the water, she might recognize some feature on shore that would help focus the rescue effort.

Bunkered in the old ship's sickbay where Ben worked, the two women had not heard the approach of Maynard Chalk's rented fishing boat, or

Clyster's boarding at the *American Mariner*'s exterior accommodation stair which was rusted in place close to the stern.

Despite the angle into the space, the pitch of *Winnie's* deck, and the weird, thin light inside and out of the hold, the Nightforce NXS scope mated to Annie Vo's CheyTac M300 rifle brought the threat into clear focus. Even at the fifty yard remove from *Winnie Estelle*, the Cheytac's report must have cracked like thunder in Hold No. 2.

The bullet, weighing four hundred nineteen grains, just shy of one ounce, screamed out of the gunbarrel at three thousand feet per second, and struck Clyster's leg like the 5:15 Memphis-Oklahoma Redball. Hydrostatic shock overwhelmed his brain function in little more than an instant. Clyster dropped over the skiff's side and sank under the weight of his gear with even money on his drowning or bleeding out first. Either way, dead was dead.

Annie Vo regretted missing a chance to chat Clyster up and search his gear, but in the circumstances, with his aggressive behavior toward—well—family, punching his ticket with a lower extremity shot that would bury the bullet in the skiff instead of sending it caroming around the hold to do collateral harm seemed an acceptable trade-off.

Ben's half-sister explained she had then swamped the skiff in place to prevent its attracting attention when someone came by to retrieve Clyster; not that there was much chance of that now, not before decomposition gasses bloated and buoyed him back to the surface. At least the cold water would slow the microbiological action and conspire with Clyster's hardware to keep him down for a time.

"Who was that strapped-on fuckface back there at the ship?" asked Annie Vo.

"Never seen him before," admitted LuAnna.

Tally surprised LuAnna and Annie Vo when she said, "He's one of the men holding us prisoner."

Annie Vo exhaled slowly, and said, "Put me in possession of the facts, why doncha?"

LuAnna remained silent. It was Tally's story to tell. "There are at least ten of them. And one woman that I've seen. Maybe many more. All armed. And dogs."

"*Prisoner* sounds like you did something wrong," observed Annie Vo.

"No! *Hostage* then," said Tally. "We were brought here like animals. They mean to use us. I think they mean to kill us. For some kind of sport. It begins tonight."

With an unholy glance at the dog, Gertie, whose digestive tract was once again venting malodorous puffs of disagreement with her diet, Annie Vo said, "Let's take this forward. Conrad should hear it."

With a coffee mug for Conrad in LuAnna's hand, the three women left the dog in the galley, made their way forward, and climbed up the two steps into the buyboat's wheelhouse. LuAnna greeted her grizzled uncle with a hug and a kiss on the cheek. He thanked her for the coffee. She introduced Tally, and caught him up on the young woman's story so far.

Conrad asked, "They brought you here from where?"

Tally took heart from LuAnna's and Annie Vo's obvious trust in Conrad Bryce, and continued. "My sister, Chamaiyo and I are from Kenya. She's eleven. We ran from home when my auntie began discussing Chamaiyo's circumcision. Do you know what this is? What it is to do this to a girl?"

Annie Vo nodded, her face barely concealing her revulsion.

Conrad asked, "I'm sorry, but what do you mean?"

LuAnna said, "I know they take the hat off boys when they're babies, but yeah, what's there to lop off of a gal's suzy?"

"Everything." Tally was either matter-of-fact, or masking a painful memory with practiced reserve. "With a dirty blade, the old woman cut everything away from me. She was nearly blind. Back and forth she cut me, like a saw. I thought I would die from pain. Then she sewed me all together again. Inside, I am still a woman. Outside, I am scars on scars. There was bleeding and infection. I was close to death for months."

LuAnna's hands involuntarily covered her groin. "Jesus wept, honey-girl. That's horrible!"

Tally went on, "Auntie is my father's brother's wife. She is from the Samburu people, and she has money, so my father and mother listen to her. It was too late for me, but I would not let them do this thing to Chamaiyo."

"Of course not," said Annie Vo, with a glimmer of compassion in her eyes. "So you ran."

Tally explained, "Soon we were starving, dying of thirst. We joined with a group of Al Shabaab fighters."

"That's Al Qaeda. In Somalia. I was just shooting at them last month. Nice company," said Annie Vo.

Tally defended herself. "It was that or die! They trained us. We stayed with them for a year, until they ran low on cash. They sold us. Documents must have been forged, or stolen. We were brought here on an airplane."

Conrad asked, "How many of you are there?"

"We saw only three others, but where they held us, we could hear many more. I think there are at least twenty, perhaps thirty."

"All that muscle must be in place there to keep a sizeable bunch in line," agreed LuAnna.

"And you don't know where they kept you?" Conrad asked. "Or who's running the show?"

Tally said, "I have no idea. It was dark. I ran along a shore. I could not see any stars. I stole a small boat. With the cold, I could not stay awake any longer. But the name I kept hearing the guards mention was Chalk."

"Oh my blessing. I should call Ben," said LuAnna. She pulled out her sat-phone.

"Wait," said Annie Vo. "Is Chalk the one from before? He was in the news for a time?"

"That's him. He's no piece of work," LuAnna said, in the sideways manner of Smith Island.

Annie Vo said, "And he's likely connected to black-ops folks, which means your call could be tracked. Don't light Ben up like that. Not yet."

"If the fun starts tonight, we don't have a lot of time," said LuAnna.

Annie Vo said, "We need to find Pap."

"Do you know where he is?" LuAnna asked her sister-in-law.

"Haven't seen him in a while," said Annie Vo, "but I heard he might be local."

Conrad gave a short, grim laugh. "Ain't nobody knows where Dick Blackshaw is, even when you're staring dead at him. But I got a fair notion where he *might* be."

CHAPTER 81

THE FISHING ARK was canted at a slight angle. The scow it was built upon lay on shore, drawn up past high tide beneath the sweeping boughs of a large willow whose roots rucked the scow's bottom; the roots drew fresh water from the stream running down to the marshy shore from the small island's interior.

An older man with a salt-and-pepper beard, a dark mustache, and longer hair that was also running gray, brought a combat knife with him out the door at the end of the shanty. He carved a small patch of bark from the willow tree's broad trunk, popped it in his mouth, and softened it with spit and the occasional grinding chomp between his molars. The salicin in the bitter chew would help with the fever he had been fighting. He cut another piece of bark to make tea later, and a third slice for when the chunk parked in his cheek was spent.

He gazed around him and noted the willow was leafing out beautifully. Its roomy canopy made a fine screen to hide the ark from every vantage, particularly from the air. He was grateful the marshes of Lethe Island lay under none of the approaches or departures from any of Washington, D.C.'s three major airports. Private pilots liked their altitude over the Chesapeake, unless they were emboldened by a second engine, floats, booze, or a new girlfriend to fly lower. Privacy was important to this man.

When the hermit had first towed the old ark to the island one cool quiet night with waves nearly flat, it had been loaded with stores and building materials, wood, and tarpaper, as well as hand tools. He had completed the ark's refurbishment during the late winter months that, thank God, finally seemed to be backing off and giving quarter to Spring.

The eight by ten foot shelter was luxurious compared to many of his past hides. He had forgotten that when he lived aboard during the shad runs with his grandfather in the upper bay decades before, the warmth of the stove tended to shrink the wall boards, admitting breeze and gale as they pleased. Tarpaper and caulk helped with drafts now, but on days darkened by the foulest weather, he still kept to the lower bunk, rising from beneath fleece and sleeping bag only to refuel the smokeless alcohol stove, make coffee, or warm something from a can to keep body and soul together.

Though alone, he felt embarrassed. He hated to confess even to himself that this spring was a blessing; to witness its coming, to still be alive after all he had endured, to feel the chill slowly seep out of his body. When had he gotten so old?

Returning to the ark, he checked on the plump coot simmering in the pot. It was coming along nicely. He had trapped the bird earlier that morning. The thing looked like a duck, but it was more closely related to the crane family. True to form, it had fought him like hell to the end. The few seasonings he added brought back more memories of his grandfather, and his cantankerous brand of wisdom. He marveled at the way the aromas acted like a time machine, or worse, a witch's concoction. He was never sure if he did the traveling back to earlier days, or if his specters were tracking the cooking smells from the other side of the veil, and tolling in to haunt him in the present hour. The thoughtful man stirred the pot, wondering if he were a grandfather yet.

The sound of a boat engine intruded on his musings. He listened for a few moments, and determined the rumble was drawing closer. He turned off the stove, reached for his Beretta 96 A1 .40 pistol, and tucked it in his field jacket's lower cargo pocket. Then he grabbed the carry handle of his L1A1 Self-Loading Rifle, which was the Commonwealth version of the Belgian FN FAL. Stuffing extra magazines and Cliff Bars in his other pocket, and slinging a canteen across his chest, he opened the ark's door and disappeared.

CHAPTER 82

CHALK DESCENDED THE stairs toward the holding corridor. Just behind him followed Seb Kentish and Rolly Mulgrew, their Glocks and LED flashlights trained into the darkness. As they stepped past Martin Jasper, nobody stopped to check his pulse. He lay flopped on his side, his head down on the staircase, his boots splayed toward the top landing, with a drying seep of blood to point the way down the next few steps.

Chalk said, "If Jasper here is still breathing, he's making a damn shitty job of it."

"Dirt nap," muttered Mulgrew.

"How old is this kid supposed to be?" Chalk had quizzed Rookard about anything Jasper had told him, but the little man was rattled and shaky on details. Best he could tell, this escapee was the little sister of the day's first runner. So it seemed that being a complete pain in the ass was part of this family's DNA.

Kentish answered, "At least twelve."

Chalk said, "Right. Said something like that on the roster."

They reached the second landing, and Chalk did not scruple at Mulgrew being the first to put his face and gun barrel around the left-hand corner and look down the next flight of steps.

Mulgrew leaned over the landing. Suddenly, his pistol discharged, deafening in the confines of the corridor, and he staggered back clutching his face. The back of his hand also bled in a rush.

"Damn!" shouted Mulgrew. "She cut me! My eye!"

There was a whisper of shuffling around the corner. It receded down the stairs to silence.

Seb Kentish said, "Where's your weapon?"

Mulgrew was yanking a trauma dressing out of his right thigh cargo pocket. Then he tore it open with his teeth and slapped it against his face. "She was right there! I looked around and she fucking cut me and grabbed my gun! *Fuck* this!" Mulgrew retreated up the stairs, swearing as the slash into his face really started to burn.

Kentish pointed his Glock at Mulgrew's retreating back. Chalk put his hand on his operator's wrist, and nodded back down the stairway. "Nice thought, compadre. I hate inefficiency like crazy, myself, but I need you to *not* finish that bitch's dirty work for her."

Kentish seemed reluctant to pull his sights off of Mulgrew's T2 vertebra, but he harnessed his homicidal urges, and refocused on the escapee. Before rounding the corner that had proven Mulgrew's undoing, he stepped back a pace from the left wall. Chalk drew his pistol, and nodded. Kentish lunged around the corner and pushed down the stairway, his under-the-barrel mounted LED cutting a swath of light through the dark.

Chalk waited patiently until Kentish said, "Clear! Boss, you're gonna-wanna see this."

"What ya got?"

"All the pens I can see are wide open. For sure all six in isolation," said Kentish. "They're empty."

Rage surged through Chalk. He was about to round the corner and head down the stairway to the holding level when a gunshot exploded against the cast cement walls and set his ears ringing.

Kentish was shouting, "Dammit! Shit! I'm hit! She fucking shot—"

Two more punishing reports echoed from below, and Kentish went quiet.

Chalk checked his descent and hugged tight against the wall. "Kentish? Seb?" He waited a moment and mumbled, "Not so clear after all." Then he shouted, "I'm coming for you kid! I'm coming for all of you!"

And with that, Chalk turned and scuttled quickly up the stairs through Jasper's and Mulgrew's blood for reinforcements.

CHAPTER 83

THE THOMPSONS WERE finally back at their home in Prince Frederick, Maryland. Special Agent Wilde had left them there with Special Agent Judith Heck and two other agents, all of whom had orders to continue learning as much as they could from the bereft couple, as well as to monitor every mode of electronic communication to the house.

The idea was for the empathetic Agent Heck and her team to provide Abigail and Mark a compassionate ear, a realistic sense of hope that their children would be found, and to constrain any rogue search and rescue efforts by the couple that were not part of the bureau's playbook.

They were also supposed to keep a watchful eye on the mailbox on the sidewalk thirty feet from the front door in case a ransom demand was delivered by hand, but that was unlikely, because at least eight local and national TV trucks were now stationed on the street. Reporters loitered waiting for statements, for interviews, for any change in the situation that they could spin into progress, or even restatements of the facts from a slightly new angle. It irked Wilde that all the arrayed investigative powers of the media were solely focused on the Thompson house where the emotion might first erupt, and not on finding the kids, which would do the most real good.

Molly Wilde finally had something she wanted: a few minutes alone in the bureau-issued Crown Victoria on her way to Calvert Memorial Hospital. She also had the Thompson's Kindertrek tracking device that at one point, perhaps as long as two years ago, had received a signal from Nicole

Thompson's flip-flop; a signal that would reach all of two miles. Wilde was not holding out much hope. The children, their shoes, and the dead chip could be hundreds of miles away already.

Senior Resident Agent Lowry wanted to meet her at the hospital to interview the French, possibly Canadian, John Doe recovered alive from the whirling boat that Wilde had spotted on the Chesapeake, and that the Natural Resources Police had intercepted. Doe was still in and out of consciousness. Lowry had all but begged the attending doctors to back off the sedation. Whenever Frenchy came to, word from his protection detail was that he continued to exhibit signs of shock and trauma, including altered mental status. Wilde knew why Lowry was eager to meet John Doe sooner rather than later. The woozy patient might blab something interesting in his delirium before he rallied his wits and lawyered-up.

En route to Calvert Memorial, Wilde detoured back to visit the waterfront crime scene, in case anything jumped out at her as unusual, off, or weird. When she was alone, she felt as though she had a different pair of eyes with which to see the world, and to understand how the case fitted into it. On a whim, she pressed the Kindertrek monitor's power button. The LCD screen was so pale a green, and so feeble, that Wilde's quick glances from the road to the monitor left her unsure if it was on, or if she was seeing the burned-in graphics one could always observe on such a device after even a few hours of use. She rooted in her purse, and was pissed to realize that her usual stash of AAA batteries was gone; she remembered that, weeks ago, she had given them all to a friend who still took pictures with an actual camera instead of a phone.

She turned on the radio to WMJS and tried hard not to tune away from Jackie DeShannon's *Put a Little Love in Your Heart*, lustily rendered by Annie Lennox. It was such a hopefilled song, but the lyrics ran strongly against the current of her downcast mood. Where were Nicole and Barry Thompson? Who had them? Who had so little love in their hearts that they could whisk kids away from all that was good in their lives?

Something was wrong with the song. Maybe the DJ left the mic open, and his mobile phone was chiming somewhere in the studio. There was a faint *bleep* that cropped up every few measures well off the song's 4/4 beat. She checked the dashboard. There were no check-engine lights or other urgent warnings that the oil pressure was dropping, or that the brakes were on the verge of failure. Perhaps it was her phone, warbling some kind of notification she had never heard before. The thing was new, and kept surprising her, sometimes in the middle of the night, with chirps and buzzes she had yet to fathom with anything but annoyance.

Something told Wilde to pick her shoulder bag up off the passenger seat. The Kindertrek, which had slipped beneath the satchel, bleeped at her. It was *working*. Her heart pounding, Wilde pulled over to the quiet roadside. She had to angle the Kindertrek's screen toward the windshield to improve visibility. The sound was probably nothing more than an audio alert that the device was powered up. Then she saw a dot blink, and when it did, the beep sounded again. Wilde turned off the car, and the song on the radio died with the engine.

She leaped out of the Crown Victoria, and held the Kindertrek aloft, like a desperate mobile phone user trying to eke out an extra signal bar on the edge of spotty rural cell coverage. She took a risk, and opened the little unit's battery compartment. Without shutting the Kindertrek down, she rolled the batteries around in their slots to rub any corrosion off the contacts. Closing the compartment, she looked back at the screen. It seemed just a little bit brighter. The dot winked again, and the little sound chip bleeped.

"Yes!" shouted Wilde. She quickly oriented herself with respect to the dot on screen, and found herself looking into a pine forest by the road. Without a second thought she jumped over the roadside ditch, and ran in among the trees. She glanced at the screen every few seconds as she jogged further through the pines. Maybe Wilde imagined it, but the dot seemed closer to the triangle fixed at the center of the screen, which represented her position. She pushed into the woods further, snagging her pants on sharp briars that were just starting to turn green. The dead pine needle carpet on the ground whispered to the living needles swaying in the trees above. She was going to find Hansel and Gretel with electronic breadcrumbs.

One more study of the Kindertrek screen, and she bore off to her left, to the north northeast, as far as she could determine. It was hard to understand the scale of the screen, except that the two mile range seemed to be represented in the one inch radius from triangle to the monitor's edge. By now, she saw that she had managed to bring the winking dot half the distance toward the triangle from where it first appeared. She was getting closer, but the scale was too small, coarse, and imprecise to really understand how far she still had to go. She kept running, but she also examined the sides of the Kindertrek case to see if there were some way to zoom the image in for more clarity and accuracy. The bleeping suddenly stopped.

"Fuck! No-no-no-no!" With a growing sense of fear, Wilde reopened the battery compartment, and rolled the batteries again. She snapped the compartment shut, and pressed the power button. The LCD screen illuminated, but the graphics were now very faint. She saw one blink, heard one bleep, before the screen completely shut down. She started running again in the last direction the device indicated. She tried to wait to let the old batteries rebound a little before pressing the power button again, but after only a few steps, she could not resist, and tried to start it. With her entire being concentrated on willing the little screen to light up just once more, Wilde sharply twisted her ankle on a fallen branch, and went down hard.

"Dammit!" she shouted. She tried to stand up, but her ankle shot spasms of pain up through her leg. As she collapsed, she loosed a barrage of epithets that momentarily silenced every bird within hearing. She reached for her shoulder bag. It wasn't there. With another curse, she envisioned it back in the car with her phone. After so jubilant a discovery as the semi-functional Kindertrek, her procedural deficiencies now brought her very low, filling her with self-recriminations. So stupid to run into the woods like an idiot. She should have checked in at the office first. She should have waited for another agent to join her. She should have watched her step like any normal person.

Wilde tested the branch that had tripped her up to see if it might now serve as a crutch or cane to get her back to the road and her car. She tried to stand again, but the branch's wood was punky, and it collapsed into crumbly brown fragments beneath the weight of her first step. She fell, and swore in utter frustration as much as acute pain.

"Lady? You okay?"

Wilde turned to see a woman looking at her from behind the giant dirt-caked root system of a fallen tree. "Oh thank God. I hurt my ankle. I'm an idiot. Could you please help me?"

The woman did not move. Instead, she said, "Hell of a day for a hike. And quite the outfit."

Wilde was still catching her breath, which the ankle pain had swept away. "I just need a hand to my car. It's back at the road." Wilde dug into her jacket pocket for her bureau identification. Something told her to stop, but once again, lower functions of thought overpowered her instincts, and she opened the wallet to reveal the ID. "Special Agent Molly Wilde. Federal Bureau of Investigation. What's your name?"

The woman stepped out from behind the wall of tree roots, and Wilde was not prepared for what she saw. Dressed in BDUs, her rescuer had a Glock in a holster at her thigh. The stranger carried a submachine gun, an MP5 by the looks of it, and it was aimed directly at Wilde's face. She also had a mouse brown mullet spiking out from beneath her fatigue cap.

Wilde's heart sank as her recollection kicked in. This was the woman from the barber shop.

Earline Byrd said, "My name is Take-Your-Fucking-Gun-Out-Nice-And-Slow."

CHAPTER 84

THE GATLING GUN was first conceived in its modern, multiple rotating coaxial barreled design in the 19th Century. Ellis believed that the larger caliber models of the weapon, and their most exotic ammunition, were created later in the 20th Century. During his time in Vietnam, he had always admired these armaments, particularly when twenty-millimeter types were hung out the port sides of AC-130 Spooky gunships providing him and his buddies with accurate, terrifying, and devastating close air support in tight firefights. The forward mounted, two-ton GAU-8 Avenger, with its six thirty-millimeter barrels and tank-busting spent-Uranium rounds became the favorite of later ground troops when it was brought to bear in a fight by the doughty Republic A-10 Warthog. But the unhallowed thing Ellis beheld in that dark old bunker turned his understanding of early rapid-fire weapons on its ear.

"Ben, what in the name of God is that thing, and why're you grinning?"

"I'm not sure, but swagger die, she puts our old market guns sorely to shame," said Ben, stepping closer to the murderous engine before him. He drew his thumb through the greasy dust obscuring the maker's plate machine-screwed to the monster's side beam. He read, "*Havokker.* Havoc, I'm guessing. Maybe Swedish? German? I don't know. Says here, *1877 No. 1.*"

Ellis said, "Bet she was the first and the last of her kind." Ellis approached the business end of the piece for a closer look. Six muzzles, each one sealed with an old wood and leather tompion, were arrayed in a hexagonal clock of death. He pulled one tompion out, and peered into the barrel. "Rifled," he observed. Unable to resist, he made a fist, and inserted it into the barrel. The great bore swallowed his entire hand without touching.

Ellis absently asked, "Ben, did I ever tell you about a gal I knew, Miss Tara Lee? I haven't thought of her in years."

"No, and you best not reminisce on her now. Disgusting."

Ellis said, "Didn't mean to offend your delicate punk-ass sensibilities." But he was still smiling. "How did ol' MacCatheter get ahold of this thing?"

"Money," said Ben. "And I bet she went cheap. Look at the workmanship on her. Beautiful even for an age where the most functional crap sported a grace note or two. Look at the tight tolerances. There's steel, brass, and bronze here. She was a whole lot o' Rosy even for this man's army. Gatling's smaller caliber stuff worked fine. This baby must have cost way too much for mass production."

Ben angled his light over the length of the weapon. "And the weight. She's got to be nigh on half a ton if she's an ounce." He ran his hands along the greased breach with its florentined arabesque etchings. "Maybe she was meant to guard a harbor from out of a fort, or mount an ironclad. Weren't no tanks to carry her back then. You'd need a team of draft horses to move it, and that's on dry, clear ground. Or a rail car, provided your fight was local to your train line. Those shorter barrels wouldn't give her much over-the-hill-and-through-the-woods kind of range."

Ellis respectfully noted, "But up close, she'd knock six good holes in something bad."

"I reckon more than that." Ben flipped a catch on the Havokker's breach, and extended a heavy brass two-foot crank with a mahogany handle. He pulled the crank through a half turn, and beautifully milled bronze reduction gears revolved the six barrels through a quarter turn of their own. "This is a Gatling style mechanism. Six locks would be plenty to fire six barrels if that's all you wanted to do. Then you could reload, and pop six more. But she was built for sustained, rapid, big-bore fire. But being so huge, she was ahead of her time."

Ben pulled a rotting wax cloth tarpaulin off the rest of the breach. "There you go." Two rectangular tompions lay in two recesses in the top of the breach. "Two receivers. Two feeds. Two magazines. Either two barrels fired at once, or—" Ben searched the back of the breach. "Now that's sweet. There's a little lever right there."

Ben moved the lever. "It toggles between two fancy etched letters, A and B. I reckon you could fire from one magazine, A, while a second magazine, B, got swapped out by the crew. Then flip that switch to letter B, and don't you think she fired out of magazine B while mag' A got changed out. She could shoot and shoot until she melted."

"Groovy. Why are we gabbing about this?" asked Ellis. "There's no ammo for it. And that, by the by, is another reason MacCatheter could snap her up for a surplus song. Every round would have to be turned pretty on a lathe. She was a cost-overrun before she ever let blood."

Ben looked around the cluttered low space. Toward the back, deep in the shadows of the bunker, he saw two wood crates. Using the old leaf spring as a crowbar, he jimmied the top crate open. Inside lay six enormous verdigris brass magazines in greased cloth wraps. Each magazine had an ornate handle bolted on top. He grabbed the handle and lifted. Outside of the crate, the magazine was shaped like an inverted teardrop. Ben guessed it weighed in north of fifty pounds. He shuffled over to the Havokker, removed one of the breach tompions, and wrestled the magazine up onto the breach until it snapped into its receiver. He repeated the process with a second magazine.

Ellis's head tilted sideways regarding the weapon. With the big teardrop magazines paired in place on the breach, they resembled the ears of a large mechanical mouse; the six barrels formed a deadly snout. "If Disney was a gunsmith, this is what you'd get."

Ben said, "Nothing funny about her. Let's break her down as small as we can, and get to hauling."

"Knew you were going to say something like that," Ellis unsnapped the first magazine, and carried it out of the dim bunker into the gray wet day.

CHAPTER 85

THE QUIET ROOM of Calvert Memorial Hospital was made easy to pick out by the presence of one female nurse, acting as a sitter, one male hospital security officer, and Sheriff Williams standing outside its door. Senior Resident Agent Lowry was disappointed that Special Agent Wilde was not already there. She'd had less distance to travel from the Thompson place than Lowry had to come from the office.

Sheriff Williams was holding a small water bottle in an awkward manner, by the cap. He stepped away from the Quiet Room door, and met Lowry halfway down the hall out of earshot from the nurse and the guard.

Williams spoke softly, "Jacques Doe's still in and out. The doc is easing up on the sedation like you asked, but that meant four-point restraints. You thirsty?" He held out the water bottle to Lowry.

"No, thank you—"

"I think you are," said Williams. "If you don't take this water, I'm going to get my feelings hurt."

"Sheriff?"

"There was a time about a half hour ago that the doc and the nurse were both out of the room. Jacques looked thirsty to me. I offered him this bottle."

"While he was restrained?"

"See, Agent Lowry, that's why you're a fed', and I'm just a county mounty. I didn't think it through. He took the bottle in his bare hand, but with his wrist strapped down, he plain refused to lift the bottle up to his mouth to drink from it, poor guy. So I took the bottle back. It felt like rejection."

Agent Lowry came close to smiling. He accepted the water bottle, and held it the way Sheriff Williams had held it, from the cap, knowing a decent set of Doe's prints could likely be lifted from its smooth sides. "Thank you sheriff. Seems I am a bit thirsty after all."

"Don't get me wrong, Agent Lowry. I'm this close to arresting him. He was aboard a boat full of bodies and body parts. Suspicion of murder would be easy, except that he was trussed up himself."

Lowry said, "I understand. So he's a person of interest for now."

"Exactly. He is not under arrest. So at the moment, he has neither waived nor requested an attorney."

"Good. About those body parts," began Lowry.

"By a show of hands, so to speak, one hand is missing," said the sheriff.

"Like, perhaps the one we found at the light station?"

"We've received no calls to be on the lookout for other missing hands today. I'll check my messages, of course, but for now, in this case, I think the hand at the lighthouse might go with the assortment of parts on the boat. There's definitely crush, disarticulation, and avulsion trauma, and burns on it."

"Two of a kind?" asked Lowry.

"Just playing the hand I'm dealt," said the sheriff without cracking a smile.

Agent Lowry checked his cellular phone. There was nothing from Agent Wilde to explain her absence. No voicemail message. Not text. No email. He felt the first stirrings of worry, but set them aside, unsure once again if this were normal, professional concern, or a symptom of his undeniable affection for her. "Sheriff, let's go see if Jacques Doe wants to chat."

CHAPTER 86

GERTIE THE DOBERMAN got loose from the *Winnie Estelle*'s galley when Uncle Conrad went aft for a coffee refill. She scampered up the two steps into the wheelhouse. With coaxing from LuAnna, Annie Vo, and Uncle Conrad, Tally eventually climbed down from the top berth where she had fled upon Gertie's appearance; petting the fierce-looking dog was still not something the refugee was prepared to do. Though LuAnna was chilly, she kept the wheelhouse doors and windows open because the dog was still a source of challenging aromas.

Kneeling by the lower berth, Annie Vo referred to the old charts that Conrad Bryce rarely glanced at anymore, and then she rose and looked out the forward window. "That's it? The one with the big willow tree?"

"Yep. Lethe Island," confirmed Conrad.

LuAnna said, "Sounds like a place you go to forget."

"Or to be forgotten," said Annie Vo.

"Water's deep enough for *Winnie* on the southeast approach," said Conrad. "Get us in right close to shore." Conrad looked down at his dog and said, "Gertie, *boots!*"

Gertie dashed out of the wheelhouse, and negotiated the steep stairway down into the hold like a goat. In less than a minute, she was back with a pair of rubber boots in her mouth. Conrad repeated the command twice more, and the dog left on two more trips, and returned with two more pairs of boots. LuAnna silently gave thanks she wore her own. Gertie fetched boots like a champ, but she had no notion of grabbing them in matching pairs.

Conrad goosed the throttle, nosing *Winnie Estelle*'s bow into a gut wide enough to afford a dignified step from the mid-ships ladder into the marsh. He walked a small anchor forward, and swung it hard into the wet earth. He said, "We won't be here long."

"If we surprise Pap," said Annie Vo, "it won't be long at all."

"If he's here, reckon he already knows we are," avowed Conrad.

"You like to make him sound spooky," LuAnna said. It had been more than fifteen years since she had set eyes on the object of their search.

Conrad smiled, "If the shoe fits—"

The three women sloshed after Conrad into the reeds lining a planked gut, crossing a small peninsula. The gut wended toward the great willow tree. Gertie ranged ahead. They heard her splashing in the cattails after a muskrat, a Doberman raised like a Chesapeake Bay retriever. She bounded happily back to Conrad wet and stinking.

Fifteen minutes later, they stepped out of the gut into the shade of the willow. The ark, with its shanty, lay to the left, but Conrad's eyes were on the willow tree's trunk. "He ain't ailing none."

Conrad pointed to the places where bark had been freshly cut from the trunk. In spite of their disparate backgrounds, the women, who at some point had all lived and breathed in close harmony with the land and water, understood what the excisions in the willow meant.

"Hello the boat!" shouted Conrad.

They got no answer. Gertie put her nose to the ground, nuzzling the ark near the shanty's doorway. With her stump of a tail wagging from her heat diaper, she barked once and dashed into the reeds, but not the way they had walked in.

LuAnna quipped into the quiet rustle of cattails and swaying willow tendrils, "Reckon Timmy's stuck in the well, or some such."

Conrad chuckled, but Annie Vo and Tally gave LuAnna baffled looks.

Sitting down with a groan on the ark's gunwale, Conrad produced a flask from a coat pocket and nearly tilted it to his lips when he caught LuAnna's disapproving eye. "It's black tea, all right? No cream nor sugar. Don't let it get around it ain't whisky nor coffee, or folks won't know it's me."

"Your secret's safe," assured LuAnna.

In the distance, they heard Gertie bark, and then whimper.

Conrad said, "Everybody got your hands empty and plain to sight?"

Tally pulled her chilly fingers slowly out of her pockets. LuAnna and Annie Vo stood still. They watched the reeds from the direction of Gertie's ruckus.

A low graveled voice spoke from behind them. "I got a coot in the pot. Won't be much to go around. A taste might be worse than nothing."

Without moving, Conrad said, "True enough, the way you cook."

LuAnna turned slowly and saw Richard Willem Blackshaw grinning at them. He stood ten feet from the reeds, and well into the clearing. How he had got there unseen and so quietly was anyone's guess.

Conrad asked, "What you done to my dog, Dickie-Will?"

Dick Blackshaw pulled the wrapper of a Cliff Bar from his pocket. "Puppy crack. Also known as peanut butter crunch."

Gertie trotted happily into the clearing, her tongue working forcefully around inside her mouth to dislodge delicious morsels of the treat from between sharp white teeth. She bustled straight over to Dick Blackshaw, her hindquarters swinging, and her head low in submission to this human god of earthly delights.

"Hey Annie Vo." Blackshaw pecked his daughter on the cheek. "Lordy go to fire, is that LuAnna?"

LuAnna gave her father-in-law an awkward embrace. "Been a while, Mr. Blackshaw."

"Now I *do* feel old," said their host.

"You look it, but I'm still not going to call you Dickie-Will," said LuAnna.

"For which I'll thank ye kindly. How's about *Pap*? Will that suit, seeing as how we're family'n all?"

"We'll have to see about all that," said LuAnna.

Blackshaw cast a look at Tally. "Let's get inside out of this chill," he said. The others felt the day to be mild enough compared to the winter dwindling behind them, but they followed him inside.

Thirty minutes later, when clean dishes lay drying on the small sideboard, and the coot's carcass simmered in broth with vegetables for soup,

Blackshaw mused aloud, "I hadn't planned to saddle up again for a good month or three. My dose of lead poisoning in Mali left me feeling puny. Friends, never get shot in the buttock unless you like to be the object of ridicule. And what the heck is Forrest Gump anyway? Swagger die I been called that plenty since my wounding."

LuAnna said, "Sorry to wreck your me-time, but I think Ben's already committed to the mission, on the strength of Tally's situation."

Tally said, "He cannot do this alone."

Dick Blackshaw groped, "He's got you. All of you. And Ellis! Him and Ellis are unbeatable. They'll get your sister back ship-shape, Tally, if you all throw in together and pull your weight."

No one looked Blackshaw in the eye; too embarrassed.

LuAnna said, "If not for her sister, then help your own son! My husband! What changed between last fall and now? What happened to you?"

"I was out of my depth then. I'm out of the game now," said Blackshaw. "There comes a time in every man's life—"

Conrad blurted out, "Oh shut up, Dick. I thought you were the big bad merc', but now I get it."

Conrad got up and made his way over the tangle of feet and around knees in the tight quarters toward the shanty's door. "Thanks for the coot, anyway. It tasted terrible."

Annie Vo was the next to depart. As she went, Blackshaw said, "Annie-honey, you're young. You don't know."

Annie Vo did not answer. She didn't even look at him.

As the door slammed shut behind Annie Vo, LuAnna quietly rose to follow her. Blackshaw said, "LuAnna, you was ever the prissy little prig."

LuAnna's hand twitched and jerked, and before Dick could move, her knife was pressing at the crotch of his pants. "And I'm quick, Mr. Blackshaw. You forgot *quick*."

Now Blackshaw was alone with Tally. She gazed at him with the kind of loathing that she had first shown Ben. She said, "Your son is a good man, sir. But not because of you. You have nothing to teach him."

Blackshaw yelled at her back, "Thanks, kid. Sorry they cut up on your suzy!"

After Tally left the shanty, Dick Blackshaw listened to the wind building through the willow tree. It shuddered the ark, and though the stove was on, he felt the chilling gusts work deep into his heart. Why had he said such a horrible thing? Something had taken him over, and made him lash out at a young woman who was already grievously wounded by the brutal custom of her people; by her own family, to which she could never return. He was less a man now for speaking like a petty fiend. Dick Blackshaw suddenly felt the cumulative effects of war after war, firefight after bloody skirmish, the agonizing death of friends; it all welled up into his frayed psyche. He wrenched the collar of his coat open and burst out of the close, choking shanty to draw a breath of air. Cold sweat coursed down his back. His body shook.

The clearing under the willow was empty. His needful drop-in guests were gone and good riddance, but a resurgence of fog was making it hard to see all the way across to the reeds.

"I gave plenty!" he shouted to the wind. "I gave everything! I *bled*! I made you rich! I saved your hides. You'd be dead a hunnerd times without *me*!"

Richard Blackshaw heard the warble and skirl of a red-winged black bird. Then the Caterpillar engine of *Winnie Estelle* roared to life. He stayed outside until the throb of the motor receded from his chest, leaving a galactic emptiness in the air around him despite the whispers of the marsh.

"Dickie-Will, I might have gone off loving you, but I was never, ever ashamed of you 'til now."

Blackshaw picked the lone figure out of the murky distance. "Who's there?"

The figure drew closer, but Blackshaw did not retreat. He had not seen this woman in more than fifteen years, but in that time she often appeared to him out of the scorched wastes of his past. His son had located the lonely spot in the marsh where she had been murdered a decade and a half before. She had loved the wild, free air of the place in all seasons. With love and wisdom, Ben had left her remains undisturbed after the grim discovery.

She never spoke in these visions. She would manifest, sometimes when he dreamed, sometimes when he woke. She would give him that look of hers, the one glance, her head cocked a little to one side; that quizzical regard that spoke volumes of his shortcomings. Then she usually faded away, leaving him alone to stew in his regrets, like the coot in the pot on his stove in the shanty, but never so savory.

Instead of vanishing, she was now drawing closer to Blackshaw through the mist. He watched her approach with particular care this time. Usually, she appeared to be as young as the day he first met her. This apparition was older. The beauty was all there, and the agitation it caused in his heart, but so were streaks of gray in her hair, and lines around her eyes.

She stood directly in front of Dick Blackshaw now. The fever must be doubling back something fierce. He imagined he could hear her breathe, see the rise and fall of her breast, discern tears in her eyes. The phantom woman coiled her arm behind her and swung hard. The sting of her open-handed slap blazed across his face, dazing him into a tripping stagger, and assaulting him with an impossible truth.

CHAPTER 87

CHAMAIYO YANKED NICOLE by the hand through the dark corridor; she in turn drew Barry, her sobbing twin brother, along behind her. A younger white man, Abel, with an angel's eyes and a belly swaying down nearly to his private parts assisted a pregnant woman of Hispanic descent along the passage. Ascensión ran in a half-crouch, covering the nipples of her swollen breasts with a forearm, and her pubis with her other hand, keeping her rump toward the wall. All but Chamaiyo, who had stripped Kentish of his shirt, were still naked, the way they had been held captive; the way they had been born. Their will to live, to move away from those cells, overcame their natural modesty.

Chamaiyo still carried the guns she had taken from Meeker and Kentish, as well as a knife, keys, and radio all curled in the crook of her thin brown arm like loose groceries. They were three turns into the corridor, but only fifty yards away from their holding pens.

Abel said, "Little lady, you sure you don't want me to hold one of those guns?"

Chamaiyo stopped the small procession, dropped the keys and the radio, shined the searing light directly in Abel's pretty eyes, and aimed the pistol at him. "I am sure. If you try to take it from me, I will kill you." Then she handed the knife and a pistol to Ascensión. "I will try to get you all to safety." To Ascensión, she said, "If he gets close to me, you can stick him. Or shoot him."

Ascensión nodded to Chamaiyo, then glared at Abel. She growled, "Damn right, Penis de Milo. And if you rub your dick on my backside one more time I will cut it off, shoot it, and make you eat it. I'm pregnant. There are children present. Show some fucking respect."

For Abel's part, he took Chamaiyo and Ascensión at their word, held up his hands palms outward, and said, "Take it easy. No harm meant."

Chamaiyo collected the keys and the radios, and led them onward through the dark maze.

CHAPTER 88

ELLIS EXAMINED THE Havokker gun belayed on *Miss Dotsy*'s deck. Then he checked the lashings on the weapon's dismantled carriage, which now lay forward of the engine box. The waves were mounting, and if any of these heavy elements began to work loose, they would punch out the deadrise's sides taking everything and everyone to the bottom in a few hectic seconds. Ben worked the tiller fore and aft with vigor and care, as though he were stirring a death-defying recipe in the waters of the Chesapeake Bay.

It was clear to Ben, to anyone, that this was no ordinary fog. It seemed that an entire low pressure weather system of purple-gray nimbostratus cloud, complete with embedded thunderstorms, had descended to earth across a front of hundreds of miles. It was that, or the hand of God, and Ben was not sure which worried him more.

Ellis yelled aft, "Ben, are you sure you want to do this? I'm experiencing grave misgivings."

"This isn't exactly top of my druthers either, but Chalk's got to go. Problem is, soft targets in amongst the hard," said Ben. "This Havokker's strictly a last resort."

"You ever lay hands on a gun you didn't come to use?"

Ben did not answer.

Ellis said, "That's what I thought. *Last resort*. That's rich. So what's the game?"

Ben regarded Ellis quietly for a moment. Then he said one word. "*Herculaneum.*"

Ellis let his breath out slowly. "In that case, I got a couple calls to make."

PART III
HERCULANEUM

CHAPTER 89

TALLY TOUCHED LUANNA on the arm. With no cargo as ballast, *Winnie Estelle* was rolling hard over the quartering waves. In the pitching wheelhouse, LuAnna first thought Tally had grabbed hold to steady herself, but a look at her face set her straight.

"What is it?" LuAnna asked.

"I remember something, but I cannot understand it," said Tally.

Annie Vo and Conrad began to listen.

Tally said, "Moons. I was running away this morning, from that place. It was dark, and there were clouds and rain, but I saw great moons. Two, maybe three. Pale and yet dark. I thought they would crush me. How can you see moons below clouds?" Tally paused, frustrated by this germ of a memory that refused to grow. "It must have been a dream when I was sleeping in the boat."

Annie Vo asked, "Conrad? Do you know what she means?"

Conrad shook his head. "Ain't seen sun, nor stars, nor moon in a couple-two-three days."

"Chamaiyo is there," said Tally, her spirits low and aching. "How could I leave my sister, and not remember the way back to her? I promised I would come for her."

LuAnna asked her, "Were the moons all close together like?"

Tally looked up with a glint of hope in her eyes. "Very close together. In the rain and fog, they left me wondering. They could have crushed me though I ran away from them." Tally looked at the cuts on her hands, and remembered more. "And I climbed under a high fence through a stream."

LuAnna said, "Moons and a fence. I think I know where they had you, girl. Reckon I know where your sister is."

Annie Vo cleared her throat, and said, "Uh, Sis? Would you help me vang down the main boffindangles by the forward poopdeck bumkin-sprit?"

LuAnna raised her eyebrows. "They come loose *again*?" She scolded her bewildered uncle, "Told you to have them boffindangles seen to."

Annie Vo and LuAnna made their way forward along *Winnie Estelle*'s heaving deck. LuAnna was glad the old boat's yachtification from her original design included bronze stanchions, lifelines, and top-to-bottom webbing to keep the landlubbers from rolling into the soup after a highball. The women began idly recoiling and bowsing the forward mooring lines while they spoke. Waves and spray drenched them to the skin.

"We couldn't have gone aft to the galley for coffee?" complained LuAnna.

Annie Vo ignored the lament. "You believe her sudden recollection? *Crushing moons and fences* and all that?"

"Oh *hell* no," said LuAnna turning her back to a wave dashing over the bow. "Tally's been trying to marshal some help all day. I think that operator back on the old ship made her think twice about going in with just me once we didn't meet back up with Ben. And when Dickie-Will went piss-yellow on us, she likely figured the head-count's as good as it's ever going to be before the deadline. No offense to your pappy."

Annie Vo asked, "None taken. I've never seen him like this. You think that's all Tally's angle is. Wrangling conscripts?"

"Can't know for sure 'til we're there."

"Okay," said Annie Vo, still looking troubled. "Then we're good going in, just us. Still want to call Ben?"

"He's probably worried sick. And Ellis is a dab hand on a gun, but they've both been through the mangle lately, I don't have to tell you." LuAnna's resolve stiffened. "No, Chalk would kill Ben on sight for a few million personal reasons. Without Ben along, Chalk likely won't know me to see me. His goons might back off if we make it hot enough and not worth the trouble to stand and fight."

"So it's just us girls, and Conrad. I like your style, lady."

"Don't forget Gertie. And who in fuck are you calling *lady*, anyway? Let's get back to the wheelhouse."

"No," countered Annie Vo. "Let's go below to the hold. Got a few toys to show you."

CHAPTER 90

CHALK LED ROLLY Mulgrew, whose slashed cheek was now crudely stitched and dressed, and Wendy Peltier down the dark echoing stairway past Martin Jasper's body. Chalk reflected that it appeared too late for Jasper to benefit from chilling in the walk-in freezer.

Peltier stopped to examine the dead man. She said, "Sweet Jesus. She shanked him up from under the bottom of his vest. A *kid* did that?"

"She's short," snarled Chalk. "Scalping wasn't in the cards, hermana."

They continued down the stair to the next turn. With a nudge from Chalk, Mulgrew went down and around the corner first, quickly followed by Peltier. After a tasteful interval of quiet, Chalk followed. They stepped farther downward.

"Where are the lights?" demanded Chalk.

"Off," observed Mulgrew.

"Thank you, Overlord Cocktard of the Obvious. Here." Chalk passed Mulgrew and Peltier two night vision goggle sets, and donned his own. After a few moments warming up, the corridor glimmered from twilight to a sparkling tourmaline. Emboldened by a better view, they descended to the next corner.

"Bunch of Slinkys is all you are," muttered Chalk.

The NVGs pressed painfully on Mulgrew's cheek stitches. In a foul mood, he got pissed. "What the hell do you mean, *Slinkys?*"

"Completely useless, but still kinda fun to shove down a flight of steps." Chalk did not openly acknowledge an operator's secondary value of absorbing bullets meant for him.

They came to Sebastian Kentish's body next. He had had been stripped of his gear, and his shirt.

Quickly examining the remains, Peltier said, "One shot to the leg. One under the vest in his gut. One above the vest in his neck. Kid's got a real knack."

"It's all these open, empty stalls that're getting me down," said Chalk, surveying the dungeon.

Mulgrew said, "Here's the light switch."

"Keep them off," ordered Chalk. "I want to see this runner before she clocks me."

The trio moved forward again.

"Isn't this something we should be reporting to DePriest?" asked Peltier.

"Big fat no," said Chalk. "Let's not worry his bubble head about it. We'll have this set right in under an hour, tops. Be the dark, Wendy. Be the dark."

They carefully rounded two more turns.

Mulgrew whispered, "You hear that?"

"Nope," said Chalk. "What you got?"

"Up ahead. Sounded like—"

A single gunshot assaulted their eardrums. The back of Mulgrew's skull voided most of his brain matter through a gaping exit wound as he dropped to the floor. Chalk and Peltier slammed their backs to the walls. They both snapped off a few rounds down the corridor for suppressing fire, and maybe a lucky hit.

Chalk pulled out his handkerchief and wiped blood from the lenses of his NVGs. "You good?"

Peltier said, "Yeah. Mulgrew bit it."

"I noticed. Which means we're getting close! On me, baby! Let's run the little fox to ground!" Chalk holstered his pistol, swung his MP-5 from his back, and dashed onward down the corridor, baying like a rabid hound and blasting singles and double shots into the distance, thrilling whenever a ricochet hummed, zinged or trilled off the walls like an old Western.

CHAPTER 91

AGENT WILDE HAD heard of a rifle butt to the head, but coming to with the mother of all migraines brought the concept home hard. The woman who took Wilde prisoner had walked her at gunpoint into a building that lay in the shadow of several gigantic above-ground spherical tanks. Wilde knew where she was, but no one else did. At least, not anyone she relied on for help.

Once inside the building, her captor had simply struck her down without ceremony. Now, the welting knot on the back of her head throbbed, but rubbing her fingers together after touching the wound, she was relieved to discover she had bled only a little. The shattering pain in her head and twinging through her ankle added to her ripening sense of futile stupidity. There was no reason for her to be here. With a modicum of patience, she could have avoided putting herself in mortal danger.

She lay in a total darkness that stank of animal filth. The chills running along her body let her know she was utterly naked before she moved an inch. Now humiliation fused with her newfound shame.

Wilde carefully crawled on hands and knees until her fingers detected a cinderblock wall. Slowly standing, and testing the ankle, the darkness and the head injury teamed to whirl her equilibrium into nauseating spins, dips, dives and loops. She pressed against the wall with both hands until the dizzy black world steadied. Edging along the wall to her left, she kicked what felt and sounded like an empty metal bucket. That din rebooted the pain in her head and unleashed another woozy spell. Groping for the bucket, she threw up in it, which compounded the blitzing headache. Slowly, she began to fear she might be more seriously injured than just a crack on the noggin.

She was thankful the bucket turned out to be the only obstruction other than the three corners of her cell before she encountered the door. There was no nob or lever, locked or otherwise, to yank on. She let her hands trace a grid pattern to see if there were some other kind of locking mechanism. She discovered a gap about three inches high and one foot wide at the bottom of the door, likely for passing in plates of food. At eye level, she found a window about one foot square with a welded metal lattice that permitted observation of the captive.

Wilde skipped back involuntarily when she heard a series of gunshots and distant shouts echoing down the hall. She thought she heard a howling dog, but could not be sure. Groping blind, she limped to the cell's back wall and crouched down, making herself small.

In the quiet, Wilde heard the furtive footfalls of several heavy-shod in-dividuals approach. The steps halted at her door. An older man's gravelly voice said, "Who the fuck is *that?*"

A woman answered, "Earline said she detained a snooper."

Gravel Voice carped, "Jesus H. Christ of the Housatonic! Who are you honey?"

Wilde remembered the man's tones from her eerie encounter with the fog-shrouded fishing boat that morning. With the barriers of water, mist, distance, and clothing stripped away, she felt a dread she had never before experienced. For this man to see her in this pitch blackness, he and his partner had to be using night vision gear.

Wilde said, "Hi Maynard. How're they biting?"

She heard a snort, an intake of breath, and a few scuffs, as if someone stepped back in surprise.

"Who are you?" demanded Chalk.

"Special Agent Molly Wilde, Federal Bureau of Investigation."

"I see. I didn't recognize you with your clothes off."

Wilde held up the middle finger of her left hand. "Green's not my color."

"Hey, missy! I'm going to bite that finger off myself."

Now Wilde was sure he could see her plainly.

"How do you know my name?" demanded Chalk.

"You're famous," said Wilde. "Taking the twins was a real mistake, Maynard, like taking me. Not to mention leaving body parts of your crew all over town. Sloppy. There's a task force looking for you right now. This would be a really good time to open this door and fade away. We'll catch you, but I'd remember you let me go instead of fucking up my manicure."

Chalk was quiet for a moment. "Hah! I'm going to *start* by eating your hand."

"Great. Then I can fist you from the inside. You're call."

The woman with Chalk said, "I think I hear them, sir. Down this way."

"Hey, don't run off," said Wilde. "You just got here. Could I bum a cigarette? You know. For the condemned."

"I don't smoke," growled Chalk.

The woman with Chalk said, "Sure, I got one."

"Hurry it up," ordered Chalk. "Think I'm going to get some fags for next time, and put the whole pack out on your rosy little neeps."

The female operator ignored Chalk. "Menthol Newports okay?"

"I heard they make your lungs bleed, but under the circumstances—"

When the woman spun the striker wheel on her Zippo, the light from the little flame was dazzling. While the woman pushed the butt of the cigarette through the grate, Wilde got a clear look at Maynard Chalk. He had taken his night vision gear off look back at her, too. He was older, puffy, with a white scar across his receding hairline. His eyes were piggy, but bright with madness and hate. Wilde would not forget him.

The female operator made sure the cigarette was glowing and snapped the lighter shut. In the renewed darkness, Wilde took a deep drag and felt her lungs open to the acrid smoke like an old friend.

Chalk said, "I'll be back to deal with you, Sugar-Tits. You and I got a date."

Wilde heard the steps quietly recede down the corridor. Her body began shaking with fear. After a few blind, halting steps, she crouched like an animal against the back wall again. Antagonizing a captor ran against every chapter and every verse of her bureau training. She was losing her mind on this case, but the cigarette tasted wonderful. After a few more drags, she jammed it into the wall and watched the tiny orange sparks cascade and wink out.

Suddenly Wilde heard another sound at her door. It was the unmistakable clunk of a big lock turning. Wilde whispered, "Who's there?"

In answer, she heard a scraping along the floor that stopped several feet from where she crouched. She twisted into a ball, thinking Chalk snuck back and rolled a grenade in through the door gap to keep her company.

When nothing exploded after several moments, she whispered a tentative, "Hello?"

She heard nothing more. She crept forward, gently patting the floor, not sure what she might find. To her astonishment, her left hand came to rest on top of a pistol. By feel, she instantly knew it was a Glock. She slowly racked the slide, and found a round already chambered. Then she ejected the magazine and probed it end to end. It was full. She replaced the magazine immediately in the pistol with a satisfying snap.

Hope flooded Wilde's nervous system like the nicotine had done moments before. She inched forward again on all fours through the dark until she reached the wall with the door in it.

"Hello?" she whispered.

She heard no shouts of alarm; no murmurs of conspiratorial intrigue. No answer came at all.

On impulse, Wilde pushed the door. To her surprise, it swung open with a few pounds of pressure. She suspected it was a trap Chalk had laid to buoy her spirits before he got serious about torturing her to death. She failed to understand who would go to the trouble of taking her prisoner, and then cut her loose. Her head still blasting with pain, she laid that question aside.

For now, no one shot at her. Nobody kicked or punched her. No phantom maniac in the dark slashed at her. She was free. She was armed. Wilde turned in the direction Chalk had taken, and feeling carefully along the corridor wall, she hobbled after him.

CHAPTER 92

THE HAVOKKER CARRIAGE weighed nearly as much as the weapon by the time Ben and Ellis had it assembled on the wooded shore north of the LNG terminal. When they lowered the trunnions down onto the carriage, its two wheels began sinking in the rain-soaked soil; no matter that their double-spoke design was widened with sheet metal rims like the drive wheels of an old steam tractor.

"No wonder this thing never found a market," said Ellis.

Dusk was closing in around them, adding to the fog's gloom. Both men turned when they heard rustling in the distant ground cover. Two silhouettes approached through the mist.

Ben recognized Sonny Wright's voice immediately when his grouchy neighbor said, "Found this one looking all lost and forlornsome, and throwing your name around, Ellis. Should I kill him?"

Sonny materialized out of the fog with his shotgun trained on a young man in fatigues toting a tactical medic's backpack. He also sported a holster meant for a sidearm, but that was empty.

Ellis said, "I wish you wouldn't just yet. How you been keeping, Vincent?"

"Never better, 'til a few minutes ago." To Sonny, the new guy said, "Can I have my piece back?"

Sonny grinned. "Any friend of Ellis is probly a sumbitch, but it's good enough for me." He drew a Beretta from the depths of his coat pocket, and passed it to Vinny, who checked the weapon and holstered it.

"Vinny's our patch-up man. You want him in your corner. Wished we had him on the last couple go-rounds," explained Ellis. "Anyway, I served with his grandfather. I said I'd help the kid with a new set of rims for his truck if he threw in with us tonight."

"Rims is coming out of your end of the money, Ellis. That's all I've got to say on it," declared Sonny.

Ellis glared as if Sonny were actually reaching into his back pocket. "Like always, Sonny. No fear on that."

Ben held out his hand to the newcomer. "Ben Blackshaw. Welcome aboard."

"Vinny DeRosa. Happy to be aboard."

Four more figures took shape out of the fog. Reverend Mosby led Art Bailey and Orville Hurley. Last, and most disturbing to Ben and Ellis , came Mary Joyce, widow of the late Wade, whom Sonny had gunned down only this morning. Everyone carried 12 gauge pump guns; some weapons were newly fitted with ten-shot magazine extensions.

Ben took Sonny aside and spoke softly. "Care to explain how Mary comes to be here? Or any of the others, for that matter?"

"I was so mad at how folks done you down when you called on us, I went 'round and had a talk with them," said Sonny. "It didn't take much. Seems they don't like the way all the new money from last fall is making them feel, how to put it—*soft*. You woke the picaroon in 'em, Ben. In all of us. Over winter, I guess they dozed off. You're welcome."

Ben glanced over his shoulder at the widow, who smiled at him. "And Mary? Does she even know about Wade?"

"I told her first thing," said Sonny in a matter of fact way Ben could not reconcile with the grim circumstances.

"You did? That's—bold."

Sonny looked down at his boots, abashed. "You been gone off the island, Ben. Facts are facts. Mary didn't like how the money changed Wade. I won't carry tales, nor speak ill of the dead, but them two ain't been how you'd say cozy in a long half-while. It was stormy betwixt 'em. He laid hands on her, and more'n once. Mary and I, truth is—we've been keeping company. There. I said it."

Ben was stunned. He escorted Sonny back to where his friends were admiring the Havokker. Mary slipped her hand into Sonny's and gave it a squeeze before letting go.

Ben signaled to Ellis for a short confab. When they were far enough from the group to be out of earshot, Ben asked his friend, "Did you know about Sonny and Mary?"

Ellis said, "Can't say I felt like Cupid exactly, helping bury Wade, but let's face it, one double-ought shell and a drop cloth is a hell of a lot less trouble than a messy divorce."

"Point taken. And I'm the last to know."

Ellis grinned. "Oh, don't get all bent. See the fun you been missing playing the hermit goldsmith?"

CHAPTER 93

SENIOR RESIDENT AGENT Pershing Lowry and Sheriff Williams were unhappy after the hospital interview with Jacques Doe, but for very different reasons. Lowry had passed the water bottle to an agent who had pulled a very clear set of prints from the bottle's smooth surface. This time, Lowry did not have to resort to the MiSLED database to scare up a name. Gläans Bellendre had been busted three years earlier on a DUI in Vienna, Virginia, and his prints popped up in the Integrated Automated Fingerprint Identification System. A further check revealed that he, too was billed as a Right Way Moving & Storage employee who, as of one month ago, had overstayed a work visa. Bellendre would soon be under arrest as an accessory to kidnapping and murder, and though Lowry's contact at Immigration and Customs Enforcement was frothing to begin deportation proceedings, ICE was willing to take a back seat while the bureau's charges against the patient were developed. Sheriff Williams was pissed because Bellendre had refused to speak a word before his doctor returned with a powerful sedative to calm his agitated patient.

The unflappable Lowry was now sick with worry because Special Agent Wilde was still a no-show. She had not answered several calls, nor even his text messages, which ordinarily Lowry never bothered to thumb into his phone.

Driving back to his office from the hospital, Lowry made his second call in an hour to Special Agent David Pratt, an older operative in the Calvert office who had given up climbing the bureau career ladder in favor of spending his few remaining years quietly manning his desk before retirement.

When Lowry heard Pratt answer, he skipped salutations, and asked, "Anything?"

Pratt sounded worried when he said, "No. No one has seen her, or her vehicle."

"What about her phone?"

Pratt wheezed, "Her last call was from the kids' parents' residence to your number. Did she say she was making any stops before going to the hospital?"

"No, she didn't," said Lowry. "But she sometimes backtracks. She likes to visit scenes after the techs are done to get a second look without the personnel crawling all over the place."

A very conventional Pratt said, "That seems strange."

Lowry felt himself get defensive on Molly Wilde's behalf. "She says it gives her insights. What about the tracker on her vehicle?"

"I checked," Pratt said. "It's one of the older model cars. Scheduled for public auction. The tracker might have been stripped out before sale. I'll get on it."

"Delegate that one, Dave. I want you to start for the Thompson's house in Prince Frederick right away, and drive the route from there to the scene at the grandparents' place on the bay. Get the local and county police on this as well, please. And run the routes between those two places and Kyle's Barber Shop in town. Check hospitals. I want her found within the hour."

Then the unorthodox idea struck Lowry. He called Sheriff Williams again, and after a few moments of conversation it was decided. Gläans Bellendre would be set free. Not so much set free, as intentionally allowed to escape.

CHAPTER 94

ROLLING THE HAVOKKER through the woods was tough going with the ground so soft, but the reverend, Vinny, Orville, and Art switched out with Ellis and Ben every few yards. Mary Joyce toted the shotguns of those taking their turn hauling the great bombard's trail and pushing at the spokes of the large wheels. Once they moved deeper into the trees, a layer of pine straw on the forest floor kept the wheels from bogging down as often.

Sonny asked DeRosa, "So you're a medico who carries a gun? To shoot folks so's then they need a medico?"

"No irony, no fun," answered Vinny.

"That's what them MBAs call a solid business model," Sonny mused.

"But I'm a decent shot, so doctors don't always factor in," vaunted Vinny. "I look out for me and my patients."

Dusk swiftly fell into the fog, and they halted two hundred fifty yards from what Ben believed would be the best firing position in range of the planetary LNG tanks. Their voices were hushed in the hugger-mugger tones appropriate to the mission as Ben revealed his plan for this evening's revels.

Ben and Ellis would directly assault the terminal's main building. Reverend Mosby, Art, and Mary would provide flanking fire. Vinny would rally to the side of anyone who took a bullet. Orville would man the Havokker.

They all huddled in the mist. Each was certain that a few, and perhaps everyone in their small force would die tonight. The grim prospect dampened no one's spirits. The silence of the woods was quickened by whispers of encouragement.

Ben gauged the sky and fog, and finally asked, "Reverend Mosby, would you care to say a few words?"

The minister looked around his small flock, and said, "Gave it some thought on the way over." He cleared his throat as he did every Sunday at the start of his sermon, and a heads bowed for a listen. "*Lord knows what we're about. He knows just what we need. It's been written how it'll all play out; who'll live and who will bleed. Our cause is surely righteous; good, our only gain. It falls to us to give them hell. Upon our foe, we'll bring the pain.*"

"Amen," said Ellis and the rest.

The outdoor floodlights at the terminal blazed to life. Through the fog, they gave a great pinkish white refractive loom behind black trees in the south.

"Hosanna," said Ben. "Let's move."

But Ben's pace was slower, and he dropped back while the others took their turns moving the gun forward. Reverend Mosby was next in line to put his shoulder to the wheel; but with a well-developed sixth sense for when folks needed to talk, he hung back with Ben and said nothing.

After a few more steps, Ben came out with it. "Lately, I'm not feeling God's so close n'mare."

Mosby said, "Then who moved?"

"You think it's all on me? How come? Look at me, Rev', stumbling around in the dark."

"First, I'd say this is not the best time for an existential gut-check, Ben. And second, stop looking where you *fell*. Start looking where you *slipped*."

Orville stepped away from the gun, and without another word, Mosby walked forward to take his place.

DeRosa pushed ahead of the main party as a scout while they drew the gun west and south to line up on the first spherical reservoir, the tank that was still filled with natural gas.

Ellis told Ben, "We don't know if that Havokker's ammo is stable, or functional."

"I'm betting no, and no again," said Ben. "But it looks to be an exploding, incendiary round in those mags. Best case is we don't need the thing. Hate to blow up a neighbor who's firing it for no reason."

Several sets of limousine headlights measured the terminal's long lane through the woods from the local road.

Ben grunted as he stepped forward to haul the gun's trail. "I thought this was just an Internet play."

Art Bailey said, "Looks like somebody's come to see the doings in person. Hope I get a couple of 'em in my sights."

"It's them's with the big money and the sickness who're making this whole thing go," said Sonny. "Without that particular shitwad of deviants, it'd be just another day in Paradise."

Orville said, "Yeah, that ain't no building over there. It's a septic tank, a slough hole for monsters. I'm with Art. Wrong as it all is, if we can sieve a little scum out of the gene pool tonight, we're doin' the Lord's work."

Vinny DeRosa returned from his recon ahead, and whispered, "This is it. There's a picket about one hundred yards from the compound. Even with the wind in these pines, I can hear you all humping this gun from pretty far out. Do you maybe have a shot from here?"

Ben studied the gigantic gas tank and the intervening trees. He took a few steps to the left, then more to the right, gauging trajectories at various elevations. Then he looked closely at the Havokker's coigning mechanism that would elevate the six barrels in unison. "She cranks up pretty steep, like a Howitzer, or a mortar. She doesn't lay out like a long range gun. Looking at more of a high arc than a low, flat, high-velocity shot—"

"Lordy go to fire, Ben!" interrupted Mary Joyce. "Will she hit home from here, or do we still have to haul this brute around the wilderness half the night 'til you're happy?"

Ben grimaced. "Honestly, Mary, Ellis is right. I don't know how much powder's in those cartridges, nor how much of it's still good. Brand new, she might hit that tank. The trajectory's clear enough from right here. But Orville, you know you might get a short round. The whole gun, and every round in it might blow up in your face. Sure you still want that job?"

Orville said, "I told you I'm in. Let's get at 'em."

Satisfied, Ben turned to Sonny. "I need you back aboard *Varina Davis*. For what I'm planning, I need you to loiter out of rifle shot off that T pier. When you see friends there, toll in to the pier's shore end quick as you can."

Sonny looked mad. He had not come all this way only to be sent packing back to the boat. "What if I don't see nobody?"

"Use the Jiffy Pop clock," said Ben. "When most, but not all of the small arms fire dies down, you toll in."

Sonny reeled in his anger. "And once I'm there?"

"Think *Dunkirk*."

Sonny grinned, gave Mary a smart, hard kiss on her mouth, and jogged back into the fog toward the Chesapeake.

CHAPTER 95

LUANNA'S UNCLE CONRAD eased *Winnie Estelle* down the main channel of the bay at a slow 500 rpm. He was watching his Simrad Automatic Identification System radar system, and marking the progress of the large container ship that was outbound south through the waning day from Baltimore Harbor.

He nudged LuAnna and pointed to the container ship's small AIS triangle on the screen. Then he brought up the ship's information, and said, "*Akuma Maru*. Reckon with her heading and speed, she'll be down around Dove Point in under an hour. See my heading?" He laid the edge of his hand over the screen in a line that intercepted the *Akuma Maru*'s course just off the LNG terminal's T pier.

"I get it," said LuAnna. "We come in at the right speed, and the right time, and the right heading, and the ship hides us. Masks our noise, blocks a radar return, if anybody's looking, and blocks sight of us too, if it's still light enough to see, or if some fonny boy's hooked into some night vision gear. The fog's going to help."

"Got a headpiece on ya, girl, I'll say that," said Conrad.

Annie Vo and Tally were checking over an array of weapons spread out on the upper and lower berths at the back of the wheelhouse.

Tally said, "I like this 1911 pistol. I want nothing else. Except a knife."

Annie Vo did not question Tally's simple taste in arms. She reached into a side pocket of her duffle, and withdrew five loaded 1911 magazines, and a sheathed Gerber LHR combat knife.

"Thank you," said Tally, accepting the gear.

"Aw hell," said Conrad, as he began to turn the helm wheel hard to starboard, as he pushed the throttle to 1600 rpms.

"What's the matter?" asked Annie Vo.

Conrad said, "Forgot that Tally talked some about guard dogs at the terminal."

Tally said, "There are at least males. Males."

"Depending on how well they're trained, we can upset them." Conrad almost giggled. "Gertie's crazy in heat. We're going to give her a little shore leave. Let her have some fun."

Tally said, "I'll go on land with the dog." When her statement was met with silence, she said simply, "I can keep up with Gertie."

CHAPTER 96

BEN AND ELLIS crept forward through the wet pine needle straw. Black tree trunks loomed out of the mist in silhouette. They were approaching the sentry position that Vinny DeRosa had identified in his scouting sortie. Vinny, Art, Mary, and Reverend Mosby were following them in through a path the two-man vanguard had cleared, with a plan to fan out left and right as soon as they were closer, to provide flanking and suppressing fire.

Ellis was half serious when he asked, "Any Rules of Engagement you got in mind?"

Ben was not amused. "Rules of *what?*"

"Attaboy," said Ellis with a tone devoid of mercy.

After a moment, Ben asked, "You see him?"

Ellis peered ahead through a night vision AN/PVS-22 site on his Surefire suppressed M40A5 rifle, slowly collapsing the forward sectors. "Negative."

"Shouldn't oughta done that, dummy," said Ben softly.

"Beg pardon?" Ellis trained his rifle roughly in the direction Ben was aiming his monocular.

"That cat yonder, a hundred twenty-nine yards. He slapped a mosquito. Smarty pants is up in a tree stand fifteen feet or so, far side, and all but blanked by the trunk. Wind is—no factor."

"One hundred twenty-nine yards," said Ellis. "Up fifteen foot—now I got him. Dearie me, the skeeters are messing with him something awful.

You'd think the weather would keep them down." He was quiet for a second. "I got a line on his coconut, left side of the trunk. Shooter ready."

"Send it," said Ben immediately.

Ellis squeezed the rifle trigger, and the gun made a crisp *snap*, which was followed by a momentary *hiss* as the 7.62 NATO bullet streaked away at 300 meters per second. An instant later, the sentry in the tree jerked, and slumped against the trunk. The sentry's weapon, along with something else Ben could not identify, dropped to the ground.

"That'll do," said Ben.

"Hold on," said Ellis. "He's belayed to the tree. Or he's playing possum."

"Possum's giving you some torso now. No movement. Range and elevation the same. No factor, wind."

Ellis worked the bolt open. Smoke wreathed from the breach. He closed the bolt chambering the next round, and aimed. "Shooter ready."

"Send it."

Ellis squeezed the trigger again. Another *snap* from the muzzle. The sentry in the tree stand twitched, more from an impact force than a nervous system reflex to the second bullet going home.

The headlights of another car pierced the growing darkness along the access lane to the facility. Ben said, "We best pick up the pace."

They moved forward with deliberate swiftness, soon flanking the sentry's tree stand. Ben held his rifle low, while Ellis kept his weapon trained on the sentry's still form perched above. A few feet from the base of the tree trunk, they found a dropped MP5, and an upside down tan fatigue cap neatly cupping frontal and parietal skull fragments, a gory scalp flap, and a chunk of brain.

"Lookee there," whispered Ben. "He tipped his cover in welcome."

"I like when a corpse shows proper respect."

They moved forward again through the murk toward the bright lights of the terminal.

CHAPTER 97

UNCLE CONRAD BRYCE backed *Winnie Estelle* away from shore. For only a moment, Tally watched the boat retreat. Gertie sprinted through the waves to dry land unencumbered by her heat diaper. Soon, a howling of dogs scented and acknowledged Gertie's redolent, fecund presence. Gertie charged south toward the sound. Tally followed at an easy loping run, her pistol in one hand and knife in the other.

CHAPTER 98

CURTAIN TIME WAS nearing. Armand and Wallace were still welcoming the guests partaking of the festivities in person. Armand wore a gold *guipé* sleeveless dress that showed off his sinewed arms. For the sake of comfort, he wore dyed-to-match gold Capezio character shoes with a single thin instep strap and a heel somewhat wider than a stiletto. He was going to be on his feet late into the evening. Armand's orders were simple. Monitor the buffet, and kill any guest who got squeamish at any point in the proceedings and who wanted to bail out of *L'Abattoir* early.

Wallace kept it simple in his way, with full black latex body paint, a leather hood and mask with zippered eye, nose, and mouth openings, a thong encrusted with red and white crystal beads, and ten-inch black tactical boots. He was to stage manage the acts in accordance with the plans that DePriest and Rookard had made. Before wrangling the next act from the holding pens into the studio, he would assist in trundling the talent from the last performance off the stage and into the freezer. Waste not, want not.

DePriest watched the many flatscreen monitors in his lair. The studio was ready for the first act, a pretty, pregnant Latina. On a whim, he played his fingers over the tablet that served as his electronic command unit, and brought the cameras in the holding area onto his screens. The screens were black. This was not right. This was not right at all. Suddenly, two flashes winked brightly on the screen to his left. Muzzle flashes. The screen should have been showing the isolation wing of the dungeon. Closed pens. In the instant flash of the gunshots, he had seen nothing but open doors. He stared at the black rectangle in disbelief.

Then he shouted, "*Maynard!*"

CHAPTER 99

THE MAIN ENTRANCE of the terminal was guarded by three armed operators. From a concealed position not fifty yards from the metal double doors, Ben observed a fourth armed man driving a large passenger golf cart with several rows of seats. The cart served as a shuttle from the parking area where well-dressed guests had left their Maseratis, Rolls Royces, and Maybachs. Ellis would be pleased to note that, despite all the high end rolling stock represented here, his Bugatti back on Smith Island remained the only one Ben had ever seen in person.

Ellis lurked out of sight at the utility garage where a large metal panel protected the electrical busses for the terminal's exterior, and possibly interior power. He was setting up an Easter egg hunt of explosives and flash-crash grenades from a rucksack filled with boom and doom.

Ben checked his watch, and as the second hand swept toward twelve, he powered up his NVGs. He was looking at men, and likely women, he would need to kill to rescue LuAnna and Chamaiyo. He had long ago crossed the line where killings in civilian life, based on no laws of this land, were more like summary executions. If the condemned shot back at him, it evened the odds, but eased his conscience very little. The blessing of Reverend Mosby, and his willing hand on a weapon to aid the cause helped Ben reconcile his deeds with the God of his youth. Ben was not so sure the reverend's words were going to save him from the God of his more mature understanding. Kindly Preacher Mosby seemed to be getting bloodthirsty in his golden years. Could such a man guide Ben to any kind of redemption, or help weave him some kind of cloak of salvation? By disobeying the laws of man to vanquish preternatural evil, Ben wondered if he could win favor in the eyes of the Deity. He could soon get his answers if an enemy's bullet or blade knocked him from this world to the next.

Ben's ruminations were shattered with the blast of Ellis's first flash-crash grenade, which he'd somehow rolled under the passenger golf cart. Six well-dressed guests scattered, disoriented, staggering in all directions, tripping over their feet and each other in flight from an unseen enemy. The guards bravely, foolishly dashed away from the main door toward the cart.

In the next instant, another explosion at the utility garage took out the surface power. All the big floodlights winked out. A fast sequence of gun-shots from Ellis destroyed the four battery powered emergency lights that had stayed on. The darkness was complete and blinding for everyone except Ben and his cohort.

Art Bailey, Mary Joyce, and Reverend Mosby opened fire with their pump guns. With a fresh magazine, Ellis went to work with his M40 rifle. The armed driver of the golf cart spun and rolled headfirst out of the driver's seat onto the ground. The other operators loosed sprays of fire from their submachine guns, but they had no clear targets. They died of bewilderment as much as bullet wounds. Then the Smith Island shotguns went to work on the guests. There were screams of panic and terror. A fat woman in a fur coat went down like a wounded grizzly and lay still. Then came a moment of righteous silence.

Ben made his run for the facility's main door. Single shots came down around him from somewhere high on the nearest natural gas tank. Then two shots blasted from the building's roof, but not at Ben. He glanced up, and could have sworn he saw his father, Dick Blackshaw, sniping from the roof at the shooter on the tank.

Dogs, very large sounding dogs, were baying near the complex.

Ben ducked inside the door alone, cleared the small vestibule and foyer area opening to ground level offices, and beelined for a stairway leading down into the subsurface levels of the complex. An operator rushed toward him, gun leveled, mistaking Ben for a comrade. Ben shot him down without missing a step. Pushing open the door, he was overwhelmed by the fetid odor of a wild animal's den that had become a tomb.

He did not see the phantasm that dashed in through the stairway door after him.

CHAPTER 100

MAYNARD CHALK AND Wendy Peltier were patrolling along a corridor toward another bank of holding pens when they heard the muffled sounds of explosions transmit down through the walls, ducts, and pipes of the sub-basement area.

Chalk blustered in anger, "What the fuck is *that?*"

"It's not the sound of money." Wendy put her back to the wall, glancing upward toward the source of the explosions, and back down the corridor leading away into the dark. "This deal's screwed, boss."

"You keep searching," ordered Chalk. "I'm going to see what's what. I'll send somebody to help you." Chalk checked his watch. "The show must go on. Things should get rolling in few minutes." He planned to stop at the stage first on his way up toward the trouble to see how Rookard and his team were doing.

He set off down the hall in the dark using his NVG set to find his way. He pushed through a fire door into a stairwell. What sounded like the hurried footsteps of a small group echoed down the stairwell from above. He dashed up a few steps, and saw two little kids on the run with a group of grown-up-sized shadows. In the green of his NVGs, their naked forms made them look like frail-limbed alien beings. His newfound twins! Chalk fired at the group. One of the children screamed and fell up the steps.

"Gotcha, ya little shit!"

From somewhere on a higher landing, gunshots amplified by the cement walls to an earsplitting cacophony rained bullets down all around him.

"Damn!" he bellowed. Chalk retreated for the fire door and reentered the hall. He would head up toward the surface another way. Peltier was right. This was not going according to plan. This was chaos. Chalk felt strangely peaceful with this new realization.

CHAPTER 101

BEN BLACKSHAW SLAMMED down a flight of stairs in the LNG terminal complex. Tally had been clear that she was held underground. Chamaiyo and LuAnna would most likely still be held there.

He caught the sound of heavy footfalls approaching from below and stopped. An armed operator rounded the next landing. Ben fired quickly twice, one shot at a leg, another at the head. Everyone he had seen wore ballistic vests, and he did not want to waste a single round. The operator tumbled backward down the stairs into a heap on the landing. Ben saw the hair was longer in back, with jagged bangs spiking form beneath the cap. A woman. So much for the maternal instinct. Ben kept going down.

CHAPTER 102

THE STUDIO SEATING was only half full when Maynard Chalk entered. No doubt the ruckus outside was holding up the rest of the live audience from taking their places, perhaps forever.

The lights in the sublevels were still doused everywhere. Likely the show was over before it had even begun, since there was no power for the cameras or the servers. He wondered where in the name of all that's holy were Rookard, Wallace, and Armand? They should have the preggers Latina strapped down on the table by now.

He scanned the audience through his NVGs, and was met with the heartwarming sight of a familiar face. The evening would not be a total loss. There sat the Secretary of the Department of Homeland Security, Lily Morgan, the sole author of his current straits. She was parked next to a shrimp-faced geezer gawping in the darkness with a protective arm around Lily's shoulder.

Chalk said, "Hey Lil'. How you been?"

Lily blinked mole-like eyes and said, "Who's there?"

"Just an old friend."

"You sound familiar," said Lily. "Who are you? And what the hell's going on with the lights?"

Chalk took off his NVGs and drew a small flashlight from a cargo pocket. He turned the beam on and aimed it directly in Lily's face. "We had a good thing going, Lil', and then you turned chicken."

"Get that light out of my face—Maynard! Is that you?"

More explosions rattled through to the studio level. Dust sifted down from the concrete ceiling.

"In the flesh. Been too long, Lil'. I've missed you.'"

The geezer with Lily squinted into the light and piped up, "Dear, who is this man? I think we should leave. If you'd be so kind as to show us the way out, sir—"

"More than happy to oblige," said Chalk. He raised his pistol and fired three rounds into Lily's chest, and three more at her shriveled husband's gut for good measure. They twitched and toppled toward each other in a final ragdoll embrace.

CHAPTER 103

BEN WORKED HIS way through the corridor that gave off the lowest landing of the stairway. He stopped for a moment and listened. Someone was moving toward him from around the corner. A second later, his NVGs revealed a naked woman with a pistol limping her way along the wall.

He said, "You're Special Agent Molly Wilde."

The woman froze, instinctively covered her breasts with one hand, extended her pistol toward the voice with the other, clearly racking her memory to recognize the disembodied intruder's voice.

Ben continued, "Easy there. It's Ben, from this morning. We've met."

"Blackshaw!" She adjusted the barrel of her gun, refining her bearing on his voice.

Ben moved quietly behind a large horizontal pipe for cover in case Wilde was not in a talking mood. He said, "I'm taking off my coat, and I'm going to throw it toward you. It'll land to your left, away from your gun-hand."

"You can see me. Crap. Does everybody in this shit-hole have NVGs but me?"

Ben threw the coat where he promised. "A bunch of us do. How'd you get here?"

Wilde groped for the coat, sorted it out, and donned it by shifting the pistol to her other hand as she needed. She could not manage the zipper single-handed, so she clutched the coat closed with her left. "Like you don't know how I got here. I figured out why you dimed Chalk. You wanted the bureau to help you cut out one of your partners."

"Not even close. I'm looking for somebody. This whole thing is a snuff party. Did you figure on that? On the Internet, for big money. There are at least fifteen, maybe twenty hostages going to slaughter."

Wilde's gun lowered an inch for a moment. "My God. And you're telling me you're one of the good guys."

Ben pointed out, "I'm talking, not shooting. Killing or disarming you wouldn't be real tough right now."

Wilde had to agree. She changed her tack. "Who are you looking for?"

"White female, early thirties, blonde. Small black female, early teens. She's the one who stole the boat from the dock where we met."

Wilde pondered this. "She got away from here, and came back again?"

"For her little sister," Ben explained. "I reckon I can't cull just those three from the bunch, so we come to cut everybody loose."

"Isn't that democratic of you. Who's we?"

"Friends. And a relation. We need to get moving."

"Ben Blackshaw, I'm placing you under arrest—"

"Lordy, Agent Wilde, you don't let up! We have to work together. There's pipe conduit tunnels that lead from this building, from this level, straight to the shoreline, and then out to the end of the T pier. We have to locate every hostage and get them there as fast as we can. There'll be a pick up."

"More of your friends?"

"And a boat, yes. You hear those flash-crashes? They're from *my* people, not yours, though I reckon yours'll come running here soon enough for you. Before that, the place is going to go sky high. The shoreline will be the only safe place."

"What do you mean *sky high*? You're a terrorist now?"

"Call it housekeeping. There's one LNG tank that's still full. Remember Herculaneum when Mount Vesuvius went up? Plenty folks sheltered at the shore under a bluff."

"They all died there, Ben"

"That won't be the case this time. If you help me."

Wilde recoiled. "I've seen the plans from our ICS exercises. Every transfer pipe leads through here. We're going to incinerate."

"Hence the whole *let's get a move on* thing. Most of the pens down here are open, and I can't figure why. Reckon there are other pens I haven't seen yet. I'll head up and send hostages to you here. You send them in the direction you're facing now, and you'll get to the tunnel."

Wilde was thinking fast. "For Christ's sake, there's another tunnel that connects from down here directly to Calvert Cliffs."

"The nuke plant?"

"A-firm, Ben."

"Who thought that up? Does it have a blast door? Is it closed?"

"I'll work on that part, but I can't see to find anything down here. The emergency lights have all failed."

"And now you want my NVGs? So you can cap me?"

"You wanted me to trust you." Wilde clutched the jacket tighter around her body but held the pistol steady.

"Aren't you a coy thing."

"Ben, I can see your fancy watch dial glowing like a spot light. I could have shot you anytime."

Ben held the watch face to his thigh. It was strapped outside his wetsuit sleeve. He could not hide it any other way. Reconsidering, he took off his NVGs and set them on the floor.

"You want to see, you come over here for the goggles where I put them. If you waste time coming after me with 'em, a lot of good folks will die."

Ben, whose ears worked like eyes since he was a boy poaching the marshes in the small hours, slipped through the stairway door and started his climb.

A shadow within the darkness followed him upward in total silence.

CHAPTER 104

ANNIE VO LAY prone on *Winnie Estelle*'s wheelhouse roof with her CheyTac rifle stretching out next to her, but hidden under a pile of orange brick life vests. The Caterpillar engine's noise clattered loudly from the dry stack exhaust just aft, and a sooty pall surrounded her because of the following breeze. Uncle Conrad had the helm.

LuAnna took a seated position on the hatch cover with Conrad's stainless steel Winchester Model 70 lying beside her under a backfold of the egg-yolk yellow hatch cover tarp. She felt that sitting gave her nearly the stability of lying prone, but allowed her entire body to compensate for *Winnie's* movement beneath her. She had been shooting from all kinds of boats since she was a girl, and the troubled Chesapeake today was nothing to her. She even preferred the weapon's open sights for fog; condensation on the objective and ocular lenses of a scope was never an issue this way. Nor did she need a scope's windage and elevation adjustments either. As a Smith Islander, she handled those calculations instinctively.

Lookouts stationed on the *Akuma Maru* container ship's port side had briefly turned their binoculars on the vintage buyboat playing pilot fish to their whale shark. A quick glance at headings and relative speeds made it clear the old boat would pass under the big ship's stern with little risk of collision.

When Sonny Wright drew out of a fog bank next to the *Winnie Estelle* in *Varina Davis*, LuAnna greeted her neighbor, who was staring gapemouthed at her.

"You know Ben's been looking for you all day. For you and that Tally girl," hollered Sonny.

LuAnna said, "Expect nothing less from that man."

"It's Chalk over there. He's in on this. There's fonny boys every which way, and they mean business."

LuAnna's face clouded with this news, but she quickly brightened. "We've all got some business with that one."

"Thought you'd see it that way," said Sonny. "What's your plan?"

"If Ben and Ellis are going in, I figure they'd put friendlies out toward the water. This fog would get them clear quicker than messing on land. Tally's put in already to find her sister. Can you handle the pickup?"

Sonny countered, "Can you thin 'em out on the pier?"

LuAnna patted the concealed rifle on the hatch cover, and gestured up at Annie Vo who was watching the conversation, but completely unable to hear it over the roar and clatter of the engine's exhaust. "We gotcha covered."

Sonny asked, "Who's she?"

"That's Ben's half-sister, Annie Vo."

"No shit." Sonny accepted the news with barely a hint of surprise, and gave a small salute to the woman looking down at him from the wheelhouse roof. Annie Vo saluted in return.

Introductions made, Sonny said, "Best we get in shore to the shindig. Mind if I tag along with you behind that big fat box boat?"

CHAPTER 105

SAM ROOKARD KNEW *L'Abattoir* was imploding, regardless of whom, or what was assaulting the LNG terminal. The key was not getting caught up in the fallout. To get out cleanly, he stripped off all his clothes to blend in with the hostages, and moved from his small office space in the first sub-basement level carrying only his favorite knife. The dark did not scare him. He would know the warren of corridors with eyes closed by now.

He was making good progress up the stairs toward the main entrance level when a man called out to him from below.

"You! Where are the rest of you?"

Rookard stopped, palmed his blade, adopted a terrified mien, turned and said, "Up here! They must be up here! I can't see. Are you the police? Can you help me please? They're crazy! They're going to kill us!"

The man said, "You might get caught in crossfire up there. Turn around, hustle back down to the bottom of the stairs. An FBI agent will get you out toward the shore. A boat will get you away from here with the others."

"The FBI is here?" The last thing Rookard wanted was to spend time with his former hostages or the feds. The hostages would recognize him and turn him in, or tear him to pieces exactly as they knew he had intended to do to them. "I can't go back down there," he whimpered. "I just can't."

The man said, "I have a flashlight. I'll point the way down. Telling you, buddy, you'll get killed up there."

The man shined a flashlight, first on Rookard, then on the steps below. To Rookard's horror, the steps were not empty. The runner, that black little bitch, was standing right there on the landing. She was clothed. He was naked. The tables had turned.

CHAPTER 106

BEN WAS COOL with the hostage's nakedness in the light, and tried not to add embarrassment to his fear. Ben was abjectly surprised to discover that, when he shined the flashlight beam on the steps below, Tally was standing there with an upraised pistol. Where had she come from?

She fired the gun. The report was deafening, but Ben still heard and felt the round flick past him. The hostage grunted and toppled down the steps. A keen bright scalpel, once concealed in his hand, clattered onto the stairs. The guy lay writhing, clutching his thigh, and cursing his assailant.

Tally said flatly, "He is one of them." She moved in quickly with her knife, slashing and stabbing savagely at the fallen man who tried to defend himself with upraised hands, howling, screeching, out of his mind with panic in the face of Tally's unstoppable ferocity. At least one of his fingers was completely severed. Gouts of arterial blood flipped up on the walls in feathery arcs.

Ben held the flashlight high until the man lay still, and Tally stood over her tormentor triumphant, but panting gently.

"Feel better?" asked Ben. His wetsuit gleamed with runnels of blood.

Tally nodded, and smiled broadly, passing her coat sleeve across her face to wipe away the gore. "A little bit."

"Where'd you get that coat?"

"Your sister. She picked up L'Wana and me this morning in her uncle's boat. *Windy Steel.*"

"LuAnna's okay?" Ben felt hope well up in his chest and meld with confusion. "And Annie Vo is here?" If that actually had been Dick Blackshaw who Ben had spotted in the helter-skelter dash into the building, this was quite the family reunion.

"She said she had business with you. But no, she is still on the boat with L'Wana. Where is Chamaiyo?"

"Haven't seen her yet. If you run into anybody, hostages, I mean, send them down to the bottom level and toward the shore, that way," Ben instructed, pointing.

CHAPTER 107

BLACKSHAW CREPT THROUGH a corridor one level up from where he had met Agent Wilde, and where Tally had diced up her captor and would-be killer. Tally had remained in the catacombs below to search for her sister. Though Ben could not see in the darkness, except for quick checks of the path with his flashlight, he had no problem hearing six reports from a distant room. The lightning of gunfire defined where a doorway lay, thirty feet in front of him.

An instant later, the sounds of two sets of heavy footsteps came running toward him from corridor that joined his at a perpendicular angle. A pair of boots, and a woman's heels thudding and clacking closer. Two blue-white LED flashlight beams bumped and jumped ahead in the unseen runners' hands, and almost lit Ben up. He ducked back into a recess in the wall next to a set of manual valves as large as old Chevy pick-up steering wheels.

When Ben saw the gold dress sparkling in the distance, he was sure he was looking at a female guest who had come to the terminal to watch the psychotic destruction of other human beings.

Then Ben heard the woman say, "Since the pens are all open, we have to get the boss, now."

The golden woman's voice was lower than Ben had expected, but this was much less alarming than what she said. It was clear she was not a guest, but an active functionary in this horror show with a stake in the safety of her chief. Maybe she meant Maynard Chalk. If Ben followed her, maybe he would find the prime mover of the nightmare. The person accompanying this woman was much more difficult to pick out. The approaching flash-light beams were shining toward Ben's eyes, forcing him to squint to discern anything. All he could discern of the second person was a strange gleam in a dark void next to the woman, a void punctuated by a glittering red and white triangle approximately waist-high.

Two-to-one odds were okay with Ben. He stepped out of the recess into the corridor directly in front of the oncoming pair. The woman in the dress tried to stop, but because of her stylish, yet impractical shoes, she lost her footing and fell on her ass. Her companion slowed his approach briefly assessing Ben, then ran hard at him. The man's face was covered in some kind of mask, but the body English spelled trouble.

The attacker slammed into Ben, bulling him back a few feet. A smooth rubber material, like a wetsuit, but much thinner and more tightly fitting, tore away in Ben's grasp. Like the woman in the gold dress on the floor, this was not a hostage, not a victim. This was a murderer bent on plying his trade against Ben.

In no mood for a set-piece sparring match, Ben drew his knife only to see his assailant produce one of his own while trying to blind him with the flashlight. Ever practical, Ben dropped his knife, jammed his hand into his coat's cargo pocket, got a grip on his pistol and fired twice directly through his jacket. One round shattered the rubbery attacker's weird beaded cod-piece. Red and white crystals spun and glinted up and down the hall along with the dying screams of the fallen rubber man.

Ben turned to see the woman in the *guipé* dress scrambling to her feet. She was drawing a small pistol from her clutch. Then Ben saw the muscled arms, the Adam's apple, and realized this was also a man. Whatever scruple Ben had momentarily felt about hurting a woman dropped away, and he fired again. Blood bloomed across the gold fabric, and the man pitched backward onto the floor writhing, then doubling into a fetal curl, and moaning.

Ben snatched up his knife and sprinted down the hall toward where the six gunshots had rung out moments before his encounter with the bizarre pair. At the sound of turmoil ahead, he risked a quick beam from the LED flashlight, and found a small group of older men in suits dashing down the hall at him in headlong panic.

To this group he yelled, "Head straight up any staircase you find. Help's waiting to get you off the premises." These were the buyers, Death's customers come to see the torture and slaughter of innocents. Ben knew Ellis and company would know them for who they were, and give them more than they had paid for. He painted the stairway door with his flashlight. They pushed through the door in a scrum of arms and legs, trampling each other to climb toward the surface.

CHAPTER 108

JOACHIM DEPRIEST FRETTED in the darkness. His flat-screens were still black. There were thunderous concussions shaking the terminal somewhere above him, perhaps outside the main building. If he could trust his ears, there was also sporadic gunfire cracking out down on the lower levels interspersed with shouts of panic. The generator he had installed in case of power failure had itself failed for some reason, perhaps from the damage he was hearing wrought overhead. He had no idea who had instigated the firefight, and it did not matter. He only hoped Maynard Chalk and his cadre were looking after their shared interests with his oft-touted bloodthirsty zeal. *L'Abattoir* was in grave jeopardy. DePriest's only comfort was that the payments were all banked and safe offshore.

His own immediate safety was another matter. He played a tiny pen-light around his lair. He was still alone. Armand and Wallace were absent, not responding to his cries for their immediate presence to assist with his escape.

With a monumental effort, the like of which DePriest had not expended in an eternity, he heaved his rippling bulk up from his chaise, and took a step toward the edge of the dais and the door. His knee gave out beneath him, and he toppled heavily back onto the chaise, with a grunt and a shriek of anger. He caught his breath and tried to stand again, shifting his weight onto the other foot this time. The cracking sound, and the stabbing jolt of pain were unmistakable. Something in the knee had snapped. A cold sweat broke out over his great shelving brow as he rolled back onto the chaise again, his pen light clattering to the floor out of reach.

He was not certain, but through the agony of his damaged knee, and over his gasps for breath, he thought he heard a movement near the door to his lair.

"Armand! Wallace! Come to me. I need you!" No answer. "Who's there?" he demanded.

Again, silence was the only reply.

CHAPTER 109

CHAMAIYO HAD WATCHED DePriest for a moment during the brief flickers of his little penlight. While her time with Al Shabaab in Somalia had made a child into a stealthy killer, DePriest's time below ground had metamorphosed a man into a mole blinded by hours staring at his flatscreens. He was no good in the dark. Chamaiyo was at home.

The girl knew from this man's gigantic, yet pale larval girth, and the accoutrements of his lair, that he was responsible for her captivity and suffering. She was now certain it was a good thing that she had separated from her fellow escapees, directing them down and away from the noises of the battle above. The little boy had been struck by gunfire. The agent she had seen Chalk twitting in her catacomb cell, the agent she had later freed, was now looking after the boy, carrying him, and leading the others to safety.

Chamaiyo had stayed behind; she was a little Valkyrie with a keen sense she still had work before her, and a keener blade with which to do it. Though Chalk was her object, this behemoth was a bigger prize in every way. She could hear his stertorous gasping, sign of his easy mewling defeat from some pain. Chamaiyo was Kalenjin. She was raised with pain and the cultural imperative to press through without complaint. Dark as it was, she dashed forward.

Her feet danced lightly onto the dais at the same time her hands sank into DePriest's fat leg. Like a spider, she climbed up his greasy bulk toward the wheeze of his sour, fetid breath and darted around his shoulders onto the nape of his neck. He screamed over and over as she cut into him, jamming her blade down through the deep layers of flesh until the point must have sunk home into vitals; all the while she dodged and slashed at his big fists flailing to dislodge her. The man's movements weakened, grew slow and heavy, while his wailing became bubbling, gargled whimpers of petulant self-pity. And then finally silence. When Chamaiyo believed this Pantagruel was dead, she unhooked her fingers from his eye sockets and slid back to the floor through a warm river of blood.

CHAPTER 110

AGENT WILDE PUSHED through the corridors with a small troop of former hostages that Chamaiyo had already released. In their brief meeting, the little girl had handed over not only her pistol, but a set of keys to all the holding pens, including those that remained unopened. With a few quick directions from this clear-eyed child warrior, Agent Wilde was sent to save as many captives as she could. Of course, the kid was right. The discomfort in Wilde's head and ankle were nothing compared to the pain of shifting away from her immediate desire to detain Maynard Chalk. Though Wilde went to lead the others to safety, she was disgusted and astounded by turns at the scope of the diabolical operation.

Checking the orientation placards at every intersection, Wilde knew that from here, her quickest line to safety was not toward the shore as Blackshaw had suggested, but through the mile of access tunnel that led toward the Calvert Cliffs nuclear power plant. On the far side of the blast door separating the two main elements of the Chesapeake energy conglomerate, they would be safe.

Wilde and her blind, confused, panicked charges made the two turns shown on the placard, and there, finally, was the tunnel entrance. Her sharp ears picked up the sound of distant boots approaching fast. The captors were coming, either to retake their prisoners, or to flee the battle on the surface and fade away into the countryside via the tunnel's less protected end. Either way, Wilde could not let them pass.

Overruling the balking complaints that going further without clothes was too embarrassing, Wilde collected the second pistol and shooed her band into the tunnel, telling them to follow the wall, run like hell until they came to working lights, and then keep running until they found help, and a phone, and could summon reinforcements and ambulances. The little boy, Barry, one of the twins abducted only that morning, was grazed in the hip, and any hurt to a kid, even the least scratch, deeply disturbed Wilde.

With bootsteps of the enemy approaching along the corridor, and bare footfalls of the freed hostages slapping away down the tunnel, Wilde took a position down low behind a large pipe, laid out her spare magazines on the floor in easy reach, and waited.

Two operators, one man, and one woman, each armed with a submachine gun and equipped with NVGs, sprinted to the entrance of the tunnel twenty feet from Wilde's position.

Wilde yelled, "Freeze! Drop your weapons right there! You're both under arrest for the—"

The operators skidded to a halt in stiff attitudes of surprise, but rather than surrendering to the voice accosting them, they opened fire. Bullets flew into the tunnel, fragmenting and blowing pieces of concrete off the walls. In the buzzing hail of jagged detritus, which a part of her brain registered as kin to the sound of the Hornet's Nest of the Battle of Shiloh, Wilde kept as calm as possible. She sighted on the man who crouched shooting in the lead position. She loosed a pair of bullets, taking the man in the face. He dropped in a welter of blood, and shattered maxillary bone, choking on his own teeth.

The female operator retreated, but she refocused her fire on Wilde's position, spraying with a machine gunner's élan, taking advantage of the slugs' compounding interest in maiming shrapnel and blinding grit.

Wilde lined up on the operator and squeezed the trigger smoothly three times. The woman grunted and sank to her knee. Wilde fired twice more, and the woman rolled forward onto her face.

Listening with a hunter's care as the gunshots died away, Wilde heard no more of Chalk's crew running in her direction. They might be stalking in quietly, but if so, they would never catch up with her headlong flight. She rose, feeling blood on her face from the many lacerating wall strikes. Then dizziness nearly overcame her.

She pressed on down the tunnel to the mammoth steel blast door and weak-kneed, staggered across its threshold. She realized the lights in this portion of the passage were blazing bright, and tearing off her NVGs, she slammed the butt of her palm onto large button actuating the emergency door's closing mechanism. The blast plate swung out from the force of a powerful motor and gonged tight against its stops. A further mechanical clanking announced that multiple locks secured barrier in its massive frame, a cosmic bank's steel vault door that separated two variations on the theme of hell.

As she wobbled onward along the tunnel in lightheaded confusion, she found a sticky wet hole in the shoulder of her coat. Probing the hole in the fabric, she found the wound, and a large splinter of concrete jutting out of it. She took a few more drunken steps before her world spun and all went black.

CHAPTER 111

BEN HAD FOUND a few more captives on his sweep toward the underground passage leading toward the shore and the T pier. There was no sign of Chalk. He did find a door with a plate glass window the size of first base. He shined his flashlight through the window and took an involuntary step back. At least six men pressed their faces against the glass, and two were pointing vigorously to the door's heavy lock. They seemed to be more prisoners.

Ben yelled through the heavy glass. "Who are you?" These men wore clothes, which was reason enough to make him suspect they were not on the side of angels after all. Still, Ben fished out a set of keys he had grabbed from a dead operator.

A guy in a tank-top pushed to the front of the group, and in a muffled shout asked. "Where's Maynard? What's happening?"

At the same moment, Ben saw the tattoo high on this man's shoulder. It portrayed a little doe-eyed girl, naked, and suffering an obscenity at the hands of a male attacker who bore a strong resemblance to the guy yelling at Ben.

On a gut hunch, Ben did not want those men coming near the former hostages he was already leading. He stepped away from the door without opening it, and allowed the five freed prisoners with him to file past and continue down the corridor. Some of them wore fragments of clothes scavenged from operators Ben had felled during their brief freedom from the pens. Others were still bare, covering themselves with their hands in hunched-over shame postures. Ben closely watched the faces of the men behind the plate glass; that room was a terrarium of twisted appetites. They were transfixed by the five captives, could not tear their leering gazes away. Ben was now certain. The naked man Tally had hacked down on the stairs must have recruited fiends to help with the vile acts he had in store.

Ben checked his watch. Without a signal from him, in fifteen minutes, Orville Hurley would turn the crank on the great Havokker bombard and lob rounds at the spherical LNG storage tank. It might work. It likely would not. Ben knew he did not have time to subdue and dispatch all the brutes in this room. He said a prayer the old gun was as well made as it looked, and put his keys away. Desperate pounding from inside the door reverberated in the hall with more muffled shouts. Ben ignored it all. *Showbiz is a bitch.* He followed the hostages toward the pier tunnel.

CHAPTER 112

LUANNA'S UNCLE CONRAD helmed the *Winnie Estelle* along the end of the T pier holding just a few hundred feet off. As hostile operators dashed out of the dark and fog with flashlights to investigate what boat was powering past, Annie Vo and LuAnna shot them down. Then somebody caught wise and held back from the growing line of dead comrades, and just let fly out of the fog with a light machinegun toward the sound of *Winnie's* engine. Bullets made her lifeline netting dance, sent up splinters from her gunwales, or buzzed through the air overhead.

Sonny Wright vectored in from the south at the helm of the more nimble *Varina Davis*, and passed nearly to the shoreline in hopes that a friendly or two would be there for a quick dust off. He was grateful for the dead accuracy of the suppressing fire coming from the buyboat, but noticed friendly gunshots were suddenly slacking right at the moment he needed them to pick up. Maybe somebody on the buyboat got winged in the fusillade from the pier.

Under the pier, the fog-shrouded moon revealed a small group of folks with Ben standing in front of them; he eyed the underside of the pier catwalks for trouble. Sonny barely slowed *Varina Davis*, and Ben helped, and sometimes threw the former hostages aboard. Then Knocker Ellis, Mary Joyce, Vinny DeRosa, and Art Bailey exploded from the tunnel, followed by a sprinting Dick Blackshaw himself. They all looked badly clawed in the action, but like Tally and her sister Chamaiyo, they were breathing, moving, and likely to survive. Ben leapt aboard last, as Sonny rolled the deadrise's throttles forward.

When *Varina Davis* broke out from beneath the pier, someone fired down at the boat. Ben saw a plum-sized shadow drop out of the night sky, and with an outfielder's prowess, he snagged the grenade out of the air and whipped it back up where it came from. It cracked and flashed in the grey dark, and though the shooter on the pier went quiet, there were yelps and cries aboard the deadrise as grenade fragments caught meat. Vinny dug into his pack and went to work on the worst of the hurts even though he had taken a wicked cut on the back of his own scalp.

Winnie Estelle veered from her track, and with a white bone in her teeth, *Varina Davis* gave chase and closed. The transfer of former hostages to the deck of *Winnie Estelle* was performed at the buyboat's top speed. Ben kept checking his watch as he lifted, hoisted, or simply pushed the haggard passengers from the deadrise to the larger boat's deck.

There was his half-sister, Annie Vo, and his father helping without a word. Annie Vo was studiously not meeting Ben's eyes. But when she pulled Vinny DeRosa aboard, she caught sight of his medical pack, and whispered a few quick words into his ear. Right away he hustled up to the wheelhouse. Ben was suddenly sick in the pit of his stomach. He knew something was terribly wrong.

With the able hands all helping their injured, weaker friends to board, Ben vaulted over the rail and sprinted the short distance to the wheelhouse. Vinny DeRosa already had his kit open, and was applying hemostatic dressings to a still form stretched out on the lower berth. From Ben's initial glance, all he could see were small feet propped up on a duffle bag in the first responder's go-to shock position. There was blood everywhere.

Looking down over Vinny's shoulder, Ben saw him place a large bore IV into LuAnna's left cephalic vein in her upper arm. He handed the bag of saline to Annie Vo and told her to squeeze it while he started another line in her right arm. Conrad kept looking back at the blood-soaked berth from the helm with fury and sorrow sharing his features.

Ben moved around Vinny and Annie Vo and kneeled by LuAnna's face. She was so pale she was almost blue-black in the red loom of the wheelhouse's night running lights. He had no idea what anyone was saying.

He gently smoothed the sweat-damped hair from her face. Ben let his eyes move down her form where two gunshot wounds marred the beauty he loved. In a moment, his father was up in the wheelhouse squeezing the second IV bag as he held it high.

LuAnna opened her eyes and smiled directly at Ben. Then her gaze trailed away to vast and distant spaces. Vinny shoved Ben aside to apply the leads from a compact defibrillator to his patient. *Red-rib, white-right,* Ben silently recited to himself. Vinny snatched the IV bags from Annie Vo and Dick Blackshaw, and rested them on the upper berth as he shouted, "Clear!"

LuAnna's body shuddered once, and in the next moment, Vinny had a light finger's touch on her throat. He shook his head, and everyone immediately help lift LuAnna to the cabin sole. Vinny's rapid, deep chest compressions restarted her wounds' external bleeding.

Well past all protocols of shocks and compressions, and with epinephrine boluses flowing in through the IV lines and failing to make a difference, Ben's world went dark. He talked to LuAnna. He held her. He talked to God. He held LuAnna more. Rage, stoked with inhuman grief, ran through Ben's core.

Mary Joyce put her head in the wheel house and said, "Annie Vo, there's some asshole on that pier screaming bullshit, but we're too far out. I can't tag him with a pump gun."

Annie Vo snatched her CheyTac off the upper berth and made for the wheelhouse door, slipping in the blood. Knocker Ellis and Dick Blackshaw both got hands on the rifle before it struck the deck. They let go of it again when Ben grabbed the rifle, stepped over Annie Vo and cut aft as fast as he could. When he scanned the T pier through the night scope, he saw the figure, fists shaking at the sky.

Ben yelled forward, "Kill the engine!"

As the big Caterpillar died, the madman's voice carried over the water from the pier. "Fucking Blackshaws! I'll fuck you up! I'll assume my true godlike form and tear you all to shitty little pieces with my hate!"

Ben removed the CheyTac's magazine, tapped it on *Winnie Estelle*'s taffrail to seat the big rounds. He pressed his thumb into LuAnna's blood on the back of his other hand, and carefully rolled his print onto the topmost bullet. He reinserted the magazine in its receiver sleeve, worked the bolt, and chambered the marked bullet in one fluid motion.

He settled the crosshairs on the raving lunatic, firmed up his welds to the gun, and slowly squeezed the rifle, drawing his trigger finger in a line toward his eye. The CheyTac cracked and kicked. Ben held the sight on his target as he worked the bolt and sent a hot spent casing into the air. As the casing rang on the afterdeck, Maynard Chalk's head exploded in a puff of wet medical waste. The decapitated body slowly teetered forward off the pier into the night, into the Chesapeake Bay, and down into oblivion.

CHAPTER 113

ORVILLE HURLEY CHECKED his watch. The moment had come. He could still hear gunfire to the east, and that meant his friends were still engaged with the uglies. Yet it was not for him to judge the situation, but only to say a prayer and do as he had promised, and at the precise time.

He grabbed the great crank on the multi-barreled Havokker gun, and wrenched it around hard.

Whether by curse or by miracle, the gun blasted forth long gouts of orange fire as each barrel was loaded and discharged with its finely turned ammunition. The gun shook, heaved and jumped like a mad iron bull with every shot, almost spoiling her lie and aim. One of the big carriage wheels hopped up and came down on Orville's right foot. If the ground had been dry and hard, his extremity would have been crushed outright. As it was, Orville kept winding the crank, loosing holy hell down range.

The first magazine emptied in only a few heartbeats. Unperturbed by the gun's frisking, its thunderous din, or the killing pain in his foot, Orville switched the magazine selector, and started cranking again from the other feed.

Before the second magazine was empty, the old shells from the first magazine started falling home in the LNG terminal compound. Explosions erupted over a wider field of fire than Orville expected, striking the main building as well as outlying structures. It was then the sun came up at midnight with an ear-shattering roar.

The sphere of the still-full LNG tank detonated with the fury of a stockpile of MOABs, or a depot of daisy-cutters. Orville watched as a pyroclastic shockwave bent the trees double, snapped them, and flung them toward his position. He threw himself to the ground, and boggled at the sight of the ponderous Havokker lifting into the air as if it were a child's tin toy, flying directly over his head. In the next instant Orville was also airborne in a searing cyclone of raw energy. There was no thought of where he would come down. He flew ever skyward, the earth twisting and reeling beneath him in a reckoning and a rapture.

CHAPTER 114

JOACHIM DEPRIEST LIVED. Though badly wounded, and all but blinded, the little child's stabbing blade had missed his vital organs. His thick walrus hide of leathery scar tissue and fat had saved him once again. Yes, he was grievously hurt, and unable to move, but he could heal. He could come back stronger and more terrible than before, just as he had when the entire Serbian army had tried to kill him and failed. His wheezing laughter whispered and fluttered into the den's darkness like the passage of a bat on the wing.

Then the ground shook and jumped, tossing DePriest off the chaise and onto the floor. The thunderous rumble became a roar, and a gale of superheated wind rushed in at his chamber door. Then came the light, white, and glaring bright, as if the a star were reaching down into the earth to find him. Primordial horror overtook DePriest. This was *fire*, far greater than the trickle of burning gasoline that had disfigured him in the pit. He struggled to rise, to flee, but his own weight pressed him down. The flames, hot and fast as a rocket engine, rushed in. For an instant, he screamed, and smelled his own flesh burning like tallow as he died.

CHAPTER 115

PERSHING LOWRY SAT near Molly Wilde's hospital bedside waiting for her to surface from the general anesthesia of her surgery. He had been at the hospital for two hours, and would have been there sooner, but there were so many details to address before the delegating could begin.

Molly took a slow deep breath, took in her surroundings, and let her groggy eyes rest on the IV line. "Now thaaat's the good stuff. Waaay better than Nicorette."

Lowry caught his breath and leaned forward. "Molly?"

"Hey Persh'. What's the haps?"

"It's over, Molly. Done. The twins are back. The boy's in here with you, but he'll be okay. You saved them, and quite a few others."

"The others I missed? More?" Molly was downcast.

"Scrapes, cuts, bruises, malnutrition for the ones abducted earlier. They need plenty of trauma therapy and time more than anything. But they're not talking about how they got free. Won't say a word."

"The word is *Blackshaw*."

"Interesting," said Lowry. "Because we found the group you freed along with you at Calvert Cliffs. But the others were waiting down on the beach, miles from the terminal."

"What about the doers?"

"The Federal Bureau of Investigation is not in the habit of arresting corpses. That's all we've got. There's the one who was tied up on that speedboat, Gläans Bellendre. We cut that one loose to follow him, and after

a few drinks at a bar, he went back to the LNG terminal just in time for it
to blow sky high. I'll have some explaining to do on that. The fire is a four
alarm thing so far, with more companies likely to respond. Nobody's walking out of that. It's like Dresden there. I'm not sure even dental records will
identify some of the remains we've found. The investigation will prove interesting. Your particular insights will be needed."

Molly frowned, "I'll be back at the office tomorrow."

"Fair enough. Because you're in charge there, Acting Senior Resident
Agent Wilde."

"Hold it. No. No way. What about you, Persh'?" Wilde winced as she
tried to use her injured shoulder to sit up.

"Take it easy. The director has accepted my recommendation about
you, and my request for a transfer. He wasn't happy about my late night
call, and there will be paperwork by the truckload, but it's true. You're top
dog. I'm moving on. First, there's going to be a short leave of absence for
me. Later, a new posting where I've been guaranteed I will have no supervisory responsibilities over you."

"That bad?" Wilde lowered her eyes.

"How are your pain meds, Molly?"

"Working like a charm, because I'm pretty confused by all this."

"Excellent. That improves the likelihood you won't remember what
I'm about to say."

Emboldened, Lowry sat up, and pulled his chair closer to the bedside.
He cleared his throat. "Molly Wilde, I must inform you that I'm completely,
utterly, and hopelessly in love with you. I have known this for some time.
There is nothing I can do about it. Believe me when I say I've tried. No
woman has ever touched me as deeply as you do when we are together.
When we are apart, you are constantly on my mind. When I learned you
were injured, for a moment, I actually thought *I* would die. When the
surgeon told me you'd survive, it changed everything I've believed to be
important, and every dream I once held sacred. If you like, we can discuss
all this when you feel better. I promise I can be more poetic, given time.
Or—we need never mention this again. Up to you."

Lowry stood to leave, but turned back, and stiffly bent to kiss a wide-
eyed Molly on the forehead. She looped her good arm around his neck,

pulled his mouth down to hers, at once blissfully happy, and acutely self-conscious of how long it had been since she'd brushed her teeth.

CHAPTER 116

BEN BLACKSHAW DREW *Miss Dotsy* through the inner guts of Lethe Island, making for the great cascading willow tree.

Orville Hurley had been found north of the Havokker gun, broken and singed, but alive. He was rallying under the watchful care of friends.

LuAnna lay in their saltbox on Smith Island. At the rise of the parlor prayer service, with many well-meaning neighbors banished outdoors for want of space, Ben and Ellis just stared at one another in disbelief; both knowing they had come through this trouble tired and bloody, but nowhere near as wounded as they had ended up after other sorties together. Their sole casualty was LuAnna, as if she had borne the full brunt, the sum of all the wickedness in the LNG terminal. They might never stop asking themselves how they had come through, and why LuAnna had been so stricken. The question pressed heavy on their shoulders, a yoke of cold, rough-hewn stone.

Vast sums of new Smith Island money had brought in two of the best trauma surgeons in the Washington, D.C. area, as well as three nurses, and every piece of equipment normally part of a rapid response medical unit. Helicopters flew in with additional supplies, including blood of her type. The money paid for silence as well as materiel and skill. But still, LuAnna was unconscious. She had lost so much blood, and been in hypovolemic shock for so long before the transfusions and other interventions began in earnest. Everyone was amazed she was still alive, and not a few quietly wished her suffering to be over. Ben heard all the kind, encouraging words about how she would recover, often tailed with that sad phrase *bless her heart* that was almost always reserved for hopeless cases.

It had been such a long ten days since the fight. Tally and Chamaiyo had recovered themselves enough to travel. With rest and food, and a few dollars in the pockets of their borrowed clothes, it was agreed they would be dropped in Salisbury on the main, to make their way in the world as best they could. They had a better chance than most, with their quick wits and deadly skills. Ben and Ellis wondered if letting former terrorists loose on American soil was a wise thing, but the girls had been forced into whatever crimes they had committed in East Africa, and their time at the terminal was adequate for penance and pardon.

Wade Joyce got his proper grave, and some kindly words, but his rites took place at night, and then no one wanted to speak of him anymore.

Annie Vo stayed close by, but as stories of the terminal explosion began to share the news cycles with the disappearance of Lily Morgan, her husband, and many other international notables, she realized she was done on Smith Island, and her place was back home with her Janie.

With a rucksack slung over his shoulder on the way out the saltbox door, Dick Blackshaw had suggested that the family's old fishing ark on Lethe Island might be something for Ben to see again. Dickie-Will declared he wasn't going back to it. Ben could have it. Something in the way his father said all this lent some urgency to Ben making a visit to Lethe sooner, rather than later. Friends, including Ellis, encouraged Ben to go. LuAnna's status was unchanged, and every medical prediction said it would never be any different, certainly never any better than the vegetative state in which she now persisted. Reluctantly, he set out aboard *Miss Dotsy*.

A solitary trip on the Chesapeake in a deadrise seemed a good way to fill Ben's unending hours of grieving and of self-recrimination. He was near exhaustion from sitting up with LuAnna, and still refused go to sleep just yet if he could help it. Gremlins, demons, and old enemies reared at him out of his dreams. If LuAnna's face were to appear suddenly among those phantasms, Ben knew that he would happily go to her side forever, never to wake.

With *Miss Dotsy* moored by her day-hook into the Lethe marsh, Ben hiked along the sunken planks toward the place his father had described.

He pushed through the willow's leafy curtains into the clearing. There was the shanty pulled up on the hard, improved by his father's recent efforts, but still easily recognizable as the Blackshaw family ark of old.

Ben struggled to recognize the lone figure seated in the door looking out at him. Then he knew her. Would know her anywhere after fifteen minutes, or fifteen years. He was unsure whether she was real, or if exhaustion and the upwelling of deep-cut traumas were rattling his senses. Unable to help himself, and with a man's younger voice, he said, "Afternoon, Ma."

EPILOGUE

BLACKSHAW HAD SO many questions to ask his mother about what happened on the appalling night that sundered their family fifteen years before. After an awkward embrace, they retreated inside the shanty out of the drizzle, and he began with the simplest, yet most confusing matter.

"I thought you were dead. Everybody thinks you're dead."

Ida Beth sipped at her coffee, gathering herself to explain. "I won't make excuses here, nor ask you for quarter. But so's you know, things weren't right with your father after he come back from Vietnam. He was a mess. We married anyway. It was expected, and we were young, and didn't know better. Then trouble followed him home. There were things he'd done overseas and under orders that some bigwigs wanted forgotten. Hired men come at us. Tried to kill us. You remember. Ran us clean off the road into a ditch that night on the main."

"Ellis told me about it. You and Pap said it was an accident." Ben returned to his original point. "But out in the marsh, I found the pins they put in your busted-up arm."

"Not quite. Don't get ahead of me here. By then, after the wreck, your pap and I knew we had our own troubles, nevermind. The death sentence on him kinda meant the same for us as a pair. Ben, what you need to know is this, I was fixing to leave your father. To leave Smith Island."

"And me." Ben tried to hold Ida Beth's eye, but she looked away.

"Yes. You were a man already."

"I was a kid." He felt anger building inside.

There was pride in her voice when she countered, "A *man*, Ben. On Smith Island you was nigh middle-age. Later on, the next time when them fonny boys tore into your pap, and cut him up, he knew he had to light out and lay low. I was supposed to go, too. Well, I did. But not with Dickie-Will."

"With somebody else?" asked Ben.

"Alone. Without your pap. And yes, without you neither. Ellis was watching out for you. Dick, he said we'd sure come back when the trouble passed. Maybe a few days in the mesh, n'mare. But I promised myself that I never would set foot on Smith again. It was so blessed small. Anybody could see your father was restless after the war, a rover, and a life following the water would never do for him in the end. Nobody figured I was the same way. Surprised me most of all."

"A woman's got to do what a woman's got to do."

Ida Beth fixed her son's gaze. "I can live with that, Ben. So the night your pap left, I did, too, like we planned. But I never did meet up with him in the Martin Refuge where we was to hunker down and bide. I waited 'til he gave up watching for me, and he moved out of the mesh to our fallback spot on the main. Oh, I thought long and hard on it, but when the time came, I didn't go meet him there neither."

Ben had to point out the obvious. "The pins from your arm. The buttons off your sweater. The flattened-out bullet, all there in the marsh. I found where you died."

Ida Beth was reflective. "You found where I started to live. The real pins are still right here." She touched her arm. "And don't they ache like billy-o in weather like this. What you turned up was window dressing. Covering my tracks lest some day Dickie-Will came a-looking."

Ben ruminated on the facts. Both his parents, as well as LuAnna, and he himself had at one point feigned death to avoid trouble. Only now, LuAnna was the only one truly murdered and gone, whatever the heart monitor might indicate to the contrary.

He said, "That's the *why* of things. Where did you go?"

Ida Beth said, "Don't laugh."

"That's not likely."

"I roamed around some. Had my fill and plenty of foreign parts. Then I settled—in Bal'mer these last years. I got fixed up with a new name, of course."

His mother had abandoned him for a world of adventure, and had settled just up the road and across the bay. Not once had she reached out to him in all that time. Ben tried not to show his disgust.

As if to make up for her maternal derelictions, she said, "I kept tabs. You did us all proud in the service. And you don't know it, but I picked up a piece of your flat-work at the waterfowl festival. Prettiest little merganser sketch. It's on my wall back home."

Back home in Baltimore.

She went on. "Ben, I'll love you 'til the end of counting, for aught that's worth, but sometimes love just isn't enough to make a damn bit of difference with all the rest of it."

They talked for the rest of the day, and ate together in the shanty that evening. Ben shared more than he expected about the intervening years, about LuAnna. He spoke of her most. He could tell Ida Beth sensed what his bride's loss meant to him. He could hardly go back to the saltbox on Smith without LuAnna there to greet him. And he had no idea what moving forward could possibly feel like without her by his side. For now she lay there on Smith Island sleeping like a fairytale princess, perhaps 'til the end of counting.

Ben bunked aboard *Miss Dotsy* that night. In the morning, he sloshed in to the clearing beneath the willow, and found the fishing ark abandoned, and his mother's few things stripped away. She must have kept a skiff in another gut, and decided she had said her piece. Once again, there was no note from her. Ben would not trouble her in Baltimore. He knew it was unlikely she would go there again now that she had tipped her hand, but the fact was, he did not care—or so he told himself. He moved some provisions and gear from *Miss Dotsy* into the shanty that morning, not sure if he would ever leave the quiet place.

That afternoon, Ben's sat-phone buzzed. He opened the line and heard a familiar query, "You know who this is?"

"Hey Mike. What do you want?"

"Sorry about LuAnna."

Ben was a few moments in responding. "Thanks." What else could he say?

"I've done a little hacking since we talked."

"Good to have a hobby, reckon."

"It's about all the fees those doodlebugs spent on the show," said Mike Craig. "I mean the revenue from the ticket sales. My little photons traced it along the way into a bank account in the islands. Every nickel went by wire around the world forty-six times. Amazing encryption effort. Then I did some more work. I have it."

Ben was loading his shotgun with a single double-ought shell, holding the phone between his ear and shoulder. "You have what, exactly?"

"The money. All of it. I changed the number on the account by one digit, and put it in my name. Then I created another account under an alias for you. Does a fifty-fifty split sound okay?"

"No argument. I appreciate it, Mike. Anything else?"

"You don't want to know how much it is?" asked Mike.

Ben racked the shell into the pump gun, and said. "Okay. I'll bite."

Mike paused for effect. "Two hundred million dollars."

That was a big figure, even for a man with a fortune in gold, albeit in stolen unspendable bullion. "Split two ways?"

"Nope," said Mike. "That's what's in *your* account."

"That's something. But it won't bring LuAnna back, will it."

Mike said, "I heard you rack that weapon, Ben. Think about what you could do with scratch like that. Think long and hard about it before you do something stupid."

Ben broke off the call, and wondered how many times in his life he'd been shown the business end of a gun. Plenty. But never with his own hand so close to the trigger.

For Discussion

Human trafficking spreads misery throughout the world for victims of all ages, but the multi-billion-dollar revenue makes the practice lucrative for traffickers at every level.

For thirty years, The National Center for Missing and Exploited Children has served as a core organization for the prevention and resolution of cases of child abduction and child sexual exploitation. Consider learning more about their important work, particularly since, despite the measurable successes of law enforcement efforts, crimes against children continue to rise at an alarming rate.

www.missingkids.com/home

UNICEF is also working very hard to protect children from this practice.
www.unicefusa.org/mission/protect/trafficking

To quote Orchid Project "Female genital cutting is an abuse of human, women's and child rights."

The barbaric practice is not just an overseas problem. Young girls are victimized in this terrible way all over the world, even where you live. Please learn more about what you can do to halt this savagery and empower young women everywhere.

www.orchidproject.org

www.trust.org/item/?map=female-genital-mutilation-on-the-rise-in-the-united-states-report

www.endfgm.eu

ABOUT THE AUTHOR

Robert Blake Whitehill is a Maryland Eastern Shore native, and an award-winning screenwriter at the Hamptons International Film Festival, and the Hudson Valley Film Festival. In addition, he is an Alfred P. Soan Foundation award winner for his feature script U.X.O. (Unexploded Ordnance). Whitehill is also a contributing writer to Chesapeake Bay Magazine.

Find out more about the author, his blog, upcoming releases, and the Chesapeake Bay at:

www.robertblakewhitehill.com

Enjoy the opening maneuvers of the next Ben Blackshaw thriller!

GERONIMO HOTSHOT

PART 1
RESURRECTION

CHAPTER 1

THE FIRE RAGED on the mountainside below him. Delshay Goyathlay was trying his damnedest to regroup with his squad on the fire line farther down the crag before dark. The light was already failing. He knew he was lucky to be alive, but he was still cut off. The high Arizona woodland wildfire he and his men were struggling to contain had hopped sparking through the trees over the firebreak that they had cleared of its tinder-dry undergrowth and ground cover. He should have seen that flash-over coming.

Del could hear his squad boss yelling intermittently for him over the walkie on his chest, but it was plain his replies were going unheard, either because of signal blockage from the mountains or from the walls of this crevasse, or because of damage in the fall he had taken. The battery meter was still in the green, if on the low end.

He wanted to rejoin the crew as much to get back to work as to stop his friends worrying about him. Del would never hear the end of this. If he wasn't back on the line soon, manpower would be yanked from the real work to locate him. Getting separated had been stupid, but he was on the line's end closest to that stream up the mountain, knew the way better than anyone, and all the water bottles needed a refill. That was another problem. Except for the camelbacks built into the three newer packs down with the crew, Del now had all the squad's canteens. He had to get back to the guys or it would be a long thirsty hike back to camp with a fair amount of cussing, and most if it directed his way.

When the flashover had ignited the trees downhill from him, their trunks had blown up bright in an astounding roar and rush. It was like some kind of thermal bomb had gone off in his face. He'd staggered back involuntarily from the heat, and tumbled down twelve feet into this crevasse in the rock. Many decades' accumulation of tree litter had recently burned down here, and the ash and charred branches had broken his fall. Now he was choking in the smoke of the flashover, and the fine ash he'd kicked up on impact.

Del's right knee was twisted and hurting from the tumble, but other than scrapes, that was the worst of it. He retrieved his clear-lensed goggles, and swept his black braid on top of his head before replacing his red fiberglass helmet. The drip torch for lighting backfires seemed sound, so he lashed it onto the pack for the climb. One less thing to get hollered at for busting or losing.

He scrambled a jagged path over the steep uphill face of the rock fissure as handholds and footholds allowed. The rock was still warm through his leather gloves. As he climbed, he managed to recover his Pulaski axe out of a tangle of roots.

Toward of the mountain's peak, he hoped he could catch a quick breather without fear of immolation, and figure out his next move. Lightning from a storm two months before had already scorched at least three hundred wooded acres to black stumps in that direction. There was no fuel left there.

Del kept climbing. His knee loosened up a little bit, though it still hurt. Five feet below the lip of the fissure, Del noticed a smaller crack in the rock about two feet wide. Despite his problems, anger surged in his chest. The glint of metal, like part of a buried aluminum soda can caught his eye in there. He could not fathom who would hike into this country to be one with nature, and then leave trash behind.

He reached in for the can, but it folded like fabric in his grasp. It wasn't metal at all. This was an ash-covered, scorched space blanket, and it flexed, then crumbled and tore in his fingers. He pulled a few more silvery fragments out of the rock gash, and tucked them into a pocket in his yellow brushcoat. Del sure has hell wasn't going to make the trash problem worse by dropping crap into the crevasse. He wondered if a hiker had lost the blanket, or perhaps a firefighter attacking the earlier blaze.

A larger swatch of the blanket ripped away in Del's hand all at once, and that's when he saw the human head. It was very well-preserved, likely from the dry elevation, with short bristling hair; it was gray-black with soot. *Oh hell*, he thought. This is exactly the kind of niche in just this kind of crevasse for an old native or prehistoric burial. Del wondered if he was disturbing an ancestor.

The head opened its eyes. Del shouted in shock, lost his footing, and slid down the crevasse's slope a few feet before he caught himself. The eyes stared down at Del.

Then the mouth opened. "Got any water?" The voice rasped.

"A little," Del said. He still had to get to the stream, but he unscrewed the top of a water bottle and passed it up toward the head.

Lower in the niche, blackened fingers jutted through the tatters of the space blanket in a puff of ash, seized the bottle, and tipped it to soot-caked lips.

The voice, a little less raspy than before, asked, "What day is it?"

"Wednesday," answered Delshay.

The dark face seemed puzzled. "Wow. Okay. I need to get moving."

The cover of detritus in the niche shifted beneath the blanket as a very big cinder demon bent to extricate himself.

Del climbed to assist the specter. "Man, for a minute I thought you were a dead mummy."

"I'm okay. But this bastard wedged in here beside me is a gonner for sure. What's your name, friend?"

The firefighter could not speak for a moment, but he soon said, "Del."

"I'm Ben. Now, Del if you could help me out of here, we might-could save a couple-two-three million folks before breakfast."

"What?" asked an incredulous Del.

"You're probably right," reflected Ben. "By tomorrow supper at the latest."

CPSIA information can be obtained at www.ICGtesting.com
Printed in the USA
BVOW05s0542150914

366576BV00002B/7/P